DESOLATION

A RALPH DE MANDEVILLE MYSTERY

KEITH MORAY

B
Boldwood

First published in Great Britain in 2025 by Boldwood Books Ltd.

Copyright © Keith Moray, 2025

Cover Design by Dan Mogford

Cover Images: Open Access - The Met

The moral right of Keith Moray to be identified as the author of this work has been asserted in accordance with the Copyright, Designs and Patents Act 1988.

All rights reserved. No part of this book may be reproduced in any form or by any electronic or mechanical means, including information storage and retrieval systems, without written permission from the author, except for the use of brief quotations in a book review. This book is a work of fiction and, except in the case of historical fact, any resemblance to actual persons, living or dead, is purely coincidental.

Every effort has been made to obtain the necessary permissions with reference to copyright material, both illustrative and quoted. We apologise for any omissions in this respect and will be pleased to make the appropriate acknowledgements in any future edition.

A CIP catalogue record for this book is available from the British Library.

Paperback ISBN 978-1-83703-432-1

Large Print ISBN 978-1-83703-433-8

Hardback ISBN 978-1-83703-431-4

Trade Paperback ISBN 978-1-80656-029-5

Ebook ISBN 978-1-83703-434-5

Kindle ISBN 978-1-83703-435-2

Audio CD ISBN 978-1-83703-426-0

MP3 CD ISBN 978-1-83703-427-7

Digital audio download ISBN 978-1-83703-430-7

This book is printed on certified sustainable paper. Boldwood Books is dedicated to putting sustainability at the heart of our business. For more information please visit https://www.boldwoodbooks.com/about-us/sustainability/

Boldwood Books Ltd, 23 Bowerdean Street, London, SW6 3TN

www.boldwoodbooks.com

For my fabulous wife Rachel, my companion of many adventures, with thanks for her continued support, advice and encouragement.

That day will be filled with wrath, a day of trouble and tribulation, a day of desolation and devastation, a day of doom and gloom, a day of clouds and shadows.

> — THE BOOK OF ZEPHANIAH, HOLY BIBLE

The plague began to show its sorrowful effects in an extraordinary manner. It did not assume the form it had in the East, where bleeding from the nose was a manifest sign of inevitable death, but rather showed its first signs in men and women alike by means of swellings either in the groin or under the armpits, some of which grew to the size of an ordinary apple and others to the size of an egg, and the people called them *buboes*... And just as the *buboes* were a very definite indication of impending death, in like manner these spots came to mean the same thing for whoever contracted them. Neither a doctor's advice nor the strength of medicine could do anything to cure this illness.

> — *THE DECAMERON*

'It was not for nothing that my nose fell a-bleeding on Black Monday last, at six o'clock i' the morning...'

— *THE MERCHANT OF VENICE*

PROLOGUE
THE ABBEY OF ST LEONARD

16 March 1361

Osbert Flood, the bailiff of Axeton in the wapentake of Langbarugh, gradually emerged from the hellish nightmare he seemed to have lived through for many days. He became aware of his surroundings, the dank cell illuminated only by a solitary slit window and the cot upon which he lay. He vaguely recalled being carried by monks following the instructions of their hospitaller, Father Alban.

Am I dead?

How many days he had lain there raving he did not know. Even now he was barely able to move, yet he realised that he lay in his own soiled clothes. His arms and legs hurt, his elbows and groins burned and his limbs felt as heavy as lead. Raising his head with difficulty, he blinked repeatedly to try to ease the burning of his eyelids, and slowly the blurring of his vision cleared.

Crude bandages covered various parts of his arms and legs, all of them stained with blood.

Nausea overcame him and his stomach heaved. He managed to turn over and vomit over the side of the cot into a bowl that contained older vomitus.

If I am not yet dead, am I dying?

His thoughts were jumbled. Where was he? Why was Marion not near him? Where was Dickon?

Dickon, my son!

His retching over, he rolled onto his back again, exhausted by the exertion of emptying his stomach of thick greenish-yellow liquid. He knew the taste of bile.

When in good health he was a strong man with a robust constitution, but now he found any movement the greatest effort. He managed to raise a hand to wipe his beard with the back of his hand and then winced for it smelled foul. His very flesh reeked as if it was corrupted and rotten.

Dickon? Where are you, boy?

Dimly he recalled travelling with his young son Dickon whom he had taken with him on the rounds of the Manor of Axeton, owned by his lord, Sir Hugo de Braithwaite, one of the wealthiest landowners in the Langbarugh wapentake. The lad was eight years old and Osbert was teaching him the way that a manor worked, and how it was the bailiff's responsibility to manage it on the lord of the manor's behalf. In general, a round of the manor farms, the nine villages and numerous smaller hamlets once every quarter year would take him the better part of a week and all those due to make payments knew on which day he would visit them.

Marion, his wife, had not wanted him to take Dickon this time as she was fearful of the rumours that had been coming to Axeton that the pestilence was returning. But Osbert was the bailiff and he had overruled her, saying that his son had to learn if he was to advance himself and hopefully one day take over his position. In this Dickon had rejoiced as he worshipped his father and wished for nothing else than to please him.

The weather had been against them and Dickon had been sneezing, sniffing and coughing and Osbert wanted to get him under cover for the night. He had only the haziest of memories of that wet and dank evening. They had stayed at the home of Robert the Hayward in a small hamlet where he as the bailiff and his son were welcomed and expected to stay. After they had supped a meal prepared by the hayward's wife, the bailiff and his son had gone to bed. Osbert had wondered if the food they were given had turned bad, for in the night he became ill, as did Dickon. The hayward seemingly panicked lest they should be carrying illness and took them in his own wagon to the nearby Abbey of St Leonard.

Osbert had never been to the abbey before as it was not part of Sir Hugo's estate, but like so many monasteries it had been gifted to one of the holy orders by one of the Norman nobles in the twelfth century as an assurance of gaining entry to Heaven when their end came. It still had patronage from a neighbouring manor lord. Osbert had heard that there had been a dozen or so monks and a few lay brothers before the pestilence of 1348, but that more than half their number had perished as the disease had spread.

Everything from that night was a blur. He had an almost dreamlike memory of being buffeted in the wagon and of them being half carried by monks into the abbey. He remembered seeing his son settled in a cot in the small hospital quarters after he had also been given a draught of physic of some kind by the kindly old hospitaller, Father Alban.

Then Osbert himself began to worsen and he lost all sense of where he was, who he was or even whether he was alive or dead. His throat burned, he felt unquenchable thirst and utter weakness. Nausea, thundering headache and drenching perspiration. From time to time he saw dark cowled figures, he wasn't sure if it was one or more, bending over him and holding him down, wielding a blade. He felt shooting pains and heard the zinging sound of blood spurting into a metal bowl. And then being helped to sup physick or gruel and then nothing more but the nightmarish sleep.

'So, you have awoken at last, my son.'

The voice startled him and he opened his eyes from yet another sleep.

'What... Who...?'

The male voice was kindly but seemed strangely distant and deliberate with an accent that was not of Osbert's wapentake. 'I am Father Alban. Do you remember me? I am the abbey chamberlain and hospitaller.'

Osbert shook his head and blinked, trying to clear his blurred vision. 'Ah yes... yes, I remember.'

'Abbot Joseph has been unwell and instructed us to care for you, so I and my assistant Brother John have been looking after you these six days while the fever raged. But the physick and the bleeding I have done on you has broken the fever and you will live.'

'Is it... Was it the pestilence?'

He thought again of Marion begging him to delay leaving the village with Dickon as everyone was aware of the rumours about the plague returning. But he had been pig-headed because they had not been affected those years before when half of the population had died from it. Besides, he'd felt confident he could look after his son.

Struggling again to clear his eyes, he saw the two monks. The older Father Alban and a taller one who looked to be about thirty beside him. Both wore their cowls up over their heads and with neckcloths pulled up over their noses. Osbert realised that this was why the monk's voice sounded distant. His voice was muffled.

'Yes, my son, it was the pestilence, but the Lord has spared you,' the elder monk replied.

'And Dickon? My boy, is he well? Where is he?'

Father Alban dropped his head for a moment. He took a deep breath then looked down at the bailiff with sad eyes.

'It grieves me to tell you, but your son has left the world this morning and will now be on his way to Heaven. I had hoped that you would recover so that you could see his body first, before we must bury him here in our graveyard where so many of our order died last time.' He took another breath. 'I am afraid that the illness has ravaged his body, so seeing him will be a shock for several of the pustular bubos that grew upon his neck and groins had burst and haemorrhaged.'

Osbert Flood felt a huge lump rise in his throat and then he dissolved into tears. 'May I see him?'

'Of course, my son,' the old monk replied. 'We will show you his small body and pray with you. We have already prayed for his soul, but the presence of his father may speed his journey. In one so young it is unlikely that he will have sinned much, so he may be spared a time in purgatory.'

They gave him water and stood and watched him for some time to ensure that he could keep the liquid down without vomiting. Then Father Alban led the way and Brother John and another monk each draped one of Osbert's arms around their shoulders and supported and half carried him along a dimly lit corridor and down steep steps to an underground room lit by guttering candles. Two more monks stood at the open door.

The room stank of death and decay. A small incense burner did little to assuage the odours.

Upon a table, his body wrapped in a shroud apart from his head, lay his son. An empty wooden coffin was on the stone floor. Osbert gasped and put a hand to his mouth as he saw the abdomen was bloated and that his son's tongue was swollen and protruded through his cracked blue lips.

'Dickon, my son!'

His unmistakable mop of blond hair had always looked so angelic and seeing him as they approached brought a sob to his throat and filled him with a cold feeling such as he had never felt.

'His face looks so purple and black,' the bailiff managed to utter. 'He... he looks so changed. And his neck is so swollen with those horrible lumps, and his beauteous face is so bruised.'

'His neck is swollen because of the bubos,' Father Alban explained. 'They are glands that swell and then they haemorrhaged, which means that they burst and bled into the skin. That is why his skin is so mottled purple.'

'I... I remember seeing people with the pestilence all those years ago. And those awful bubos,' said Osbert in horror. He felt guilty at feeling revulsion in the presence of his son's dead body.

Indeed, who but a child had not seen these horrible signs of the pestilence? It had been a little over a dozen years since the plague had ravaged the whole country, killing almost half the population. Osbert himself had lost his parents and a sister to the disease.

'I... I would kiss his head,' Osbert said, turning to Brother John. Despite himself he shuddered, for in reality he had no wish to get so near to the corpse, which was already surrounded by the stench of decay, but he felt it his duty to say farewell properly. To touch his son one last time.

Father Alban immediately put a restraining hand on his shoulder. 'I am afraid not. This is as close as you can come to your son. Only the brothers who are totally covered can go near when they carry his body to the graveyard where he will lie with the monks of our order who have already succumbed to the pestilence. We have given him the last rites, and should have buried him already, but I hoped you would recover enough to see him and say your farewell to him before he travels to paradise to be forever with his maker, the Lord.'

Osbert hung his head and sobbed uncontrollably for some time.

'You have lost others?' he managed to ask at last, his thinking proving difficult as the wave of inconsolable grief swept over him. 'Already?'

'We have lost a canon and two brothers,' the kindly monk replied. 'Yet there will be more, I fear. Our beloved Abbot Joseph clings to life by a thread in the Abbot's house.'

'We pray for them every day,' said Brother John. 'As we should now pray with you for your son, before we must bury him.'

And so, they prayed, then Osbert wept copiously as the two monks who had been attending at the door came in and gingerly covered his son's face with the shroud before lifting Dickon's body and placing it in the coffin.

Osbert fainted and fell to the floor as they nailed the coffin lid down.

When he came round after Father Alban wafted incense under his nose, he saw that the coffin had been taken out. By sheer force of will Osbert made himself walk outside into the mist and rain, once more assisted by Brother John and the other monk to see the open grave where his son's coffin had been lowered into.

As they stood at the graveside, Father Alban presided over the short funeral service. He read a passage from the Bible then invited Osbert to toss some clods of earth into the grave and then sprinkled holy water onto the coffin.

'Go forth, young Dickon, son of Osbert Flood, Christian soul, out of this world,' he intoned. *'In nomine Patris, et Filii, et Spiritus Sancti, Amen.'*

They all made the sign of the cross, and then the monks began to cover the coffin using wooden shovels to move soil from the heap they had excavated in digging the grave.

'And now we shall pray for all of us,' said Father Alban as the monks broke off their shovelling at a sign from him. 'Now that the pestilence has returned.'

1

THE COFFIN

Axeton, Langbarugh wapentake
19 March 1361

'The bailiff's coming!' cried Nigel, the youngest son of Piers the Pinder.

'You'll be pleased to see Dickon then,' replied his father, who was kneeling to wipe cow dung from his boots after they had left the cattle in the pinder-field for the last time that day.

'He's not with him. It's just Master Osbert riding his pony and leading Dickon's.'

Martin stood up abruptly and put an arm about Nigel's shoulder as he looked up the road leading into Axeton. It was late afternoon and it was starting to rain.

'You run home now, Nigel.'

'But where's Dickon?'

'Home, lad, and tell your mother I'll be along soon. I'll have a word with the bailiff on my own.'

All the way back from the Abbey Osbert Flood had been dreading having to tell people that his son was dead. In particular he did not know how he was going to give Marion the news that would undoubtedly break her heart, but he knew there was little chance of being able to talk to her first.

'Master Osbert, are you unwell?' Piers asked in alarm when the bailiff stopped in front of him and looked down from his pony. 'You are alone?'

'I have had the pestilence and it has taken my Dickon,' Osbert replied, his voice quaking with emotion. 'I must tell my wife, so I pray you tell no one except the reeve. Tell him to come to my house in an hour's time, for I will need to comfort Marion before I inform Sir Hugo and Lady Honoria. They will want us to take precautions to protect the village.'

Piers stared at him as fear overwhelmed him upon hearing the word pestilence. He made the sign of the cross as he struggled to find words of condolence, being more used to talking to cattle than people.

'But my lad has seen that you are leading Dickon's pony, Master Osbert. I sent him home to his mother.'

'Then for now tell your wife and family only that Dickon fell ill and has died. Once I have talked to the reeve he and you can give these sad tidings to the village.'

'Poor Dickon,' Piers said. 'All my lads adored him.'

Tears welled up in Osbert's eyes and he nodded. 'As did I.'

* * *

When Marion heard Osbert's pony's hooves on the cobbles of their courtyard she rushed out to greet him. He had dismounted and handed the reins of both his and Dickon's mounts to Thomas the Ostler, who was looking shocked and confused.

'Where is Dickon?' she asked, holding up her skirts and running to him.

Desolation

Osbert bit his lip and held out his arms to her. 'Our son has gone, my love. We... we both caught the pestilence and he... he succumbed. He has been buried at the Abbey of St Leonard's.'

It was as if she had run into a wall. She stopped short and stared at him in disbelief. Then with a shriek she covered her face with her hands and started to sob.

Osbert suddenly felt utterly exhausted but signalled for Old Thomas to stable the ponies while he went to Marion and folded her in his arms.

She buried her face against his chest and wept for a few moments, then she looked up at him.

'You look ill, husband,' she said. 'Come, you must rest and tell me all.'

He had always loved her but at that very moment he loved her even more. There was no tantrum, no recrimination, when he knew he deserved both. Marion had always been a dutiful and loving wife and mother.

And mother!

Weeping himself he took her by the hand and they entered their family home.

* * *

The whole village was thrown into a panic. The bailiff had almost died from the pestilence and it had killed his son Dickon, which meant that the rumours that came to the village from travellers, mendicants and mountebanks attending the fortnightly market must be true. They told that plague was gradually spreading up the country, and that they had both heard and seen people die, and gravediggers were busy, working hard to bury the dead. The Great Death seemed to be about to return after all those years.

No one but those who were children could forget the way the Great Death had swept across the manor taking men, women and children to their graves, regardless of their positions. They had heard all the rumours that were brought to them by travellers and pilgrims who said how the disease had come from distant lands, spread through the low countries and France, then across the channel in 1348 to eventually reach the great city of London. Then it inexorably crept northwards affecting all of the hamlets, villages and towns until it reached the West Riding of Yorkshire a year later.

And yet some said that it seemed to have struck in the east of the country first, which many thought was due to it spreading from the countries across the North Sea, from the ports that traded in wool and cloth, and that it was those returning merchants to the ports of Hull, Flamborough and Scarborough that brought it inland towards them. For this reason it was believed that the wool had something to do with it, as the fishing towns of Whitby and around it were slower to be affected.

It wiped out some entire monasteries, abbeys and priories, especially those with hospitals where people fled at the first sign of illness to get some medicine. It killed two thirds of the populations of some towns, while some were lucky to lose only half their number of people, and yet for others like the village of Axeton it only took about one person in every three.

Yet it was the manner in which the disease spread that alarmed everyone. It began with a cough, a sore throat or a sudden high fever. Within hours someone could be stricken and be unable to move, but had to lie down to vomit, or lose control of their bladder and bowels so that they would lie in their own urine and excrement. They would be racked with pain for which there was little relief from even the strongest medicine.

Coughs would rob them of breath. Almost instantly, large black or yellow pustular swellings the size of eggs or apples, which were called bubos, would appear in the neck, under the arms or in the groins, stretching the skin so that it burst to leak blood and yellow pus. Bruises would appear, skin and lips would turn purple or black and then they would mercifully slip into deep unconsciousness or start to convulse. Death was common within a mere two days.

Terrifyingly, it was sometimes less. Many had seen people who seemed to be perfectly healthy bid goodnight, go to bed but be dead by the morning.

Everyone was aware that this invisible hand of death seemed to reach out several feet from an ill person. Merely touching a sufferer's clothes appeared to spread the malady to the toucher.

When the plague struck thirteen years before many sufferers were taken by relatives to monasteries and priories to seek treatment, or if too ill to travel doctors, apothecaries and surgeons were called and attempted to treat by bleeding, purging, fumigating or giving medication or whatever treatment they thought could help. Most commonly they would lance the bubos to let out the stagnant blood and pus. Opening a pigeon and applying its warm body to a bubo to draw out the ill humor, which they believed was the cause, was often done.

Wise women would make remedies, stoke fires or attempt to remove the illness by letting snails or slugs touch the blood, vomitus or excrement from a poor wretch, seal it in a jug and bury it in the hope that this would transfer the illness to the creature and that as it died, so it would take the illness with it.

And of course, clerics would pray for the souls of the people and for the sick to recover if God willed it.

Pardoners went from village to village offering for sale

supposed relics of saints, indulgences or pardons, which might heal, but at the very least would reduce their sins so that if they succumbed to the pestilence and died then their souls would be absolved and they would avoid the pits of Hell but enter Heaven instead.

From the low countries, from Flanders and Zeeland and Holland, men calling themselves flagellants came in large groups, travelling about the towns and villages, dressed in cloth from thigh to ankles, but bare from the waist up. Each wore a cap with a red cross on the front and the back, and in one hand they carried a scourge with three heads, each with a knot tied in them and often with a nail through them. They would march in single file through a village to the church and they would whip themselves until they bled. They would chant in their native tongues and then sing a litany. From time to time they would lie face down and spread their arms as if they were a cross. In this manner they said they were making penance for the sake of the villagers. Pope Clement the sixth of that name condemned them and ordered all clerics to suppress them, so that they disappeared.

Doctors and apothecaries grew reluctant to treat patients at all, and only did so at the distance of a six-foot staff, and people simply died. They died in their homes, they perished outside in the fields and in the streets. Cemeteries and churches were overwhelmed and the traditional respectful burials could no longer be performed. Soon the streets of villages and towns became littered with the dead.

In the early days of the pestilence when people died their bodies were treated with respect. Clerics, be they priests, monks or friars would administer the last rites and the bodies would be reverently placed in coffins and buried in the churchyard in consecrated ground. Then as the numbers of the dead grew too numerous and their mortal remains were left to bloat and decay, the stench of death pervaded the hamlets and villages. Body collectors, often women, would collect corpses from houses, from the street where relatives lay them, and instead of being laid to rest in an individual grave they would be roughly tossed into mass burial pits.

The number of clerics who died was phenomenal so that there were either too few left alive, or those that were alive made themselves unavailable to conduct services over individuals but would say a few words after a burial pit had soil shovelled over it. When the numbers of them were even further reduced, Pope Clement the Sixth granted remission of sins to all who died of the plague, and declared that the dying could make their confession to anyone present, whether that be a man or a woman, and that would still lead to salvation.

* * *

Osbert Flood felt guilty that he had not told Marion all about their son. He was unable to describe how terrible he looked to her.

A week after he returned he offered to take her to the Abbey of St Leonard to show her Dickon's grave, but she could not bear to go, so he went alone despite being still so weak.

To his horror he discovered that soon after he had left the abbey on his way home, Father Alban and Brother John had both fallen ill and died from the pestilence. They had been buried close to Dickon's grave. There were only five brothers left and they told him that they were considering abandoning the abbey.

Osbert knew he had to support Marion the best way that he could, and he thought the best way was to let her wallow in her grief until time brought some crumb of solace. Everyone had expressed their sadness at the death of Dickon when Osbert returned to Axeton on his own. He was himself in a sorry state, emaciated, having lost the paunch that he had been so proud to have, the sign that he was a successful man, the well-respected bailiff of the manor belonging to Sir Hugo de Braithwaite. His eyes were sunken and his skin was pale, almost yellow. He walked with a little difficulty as his groins, backs of his knees and his inner elbows had wounds from where he had been bled by the hospitaller, Father Alban.

His Lord, Sir Hugo, was not a well man either. He was sixty-two years of age and had been showing signs of failing ability to manage his affairs, hence his increasing reliance upon his wife and his bailiff. While once he had been a forceful and confident man who had run his manor in an authoritative manner, he had been ever more willing to rely on his wife's counsel and to delegate more and more to the bailiff. He had developed a tremor and was subject to twitches of his face and odd mannerisms. Nonetheless, when Osbert had returned from his round of visits an ill man and with the news of his son's death, Sir Hugo had been upset for his servant and had stirred himself to personally give his condolences.

Sir Hugo's wife, Lady Honoria, was in her middle forties, a handsome and intelligent woman who carried her own past tragedies with dignity and concealed the melancholy that she felt every day of her life. She had given Marion a posy of flowers and a kerchief that she had embroidered herself, and had sat with her and tried her best to comfort her as she sobbed in Lady Honoria's presence, aware that doing so breached the chasm of class that divided them. The fact that the lady of the manor empathised with her, weeping herself, had permitted Marion to visibly mourn, for she was aware that Lady Honoria had suffered a number of miscarriages and that she and Sir Hugo had lost their only child to have survived to infancy, a son, when he was only two years old during the last plague. So it was that they grieved together. Osbert was grateful for Lady Honoria's support of his wife even though he was party to some of her secrets.

The reeve, Gideon Moor, and the other servants all had tried their best not to make any mistakes in their various tasks and to try to anticipate any of Osbert's instructions. In this Osbert was fortunate, for the reeve could read and write and was a competent tallyman. With Sir Hugo and Lady Honoria's blessing, as Osbert took on more and more of the administration of the whole manor so too did he delegate many tasks to the reeve, so Gideon Moor effectively became an assistant bailiff, able to visit holdings and nearby villages and hamlets to collect rents and tithes from the smaller holdings.

Osbert himself had been almost inconsolable, of course and had tried to show Marion his love. Dickon had been their only son and she, like himself, was in her middle forties so was unlikely to have another child. He knew that even thinking of sleeping together at this time would be most unwelcome to her, even if he had had the interest himself, which he certainly did not. Yet losing Dickon made him at least think that once he was more recovered they should try for another child.

It was about two weeks after his return from the Abbey of St Leonard when he was starting to feel stronger that he saw the wagon with two coffins coming along the road as he was heading to the stables to collect his horse. He noticed that the wagon driver was dressed in a thick gown with his hood drawn over his head. He assumed it was George the mute and did not take too much notice of it but continued into the stable.

No sooner had he entered than someone stepped out of the

shadows behind him and cudgelled him on the back of the head. It felt to him that he was diving into a pit of utter blackness.

* * *

How long he lay there face down on the straw-covered ground he did not know. He opened his eyes and tried to move, realising immediately that his hands were bound behind his back and that he had a gag in his mouth.

He heard horses moving restlessly in their stalls. They were snorting.

What had scared them, he wondered.

Then he heard the sound of someone moving towards him, feet crunching straw.

Was it Thomas the Ostler?

He turned his head as far as he could and saw a man's legs standing near him. In his hand he had a bulbous cudgel. He gasped as he saw blood on it.

Is that my blood?

He could not see above the man's knees and hesitated to try to turn lest he receive another strike to his already aching head.

'Ready yourself, master bailiff,' a gruff voice said. 'You are going on a journey.' There was a chuckle, then the man added, 'You both are. You and your ostler.'

He felt scared. Was Thomas similarly bound and helpless like him? But who had done it and why?

The man retreated to the far end of the stable and Osbert heard the large back door being creakily pushed open as it scraped along the ground. He heard another horse and voices. Stretching his head round, he saw the lower legs of two men approach him again.

'We'll take the ostler first, he's already dead.'

Osbert felt his bladder squirt piss and his heart race with fear.

Dead? They said Thomas is dead?

They passed him and went into one of the stalls. Immediately the horses started stamping, kicking the walls of the stall and snorting. He heard a voice trying to soothe them with strange words and what seemed like firm patting. Someone who knew animals it seemed, for the horses did seem to calm and stopped snorting.

There followed the noise of two people grunting as they applied some effort, then he saw the legs of the man who had spoken, and a thick gown above leather boots. He presumed this second to be the wagon driver. He saw them carry the body of Thomas the Ostler who he had known for twenty years being carried by his feet and arms. As they passed he saw the ostler's head dangling backwards, blood dripping from his greasy grey hair.

'Put him in the first one,' said the voice he recognised as the one who had spoken to him.

He heard noises outside the stable and a creaking but could only guess at what they were doing.

Moments later they came back for him. He was grabbed by the feet and by his bound arms and lifted. It hurt incredibly as he felt his shoulders were yanked backwards into their joints as they lifted him like a dead pig. He could make no noise because of the gag in his mouth, but groaned with the agony of it. He looked at the ground as he was carried, his face mere inches from it. They took him outside and then he was able to see the wheels of the wagon and he realised that it was the one he had seen with two coffins on it. There had been only one driver, so he guessed that the other had somehow already gained entrance to the stable and murdered Thomas.

His legs were dropped momentarily as one of the men climbed onto the wagon, then they both grabbed an arm and hauled him up. There he saw Thomas lying in one coffin, his sightless eyes staring up at the sky.

What was happening to him? He struggled to think.

'You're going for a journey, bailiff,' the man told him as he was lifted and placed in the second coffin. 'Rest your eyes in the dark now.'

He heard deep-throated chuckling as the coffin lid was lowered unceremoniously, and all was darkness and he felt terrified and thought that he would suffocate.

Close by he heard another lid being lowered onto Thomas's coffin.

Marion! Will I ever see her again?

'Bring one of the horses to make it look right,' he heard the man order the other.

Soon he felt the wagon trundling along the rutted road to who knew where.

He had never been so terrified in all of his life. He was hurled from side to side inside the coffin as it trundled along and from time to time as the wheels hit a bump he felt himself suddenly flung upwards to strike his head upon the coffin lid. In an attempt to cushion himself as best he could, he pushed in one direction with his shoulders and in the other with his legs, basically the only movements he could make in the darkness and the confined space in order to buttress himself against sudden lurches to avoid further injury.

The gag in his mouth was both uncomfortable and nauseating. There was a taste of dirt and every movement made it chaff against the sides of his mouth and he felt it almost graze his tongue. He was sure he could taste his own blood, which heightened the dreadful thirst he felt. Yet that was nothing compared to the fear that engulfed him.

Thomas is dead!

He could not shake the fleeting image he had of his faithful ostler, Thomas. The old man's head dangling backwards, blood dripping from his greasy grey hair.

I am in a coffin, but why am I not yet dead?

The wagon jolted and he felt a lurching as the coffin he was in was struck by the other containing Thomas's dead body.

It was accompanied by laughter from close by. Then he heard the voices for the first time. The two men who had captured him must have been sitting in silence. Now all of a sudden they were jesting and laughing, although he could not make out what they were talking about.

Are they planning how to kill me?

He felt a wave of nausea sweep over him, but he forced himself not to vomit. The smell of his own urine-soaked breeches was already bad enough.

He prayed that if the men who had put him into the coffin were going to kill him, that they did so quickly so that he could depart this horrible pestilential existence and see his beatific son once again.

* * *

It seemed an interminable time before the wagon finally drew to a halt and he heard the creaking of the wooden seat and a thudding as the two men jumped down to the ground.

Then he heard other voices and it sounded as if the ones who had taken him and Thomas were explaining something to others. Then one voice sounded above the others, a more sophisticated voice. It spoke with authority and barked orders.

'Bring them both in. Take the one with the corpse inside to the first cell and then bring the bailiff's coffin up to the special room.'

Osbert felt his coffin being slid off the wagon and then carried into a building, boots sounding on stone flagstones. There were other footsteps that sounded different.

Where are they taking me? What sort of special room?

It took a while and he heard heavy breathing as if it was an effort to carry the coffin.

'Put it upon the trestle table.'

There was a sudden knocking on the coffin lid, then he heard the authoritative voice again.

'Listen to me, Osbert Flood. I have someone here who has something to say to you.'

Inside the dark coffin the bailiff could hear his own quick breathing and the pulse of his heart in his ears.

'Father! Are you in there? Please, help me. They say... they say they will kill me.'

Osbert kicked the coffin lid as hard as he could and knocked it with his head.

It is Dickon. My boy is alive!

He wanted to yell, to ask his son if he was really alive, but he could make no noise for the gag in his mouth. Frantically he started kicking at the coffin lid again.

'Shut the boy's mouth,' the voice said. Then there was another knocking on the coffin lid. 'Now listen very carefully or the coffin that you are in will be for your final home, buried deep and the wood left to rot so that when you eventually die, your dead body will become food for worms.'

Osbert did not know what to do. He wanted to scream, to break out of the wooden coffin and fight, do anything to get to his son, to hug him and tell him that everything would be fine. That he would take him home to see his mother.

'Knock once if you understand,' the voice said.

Plaintively this time he knocked against the coffin lid with his head, his pleas merely coming out as a gurgle in his throat.

'There now, Osbert Flood,' the voice cooed through the wood.

The bailiff could hear drumming of fingers on the wood mere inches above his face. But all he could see was the dark interior of the coffin. 'Hush! Hush. Don't hurt yourself any further than you have. It must hurt banging your head like that. Just listen to my voice.'

Osbert lay still, hearing now only his own rasping breath.

'That's better. Now understand me. You are going to do exactly what I tell you. You will know me as the Magister. I am your master and you will promise to do whatever I say. If you understand me, knock once.'

The petrified bailiff knocked once with his head.

'That is good. Now this time I want you to make a promise to obey me. Knock once more if you promise.'

Osbert hesitated.

'I said knock if you promise!' the voice came sharply. 'Disobey me and the next you will hear is the scream of your son before I cut off one of his fingers. How loud will he scream, Osbert? Shall we find out? Knock if you will obey me.'

He knocked his head hard on the lid, oblivious to the hurt it caused.

'That is good. Now understand this. I will know if you ever disobey me and I promise you that you will never escape me.

Your punishment for that will not be just hearing him scream as I cut off a finger. It will be the scream before I slit his throat before your very eyes.'

2

BODKIN

Axeton
14 April 1361

He had chosen both of the women well. There had been five in the village that he originally thought could be used, all of whom he could bend to his will. Yet too many could be a risk for him, and that was something the Magister had emphasised upon him must not be taken. There was too much at stake, he had said, especially for him since that would include his life.

He shivered at the thought, for the Magister had shown him that he was well versed in the art of killing.

That was why he had chosen the two women, unwed and never likely to be taken in marriage. Plain, simple and ugly women that he had heard village men jest that they would rather be caught with a pig than one of them.

As a frequent traveller to all of the villages in the manor, his presence would never raise an eyebrow, and so he had ample opportunity to talk to the women.

Megan Prole looked after six pigs and was as strong as any

man. She wasn't averse to showing it either and had bested several younger fellows in fights with her fists and her teeth.

The other woman was known as Sally Bringbucket, for she collected all the urine and excrement she could from people and animals to sell to the tannery beyond the Old Stone Bridge and to the laundry women in Axeton.

Neither woman had been with a man before, that was clear, but both succumbed to his attentions when he caught them alone. He easily seduced them, slept with them despite their body odours and made them feel special. So special that they would do anything for him. Perform any sex act however he wanted, and he made them feel that he enjoyed them.

'You really like being inside me, sir?' Megan asked.

He grunted assent. She never used his name, of course; that was how he told her it had to be until the time was right. So 'sir' was how she addressed him.

'And will I really be a lady, lord?' asked Sally. 'And live in a great manor with you?' In a similar manner, 'lord' was how she had to address him when they were alone.

'You will,' he gasped as he orgasmed inside her.

He had put the fear of death into them both. He told them that he was not the man they thought he was, but a man possessed of the demon. That the seed he shed inside them on the many times he ploughed their furrows had made them his, but that when the time came for the rise of his master, as surely he would come, they would be saved. They would have his children and they would become wealthy and look down on all those villagers who had so despised them all these years.

Grooming their simple minds had been so easy. One at a time, with Megan lying on straw in her cleanest stye, or under a blanket with Sally Bringbucket in her hovel, he stirred up their hatred of some of the villagers. Ones they would love to get even with, or even see dead.

That was when he told them that the pestilence was coming again and that he could control it. That it was a thing that obeyed him. As his helpers, he could save them and protect them from the pestilence. All they had to do was point out to him the people they hated most. People who lived on their own. He told them what they were to do in the mornings when the time came.

And that was how he selected his first two victims. Two folk whose lives were of no value and whose deaths would serve the master.

Neither of them were hard to kill. The woman was more attractive than either Sally or Megan, and like the other victim led a solitary life.

Edith Pargit was a widow of some fifty years. He had no trouble seducing her, just as he had seduced Sally and Megan. Sleeping with her was better than with his two other beauties, but while she was in his arms on her rough cot of a bed he had enjoyed the look of horror and the sudden stare of death as he shoved the bodkin needle he had in readiness into the base of her skull.

It was a thick needle such as a cordwainer would use, but he had adapted it by giving it a wooden handle that he could grip instantly and which left a full hand's span of bladed shaft. He carried it in a concealed sheath strapped to his left forearm so that he could draw it surreptitiously and put it to instant deadly use.

He knew exactly how to do it, just as the Magister had shown him on a skeleton. The large hole at the base of the skull where the bodkin would slip inside the skull relatively unimpeded. It slid up into her brain and she convulsed in his arms as he wriggled it back and forth to macerate a cone of brain tissue inside her skull.

When he withdrew it he saw that it was covered in blood and pink-grey jelly tissue, but yet the wound barely bled at all.

He dressed and began to work on her dead body. He punched and pummelled her about the throat and face with a small mallet. Bruises appeared, some of them opening up and seeping blood. Then he took a vial of vinegar and poured some into each eye, smiling to himself as the blood vessels burst and the whites became totally bloodshot.

'A pity, for I enjoyed your body,' he whispered, 'but you have a greater purpose dead than alive, and no one would wed a widow of your years.'

Taking a large chunk of cheese that he had brought for the purpose, he broke it up and, rolling it into four balls, he lay them at her side. Then with a sharp blade he made some cuts on her neck, which did not bleed too much as her heart had stopped beating. Shoving his fingers beneath the skin, he opened holes wide enough to shove the balls of cheese into them, then smeared blood over them so that they resembled the bubos that people knew about or had seen on their own dying relatives those years ago when the plague was rife.

Not satisfied, he placed both hands on her belly and pressed down hard several times, smiling as he heard gas moving inside her corpse and moments later the smell of excrement and urine were apparent as bowels and bladder expelled their contents.

Leaving in the dark, he went to Megan and told her to visit Edith Pargit first thing next morning.

'Enter the house where you will find that she is dead from the pestilence. Then go straight to the reeve and tell him what you have found, and suggest he tell the bailiff.'

It all went according to his plan. The reeve told the bailiff and he had the apothecary from the next village come. And as planned, the apothecary took one look and confirmed the first death from the plague in the Manor of Axeton.

A coffin was called for and the two women who everyone despised were the only people willing to lift the body into it and to carry it out to the coffin maker's wagon.

After discussion between the apothecary and Osbert Flood the bailiff immediately after the 'discovery' of his first victim, Megan Prole and Sally Bringbucket agreed to act as *searchers* to keep a watch for anyone else with signs of the pestilence. They were given pots of red paint to identify any houses where someone with the pestilence may be lying ill. The apothecary suspected that they were two of the lucky folk who may have survived the first plague and somehow had some defence against it as a result.

'You shall be paid for this service to the village and the manor,' Osbert told them, to which both women gratefully and somewhat obsequiously gave thanks.

'And will you be willing to attend on these people?' Osbert asked the apothecary.

Humphrey de Duncombe, the apothecary, was not a young man, but he clearly had no wish to meet his maker too soon in the future. 'If I am not over-busy with the good folk of Duncombe and the hamlets about, then call for me.'

The next day after the two women had become official searchers it was the turn of Percy the Comber who Sally Bringbucket had selected to die, because he had abused and belittled her with his friends on several occasions. Both women knew that from now on an apothecary would probably not be called, as those selected would already be dead by the time they 'discovered' their bodies.

After Sally Bringbucket's chosen person had been dispatched the pestilence had officially begun in Axeton.

He instructed the two women to choose two further victims. He told them to choose well for they would never see the living world again, but that Sally and Megan would be kept safe and rewarded when his master rose again.

* * *

Gideon Moor the reeve was a popular man in the village and regarded as being capable. He was the village baker as well as the reeve and was ever willing to help anyone within the village or in any of the other hamlets and villages within the manor, where he oft made deliveries or visited under Osbert Flood's orders. Unmarried, he was considered good looking by many with his strong baker's arms and ready smile. He had informed the bailiff Osbert Flood when the coffins of Edith Pargit and Percy the Comber were ready for burial. Yet there was a problem, for the Church of St Agnes had been without its own parson for over a year after Father David de Warter, the last incumbent, had fallen and broken his neck after drinking a surfeit of ale at the village tavern. Since it was considered a sin not to worship on a Sunday, the village had been forced to make do with either the bailiff or the reeve reading from the Bible and leading them in prayers.

Sir Hugo, who owned the manor previously, had his own chaplain and his own chapel, but the chaplain had also left and the manor lord had shown no inclination to replace him. Besides, he rarely attended St Agnes's Church.

But funerals were different and needed a proper man of God to give a Christian funeral before the burial, which had to be done as quickly as possible.

Gideon Moor the reeve dispatched a boy to the neighbouring village of Duncombe where he told the lad that he had seen a friar on one of his recent visits to the village.

'You must seek him out and ask him if he will come and take two funerals of two of our people who have died of the pestilence.'

'What if he won't come, master?'

'You tell him Gideon Moor the reeve of Axeton is asking on behalf of Osbert Flood the bailiff to Sir Hugo de Braithwaite, and he will be recompensed for it.'

'What does re… recomp… what you said, mean, master?'

'Recompensed! It means he'll be paid. Tell him it will be worth his while.'

* * *

Friar Simon was a slightly built young man of about twenty-five years, with mere wisps of hair on his chin, yet he held himself upright and spoke with an authoritative and commanding voice. He wore a grey cassock, indicating that he belonged to the Greyfriars of the Franciscan order.

Drawing a crowd had never been difficult for him, for although not handsome yet he had a pleasing, almost innocent look to him. With striking blue eyes and cherubic lips he had an ability to focus on a person and make them think that he was speaking directly to them. He could charm or instil fear depending upon what he was preaching about, or who he was talking to.

He told all of the people who came to listen to him that he had come from York, slowly making his way by donkey around all the villages, spending few days in each one in order to give them the word of the Lord and the message of the Holy Bible.

That was true indeed, for he had been inspired by Friar John Ball of York whose preaching techniques he broadly emulated. But it was not the Lord's message of benevolence he taught, but a vengeful warning. He foretold the coming of the pestilence, and of the end of the world.

It was not comfortable to listen to him but folk did wherever he stood upon a mound or a stool with his wooden bowl before him for offerings. And using all of his talents, his looks, his voice and his preaching he attracted crowds and within them he had an unerring skill at focussing upon women of any age who were drawn to him.

When he joined the mendicant order he had taken the threefold vow of obedience, poverty and chastity. Mainly it was easy for him, for he obeyed the rules of the order and he had no aspiration to be rich. Indeed, the people he preached to freely gave him coins or food and drink. Chastity, however, he had found torture to begin with, especially when women threw themselves at him in private, wanting his blessing and his protection against eternal damnation. For this he found many were willing to lie with him in their dwellings when their men were away, or they would back against a tree or wall with open legs and let him fondle their breasts and do as he wished. So, he came to accept his transgressions as merely being the guilt that he as a friar had to bear. Enjoying their flesh and their mutual sin that he forgave them for, he found that the pleasure he had been offered and which he had taken actually enhanced his preaching.

The young lad that Gideon Moor sent felt he was lucky to find the friar, who had been preaching in the village square. He joined the crowd gathered about him and when he had finished his preaching and received several offerings in his mendicant wooden bowl, with some trepidation he approached him with the reeve's request.

'The pestilence, you say? And it has killed how many?'

'Yes, sir. It's killed two. Widow Pargit and Percy the Comber.'

Friar Simon was already in a good humour for his lust had been satiated that morning behind the church by one of the village women. Now he was excited.

At last! Just as John Ball told, it can be revealed. I have been preparing for this and awaiting the sign and the signal to begin. And now I am ready.

He collected his bowl and poured out the coins left by his crowd.

'There's just one thing, master,' the lad said as Friar Simon told him to wait while he collected his donkey. 'The reeve said not to say anything about this to the villagers here.'

'I understand, and so it shall be, my son.'

He followed the boy back on his donkey the three miles to the village of Axeton. When they arrived, he went directly to the church and sent the boy to fetch the reeve and go about the village to announce that he would preside over the funerals.

* * *

When Father David de Warter's widow ran away with a travelling cobbler who used to regularly visit the village, but who never returned after that, folk suspected that the fatal fall may not have been quite as accidental as it had seemed. It was only after a few months that tongues started wagging and it became known that Father David regularly beat his wife, Myrtle, and that he had never slept with her.

'It would have been his drinking that robbed him of his

manhood,' one worthy said in the Cherry Tree, the same tavern that Father David used to frequent.

'What, the ale in this drinking house?' queried another drinker sarcastically. 'He'd have to have drunk the whole place dry on account of Old Alan keeps his barrels well-watered.'

'Old Alan heard that,' said the landlord, 'and you know well I doesn't do that. Especially not with these justices of the peace that the king has set upon us to enforce that weights and measures nonsense. Honest landlords like me have a bad name thanks to the likes of some rogues who water their beer.'

There was general laughter in the tavern.

'Calm yourself, Old Alan, I'm not serious about your beer,' said the jester. 'All I know is I've never had a problem rising to the matter with my old woman and she's given me nine young ones that I can barely feed.'

'You're the rogue in this tavern,' said Old Alan. 'You need to learn some respect. Look at that poor Percy the Comber who died only yesterday. And Edith Pargit before him. The apothecary they sent for says it's the pestilence returning.'

'Then we had best pray and keep drinking,' replied the jester.

'It isn't funny, you fool. They are both in their coffins and should have been buried already, only there's no priest to take the funerals.'

The door of the tavern was thrown open and an urchin ran in. 'There's a friar over at the church. He said he'd heard about the ones that had died from the plague. He says the Lord must have sent him to save us. I've to fetch the villagers and Gideon Moor the reeve to him.'

'What's his name, young one?' Old Alan asked.

'He said he's called Friar Simon.'

* * *

Gideon Moor was fetched, and soon the whole village trooped into the small cemetery behind the church. All of them knew the two victims of the pestilence and were fearful of it spreading and wanted to see that the bodies were buried deep in the earth of the church graveyard.

Friar Simon was standing by the church door. 'Come, all. I am Friar Simon and hear that you have two souls who have perished from a return of the pestilence.'

The group that had first arrived parted to let Gideon pass through to stand before the friar.

'Welcome, Friar Simon. You heard true. We have two people who have died most horribly and we already have two others who are dying if they be not yet dead already. Their houses have been marked with red-painted crosses so that all may avoid them.'

He made a sign of the cross over his heart and went on. 'We are anxious that they should be buried here in the graveyard of their forebears. They await in their coffins and two graves have already been dug for them.'

'Then bring them forth in the coffins, I pray you,' said Friar Simon. 'I shall hold the service at the burial sites.'

Gideon looked about him, already aware that none would voluntarily carry the coffins of those dead from the pestilence, except for Megan Prole and Sally Bringbucket.

'They are round here,' called out Megan Prole.

The two women left the crowd and went round the church to where they had left the two coffins. The friar and the villagers followed and stood looking at the two simple coffins left at different parts of the graveyard.

'We thought Edith would want to be buried next to her

husband,' Gideon said, pointing to the hole that the village gravedigger had dug. 'And Percy the Comber would have wanted to be beside the wall on the other side of the sheep, whose wool was his livelihood.'

The friar nodded his head. 'Very appropriate and very respectful. Are they long dead?'

'Not too long, but we would like to see them underground as soon as possible as they died of the pestilence,' said Gideon. 'It's only right.'

The friar told them all to gather round, which they did diffidently; none of them except the two searchers were willing to get too near. Despite having no knowledge of the two departed people, he carried out the funerals efficiently and with dignity. Then both coffins were lowered on ropes by the two sturdy women searchers, before the gravedigger began filling their graves.

'And now, come inside the church,' Friar Simon told the villagers as they prepared to leave, leading the way as if he knew the place and was the village priest already. 'I have an important message for you all about the pestilence and the message that the Lord sends with it.'

Osbert Flood had also been alerted by the youngster and arrived on his dapple-grey pony, dismounted and followed them in. Everyone thought he still looked unwell after his own illness and imagined that he was utterly bereft after the loss of Dickon his son. They all respected the way that each day he forced himself to face life and carry out his duties as the bailiff.

In truth, it was all an act that he felt bad about, for he knew that if he told anyone that his son yet lived the monster that called himself the Magister would either cut off one of Dickon's fingers or worse, cut his throat.

Keeping up his act he tried to give everyone the impression

that he was personally coping and able to shoulder the responsibilities of his office, albeit he was struggling with his grief. He marched to the front pew, which was reserved for Sir Hugo and Lady Honoria, on the few occasions they attended the church rather than worship in their own chapel in the manor house, or for himself in their absence. He sat down and waited for the friar to mount the pulpit. The two men nodded at one another.

Then Friar Simon delivered his message of doom and of the coming of the end of all things with great gusto.

3

AQUA VITAE

Langbarugh wapentake
30 April 1361

Osbert Flood had many tasks to perform as the bailiff to Sir Hugo de Braithwaite. One that he performed with great diligence, since he considered it an honour above his station to do so, was to represent Sir Hugo at the fortnightly manor court.

In years past, Sir Hugo always had a reputation for running a fair but harsh manor court. As he had grown older he had grown more irascible and less lenient. Then he had seemed to lose interest and had become extremely intolerant. His sentencing had mirrored this change in his attitude and it was Lady Honoria who had persuaded him to leave the running of his manor courts to his bailiff. This was something that had been greeted with relief by those who had transgressed or incurred debt in the manor villages, for they knew the bailiff to be of a kinder disposition than their lord of the manor. In addition, because he was not actually their lord, and was closer to their class, everyone felt sure that he would be more likely to give lesser sentences and fairer decisions.

And so it had been for some months until Osbert had been smitten by the pestilence and he and Marion lost their son. Then suddenly it seemed to the villagers of Axeton, whether because he had generally become angry at the whole of the world and its people, or perhaps because the pestilence had somehow affected his brain, he changed. He exacted heavy fines and gave out stiff punishments so that instead of people regarding him as a benevolent representative of Sir Hugo, he became every bit as severe as his lord had been at his most authoritative.

At his most recent manor court he had two people birched and nailed by an ear to the pillory. They were two brothers, Walter and Timothy Pinker, who had been found guilty of poaching for pheasants.

No one at all suspected that he was acting upon orders given to him on the three separate occasions that two cowled figures had taken him in the coffin to a place where he had heard his son's voice. Each time the threat to Dickon was renewed and he had no choice but to obey the instructions given to him.

Every fibre of his being felt utterly wracked with guilt about his deception, his newfound harshness and worst of all, the fact that he was concealing the fact that Dickon still lived from his wife.

* * *

'There is no doubt about it,' the Magister told the small group of friars in front of him in the vast cavern that he had been shown by Le Patron. It was ideal for his purpose, for he thought of it as an unholy church.

Two torches behind him flickered and made his cowled figure seem all the more frightening.

Not one of the group was a real friar, nor even a lay brother, but they could all preach and knew how to muster and talk to a crowd. They had been given nondescript brown gowns that made them look like regular friars.

'The end of the world is not far away,' the Magister intoned. 'This is the message you must give wherever you go. Tell them that the great Antichrist will be coming and he will undo all the nonsense that was taught by the one they called Christ. His name is Asmodeus. Say his name!'

'Asmodeus!' they chorused.

'Tell them he will show you how the apocalypse is prophesied in the book that the church priests tell their stories from, but yet they keep this truth from them.'

He paused for a few moments and watched them, seeing with satisfaction how their eyes gleamed and they nodded their heads as they swallowed his words. Then he went on.

'Say this to them, that he has already sent signs. Did he not already give a taste with the Great Death, and the famine that followed it, then the wars with the Scots and the French? And the day the heavens opened and stones fell from the sky, killing thousands of King Edward's army? And most important, tell them that the pestilence is returning and that only those who are chosen will survive.'

They had come some distance on foot, from different villages and hamlets where they happened to be staying, for none of them actually belonged to any village but were players and mendicants, tricksters and mountebanks. Men who went about the country to village markets with a bench or stool, which they would mount, gather a crowd and sell worthless nonsense. Cures for baldness, ague, cankers, remedies for impotence, love potions, charms to attract lovers, spells to fend off unwanted suitors, all the things that simple folk would pay coin for. Each one of them had been selected and recruited for their talents in peddling trinkets, charms and false hope, and for their essential dishonesty. They had made their way to the meeting place furtively after dark, after the curfew had been sounded.

The Magister as he called himself had lived in England for several years and knew how to lose his accent so that they only knew him as one of great learning and power, skilled in alchemy and necromancy, but knew not from whence he had come. They had been recruited willingly through the appeal by his special helpers to their avarice, but once ensnared in his web he had instilled fear in them all. Fear of death, one way or another.

His eyes blazed as he instructed them further, knowing that each time they gathered to hear him he had bent them further to his will so they would do anything, because they were rewarded each time they came with coin. They took it eagerly, like swine gobbling greedily. He thought of them as his swine.

He despised them as men, yet knew he had to use such as they for his plans to succeed.

Yet there were four others standing gowned like them, but instead of simple ropes around their waists three had yellow cord sashes to mark them out as ones that had superiority over them. Like himself, they had their cowls over their heads so their faces could not be seen. These three were his chosen *porchers*, the swineherds who would make the swine before him do exactly as he told them. Not only had they recruited the swine, but they had put the fear of the Magister into them, and as his cruel aids, they put the fear of death into them, too.

The fourth gowned figure was no servant. About his waist

was a purple sash, which indicated his importance. He did not always attend their gatherings, but they knew him as *Le Patron*.

'Do you hear me, my brothers?' the Magister called.

'We hear you, Magister,' they chorused.

You are not my brothers, you are my swine, he thought sneeringly.

'Will you tell them that they can be saved?'

'We will tell them, Magister,' they said at once.

'What will you tell them they must do when they are given the sign?'

'They must praise Asmodeus and rise against the Church,' one called out.

'But Magister, what will the sign be?'

'It has not yet been decided, but it will be a death of someone of importance. That is all they need to know. Tell them to have faith in Asmodeus. And tell them to show faith by making a donation, however small. Tell them that you will come again another day and bring the *aqua vitae*, or the *quinta essentia*, that will save them from the pestilence that is coming. It is a gift from Asmodeus, a precious gift that they may make an offering to partake.'

He gave a throaty laugh. 'And you will see the wooden bowl by your feet will be filled with coin.'

That appealed to them all and soon the cavern was filled with avaricious laughter.

He raised his arms. 'Yes! And Asmodeus, the king of demons, the Antichrist, will save you all, for you are chosen. Gather around and I shall give you all a taste of the *aqua vitae*. Unlike the wine that the priests give, but which is worthless, this *aqua vitae* is the water of life. I will protect you from pestilence.'

And one by one they came to him and drank from a wooden bowl he held to their lips.

Having given a drink to all he grasped one of the torches and held it aloft for a moment. 'Behold the power of Asmodeus!' he cried as he lowered the torch and then cast a hand at it, surreptitiously throwing a powder into it. Instantly there was a loud bang and a bright flash that illuminated the cave.

There was a collective gasp then anxious murmurs as the gowned figures cowered back.

'Fear not. The power is with us.'

He threw more powder into the torch and another explosive noise and another flash drew further utterances of wonder and anxiety.

'Feel the presence! Tell the crowds who gather round you that Asmodeus is coming just as the pestilence is coming to claim more lives. He will appear to villages everywhere. Tell them they must watch for the signs and they must rise up and obey him.'

At the back of the cavern the four were watching and smiling.

* * *

After the Magister had given orders to the three *porchers* as he liked to think of them, they sent the false friars scurrying like rats into the dark, back to sneak into the villages and hamlets from whence they came that night, taking their gowns off and hiding them before they arrived. Only once they were alone did he let down his cowl, as did Le Patron.

They were both men in their early forties. The Magister was bearded and had long black hair. Le Patron was broad-shouldered, clean shaven and had the arrogant bearing of one used to command.

Without speaking they took the two torches and extinguished them before leaving the cave and making for their tethered horses.

The half-moon illuminated their way and they rode in silence for a mile.

'An impressive showing, Magister,' said Le Patron at last as they were heading for the place they called the castle, which was a crenellated manor house known to be the home of Sir Boniface Blunt. 'You know exactly how to make them fear you.'

The Magister laughed. 'Fear is one of the most powerful tools, Sir Boniface. It is transformative and can make beggar and king alike, quake and quiver if used correctly. Indeed, if given the opportunity the beggar can have power of life and death over a king. These greedy, scared fools will spread dissent wherever they preach, just as the real friars of the Franciscan order seem to be doing already.'

They had agreed when they began their endeavours that they should restrict themselves to these sobriquets. There was too much to lose should an inadvertent slip of the tongue reveal their true identities to a minion.

'Do you think you have convinced them that this Antichrist, or Asmodeus as you called him, is actually going to come? And that the end of the world is really coming?'

The Magister shrugged. 'Some will and some won't. It does not matter much, as long as they do the preaching as I have instructed. Yet the fact is that he is going to come and when he does we will control him and by my rituals, you and I shall gain all that we desire. As for these swine, the more seeds of fear that they sow the more it will spread so that the pestilence we create will reap a rich harvest. It is like mixing the right materials to make silver or gold. Or that marvellous fire powder that Friar Roger Bacon discovered and so generously wrote about and which I have prepared.'

'The late Friar Roger Bacon,' said Sir Boniface with a hearty laugh. 'I have always enjoyed the way you speak, Magister. You can explain everything in terms of your alchemy.'

'But of course, since everything comes from the same source. Alchemy is the supreme knowledge and wisdom. Dust and earth yield the minerals from which I can extract the metals. And it is from the earth that life comes and ultimately it will return to. Everything goes in circles and cycles. Beggars and kings come, live and die. They get sick and suffer in just the same ways, unless they are fortunate enough to meet someone such as I.'

Sir Boniface laughed again. 'You mean if they can meet someone who can give them one of your potions.'

'*Mais oui*, someone like me who can make potions to cure, to love or even to kill. Or even to cheat death as the elixir of life can do.'

'And which you promise these minions of ours. They believe the *aqua vitae* you give them will even prevent the pestilence.'

'It will certainly prevent the pestilence that we are giving them,' replied the Magister, permitting himself to laugh. 'Now come, let us retire to your castle and sup food and wine before I must get back to my laboratory to carry on with my work to create the gold that you crave just as much as any beggar or any king.'

'And the other matter, that which is the true reason that I saved you and give you sanctuary to work in secret?'

'It is already working, as you know. Your mutual lust and my potions will help you achieve your desire and all that goes with it. But I need the sacred wood of the cross that you promised.'

'And that I will obtain for you. All is prepared and I leave tomorrow.'

They continued in silence until the crenellated outline of Sir Boniface's castle appeared in the distance. The moonlight shimmered off the moat that surrounded it.

'The chaplain goes with you?' the Magister asked a few minutes later as they crossed the moat.

'Yes, and he knows what part he must play. Just as do my two men.'

'The chaplain has a good heart and a good head,' the Magister said with a disconcerting chuckle. 'I almost feel sad that he only knows part of his purpose in this great enterprise of ours. We cannot afford for him to lose his head – yet.'

Sir Boniface suddenly felt a cold shiver run up his spine. He looked askance at the shadowy figure riding beside him.

This villain is as ruthless as myself. But what matter as long as all our goals are achieved?

4

THE JUSTICE OF THE PEACE

Paxton-Somersby, Allertonshire wapentake
14 May 1361

Sir Ralph de Mandeville sat on a bench behind a rough table in the Wattle Hall of the village of Paxton-Somersby in the wapentake of Langbarugh. It was a relatively modest timber-framed wattle and daub building capable of holding about fifty people at the most, which happened to be about the population of the entire village.

'It looks as if the session will be busy despite the size of the village, my lord,' said Peter Longwood, his clerk, as he sat at a smaller side table with his pile of vellum sheets, his lists and all his writing accoutrements in readiness.

Sir Ralph nodded as he watched the villagers file into the hall to take up whatever seats were available or to adopt a stance at the back.

'That suits us well, Peter. It suggests that all are interested in justice being brought to them and that they want to see justice being served.'

The clerk sucked air through his lips. 'Yet surely my lord, if there are disputes to be settled then one of the two parties will feel they have had justice and the other will feel otherwise?'

'But they will have had a fair hearing in a court and a judgment based upon the law, which is the right of all regardless of their station.'

Peter smiled, for he was well aware that Sir Ralph knew the law as well as any man in England and was always both fair and considered in his judgments.

Paxton-Somersby was tiny in comparison to the towns that the main quarter sessions were held in, and even for petty sessions such as this it was one of the smallest villages. The size didn't matter to Ralph; what did was that the whole village attended voluntarily in order to see that justice and the law were available to all no matter how wealthy or how poor they may be.

From his cursory appraisal of the villagers when they began to arrive, he could see apprehension in the eyes of many, and marked fear in others.

It had been thirteen years since the pestilence that they called the Great Death had ravaged the land and killed almost half the population of the country. Now there was talk that it might be returning, and it was only natural that people were fearful. Only fools and the ungodly did not fear the return of the pestilence. Especially if what the parsons, priests and friars told them was true, then those who were with sin would likely be swept away from this life and their bodies be cast into one of the mass gravepits that were so common with the first plague.

The common people were used to being told what to do, even though it may not seem fair, and were by and large both God-fearing and law-abiding. They were obliged to attend church every Sunday, and the manor courts whenever summoned, which was a matter decided by the lord of the manor or his bailiff. Yet now with the new Act passed by King Edward's government they had the opportunity to attend the new justice of the peace sessions willingly rather than through obligation.

There were two types of sessions or justice of the peace courts. Quarter sessions or assizes held in the larger towns at regular intervals in the year, when several justices may sit on the bench together and hear cases before a selected jury. Petty sessions were held in villages of the different wapentakes where one justice of the peace heard all manner of lesser cases on his own without the necessity of a jury.

Ralph waited until everyone had shuffled in and taken available seats or occupied standing positions towards the back of the hall. There was a considerable amount of muttering and mumbling and shuffling of feet. Sir Ralph rapped his gavel on the table three times and there was instant silence. He surveyed the hall with his practised lawyer's eyes, noting the nervous expressions and mannerisms of some of those in the audience and the looks of anger, indignation upon others, and yet on others nothing but confusion. He saw that there were men and women of all classes with the exception of the nobility. There were some yeomen, freemen, craftsmen, labourers, artisans, wives and persons unattached. In short, it was very similar to many of the sessions he had held across the riding.

Sir Ralph was a tall, well-built man of thirty-four years. He was clean shaven with collar-length dark hair, piercing yet kindly green eyes and a firm jaw. He wore a blue cotehardie with his chain of office prominent on his chest, a belt with a dagger at his left side. The dagger and the St Sophia locket that he wore on a chain around his neck so that it hung against his skin were two of his most precious possessions that he was never without, for they had been gifts from his late beloved wife Isabella, and he now considered each a personal memento mori. He patted his chest over the locket as he often did to establish his connection with her memory whenever he was about to do anything of importance.

His sword and scabbard he had placed on the table.

He cleared his throat and began.

'I, Sir Ralph de Mandeville, the justice of the peace for the wapentakes of North Yorkshire, declare that this session of the peace in the village of Paxton-Somersby is now open. My clerk of the session, Peter Longwood, will record all pleas, all cases, and judgments given today. He has already provided me with a list of pleas given to him by Jethro Turner, your reeve, and so we shall now begin.'

He rapped his wooden gavel on the table once more and nodded to Peter, who stood up and walked over to Ralph's table with a piece of vellum upon which he had written the same list that he had given to Sir Ralph.

'Robin Lister and Budkin Sharp,' Peter called out. 'Both approach the bench and state your names and make your pleas.'

* * *

Peter was a slight man in his late twenties with intelligent eyes and a good-natured temperament who had been in service to Sir Ralph's family household all his life in various capacities. When he was in court he was a paragon of seriousness, yet outside he had a good sense of humour, albeit always showing respect for Ralph, who treated him as more of a friend than a servant.

He had been taught to read and write by the family steward

after he had shown early on that he had a keen intelligence and had clearly more potential than merely to work in the manor's kitchen. Instead, he had become Ralph's personal clerk and assistant, and had accompanied him when he went to London to study law at Gray's Inn and even went with him to France as his servant and clerk when Ralph fought at Poitiers. Having learned Latin and French as his clerk in London he had been of great value to Ralph when he was advising King Edward the Third about the terms of the Treaty of Bretigny, since he could write competently in either language and kept all Ralph's documents, reference texts and maps along with his writing paraphernalia in his saddlebags and could produce them or look up details at a moment's notice.

People often underestimated Peter's physical abilities at their peril. Although he had never been trained in the use of arms or of any form of combat, yet he had learned at an early age how to hold his own. Generally, he used his quick wits to outmanoeuvre or outthink an opponent, but failing that he used agility that he had acquired to compensate for his lack of brawn. Although he carried only a short dagger, yet he had a small but heavy ball of lead sewn into each of the billowed sleeves of his black doublet and he had proved them to be effective weapons.

* * *

While Peter made both men swear on the Bible to tell the truth, Ralph read the short summary of the case that Peter had prepared for him after discussion with the village reeve.

It seemed there had been a long-running dispute between two families that had suddenly and violently come to a head.

Both Robin Lister and Budkin Sharp were villeins who

worked adjoining pastures and each had a few acres that they rented out from the manor. There had never been any love lost between the two and their families.

At the shearing time there had been a fight between them, resulting in the wounding and loss of one of Budkin Sharp's left fingers from a snip with sheep shears and a reciprocal broken nose sustained by Robin Lister from a strike in the face with a shovel handle.

'Who started it?' demanded Ralph.

'He did!' cried Robin Lister. 'He stole two of my lambs.'

'No, 'twas he. I took the sheep 'cos he stole and killed one of my pigs.'

They argued in front of the court and were reluctant to desist until Ralph rapped with the gavel and gave an order to be quiet. Until then both villeins seemed to expect that he would side with them and be strict and impose a harsh fine on the other.

'I lost a finger and won't be able to grip properly,' complained Lister.

'You mean you won't be able to steal and slaughter a man's pigs. Look what he did to my nose.'

Ralph called for silence again. 'Listen to me. Two lambs are worth one shilling each as they are not grown, when they would be worth seventeen pence each. One pig is worth two shillings. Thus, both of you have stolen the same from the other.'

Both villeins protested and were each supported by cries from their respective families and friends. Ralph rapped his gavel again.

'You have both come for justice, but this court will be treated with respect and I shall have no further shouting. Do you both understand?'

Both men hung their heads and muttered.

Peter stood up. 'Sir Ralph asked if you understand? So, answer. Do you?'

This time both answered clearly that they did.

'But there has been one lost finger that was cut off, and a nose that was broken,' Ralph went on. 'Yet it was fortunate that it was only the nose and not a gouged eye.'

'He must make amends, Sir Ralph,' cried Robin Lister.

'So must he!' shouted Budkin Sharp.

Ralph eyed them both sternly. 'I said no shouting.' He leaned forward and steepled his fingers to rest his chin upon them. 'Indeed, so how best to do this fairly. You must each pay the other two shillings.'

The gathered crowd sniggered and some laughed outright.

'Well said, Justice,' cried someone.

'Serves them both right,' said another.

'Yet what of the maiming of a hand and the breakage of a nose?' Ralph continued, looking about the crowd. 'Should Budkin Sharp hack off one of Robin Lister's fingers and should Robin Lister receive a blow to break his nose?'

A few laughed nervously but were rebuked for it by Peter.

Ralph went on. 'You shall not pay each other recompense, but are fined sixpence each, to be paid to the village communal fund.'

He addressed Jethro Thomas the reeve. 'I take it that Paxton-Somersby does have a communal fund?'

The reeve spoke out. 'We do, my lord. It is for maintaining the boundaries, hedges and for the poor of the village.'

Both Robin and Budkin protested vocally but were silenced again with a rap of Ralph's gavel.

'Another outburst and it will not simply be a fine, but there may be a corporal punishment with the birch,' Ralph said firmly.

Again both men looked as if they would like to protest and their families squirmed but made no noise lest the fines should mount and be difficult to pay, or worse be extended to other family members.

'Pay the money to your reeve and then return to your seats.'

* * *

Sir Ralph de Mandeville had qualified as a serjeant-at-law and had in peacetime established a successful law practice in London. When his widowed father died during the Great Death of 1348 he had inherited his title and the Manor of Hutton Conyers with extensive estates on both sides of the River Ure in the wapentake of Claro in the West Riding of the County of Yorkshire. The manor included the parishes of Farnham, Hampsthwaite and Kirby Malzeard. It had been a wrench to leave London and his growing law practice, but he felt the responsibility to return home to look after his estate.

Having married in London he had hoped to have a family of his own. Fate decreed otherwise and just a year after his father had died from the pestilence, his beloved wife Isabella had succumbed as well and he was left bereft, feeling purposeless and bored with the mere administration of the family estate.

It took him many months to come to terms with Isabella's death, for he had imagined they would live long and full lives together. She had a remarkable intellect and he felt that he could talk to her as an equal, seek her opinion on matters of importance and always be given good counsel. Being unable to see or touch her again was bad enough, but not being able to talk to her was torture, until he sensed her presence when he touched the locket of St Sophia, containing as it did strands of their entwined hair.

'We will ever be together, Ralph,' she had said when she first put the chain about his neck. 'I have the twin of this locket that will be with me forever and wherever we are we can think and be with each other in our minds.'

Isabella was buried with her locket and his became his reminder of his own mortality, but also his solace. He found that when he touched it and talked to her as if she was near him he could almost hear her speaking to him, giving him her counsel if he asked.

As a lord of the manor he had several times fulfilled his duty to the king by making himself available to fight abroad, taking with him a small contingent of archers and men-at-arms. Not only had he personally distinguished himself in battle, but he had shown his leadership qualities in handling the men under his charge at Poitiers and later at Chartres.

Yet it was his legal prowess that King Edward valued so highly. Ralph had advised the king and his son Edward the Black Prince after both the Battle of Poitiers and again four years later after the short-lived siege of Chartres, when the heavens had opened on what became known as Black Monday when over one thousand men died in a lightning and hail thunderstorm. At the Hotel de Sens on 10 May 1360, Sir Ralph was one of the six knights who ratified the Treaty of Bretigny with Dauphin Charles.

By this treaty King Edward obtained considerable lands, including Gascony and the countship of Calais and other major cities, and freed England from the suzerainty of John, King of France. In return Edward gave up all claims to the throne of France but consolidated the territories under his control in Aquitaine. King John the Second was to pay a ransom of three million ecus, but would be released after payment of one million, giving his two sons as hostages until the full ransom was paid.

Then Ralph was approached by the Crown to become a coroner, but he declined as he did not feel that the duties of the position held much appeal to him. The coroner was a long-established official role that had been introduced by King Richard in 1194. It was their responsibility to investigate all unnatural deaths, by calling an inquest. They would also hear abjurations of those seeking sanctuary in church, preside over shipwrecks, and deal with treasure or possessions if there was no heir apparent.

So instead of becoming a coroner, or crowner as they were commonly known, he opened another law practice in York, much to Peter Longwood's delight, albeit the practice only lasted for two years. At that point there was talk that Sir Ralph de Mandeville might be appointed as a Judge of the King's Bench in York, one of the highest legal positions in the land outside London.

'Thanks to His Majesty!' Peter had silently cursed when King Edward passed the Justice of the Peace Act early that year of 1361 and Ralph accepted the king's request that he should become a justice. 'Now it will be back to drudgery.'

But it would be far more important and dangerous than mere drudgery.

* * *

It was King Richard the First, who was called Lionheart, who with his first minister Hubert Walter commissioned certain knights throughout the land to preserve the peace in unruly areas of the country. They became known as the Keepers of the Peace. This system was maintained with some degree of effectiveness until King Edward the Third passed one of his first Acts in 1327 appointing good and lawful men in every county to guard the peace. Their powers were limited and ill-defined, so at last in 1361 he passed the Justice of the Peace Act. This stated that in every county there should be appointed four justices of the peace who would have the power to bind over the unruly.

Rather like the coroners, whose principal function was to record and investigate causes of death, the justices of the peace received no remuneration, so it was something that only those of considerable means could undertake. They were all especially selected as being men of honour, intelligence and who had a strong sense of justice.

This was seen to be a move to bring justice to the people, other than the situation that had existed since the Norman Conquest when the manor courts were held in each of the manors of the country, under the jurisdiction of the lord of the manor. The justice that was dispensed in such courts varied immensely depending upon the ability and the sense of fairness and justice of the lord of the manor, most of whom had no legal background whatsoever. They could sentence their serfs and freemen living in their manor district, which could cover a vast area of a county, to fines, or corporal punishment, or even to capital punishment by hanging. Each manor lord was effectively a law unto themselves.

The justices of the peace were given the power to hear and determine the different offences, differentiating them into felonies and trespasses, to supervise array and to enforce the labour laws, which removed some of the burden from the coroners. They also had the power to fine for economic offences, and sentence to punishment or to refer to the sheriff and the King's Bench in more serious cases.

A more tedious but important additional role was to oversee the new system of weights and measures.

They could also, if they felt it merited it, call a jury from the locality, ranging from five to twelve or so persons.

'So, let me be clear, my lord,' Peter Longwood had asked Sir Ralph when he was first appointed. 'What is the difference between a felony and a trespass?'

'They are both offences against the law, but felonies are all the violent acts.'

'Murder?'

'Yes, as well as physical theft, assault on the person, maiming, all manner of ill treatments of both persons and animals, and rape of course.'

'I fear that we shall be busy, my lord.'

'We shall, but this is an important task we have before us. We bring justice to the people. That means finding when felonies have been made and protecting the innocent and the vulnerable.'

Peter nodded. 'And trespasses, Sir Ralph?'

Ralph raised his eyebrows. 'Ah, these may be more subtle, but include extortion by threat of some kind. Stealing of horses, cattle, sheep and any goods, but not necessarily causing physical injury.'

'These may be fine lines, my lord.'

'Which is what I, as the justice of the peace, must determine and find or sentence accordingly.'

'And you mentioned economic offences, Sir Ralph? Is this anything to do with money?'

'Well, any money or valuables taken from someone is a theft, which is a trespass, but so often someone may have been cheated out of goods or possessions without any threat. Rolling loaded dice at the hazard table for example, or using trickery with cups and balls, would be an economic offence, albeit they are trespasses, too.'

'So would fooling someone by using a superior knowledge of tallying be such an offence?'

'It would, as it is dishonest and one person suffers at the hands of another person's dishonesty.'

'Yet difficult to prove, my lord, unless a trickster is caught red-handed. I have seen such trickery at markets and at fairs. And such tricksters often do not work alone, but have a helper in the crowd to make players think they are dealing with an honest man, or woman.'

'And therein is another offence. The law is quite clear on such dishonest assistants, who are deemed to be an accessory to a felony.'

'I have seen mountebanks working that way, my lord. They sell jugs of medicine that they say cure everything from tapeworms to baldness.'

'They are only an offence if they knowingly sell medicines that they know do not work.'

'Not like the apothecaries, my lord. They sell their potions that don't work, but they believe they do. Being ignorant seems to be a good defence in the law.'

Ralph smiled, amused by the sharpness and wit of his clerk of office.

* * *

Ralph went through the rest of the list of cases, which included a weights and measure case, dealing with an assault, two robberies and a number of further minor disputes.

There was no further shouting between disputing parties, for all had learned that Sir Ralph demanded that people show the court and the justice of the peace due respect. In return they were given fair hearings and judgments.

* * *

'Henricus Faker the butcher, come forth,' Peter called out when they came to the last case.

A barrel-chested man with great forearms, chapped hands and red cheeks came to the front of the hall and stood in the three-sided pen that was used for defendants in a case or for witnesses.

Ralph read the notes he had been given on his case while Peter held a Bible for the butcher to swear upon to speak honestly.

The swearing-in completed, Peter returned to his small table on which he had been writing the session roll. He had prepared a fresh quill at the start of the session, which had needed sharpening twice, and used a copious amount of ink to scrupulously record each case and each judgment as instructed by Ralph. After each entry he opened a pounce pot containing powdered cuttlefish bone then sprinkled a pinch over the ink, before tapping the vellum and blowing the loose particles away, thus drying the entry. He was proud that Ralph found few errors when he reviewed the cases, but he was mortified if his spelling or grammar fell below his high standard.

'Now, Master Henricus Faker,' Ralph said, staring directly at the man, who stood with a bowed head. 'You have been accused of a serious felony, in that one week ago you drank many mugs of ale in the Blue Sow tavern. That you were drunk and that you picked an argument with several men you had been drinking with and that you broke the nose of one, cracked the head of another, and bit the ear of a third so that he had to have the surgeon stitch a wound on it. How do you plead, Henricus Faker?'

The butcher looked up. 'Firstly, your honour, my name is just Henry, not Henricus. Secondly, I am guilty of all those things, and I am sorry. Those men are my friends.'

Ralph glanced at the notes Peter had made. 'The landlord of the Blue Sow says that you broke a table and broke a jug.'

'I had drunk a lot, your honour, but I was not as drunk as I should have been, if Samson Perkin had not watered his ale as we heard.'

There were a few laughs from the crowd, but a stern look from Ralph silenced them. He signalled Peter to draw close and whispered to add an inspection of the landlord's ale to the list, as weights and measures and the strength of beer and ale fell within his jurisdiction.

'Did you break a table and smash a jug?' he asked as Peter resumed his seat and scratched out a note on his list.

The butcher hung his head slightly and mumbled an assent.

'Have you anything to say in your defence?' Ralph asked.

A voice from the crowd called out. 'Yes, he has. Tell him, Henry. Tell him why you were drinking.'

Samson Perkin turned and glared at the speaker. He had been angered by the fine that Ralph had imposed on him earlier in the session after one of his mugs had been shown to give short measure and he was concerned that the justice's clerk had just written something else down at Sir Ralph's instruction.

'Who said that?' Ralph demanded. 'Come forth and take the oath on the Bible. I call you as a witness in this case.'

A man of about the same age as Henry came forward. He wore an apron covered in white powder. His right ear was covered in a bandage wound diagonally about his head.

He stood next to Henry Faker and swore on the Bible that Peter held out to him.

'Your name?' Ralph asked.

'William the Miller, your honour. Henry bit my ear, but as he says, we are still friends.'

'And what should he tell me about?'

Henry looked at the miller with tears in his eyes.

'Henry's son was taken a little more than seven weeks or eight weeks ago, your honour.'

'Taken? You mean he died? How so?'

Ralph and Peter glanced at one another. Like everyone else they had heard rumours about the pestilence having returned in other parts of the country. When someone died it was the first question on their minds.

'No, he didn't die, someone took him. There was a hue and cry, so the whole village went looking for him after he disappeared, but he went with no trace at all. Someone took him, that's what we all think. Is it any wonder Henry started getting drunk, him being a widower and all, and young Thomas his only son.'

'Tell me more of what happened?' Ralph asked Henry, his tone softer.

The butcher looked up through eyes filled with tears. 'It was after archery practice, your honour. I sent my Tom back to the house to put his arrows and bow away, but he never got home. We found his bow and his arrows, but not my Tom. There was... there was...'

'What was there?' Ralph asked encouragingly.

'Blood, your honour,' William the Miller answered for him. 'His bow and arrows were in the village ditch and there was blood on them. But no Thomas. We looked everywhere, the whole village did.'

Desolation

The crowd started to shuffle in their seats and mutter and mumble, and some of the braver folk called out to confirm the tale.

'Who did you report this to?' Ralph asked the butcher.

'To Jethro Turner, the reeve.'

Ralph nodded to Peter who stood and called for the reeve to come forward and take the oath.

Ralph questioned him to confirm the account he had been given. As he did so he looked across and saw with approval that Peter was busily scratching away on the vellum, recording everything in his neat Latin script.

'And so, no trace was found of young Thomas. Did you report this further?'

'I did, Sir Ralph. I reported it to Sir Robert Ingram himself, for he is the lord and he had men go to all of the villages in his manor estate, but young Thomas hasn't been seen or heard from since then.'

Ralph sat pensively stroking his shaven chin for a few moments. 'I am deeply sorry to hear this, Henry Faker. The loss of a son from illness is bad enough, but losing a son by having him be stolen and therefore not knowing if he still lives is truly a horrible thing to happen. I wish there was something that I could do to help, but it seems that all that can be done has already been done by your friends and neighbours. I know it is little recompense for your loss, but I dismiss this case against you and impose no fine at all.'

There were more murmurs from the crowd but no cheers or words of relief. Henry the Butcher and William the Miller briefly embraced, then with bows and tugs of their forelocks to Ralph they made their way back into the crowd.

Back in the room that Ralph had taken in the Blue Sow, much to the anxiety of the landlord Samson Perkin, before they ventured to eat and drink, he and Peter talked over the cases as Ralph read the recording that Peter had made of the session.

Neither of them felt in any hurry to eat as they were wary that the landlord might silently express his chagrin by spitting in their drink after having been ignominiously fined for short selling his ale. Ralph had yet to decide whether to officially investigate the strength of his ale. He thought he would rely on tasting it first.

'That was a horrible case of the stolen boy,' said Peter. 'One hates to think how Henry Faker must be feeling. But at least you were lenient on him.'

'It would have been wrong to punish him any further, Peter. He has lost his son in the worst way imaginable.'

There was a sudden tapping on the door.

Peter rose from his seat and opened it.

'Why, it is Merek of Ryedale,' he announced as a tall man in the livery of one of the York City guards was revealed.

'What brings you here, Merek?' Ralph asked. 'We were about to eat and drink, so you will join us.'

'I will right willingly, my lord. After I have fulfilled the task I was sent on by the Sheriff of York and His Grace the Archbishop of York. I have two important messages for you.'

'Have you come straight from York?' Ralph asked.

'I have, my lord. Sir Marmaduke and the mayor, John de Langton, had been visiting the archbishop at his palace and summoned me upon their return to the city. The sheriff ordered that I am to be considered your assistant until you deem it otherwise.'

Ralph nodded. 'I am happy to have you with us again. Peter will also be, as it may lessen my demands upon him.'

Peter and Merek smiled at each other for they had become friends some years earlier when going home to Yorkshire after returning from France, and after when working on other cases together. They had often drunk and played hazard together in taverns about the city, albeit Peter could only sup one tankard to every three that Merek could pour down his throat. In part it was because Peter had less capacity for ale than his big friend, and also that he had what the apothecaries called a choleric stomach that was easily upset by rich food, excessive ale or even the sight of blood. Yet it was also because he liked to keep a clear head when gambling, so he could calculate the chances of different dice combinations. There was never a shortage of drinkers willing to play dice in taverns and Peter usually left with more money in his purse than when he entered the establishment.

'Did you hear anything of the pestilence on your way here?' Peter asked as Merek opened a satchel and handed the two wax-sealed letters to Ralph.

'There is no sign of it in York, but there is certainly rumour of it having spread to some villages. People were certainly wary of me as I think people are becoming suspicious of travellers.'

'Did you notice any funerals or new graves as you passed graveyards?'

'I fear so, but there are always deaths, my lord. I saw at least three new burials and one grave being dug in a churchyard on my way here. Yet I do not know if any have been confirmed due to the pestilence. To be honest, I did not stop to ask anyone. I was told it was urgent that I find you and give you these letters. I was told to tell you they concerned matters of life and death.'

Ralph nodded and Peter shuddered. It was sometimes better not to know too much.

All three made the sign of the cross.

5

ARROWS

Paxton-Somersby, Allertonshire wapentake
14 May 1361

Ralph sat to read the two messages, first the one from Sir Marmaduke of Flamborough, the Sheriff of York.

'This is ill news indeed. The Sheriff of York informs me that the coroner, Sir Broderick de Whitby, has been foully murdered. He and his bodyguard, Adam Dalton, were found in woodlands near to the village of Axeton in Langbarugh wapentake. Both their bodies were found shot with several arrows and their bodies stripped of their valuables.'

He looked up at Merek of Ryedale, who stood by the door with his arms folded. 'Had you heard of this, Merek?'

'No, my lord. I am but the messenger and knew nothing of what the letters contain. But as you say, it is ill news that a coroner has been murdered and robbed. I knew of Sir Broderick, for he held lands in Langbarugh and Whitby Strand wapentakes, which are north of my home wapentake of

Ryedale. He was known as a good and fair lord and as a just coroner.'

Ralph looked at the archbishop's letter again. 'And do you know of Arncliffe Forest and the village of Axeton?'

'Aye, my lord. I do. When I was younger I... used to walk in the forest.'

Ralph smiled, aware that when Merek said he walked, he probably meant that he hunted.

Merek was broad-shouldered and taller by at least four inches than Sir Ralph, and almost an entire foot than Peter Longwood. He was the ideal build for a longbowman as the average longbow was six feet and a tall man could hold it without it touching the ground. He had a full blond beard and shoulder-length hair and habitually wore the leather wrist-guard of an archer. He dressed in a tunic with the York guards livery, with a great belt about his waist from which hung his dagger and sword. That he was good-looking was clear, as he rarely passed a woman or girl without drawing admiring glances.

'Outlaws, I will wager,' said Peter. 'When men are outside the law they lose respect for it and its officers.'

He suddenly looked up at Merek and wished for once that he had curbed his tongue.

* * *

Five years before at the Battle of Poitiers in France, Merek of Ryedale had fought well as one of the mounted archers. He and his fellow longbowmen had played a significant part in the victory over the French. The English army under the command of Prince Edward, or the Black Prince as he was known by virtue of the black armour that he wore, was outnumbered yet proved victorious in the three waves of the battle, the English longbowmen proving more efficient than the French crossbowmen, who were given little time to reload their cumbersome weapons while the archers could fire volley after volley. For every quarrel crossbow bolt fired, a longbowman could dispatch ten arrows, and while the quarrel could cover a distance of two hundred paces, a longbowman could flight his arrow three hundred.

As the French prepared for their third attack of the battle, the English archers had been able to replenish their supplies by retrieving their arrows from the bodies of the enemy on the battlefield.

In the aftermath, Merek's commander had ordered his archers to shoot down fleeing French soldiers. Merek and some of his fellows refused to obey the order, to their cost. After the battle was won, when the French king and many of his nobles had been taken prisoner, those English soldiers who had refused to obey their commander were arrested, flogged by some of the longbowmen who they had fought beside but who unlike them had obeyed the order to slaughter without hesitation. Merek and his comrades also had their pay, share of plunder and personal goods seized. Their commander, Sir Gregory Havelock, who held manors in the North Riding, proclaimed that they were henceforth to be declared outlaws and that when they landed once more in England they would be subject to the law.

Sir Ralph heard of this treatment of this small group of archers and intervened, declaring that Sir Gregory had no legal right to treat them in such fashion, either to submit them to a flogging, take their belongings or to declare them outlaws.

'I have a mind to dash out your brains, Sirrah,' Sir Gregory, who had a reputation as a capable fighter, threatened Ralph.

'You could try, but I would not advise it, Sir Gregory,' Ralph had replied. 'But know that I am going to inform His Highness, Prince Edward, that you have abused both the law and his valiant archers in such a despicable act. Once His Highness has heard the case then I am at your service if you wish me to teach you a lesson personally on the field.'

Prince Edward held an impromptu court in his tent that day. The prince was dressed resplendently in his back surcoat and mail, attended by Sir John Chandos, and the Earls of Salisbury and Warwick. He had Merek and the other archers brought before them. Ralph had talked to them all and they had agreed that Merek should speak on their behalf and be represented by Ralph. Peter Longwood was permitted to accompany Ralph as his clerk and to take a record of the proceeding.

'And so, Bowman Merek, what was the order that you and the other fellows disobeyed?' Ralph asked.

'Sir Gregory wanted us to shoot the soldiers in their backs as they fled, my lord,' Merek replied, his voice firm with no sign of fear speaking before his sovereign.

'And you refused, why so?'

'We shoot upon soldiers in the field, from a distance, but firing at them so that they can see. None of us have the stomach to shoot men in the back as they retreat from battle.'

Sir Gregory protested vehemently, but was silenced by the prince's raised hand.

'Your Highness,' Ralph pleaded, 'each one of these archers played their part in your victory and they have all shown themselves to have honour in their hearts. Sir Gregory's punishment was harsh; it was without legal precedent and he had no right whatsoever to confiscate their rightful pay and share of plunder, and absolutely no right to declare them *caput lupinum*, that is wolf's-heads. Effectively, upon their return to England, he was saying that anyone could kill them, like common outlaws.'

There were further arguments and protestations from Sir Gregory, but the Black Prince silenced him and conferred briefly with nobles.

Prince Edward announced that he agreed with Sir Ralph's legal arguments and told Sir Gregory in no uncertain manner that he was displeased at the law being abused in such a way. He rescinded the confiscation of the archers' pay and share of the spoils and ordered that they be further remunerated as recompense for the abuse and injustice they had suffered.

Ralph was at that time unaware that he had made an enemy of Sir Gregory Havelock.

Upon the return of the army to England, Merek had asked to accompany Ralph's contingent of archers home to Yorkshire. On the way, Merek and Peter had become firm friends, albeit from time to time Peter could not resist jibing about how Merek had been an outlaw even though only for a few hours, and that it possibly ran in the family, as was so often the case.

This clearly stung Merek, although he accepted it as part of Peter Longwood's humour, but Ralph himself noticed. When they finally arrived back in York, he questioned the longbowman on the subject and was told that his grandfather for a time had been outlawed in the days of King Edward the Second for failing to obey the muster to arms against the Scots, the reason being that his wife, Merek's grandmother, was giving birth to her only child who would become Merek's father. Tragically, his grandmother died within a week of giving birth and his grandfather was left to look after his new-born infant on his own, and had to bury his wife.

When Ralph again took up his practice in York he saw that Merek, who had no family of his own and no reason to return to Ryedale, obtained employment as one of the city's guards. From that day on, if Ralph had required physical help in any endeavour or legal task that required brawn as well as brain, with the sheriff's permission he had only to ask the help of Merek, who himself had proclaimed his gratitude to Ralph and his loyalty if he ever needed him.

Over the course of these endeavours the three men had come to know and understand each other well, to the point that notwithstanding their differences in social rank they could enjoy drinking ale and enter into friendly banter. Indeed, on occasions they had dressed in disguise as equals and acted the part of revellers or as comrades while engaged upon some quest or investigation. Several times they had found themselves in dangerous situations and had to fight and guard each other's backs. Each brought different fighting skills that somehow complemented each other.

* * *

Ralph read the second letter, which was from the Archbishop of York, then sat back and drummed his fingers on the arm of his chair.

'John of Thoresby, the Archbishop of York, does not seem to think that the coroner's murder was simply an attack by outlaws. He received a letter from the Prior of Gyseburg which informed him that Sir Broderick and his man Adam were killed, but that his clerk was missing.'

Merek frowned. 'You mean the clerk escaped or he was taken by the outlaws?'

'Or he was involved with them,' Peter suggested.

Ralph shrugged. 'We can assume nothing. The fact is that the coroner was killed, when he was on his way to see or after he had seen someone who had sought sanctuary at the Priory of St Mary in Gyseburg. The prior himself had sent a message to

Sir Broderick asking him to come to take an abjuration of the realm from this person, who he said was a friar.'

'Abjuration of the realm?' Merek repeated with a puzzled frown. 'What does that mean?'

'It is the law of sanctuary, Merek,' Ralph explained. 'If a felon seeks sanctuary in a church or other religious building, or even a churchyard, then he may stay in that church beyond the reach of the local sheriff for forty days. He may call for a coroner who will hear his confession and record it on his coroner's roll. This entitles him to abjure the realm, which means he swears to go into exile rather than face trial and punishment. He would be given a white cross to carry and would be escorted by constables to the nearest port. Many have avoided the axe or the rope by such means.'

'So this friar is a criminal?' Merek asked. 'Why else would he be seeking sanctuary?'

'The archbishop asked the same question in his letter to me. He said that the prior said in his missive that the man kept saying that he had to atone and that he needed to make pilgrimage, but needed sanctuary first.'

'Surely it was a grave crime indeed,' Peter commented. 'Perhaps he killed someone.'

'Possibly,' replied Ralph. 'And if so then that is something that the coroner Sir Broderick would have wanted to investigate, but of grave importance is the murder of the coroner himself.' He picked up the letter and read it again.

'There is more to tell you and this may furnish us with a clue. The archbishop had received another letter, but this was from the Bishop of Durham, His Grace, Thomas Hatfield. It was written two days before he wrote this letter to me. Bishop Hatfield reported the theft of the Black Rood of Scotland from the shrine of the blessed St Cuthbert in Durham Cathedral and requested help in gaining its return.'

'What is this Black Rood, Sir Ralph?' Peter queried.

Ralph read out the description given by the archbishop. 'It is an ornate ebony and gold, bejewelled cross-shaped reliquary containing a piece of the True Cross upon which our saviour, Jesus Christ, was crucified by the Romans.'

He waited as both Merek and Peter gasped and stared at him. Both men made a sign of the cross over their hearts.

'The reliquary is about the size of a man's palm, so the wood within it is about the size of a finger, but its importance is inestimable. The archbishop gives a little of its history. It was taken to Scotland by St Margaret, a Saxon princess of the House of Wessex, who was born in Hungary. When King William conquered England in the year 1066 she fled to Scotland and married their King Malcolm, the third of that name, who was called Canmore. Ever since then it was known as the Black Rood of Scotland and it was kept at Holyrood Abbey near the city of Edinburgh. Queen Margaret died with it in her arms and it has ever been considered a crown jewel of Scotland. Yet when King Edward's grandfather, the first of that name, conquered Scotland in 1296 he captured the Black Rood and took it along with the Stone of Scone as spoils of war and kept them in Westminster Abbey. Then in 1328 after the Treaty of Edinburgh and Northampton our King Edward returned the Black Rood when he renounced all claims to sovereignty over Scotland.

'But the Scots continued to raid in the northern borders, and during the Battle of Neville's Cross near Durham fifteen years ago, when William de la Zouche, a predecessor of the Archbishop of York, led the army in the north along with Lord Neville of Raby and Henry, Lord Percy, King David of Scotland had the

Black Rood carried in the battle. When he was wounded and captured, King Edward regained it and eventually had it placed for safe keeping in the shrine of St Cuthbert of Northumbria.'

'Why in his shrine, my lord?' Merek asked.

'Because apparently before the battle the saint appeared to monks of the Priory of Durham in a dream telling them that they should not allow the lands to be violated. So the Prior of Durham led his monks out to a hill called the Maiden's Bower carrying his communion cloth tied to a spear. The battle was won, and King David was wounded and captured. From thence onwards the Black Rood was kept in a wainscot wardrobe that is part of the shrine of St Cuthbert in Durham Cathedral. It is only viewed by arrangement with the keeper of the shrine. And there it has stayed until it was stolen, and the keeper struck unconscious.'

'Who stole it, Sir Ralph?' Peter asked.

'It is thought to have been a visiting nobleman, an Earl of Sussex with two squires and the earl's chaplain. The shrine or feretory sits behind the quire in Durham Cathedral and is accessed through the Chapel of Many Altars. It has to be opened specially by raising the canopy, but when this was done for the Earl of Sussex, he was struck down. When the poor fellow regained consciousness he found the wardrobe wherein the Black Rood was kept had been opened and the reliquary was gone.

'The group had left unchallenged and rode off. The bishop was informed and as you probably both know, he has a small army. Yet although the area was scoured by search parties in all directions they found nothing. The Earl of Sussex, of course, was no such person, merely a spy or a criminal. Since it is an object of such importance to the kings of Scotland it was feared that it might be taken to Scotland, where it could be used to rally an army.'

'But why would the Scots raise an army, Sir Ralph?' Peter asked. 'King David of Scotland has been returned to his land by King Edward and yet has to pay a ransom each year for ten more years, is that not so?'

Ralph nodded. 'Indeed so. And as you both know, at the Treaty of Bretigny which I helped to draw up and which was ratified as the Treaty of Calais only a few months ago between King Edward and King John of France, the French monarch was also given his freedom after the Prince of Wales captured him at Poitiers these five years afore. France too yet owes us a huge ransom and we have two of his sons as hostages. There should be no more threat from Scotland or France, as long as they pay their ransoms.'

Merek tugged his blond beard. 'And if one country sought war, the two may join together. *The Auld Alliance* as they call it!'

'Exactly,' said Ralph. 'Two countries both traditional enemies of England and both having recently had their monarchs released. Both have hefty ransoms to be paid, but if they had a rallying call around some object of veneration, such as around the Black Rood, the single most important relic of Scotland, then perhaps rather than raising ransoms they might raise armies instead. And this being the case the archbishop has written to inform King Edward. The archbishop also wonders if the so-called Earl of Sussex was a spy along with the two squires and the chaplain.'

Ralph frowned. 'It is all very alarming, and the murder of Sir Broderick and his man Adam Dalton is suspicious as it happened so soon after something as momentous as the theft of a reliquary of such importance to the whole realm of England. It cannot be dismissed as a chance occurrence. Especially not when a friar had sought sanctuary and wanted to make abjuration. To my mind this sanctuary-seeking friar is the chaplain to the Earl of Sussex.'

'And what of this so-called Earl of Sussex?' Peter queried.

Ralph shrugged. 'I do not know. If this friar is the man professing to be the earl's chaplain, then he may have killed the man claiming to be the Earl of Sussex. Or this earl and his squires could be chasing the friar, hence he claimed sanctuary and wanted to make abjuration of the realm.'

'We live in dangerous times, it seems,' said Peter pensively. 'First the fear of the pestilence coming back, and now perhaps war again.'

'The archbishop also comments on that, for he hears that the pestilence has already reached beyond London to Bath and Colchester and to some villages, but not yet York. He counsels caution. He also makes mention of a Friar John Ball, whom he says is spreading dissent against the Church, and preaching that the pestilence is coming along with the Antichrist and end of days because we have lost touch with the Lord.'

'It seems that friars are causing much trouble,' said Peter with a tinge of sarcasm. 'Mayhap they should all be considered *caput lupinum*.'

Then, seeing Merek's cautionary expression, he coughed and muttered an apology to his big friend.

Ralph suppressed a smile. It was clear that Merek and Peter were pleased to be together again and he knew that it would take a little time for them to get used to each other's humour or lack of it. He lay the archbishop's letter beside that of Sir Marmaduke.

'Both the sheriff and the archbishop request that I change my itinerary from my round of petty sessions and head straight for the Priory of St Mary in Gyseburg in Langbarugh wapentake to investigate the murder of Sir Broderick of Whitby and to see if I can find if this sanctuary seeker has already left.'

'But it is not likely he would have left, is it, my lord?' Peter asked. 'After all, would it not require the coroner to have furnished him with a white cross and arranged for constables to accompany him to a port?'

'He may have done so already, somehow. Or the sanctuary seeker could have taken his chances and left on his own,' said Ralph. 'The Prior of Gyseburg may have more information, but the archbishop did say in his message that the man said he needed to atone and that he had to make a pilgrimage.'

'Where to, my lord?' Peter asked.

Ralph shrugged. 'It could be anywhere in Christendom.'

He frowned. 'The archbishop is most concerned about recovering the Black Rood. If this person is involved in that crime of simony then perhaps he fears that he is being chased by someone and that his life is in danger, hence he sought sanctuary.'

'Might he be pursued by these spies you mentioned, my lord?' Merek asked.

'Or the king's enemies within the realm,' Ralph said, nodding his head. 'All is possible, but another thing comes to mind. There is another possibility now that I mentioned Christendom. Seeking sanctuary and abjuring might be a means of making his way to a foreign land to seek pilgrimage.'

Both Merek and Peter looked questioningly at him.

'If this Black Rood actually contains part of the cross that our saviour, Jesus Christ, was crucified upon, could he be thinking of making atonement by taking it back to Jerusalem, to the place where the son of God was crucified?'

* * *

Early the following morning after they had broken their fast Peter unrolled the maps of the northern wapentakes that he carried in the great saddlebag that also contained his parchments, vellums and the rolls of the sessions. He had already packed away his writing paraphernalia that he was so proud to be the custodian and user of as a literate person.

'It is not too long a journey,' said Ralph as he traced the route they should follow to get to the village of Axeton. 'I had not planned to hold petty sessions in the Langbarugh wapentake before next week.'

'It will be a fair climb in parts, my lord,' said Merek. 'We have to pass through the Tabular Hills which bound the south of the Great Moor, then after passing through it we follow the trail through the woods and valleys until we climb up again to enter the Arncliffe Forest. It is relatively flat but once we pass through it we descend again to reach Axeton.' He looked through the window at the grey clouds. 'Let us hope that the heavens do not open as we travel.'

Peter cringed at the prospect of rain, for if it came to keeping himself or his saddlebag with the session rolls dry, he knew he was likely to end up like a drowned rat.

'Are we going to Axeton to investigate the coroner, Sir Broderick de Whitby's death first, Sir Ralph?' Peter asked.

'We are, since we pass through Axeton before we journey to the Priory of St Mary in Gyseburg.'

'It is not too far from there, my lord,' said Merek. 'Across the moors. We can make it before nightfall.'

* * *

They set off, Ralph and Merek riding together on horses followed by Peter Longwood on a pony. They talked affably as they rode, for when out of earshot of courtroom or public spaces Ralph was content to treat them as equals since he had respect for Merek's honesty and integrity, as well as his ability to look after himself, and for Peter's wit and intellect.

There was nothing that Merek did not know about archery or single-handed combat, just as there was little that Peter did not know about gaming, for his aptitude in mathematics was prodigious and he had worked out his own system to win at dice and hazard. Ralph had seen him demonstrate how such a knowledge could increase one's chances of wagering on the roll of knucklebones or dice. Not only that, but he had studied the way that mountebanks and tricksters could manipulate by using conjuring tricks or even switch loaded dice that contained tiny weights to make them roll to certain numbers.

'Do you actually think the murder of Sir Broderick had anything to do with the person seeking sanctuary, my lord?' Merek asked at last.

'It is possible, but we do not know if he was on his way to Gyseburg or if he had been there already. I fear we shall not know until we reach Axeton and begin our investigations.'

'Would you care to make a wager, Sir Ralph?' Peter piped up from the rear.

Ralph laughed. 'There are things that I will wager with you about, Peter, but not on something as serious as this.'

'Your pardon, Sir Ralph, but I agree with you about that. No, I was looking at the clouds overhead which have been darkening this past hour. I wonder if they will burst before or after we stop to eat?'

Merek looked back over his shoulder and grinned at Peter. 'I take it the little man is overcome with hunger and would like to stop, my lord.'

Ralph nodded. 'It would make sense to stop soon and share

some food. There is a copse of trees ahead, so let us rest the horses and eat.'

'No wager, then, Sir Ralph?' Peter asked.

'Only about whether we get to Axeton dry or wet, Peter.'

The little clerk frowned. 'On balance, Sir Ralph, methinks betting on such an outcome is tempting providence.'

'Quite right, Peter,' Merek said with a laugh. 'We want the protection of divine providence so let us eat and merely accept that if it rains we get wet.'

'A good philosophy, Merek,' said Ralph. 'Let us take cover lest it rains while we eat and drink in safety.'

'Oh in safety in these dangerous days,' said Peter, looking round him as he habitually did to make sure that no one was following them, or waiting on the trail ahead. 'I am all for that. But as for food, my stomach is feeling queasy from the buffeting it is getting from riding this pony that insists on giving a lurch every few yards, so I will have naught but a little bread and honey as the apothecary ordered.'

* * *

After eating and allowing their mounts to drink and munch grass they resumed their journey. From time to time they passed shepherds herding sheep on the trail, or an occasional pedlar on a donkey or ass on their way to one or other of the many villages to be found in the moorland.

Many of the villages looked the same with houses of varied structure, surrounded by ploughed fields, some with serfs, villeins or even yeomen working them with oxen and ploughshares. They passed many churches and various religious houses some distance from the roadways. Some priories or nunneries were no bigger than village churches, others of medium size were small abbeys, probably home to up to a dozen monks, but none were as large as the huge abbeys of Fountains, Rievaulx or Whitby.

As they followed the route the terrain changed, and they passed through more woods, large swathes of undulating heather-covered moors with rugged cliffs and huge boulders, through the valleys between the great hills, and then began to climb upwards above scattered tarns to the ridge where the Arncliffe Forest began.

Soon they were riding along the ridge with precipitous drops and entered the great oak forest which had large rocks peeping out here and there. They kept to a path that weaved its way through thick undergrowth of hawthorn and blackthorn.

As they started down a slight incline beyond a great boulder there came a sudden whistling noise and Peter felt a jolt as his saddlebag shot forward and struck him on the back of his calf. Looking down, he saw an arrow protruding from it.

'Arrow!' he cried. He gave his pony kicks with his heels, lay forward against its neck and urged it forward. 'Outlaws!'

Merek and Sir Ralph, who had been riding ahead as usual, both looked round and saw Peter start to chase after them. Then another whooshing noise was heard and Ralph felt a thud on his left shoulder.

'Forward, my lord,' Merek cried. 'We are attacked.'

In a trice he had turned fully in the saddle and had his short bow in his left hand and flighted an arrow as he searched the undergrowth behind them for sight of an attacker.

'Come, Merek!' Ralph cried. 'We are targets here.'

Merek loosed his arrow and then dodged sideways in his saddle as he heard and saw an arrow coming in his direction, but which struck and bounced off an oak tree ten feet to his side.

'I come, my lord,' he cried.

Another arrow whumped into a tree trunk ahead of him, bounced off and he deftly caught it as he galloped after Ralph and Peter. All three kept riding until they knew they were out of arrowshot with the sort of bows that could be used within woodland.

Ralph called a halt and turned his horse to look back in case of pursuit. There was no sound or sight of anyone.

'Should I go back, my lord?' Merek asked. 'It would be too dangerous to go directly, but I could go on foot and scout around to try to find our attackers.'

Ralph was rubbing his shoulder and silently cursed. He shook his head. 'No, it would be foolish as one or more archers could be waiting for one or all of us to return.'

'Are you hit, Sir Ralph?' Peter asked anxiously.

'I was, but only a glancing blow thanks to the gambeson I wear under my surcoat.' He looked at Merek. 'How many were there, do you think?'

'Only one, I would wager,' Merek replied, glancing challengingly at Peter.

'I would back your opinion and would not waste time on a wager,' Ralph's clerk replied. 'A single outlaw, then.'

Ralph was still rubbing his shoulder. 'I fancy I will have a fine bruise when I take my gambeson off,' he mused. 'But as for this being an outlaw, I think it was an attempt on our lives, and a clumsy one at that.'

He dismounted and, reaching to Peter's saddlebag, plucked the arrow from it. Peter also dismounted and undid the buckle on the saddlebag and anxiously looked inside.

'Fortunately there is no damage to the rolls, my lord. Just a hole in my bag that I will stitch as good as any surgeon.'

Ralph was looking at the arrow. 'It looks a match to the one in your hand, Merek. What do you make of them?'

'They are unbarbed, reasonably fletched and with ash wooden shafts. Common enough arrows such as any villager in England may have used.' He held both arrows up and examined them. 'They have been used before, there is no doubt, but only on butts, I would say. Also, they have clearly been fired by a relatively unskilled archer. I would not have missed three sitting targets like us.'

'But you have shot upon men in battle; the archer who fired these may not have done,' said Ralph. 'The person who shot at us was either unskilled as you said, or else his hands shook when he took aim. The questions are, who was it, and why did he try to kill us?'

6

AXETON

15 May 1361

As Ralph and Merek finally approached the village of Axeton they found themselves confronted by two woodsmen armed with axes on the road leading into the village.

'You can't come into our village unless by order of the reeve,' said one, a burly fellow in a smock and a shapeless cap.

'Why not?' demanded Ralph without identifying himself or his position.

'We have the pestilence,' a slighter fellow replied. 'We don't want travellers bringing more of it.'

'Or catching it from here and taking it elsewhere,' said the first woodsman. 'Only folk with important business with the bailiff or Sir Hugo de Braithwaite, or any of our regular merchants and market folk that we know are allowed past us.'

'Who is your reeve, fellow?' Merek demanded.

'His name is Gideon Moor. We're here on his orders, so just turn about and be off with you all.'

Ralph lifted his chain with his seal of office from under his surcoat. 'Then know this, I am Sir Ralph de Mandeville, justice of the peace, and I have important business in this manor. I am going to see Sir Hugo de Braithwaite and then I have come to investigate murder done here.'

The two men looked in panic at each other.

'He must mean the crowner and his man,' the burly one whispered to his companion.

The other gave a curt nod and bowed his head to Ralph.

'Your pardon, my lord. We just had orders. You can—'

'Tell me of the pestilence,' Ralph cut him short. 'How many people have been affected? Have you had deaths?'

'We have, sir,' said the slighter woodsman. 'About eight of our village have died these last few days.'

'Has a physician or surgeon confirmed the pestilence?'

'The apothecary from Duncombe has, my lord. He saw some of the first cases.'

Peter's pony had been some distance behind, for the clerk had worried that it had been upset by being shot at and he had spent much time singing to it and stroking its neck as he rode along. When he came alongside Ralph and Merek he saw that the two woodsmen put on guard with their axes looked cowed in the presence of the justice of the peace and Merek.

'Now, good fellows, can you tell us much about the outlaws in the Arncliffe Forest that we have just come through, and who shot at us?' he asked.

The two men again looked aghast at each other, unsure how to respond and hoping that the other would lead. At last the slighter of the two shook his head.

'We have never known outlaws in that forest, sir. Not until we found the bodies of the crowner and his man.'

'Who found them?' Ralph demanded.

'We... we did, my lord. I am called Douglas and my friend is named Luke. We work in the forest and were on our way to do more coppicing when we found them. Both shot with arrows, three in the crowner's back and his man in the chest.'

'It was a horrible thing to see, sir,' said the man now identified as Luke. 'We had our wagon and took them into the village and called Gideon Moor, the reeve. He sent a message for the bailiff to come to tell him what to do with the bodies.'

'Did you know who they were?' Ralph asked.

'Yes, my lord,' Luke replied. 'Sir Broderick of Whitby had been to Axeton several times before. He had gone to see Sir Hugo and Lady Honoria when a messenger, a monk, came to get him from Gyseburg Priory.'

'How do you know all this?' Ralph asked.

'Gideon Moor told us and said that the crowner wanted to know the quickest way to get to Gyseburg Priory.'

'And what is the quickest way?'

'Straight through the forest, sir. We know it better than anyone and we directed them.'

'How many do you mean by them?'

'Three of them, my lord. Sir Broderick, his man Adam Dalton and his clerk, Robert Hyde.'

'You knew all three?'

'Aye, sir, by sight.'

'And they were seen to set off for Gyseburg Priory?'

'Aye, sir. The monk had set off back to the priory ahead of them. Then the next time we saw them was when we found them dead.'

'But there were only two bodies found? What about their horses?'

'Only two bodies, sir. Douglas and I searched this neck of the forest and there was no other body. We don't know what happened to Robert Hyde. Whoever killed the crowner and

Adam Dalton must have taken their horses as well as all the valuables and weapons they carried.' He shook his head as if it had been a mystery. 'But we found more blood.'

'You mean there was blood elsewhere apart from that you found by the bodies?'

'Yes, my lord,' Luke took over. 'A trail of it, but it led to the beck that runs through the forest before it runs into the Esk river. We went up and down it, but didn't find anything else.'

Ralph nodded. 'I may need your help later to show me where exactly you found the bodies and the other blood.'

'Gideon Moor can always send for us, my lord.'

* * *

The Manor of Axeton held by Sir Hugo de Braithwaite measured some six leagues by three leagues and consisted of nine villages and several hamlets scattered within the moorland and pastureland, coppiced woods and much of the Arncliffe Forest. The River Esk flowed through it and along its way had many becks running into it and itself went through many steep-faced gills. The pastures and moors were ideal for breeding sheep and grazing cattle and the land around the various villages was arable and grew crops of wheat, barley and oats.

Axeton was a large village in the centre of Sir Hugo's Manor of Axeton on the bank of the River Esk, and the manor house itself was the grandest building in the whole area. It was a mere ten miles from Whitby which was reached to the north over swathes of sprawling moorland. To the east and west of the village, open farmland was worked in strips throughout the year by the yeomen farmers who rented the land from the manor, or by labourers in thrall to the manor lord. The village ran parallel with the river and on either side of the single street and scattered around a duckpond and a village square with a large oak tree at its edge there were a varied collection of dwellings. Like most villages Ralph held petty sessions in he knew that these would be home to virgaters, half virgaters, cotters, craftsmen, woodmen, swineherds, shepherds, and assorted labourers. Thus there lived together serfs, villeins and yeomen.

The dwellings reflected people's status and were built of a variety of materials and ranged from simple one-roomed hovels to multiple-bayed houses with thatched roofs and small enclosures for animals and chickens. The more affluent villagers, people like Gideon Moor the reeve, had two-storied dwellings with an undercroft for their animals.

At the east end of the village was the church and at the other end up a rise on higher ground stood the sprawling three-storied stone-built manor house with its stables, outhouses and an actual walled garden.

As Ralph and the others rode into the village square they passed a large barn-sized wooden building with a coat of arms painted above its doors, indicating that it was where the manor court was held, and by its side a smaller square building made of stone with a heavy door and a grille that was obviously the village jail. In front of it were two pillories and beside them two sets of stocks.

'That looks like old blood on the pillory, my lord,' said Peter. 'And there have been nails there.'

Merek frowned and made a growling noise in his throat. Both Ralph and Peter knew it was because of his loathing for corporal punishment, having himself been unjustly on the receiving end of it in France.

'There will be people with holes in their ears,' Peter muttered, careful not to mention the word wager.

Ralph nodded. 'The lord of the manor has the right to pass such sentences as nailings, as well as severing ears, branding, or even that.' He pointed beyond the great oak tree where the wooden frame of a gallows stood.

'There is a tavern opposite it, my lord,' said Merek with distaste. 'I can hardly think of anything that would curb a man's thirst than seeing a dead body swinging outside. Much as I like ale. I hope it is not often used.'

'I had heard that Sir Hugo de Braithwaite has always dealt sternly with miscreants in his manor court,' Ralph replied.

'Are there not too many types of court, my lord?' Merek asked.

Ralph sighed. 'In my opinion there are too many indeed. The manor courts have dealt with most of the crime in England since the days of the Conqueror, King William the first. They have always had a reputation for being harsh, but it depends upon the views of the lord and his interpretation of law. The King's Bench in London and York can try the most serious cases brought before them. The county assizes have always been an attempt to bring the bench to the country and judges from London visit each county two or three times a year.'

'Then there are the Church courts,' Peter volunteered. 'They are said to be more lenient, are they not, Sir Ralph? If a rogue can speak a little Latin.'

'The Church courts certainly have their place, dealing with offences by the clergy such as apostasy, simony and also with Church matters. The benefit of clergy that you mention is an ambiguity that allows anyone who can demonstrate some knowledge to be tried in a consistory court by clerics rather than a civil court, be that a manor court, King's Bench or one of the quarter sessions run by justices of the peace like myself. In general, they are more lenient and less likely to order corporal punishments like we see have been given here, or capital punishment.'

'But they can excommunicate one, can they not, my lord?' Merek asked.

'Indeed they can, and to be excluded from the sacraments, attending church and receiving any form of blessing could be considered a more severe punishment than a birching, or branding, since it could imperil your immortal soul.'

They rode on and all three were immediately struck by how quiet it was. There were the usual sounds of hammering and sawing that one heard in a busy village, but very little of the chatter and noise of a market or of people haggling or bartering. There only seemed to be a few people about although they could see people within the various dwellings as well as smoke curling up through holes in roofs and the intermingled smells of cooking pots, boiling urine for laundry working, and burning peat and charcoal.

'Look at the crosses painted on those doors, Sir Ralph,' Peter pointed out.

'A sign that someone within is suffering from the pestilence,' Ralph said.

'And there!' said Merek. 'Inside that house with the painted cross on the open door. There is a body in a winding cloth. You can sense death here in this village.'

As he spoke they heard the rattle of a cart coming along the street. A man in a gown and with a neckcloth wrapped round the lower part of his face was behind the reins of the single pony, his head down as if he was allowing the animal to find its way. Walking alongside the cart were two large women, also with neckcloths about their mouth and noses.

'It looks as if they have come for the body,' said Ralph.

'There are two coffins. Unless I am mistaken one is already nailed down and the other is for this unfortunate person.'

They halted their horses as the cart came towards them. Ralph hailed the driver.

'Have you pestilence in Axeton?'

The driver looked up as if roused from a reverie. He stared at them for a few moments then nodded his head.

One of the women unwound her neckcloth. 'George is mute,' she said. 'My name's Megan, and this here is Sally. We're searchers and we saw poor old Jasper here yesterday.' She pointed to the body and then at the red cross on the door of the hovel. 'We had painted the sign after we saw he was ill for people to stay away, but the poor soul had passed in the night when I saw him this morning. We wrapped him in a shroud and fetched George to get the coffin. We already collected another.'

Ralph held up his chain and his seal of office. 'I am Sir Ralph de Mandeville, the justice of the peace. I heard from the two woodsmen who were guarding the road from the forest that an apothecary saw some of the bodies.'

'Not these,' replied the other woman, lowering her neckcloth from her face. 'But there ain't any doubt about it. It was the pestilence and no mistake.'

'And are you taking his body to the graveyard?'

'We are. Him and Ethel, who we just collected and put in the other coffin. George here has dug fresh graves for them both. The friar has said we've to ring the bell in the church when we've got the coffins ready for their funerals.'

'A friar, not a priest?' Ralph asked.

'We haven't had a priest for over a year. We've got Friar Simon here in Axeton and he's sort of taking care of the village while we've got this pestilence again. He said we've all got to work together, pray and repent together.'

'Can you unwrap that shroud for me to have a look at the body?' Ralph asked.

The two women hesitated then Megan wrapped her cloth about her face again and entered the dwelling. She bent down and unwrapped the top of the shroud to reveal the head.

From their elevated positions on their mounts Ralph, Merek and Peter looked through the open door and all of them felt repulsed by the sight of an old man's swollen, bruised and purple visage. His eyelids were open and the eyeballs had rolled upwards so that only the bloodshot whites were visible. The neck was horribly swollen with large matted bubos and burst skin about the throat. The swollen tongue protruded between the cracked and split lips.

'A horrible death, clearly,' Ralph said. 'I suggest you carry on and get him in his coffin, then arrange for your friar to take his funeral.'

The two women showed how strong they were. Rewrapping the shroud and one taking hold at the shoulders and the other the feet, they lifted and carried the old man's body out of the house and up onto the cart. Then they climbed on and lifted him into the crude coffin.

'Has the coffin maker been kept busy?'

'Eight times already,' said Sally Bringbucket. 'These make it ten. He's making more to have them ready.'

'Are you not afraid that you might catch this pestilence?'

Sally shrugged her shoulders. 'The Great Death spared us last time and with God's blessing it might do so again. Someone has to do this, so we work in God's hands.'

Ralph nodded. 'Where can I find Gideon Moor, the village reeve?'

While Megan nailed down the lid, Sally leaped down on her sturdy legs. 'He'll be along, I reckon.'

As the cart moved off people started to appear from their homes.

'It looks as if no one wanted to get too close to the dead bodies, my lord,' said Peter. 'Now they seem curious about us.'

'And this looks like it could be the reeve,' said Ralph, nodding in agreement with Peter's assessment as a sturdy man with a black beard, wearing an apron and a white liripipe hooded hat strode purposefully up the street towards them.

'Your pardon, sirs, I am Gideon Moor, the village baker and the reeve. Can I help you?'

'Indeed you can. I am Sir Ralph de Mandeville, the justice of the peace for these northern wapentakes. My assistants and I are here to investigate the murder of the coroner, Sir Broderick of Whitby. I understand that you saw the bodies of Sir Broderick and his bodyguard Adam Dalton and had them taken to the nearby priory?'

Gideon Moor bent low in a bow to them. 'I did, Sir Ralph. Under the orders of Osbert Flood, Sir Hugo de Braithwaite's bailiff.'

'Did Sir Hugo see the bodies?'

'Oh no, Sir Ralph. Sir Hugo has not wanted to see anyone since the pestilence returned. We rarely see him these days anyway.'

Ralph nodded and pointed at the manor house at the higher end of the village. 'I will pay a visit to Sir Hugo, but first, where can I find the bailiff?'

'Ah, if you go down beyond the church you will see the vicarage house and then further along and with its own stables you'll find the bailiff's house. He will likely be working on his ledgers and accounts. You should know that he lost his son to the plague not long since and he had it himself. His wife is still in mourning for their boy, Dickon.'

He bowed low again. 'If I can do anything for you, or you need anything for you or your men, Sir Ralph, just send for me and I'll get it done.'

He is an obsequious fellow, methinks. But perhaps I do him injustice. A good reeve should be willing to assist.

* * *

Osbert Flood was indeed busily working in his counting house adjoining his home, which was one of the grandest houses in Axeton, apart from the manor house itself.

He heard the approaching horses and saw them through his window. With a few words to Marion, his wife, he left his counting house and went out to greet them.

Ralph introduced himself and Peter and Merek as they all dismounted.

'It is an honour, Sir Ralph. Let me have your horses taken and refreshed.' He clapped his hands and a moment later a young lad came rushing from the stables.

'See that they are watered, Ned. Remember how I showed you.'

He gave a long-suffering smile as the youngster took the reins and with some trepidation led them towards a long trough. 'The lad has much to learn about ostling.' Then his expression grew serious again. 'I have been expecting you or someone in authority, Sir Ralph. It has been a terrible thing to happen, the murder of the king's coroner and his man. I sent a message to Prior Cuthbert at Gyseburg Priory along with their bodies.'

'It seems to be a most dangerous place to live,' Ralph said. 'Murders. Then we were shot at by outlaws in the forest this very morning.'

Osbert Flood looked horrified. 'Shot at? Should I organise a hue and cry with the villagers to—'

'No,' Ralph said firmly. 'Whoever it was is not likely to be in the same part of the forest. There is no sense in putting any of your villagers in further danger. Especially now you have the pestilence.'

The bailiff's shoulders visibly slumped. 'Indeed, Sir Ralph. It seemed just a matter of time before it reached us here in Axeton. I had it myself, but God spared me, only to take my son instead.'

He pulled up his sleeves to show healing scars in his elbow creases where veins had been opened when he was ill. 'I would have given every drop of my own blood if my boy had been spared.'

Ralph, Merek and Peter all offered their commiserations.

'This is a most accursed place to live,' the bailiff said. Then he straightened as if inwardly telling himself to show courtesy and respect to the justice of the peace. 'Will you come into my home and take some refreshments and I can tell you whatever you want to know.'

As Ralph walked along with the bailiff, Merek and Peter followed a few paces behind.

'I think the fellow speaks the truth,' Merek whispered. 'I have a bad feeling about Axeton.'

'I agree,' Peter whispered back. 'And the bailiff looks as if he believes himself to be the most accursed of men.'

'He has lost his son,' said Merek. He stopped and grasped Peter's arm to stop him, too. 'He reminds me of—'

'That is just what I was thinking, Merek. He looked as tortured as Henry Faker the butcher in Paxton-Somersby.'

7

SIR BRODERICK DE WHITBY

Axeton, Langbarugh wapentake
15 May 1361

Marion, the bailiff's wife, was dressed in a long black gown with a grey wimple. She was not a small woman, but it was clear that she had lost weight. Her face looked strained and her eyes were red-rimmed as if she had just been weeping.

'My condolences on the loss of your son, Mistress Marion,' Ralph said after the bailiff introduced him, Merek and Peter.

She looked down at her hands and Ralph noticed how red and raw they looked, as if she had been scrubbing them. He had seen such a sight before in people who were grieving and trying to punish themselves.

'I thank you, Sir Ralph,' she replied. 'I beg you to excuse the state of our humble home, but we can offer you food and wine.'

'A little ale only, if you do not mind,' Ralph replied. He did not feel that they should intrude further. 'We need to get to the Priory of St Mary before the day is done, but first I must pay a visit upon Sir Hugo and Lady Honoria Braithwaite.'

Osbert called for a servant and ale.

'Of course, you must see the body of Sir Broderick,' Marion said. 'He was a most polite gentleman. He... he also gave me his condolences before... before he—'

Her voice broke down and she covered her mouth with her hands, then curtsied and muttered apologies and left.

'I am sorry for my wife, Sir Ralph. Losing my son has affected us both so deeply.'

Ralph put a kindly hand upon his shoulder. 'I understand entirely. I have never been blessed with a son, but I lost both my father and my wife to the Great Death. There are few of us who have not suffered.'

'I went to visit my son's grave at the Abbey of St Leonard only to discover that the monks who looked after us both had also caught the pestilence and died, and that the remaining monks are considering abandoning the abbey,' Osbert said as the servant came in bearing a tray with mugs of ale. He sighed wearily. 'And now we have the pestilence in Axeton.'

He hung his head. 'I feel so bad that I may have brought the plague to the manor.'

Ralph nodded sympathetically. 'That you will never know, so it will do you no good to feel guilty about it. It can only eat into your soul.'

'I thank you for that, Sir Ralph. It is what I try to tell myself.'

'I understand that you have put measures in place. That you have appointed two women as searchers and put guards at the entrances and exits from the village.'

The two men talked about the pestilence while Merek and Peter sat drinking their ales and observing.

'We are burying the dead with all due respect in single graves, but if there are more I fear that we will have to open a pit.'

'I heard from one of the two women searchers...' He looked across at Peter and asked, 'What were their names?'

'Megan and Sally,' Peter replied instantly, as Ralph knew he would. His clerk missed very little.

'As I was saying, I heard from the seeker called Megan that you have a friar who is conducting these funerals.'

Osbert nodded and ran a finger round the rim of his mug. 'His name is Friar Simon. For that I am grateful to him, but he preaches to the people in Axeton and to the other villages around that because we have been ungodly, the apocalypse is coming and the end of the world will be upon us unless we all repent.'

'Is he preaching as the flagellants did during the first pestilence? Does he flagellate himself?'

'No, Sir Ralph, but he has made everyone afraid.' He took a gulp of ale. 'Myself included.'

'I should like to meet this friar, but I shall do so when we return from the Priory of St Mary, which will probably be on the morrow. But now, I must see Sir Hugo de Braithwaite.'

'Of course, Sir Ralph. I shall go with you and introduce you to him. But I should tell you that Sir Hugo is not as he once was. He and Lady Honoria also lost their son during the first pestilence and he has gradually shown less interest in the affairs of the manor.'

Which makes your position all the more important, Ralph thought to himself. *And mayhap that also explains the great strain that you seem to be under.*

* * *

It was apparent to Ralph within minutes that Sir Hugo was not fully aware of what was happening in his manor.

Desolation

'I leave most of the running of my affairs to my good bailiff, Osbert,' he told Ralph as they sat in his hall, the walls of which were covered with large tapestries on two walls and with pikestaffs and swords arranged on another. As he talked he twitched his head several times and his right hand had a marked tremor.

Osbert Flood had remained standing like a dutiful servant.

Lady Honoria sat beside her husband with her hands clasped tightly together.

She looks nervous, Ralph thought. *I wonder why?*

'It is alarming to hear that the pestilence has claimed so many lives in the village of Axeton,' Ralph said. 'Have you taken precautions yourself?'

Sir Hugo shrugged and waved a hand at Osbert. 'I leave my affairs to Osbert,' he repeated.

Lady Honoria laid a hand on her husband's. 'But you do send messages to all the affected families, my dear.'

Sir Hugo looked at her with a glazed look in his eyes, then he looked at her hand on his before smiling at her.

'Yes, I care for my people. Is that not so, Osbert?'

Osbert bowed his head. 'You do indeed, Sir Hugo. And they are all most grateful for your support and concern.'

'You see?' the lord of the manor said, smiling at Ralph. 'A good bailiff, Osbert. We care, you see. Even if we have to teach lessons if any break my laws.'

'Your laws, Sir Hugo?' Ralph queried.

He noticed Lady Honoria's hand tightening on her husband's.

Once again the knight looked at her hand on his and then he pointed at Osbert. 'But Osbert takes care of that these days, don't you?'

The bailiff looked at Ralph and raised both eyebrows and

gave a rueful almost apologetic smile before he replied. 'I do, Sir Hugo. And it is my honour to represent you in all things.'

Ralph was determined to have an answer. 'You said *your* laws, Sir Hugo. What exactly do you mean? Are they different from the law that I know, that I studied at the Inns of Court in London, and which I practise and administer as a justice of the peace?'

Sir Hugo looked puzzled and turned to his wife. 'What is he asking, Honoria? I am getting tired.'

Lady Honoria smiled at him and patted his hand again. 'Sir Hugo has had a busy day thus far and usually takes a rest at this time. I think he would mean that he held his manor courts regularly and that he was fair but firm in his dealings with any who stole, poached or failed to pay rents.'

'And now he has delegated these courts to me,' Osbert volunteered.

'And you use the pillories and stocks that I saw in the village square near your manor court hall?'

Ralph saw a muscle tense in the bailiff's jaw before he replied. 'I have done, where necessary.'

'And I see you have a gallows. Has that been used?'

'Not recently, Sir Ralph.'

Ralph nodded, but determined to find out later more about the dispensing of punishments by this manor court.

'A good man, Osbert Flood,' said Sir Hugo. 'I can put my trust in him. I used to place it in my chaplain, too.'

Lady Honoria patted his hand again and looked at Ralph. 'If you will be staying in the village, you are welcome to stay here in the manor house, Sir Ralph.'

Osbert looked up as if suddenly roused from a reverie. 'And of course, your assistants are welcome to stay in my house.'

Merek nodded his thanks, as did Peter, even though both would have preferred to stay in a tavern.

* * *

It was almost evening and the light was beginning to fade by the time the trio reached their destination. The Priory of St Mary in Gyseburg was an Augustinian house home to fifteen canons regular and ten lay brothers. Each of the canons was an ordained priest and could if needed be seconded as a parish priest. They all wore black cassocks, hence were often referred to as the Black Monks.

The priory itself was founded by Robert de Brus, Lord of Annandale in 1119. As such it had always been associated with the Scottish royal Bruce dynasty, having hosted King Robert the Bruce in the past and his son King David the Second when he was still at liberty before his eleven-year captivity under King Edward the Third, latterly at Odiham Castle in the county of Hampshire.

It was a fine and impressive building, which had been rebuilt in the Gothic style after a fire had burned down its Romanesque Norman tower over half a century before. Its huge arched stained-glass windows with circular tracery above reflected the late afternoon sunlight. Lay brothers were still at work on the land and as Ralph and his assistants entered the priory square facing the entrance, a canon regular came out to meet them, presumably having been advised of their approach.

Dismounting and announcing himself and his two assistants, their mounts and saddlebags were taken care of by two lay brothers.

'Welcome to St Mary's, Sir Ralph,' the canon said, with a slight bow of his tonsured head, his hands hidden but linked in his sleeves. 'I am Father Benedict and I will take you immediately to see Prior Cuthbert. He has been expecting someone to come from York.'

He led them through the great oaken doors, above which Ralph had seen the coat of arms of the Scottish de Brus house, into the nave where they saw several canons lighting candles and preparing for one of the many daily services that were part of the disciplined life of the priory. They passed through the priory then along the cloister where three canons were at work writing and illuminating manuscripts in bays looking into the cloister square. They all had newly lit candles upon their desks to help in the fading light.

Finally, they climbed stone steps into the prior's house adjacent to the dorter range where the canons lived in some comfort, evidently more so than the simpler dormitory that ran behind it where the lay brothers slept. Father Benedict knocked upon the door and received a call to enter from within.

Prior Cuthbert was rising with the aid of a staff from a prayer cushion before a small simple altar with a wooden cross atop it. He was a man in his late fifties with a kindly, almost serene countenance. He was clean shaven and his snow-white hair was tonsured like all the other canons. His black cassock was distinguished by a white cowl that hung down his back. Like the others he wore a white rope around his middle. He stood and leaned heavily on his staff.

He greeted them as Father Benedict made introductions.

'You have come a long way this day, Sir Ralph, so will you and your assistants take refreshments?' Prior Cuthbert asked. 'You will, of course, stay with us tonight. We have free cells for all of you as our numbers have never recovered since the plague.'

'We will gratefully take the refreshments later, thank you,'

Ralph replied. 'There is some urgency in our mission as the king's coroner has been murdered. This must take priority over our stomachs, I fear.'

The prior nodded. 'Of course. I had hoped it would not be long before someone would come from York after I wrote to His Grace, John of Thoresby, the Archbishop of York. These deaths have been most tragic. Indeed, since I wrote I was surprised to receive the bodies of Sir Broderick and his man Adam, both of whom had broken bread and water with us here when they came to see our sanctuary seeker.'

'I understand that there was a clerk with them as well,' Ralph said.

'There was, but only the coroner and his man's bodies were brought here. I have no knowledge of what happened to the clerk, Robert Hyde. The bodies are still in their coffins in one of the cells behind the infirmary. I knew that you would wish to see them before they are buried. Father Benedict here is our surgeon and hospitaller and will lead the way.'

They followed the canon, albeit slowly, for it became apparent that Prior Cuthbert was afflicted with arthritis and walked with a marked limp. As they approached the infirmary they heard the sound of sandalled feet moving hither and thither and the moans and groans of patients. Oil lamps had been lit at intervals along the long and lofty hall. There was the sound of coughing and spluttering, and occasionally of someone retching. The hospital itself had about twenty cots arranged in two lines against the walls of the hall. Patients lay under simple blankets and it was clear that some were monks and others were people of all ages from the surrounding villages. There was a strong odour of body fluids and of pungent herbs and vinegar.

'We care for many people from all around,' Father Benedict

explained. 'They come to us from many miles and we turn no one away.'

'What conditions do you treat, Father Benedict?' Peter asked with interest.

'Anything. Injuries, broken bones, flux of the bowels, chest troubles and fevers.'

'Have you had any signs of the pestilence?' Ralph asked.

Father Benedict shook his head. 'None yet, but I shudder to contemplate the plague returning. Our house lost nine canons the first time it swept across Yorkshire. It was terrible, and I am not sure we will be any better prepared for it if it comes back.'

'We have come from Axeton where some ten people have already died from it.'

Father Benedict winced and both he and Prior Cuthbert made the sign of the cross.

Ralph continued. 'And we heard that at the Abbey of St Leonard's where the bailiff of Sir Hugo de Braithwaite's manor was treated for the pestilence, some of the monks there have died since he left. Sadly, his son also died from the plague and was buried there.'

Prior Cuthbert shook his head. 'The pestilence respects no person, even those who labour on the Lord's behalf. It is not good news to hear that it is spreading again.'

'What of women's complaints and childbirth?' Merek asked. 'There seem to be few females here.'

Father Benedict shook his head. 'We treat women for many things but not for childbirth. We are fortunate that there is a small nunnery but two miles from here and the sisters there are experienced in childbirthing.'

'That is the Nunnery of St Judith,' Prior Cuthbert added. 'One of our canons gives communion and hears confessions every week.'

'And talking of confessions,' said Ralph. 'I will need to talk to your sanctuary seeker, whom Sir Broderick came to take his abjuration of the realm.'

Prior Cuthbert stopped abruptly and, leaning on his staff, looked up at Ralph. 'Did you not know? You cannot talk to him. He committed self-murder after Sir Broderick and his assistants left the priory.'

Ralph stared at him in surprise. 'He committed *felo de se*. That is indeed ill tidings.'

* * *

Father Benedict had instructed a lay brother to go ahead of them and light candles in readiness for them to view the bodies. The two coffins lay side by side upon the stone floor of a square building behind the infirmary that was used for preparing the dead for burial. There were six guttering candles that threw out a flickering light upon the scene.

A large oak table stood in the centre of the cell with wooden buckets of water against the walls, sponges and brushes upon another table. Shelves held a variety of jars and bottles of liquids.

'Where is the coffin of the sanctuary seeker?' Ralph asked.

He had been surprised when Prior Cuthbert told him that they had found the sanctuary seeker in the sanctum cell at the end of the north transept of the priory the day after the bodies of Sir Broderick and Adam Dalton had been brought from Axeton. It was only then that Prior Cuthbert had sent another message to the archbishop, but it did not reach York until after Merek had been dispatched with the letters from the archbishop and the sheriff.

'It is in a shed behind the chicken coops outside the priory grounds, where the lay brothers keep their tools,' Prior Cuthbert told them. 'He cannot be buried in consecrated soil, so great is the sin of self-murder.'

Ralph frowned. He found the canon law harsh that forbid the burial of poor wretches who had taken their own lives. He had come across many cases when people had acted thus because their lives seemed hopeless and they were so full of melancholy that they felt the overwhelming need to snuff out their own life. Yet he did not feel that he could say any such thing as it would undoubtedly offend these men of the cloth.

'How did he kill himself?' he asked instead.

'He slit his throat with his food knife,' the prior replied. 'One of the brothers saw the blood that had flowed under the door into the transept. When he opened the door, he was horrified to find him upon the floor with his life's blood everywhere. The poor brother has not recovered from the sight.'

Peter sucked air between his lips. 'I can understand. It must have been horrible.'

'We also thought that you would wish to view his body afterwards,' Father Benedict said.

Ralph nodded. 'I do indeed, and I will have questions to ask then. But first let us look at these bodies.'

Merek offered to help and together with the hospitaller the lids of both coffins were removed. The odour of decay was suddenly released and Peter covered his nose and mouth with his hands as the shrouded bodies were revealed.

Both men were alabaster white with blue lips. Dried blood from their mouths had congealed upon their chins. Sir Broderick had been a good-looking clean-shaven man of about the same age as Ralph. Adam Dalton had the build of a man-at-arms and a misshapen nose from an old injury that had broken his nasal bones.

'We removed most of their clothes to put them in their shrouds,' the canon explained, pointing to the rolled-up clothes that lay at the foot end of both coffins. 'There were no valuables on either of them. The outlaws robbed them entirely.'

Ralph pointed to the table. 'Let us lay Sir Broderick upon the table so that I can look more closely at his wounds.'

Between them, Merek and Father Benedict lifted the stiff body out of the coffin and carried it to the table.

Ralph nodded and unwrapped the shroud himself to reveal his undertunic.

'No wounds on the front, so Sir Broderick must have been shot in the back,' Ralph remarked. He looked round at Peter Longwood who was looking very pale. 'Remember everything, Peter, and write it down when you have your writing equipment and the use of a table.'

'I will remember this sight forever, I fear, my lord,' the clerk replied.

With Merek's help, Ralph turned the body over onto its face. There he could see the holes in the heavily blood-stained undertunic where the arrows had entered his body. Lifting the undertunic he rolled it upwards to expose three wounds between his shoulder blades.

'They are tightly clustered, my lord,' Merek said, bending close to look. 'Skilled bowmanship I would say.'

'Where are the arrows?' Ralph asked.

'They are inside the coffins,' Prior Cuthbert replied, tapping the empty coffin with his staff. 'The villagers must have plucked them out and tossed them into the coffin before they lowered the body into it.'

Peter knelt down and took out three arrows. He held them up. 'Just the arrow shafts here, Sir Ralph.'

Merek took them from him and held them up to the light.

'The arrowheads will still be inside him and looking at how far the blood is on the shaft I'd say that at least one arrowhead will be inside his heart. Their bodies must have lain outside for many hours, so that the deer sinews that were used to lash the arrowhead to the shaft soaked up enough fluid to loosen. Then when someone tried to pluck it out later from the dead body the arrowhead came off.'

Ralph looked at Father Benedict. 'How skilled in the chirurgical art are you, Father Benedict?'

The canon pursed his lips. 'When I was a young man, before I was called to the Lord and was ordained, I was a surgeon in the army of King David. I was at Neville's Cross and assisted the surgeon who removed an arrow from our king's face. I can retrieve at least one of these arrowheads – if Prior Cuthbert will permit me to do so.'

'If it is necessary to do so,' the prior replied.

'It may be if Sir Broderick is to have any justice,' Ralph replied.

He looked at the canon as he bent to rinse his hands in a bucket. 'You are a Scot? I did not hear your accent.'

'I am and I served my monarch, but grew tired of wars and was called to the Lord. I think I have lived these many years and lost my native brogue.'

'The Royal de Bruce house founded our priory and several of our canons and lay brothers were born north of the border, as I was myself, but this is our land now,' Prior Cuthbert volunteered. 'King David himself has stayed here in the past.'

Father Benedict left and went back to the infirmary, returning after a short while with a number of surgical instruments. Laying them out methodically, he began to operate. First he used a long, thin probe to insert into each wound in turn to ascertain that they were inside.

'I can feel two of them, but as Master Merek suggested, I think one has fallen inside the heart. So, I shall try to get this other one out first.'

'Before you do that,' Ralph interrupted, 'please take the arrow shafts and push them into the wounds.'

Father Benedict raised an eyebrow, then nodded with understanding. 'You wish to see the direction of the arrows as they struck him?'

'Indeed. They may give an idea of whether they were shot from the same spot, or from different locations. In other words, whether he was shot by one or by more than one archer.'

The canon did as directed by Ralph and one by one pushed an arrow shaft into each wound following the channel that had been created.

Ralph looked closely at them and nodded his head. 'It looks as if they were fired from the same place as they are parallel with little deviation in the angles they struck.' Then turning to Father Benedict, he held out his hand. 'You can remove the shafts again and pray continue.'

Selecting which wound to use, the canon reinserted his metal probe. 'I can feel it again.' Then leaving the probe inside the wound channel he picked up a pair of long-handled forceps and pushed them down alongside the probe, in the process creating an unpleasant squelching noise. After some fiddling he managed to open the blades of the instrument and secure the claws at its end around the base of the arrowhead. Then gradually pulling it out, it came free of the wound with a nauseating sucking noise and the sudden eruption of clots of congealed blood.

Going over to one of the wooden buckets of water, he swished it about to clear off the old blood and then returning to the table dropped it on the surface beside the dead body of the coroner.

'And what do you make of that, Merek?' Ralph asked.

The longbowman picked it up and put it together with the shaft. 'It was a well-made arrow, my lord.' Holding the arrowhead and shaft together in one hand he pulled out one of the arrows that had been fired at them in the Arncliffe Forest. He compared the two.

'Totally different, my lord. The ones fired at us were simple arrows such as you would find any village archer would fire at the butts but this and the ones from Sir Broderick's coffin are quality work that a real archer would have. Not unlike my own, but yet quite different. And, of course, see how these are barbed. They were not meant to be pulled free.'

'That is true,' said Father Benedict. 'It was not easy to get this out and had I been trying to remove it from living flesh it would have torn the muscles, sinews and organs that it struck as it came out. Shall I try to extract the other arrowhead, the one that did not hit his heart?'

'If you would,' Ralph replied. 'It would be interesting to see if they came from the same batch.'

They watched as the canon skilfully operated on the wound and after some time pulled out a second arrowhead which he washed and then deposited on the table. Merek placed the first beside it and they all inspected them.

'They are virtually identical,' Ralph said. He straightened up. 'I think that is all we can usefully find. There is no necessity to explore for the other arrowhead inside the heart, so we can now replace his body in his coffin and he can be prepared for a Christian burial. I know he had no family.'

'We shall find him a sunny spot in our cemetery,' Prior Cuthbert said.

They respectfully rewrapped Sir Broderick in his shroud and lay his body back in the coffin.

'We will keep the arrow shafts and heads, Merek,' Ralph instructed. Then to Peter: 'And you shall write everything up.'

Peter tapped the side of his head. 'It is all emblazoned in here, Sir Ralph. I will transcribe it later.'

'Good. So now let us look at Adam Dalton, before we go to view the body of the sanctuary seeker.'

8

THE BODYGUARD

Priory of St Mary at Gyseburg
15 May 1361

Just as they had taken Sir Broderick's body out of his coffin they did the same with Adam Dalton. In the flickering light they saw that he had been shot twice in the front of his chest. Similar to the case of the coroner, both arrowheads had detached from the shafts when they were pulled out.

'When we see the wounds together we can begin to surmise what happened,' Ralph said as he scratched his chin. 'It looks as if they were attacked from behind. Sir Broderick was probably shot first and may have received a fatal wound with the first arrow, but two others were fired to make sure. I suspect that Adam had spun round on his horse and was shot rapidly twice.'

'How many attackers were there, do you think, Sir Ralph?' Peter asked.

'Possibly two,' Ralph replied. 'Both skilled archers as the wounds are clustered so close together.'

'I agree, my lord,' said Merek. 'One skilled archer could have done it, but that would require rapid shooting and Adam may have managed to shoot at least one arrow before he was hit.'

'But we have no way of knowing without searching the spot where they were found, if the woodsmen we saw could even point it out.'

Father Benedict took a step forward. 'Do you wish me to try to retrieve an arrowhead from this poor fellow's body?'

'If you would that would be very helpful,' Ralph replied.

'But *how* would that be helpful?' Prior Cuthbert asked.

'If the arrowheads are different, having been made by different arrowsmiths, even if the shafts were made by the same fletcher, as they seem to have been, then that could suggest that there were at least two archers.'

'Yet if they look the same that wouldn't necessarily mean that it was a single archer?' Merek said.

'I agree, but we want to gather as much information as we can,' Ralph said. 'So please, Father Benedict, can you once again push the arrow shafts found with his body into the wounds.'

The cleric once again shoved the shafts into the wounds and then stood back for Ralph and Merek to inspect them.

'He was struck full in the chest and they are parallel,' said Ralph. 'Interesting.'

Merek looked quickly at the justice of the peace but a look from him told him to ask no question.

Ralph himself pulled the two arrow shafts free and placed them on the small table. 'Please now continue to extract the arrowhead, Father. And the other, if you will.'

They all watched as Father Benedict operated again and after a few moments extracted first one gory arrowhead then the other. One by one he washed them and lay them on the small table beside the arrow shafts and the other arrowheads.

'They are identical,' Ralph said, holding them all up to the candlelight. 'Barbed and meant to cause maximum injury. Almost certainly from the same batch of arrows. I think we can replace poor Adam Dalton in his coffin and they can be buried on the morrow.'

'Shall we visit the body of the sanctuary seeker?' Father Benedict asked once they had closed the coffin lid over the body of the coroner's bodyguard.

'I think not,' replied Ralph. 'Darkness has fallen. I think we will happily accept your offer of sustenance when you have your meal, then have a good night's sleep before we view his body in the morning.'

*　*　*

A bell sounded from the tower and Prior Cuthbert and Father Benedict had one of the younger lay brothers show them to the cells that had been allocated for them before they excused themselves to attend compline, the dusk service.

Having investigated a murder in a previous case and having had an opportunity to observe the lives of monks in a monastery on the Holy Island of Lindisfarne, Ralph was well aware that a monk's life was dominated by *opus Dei*, the work of God, the unceasing round of prayers, chants and rituals. Seven times a day starting with the night office of *mattins*, then the *lauds of the dead*, when they would pray for the departed. This was followed by *prime* at first light, then by *terce,* the shortest service, three hours later, then *sext* at noon and *none* in the mid-afternoon, before *vespers* in the late afternoon.

Taking the opportunity to talk on their own, Ralph called his assistants into his cell. He told Peter to bring his writing paraphernalia and to write about everything that they had discovered during their inspection of the two bodies and the retrieval of the arrowheads, while it was still fresh in his memory.

'We shall go over the implications of those discoveries while you are writing,' Ralph said, sitting on the cot. Merek stood by the wall on which a wooden cross was nailed beside the sconce and the candle it held.

The sound of chanting could be heard coming from the church building.

Peter sat at the simple table on the single stool with his saddlebag beside him and, taking out fresh vellum, inkpot and quill, he began to write. Ralph nodded approval as soon as Peter's quill was scratching out his neat account of the matter.

'Firstly, two heinous murders were committed, and I favour the theory that they were committed by two not one killer. Not just one bowman because of the accuracy of the shots and the fact that they must have been fired in rapid succession.'

Merek tugged his blond beard and then folded his arms in front of him. 'I agree, my lord. It was not three, else the shafts would have been at different angles.'

Peter stopped writing and brushed his forehead with the feather quill. 'But how can we know that, for Sir Broderick was shot in the back, and Adam in the front of his chest. Surely we have no way of knowing where each archer, if there were two archers, stood or fired from.'

'That is true,' Ralph agreed. 'Which is why we shall have to try to visit the murder scene or the place they were found. But the fact that the arrows in each body were parallel implies that one hand killed each person. It may have been one very skilled archer firing from the same spot or two from different positions, each selecting their victim.'

'There was something else you were thinking about though,

was there not, my lord?' Merek asked. 'I saw you look interested but did not want to talk about it.'

'That is right. Adam was shot full in the chest. What does that suggest to you?'

'That he had turned to face his assailant. Either turned in the saddle or wheeled his horse about.'

'You said you thought he may have loosed an arrow,' Ralph said. 'But what is against that?'

'I see what you mean, my lord,' the bowman replied. 'If he was shooting his bow or about to do so, it would be likely his chest would have been sideways on to his killer. He would likely have been shot in the arm or the side of his chest.'

'So he probably did not have time to flight an arrow,' Peter said, snapping his fingers.

'Indeed, and if we consider Sir Broderick, I think it likely that he was shot by three arrows fired in rapid succession by the same archer, while he was upright in his saddle. Had he been shot when he was on the ground after falling from his horse, or if he had fallen forward over its neck, the arrows would have had different angulations.'

Merek nodded. 'I think you are right, my lord. And Adam also must have been killed by two arrows shot in rapid succession. Since Adam was shot before he had time to flight an arrow, that confirms that there must have been two bowmen who ambushed them from cover.'

'They must have allowed them to pass by, then attacked from behind. Adam must have turned when he saw an arrow strike Sir Broderick in the back and the second bowman shot him twice.'

Peter continued to write.

'Yet the next question we need to answer is where is Robert Hyde, his clerk? It does not sound as if he was in league with the killers, since the woodsmen who found the bodies told us that they found blood in the forest, but it stopped when they got to the beck that runs into the River Esk. That indicates that he too was shot at and may have been wounded but somehow managed to escape.'

'So he must have entered the river, my lord. It is a fast-flowing river in parts and as far as I know it is the only river that flows directly into the North Sea.'

Ralph nodded. 'Since it is a fast river that might explain why his pursuers, and we must assume that the killers did try to pursue him, could not find him. There are several possibilities, of course, and each begs further questions. First, he may have been able to swim and did escape, but if so why has he not reappeared and reported the murders? Could he have escaped but been wounded and managed to get to hiding, only to fall ill? Or they may have caught him and killed him, but then where is his body? Finally, he may have drowned and his body could have washed out to the sea.'

'Then we may never know, Sir Ralph?' Peter asked.

'We may not, but we need to try to find out if we are to have any hope of finding Sir Broderick and Adam Dalton's killers. We ourselves may have been fortunate not to have suffered the same fate.'

'Do you think we were shot at by the same people, Sir Ralph?' Peter asked, dipping his quill in his inkpot.

'No, whoever shot at us was not as skilled as the two who slew the coroner and his bodyguard. There may only have been one of them, but we don't know. We will have to search the area of the forest when we return.' He stood up and paced back and forth in the cell with his hands steepled together under his chin.

'Another question that will probably be difficult to answer is whether Father Benedict is still loyal to the Scottish throne. Indeed, the whole priory could be, as it is still under the patronage of the Royal House of Bruce. You heard the prior say that he himself was born north of the border. That inevitably brings up the question of whether any of this has anything to do with the Black Rood of Scotland. After all, we are not far from Whitby, which is itself on the direct road to Durham.'

* * *

Unlike some other religious orders, the Augustinian canons did not enforce a strict diet. Indeed, that evening Ralph, Merek and Peter enjoyed an amiable meal in the priory refectory, sitting at the top table with the prior, Father Benedict and three of the elder canons. They did not eat meat and the meal consisted mainly of vegetables grown in the priory gardens, and eggs, bread and cheese. To Merek's great relief they served ale that was brewed by the lay brothers and his wooden tankard was filled and refilled several times.

Ralph and Peter ate and drank more frugally. Peter barely touched his food as he was still feeling queasy after the bodies of Sir Broderick and Adam, his bodyguard, were examined, although he would never admit to such a thing in front of either Ralph or the seemingly iron-stomached Merek.

Ralph was more interested in hearing the canon's views on the cause of the pestilence.

'It is a punishment for forsaking God,' Prior Cuthbert said emphatically.

'In what way have we forsaken the Lord?' Ralph asked.

'By not worshipping him enough.'

'But I heard you all chanting at your compline service. You spend most of your day and night in prayer.'

'We do, but not all people do. The common people only attend church because they have to, as indeed could be said for the yeomen, the nobles and even, dare I say it, some of the king's household. They attend, but they are not necessarily sincere in their worship.'

He looked at Ralph with a smile. 'Do you worship the Lord, Sir Ralph? I mean, sincerely worship?'

'I believe that I do. Yet surely the way the Great Death swept across Christendom from distant Cathay suggests that it was something that spread from person to person. Across all those countries, across France and even badly affected Avignon where Pope Clement the Sixth lived. One quarter of his court perished from it. Surely His Holiness and those around him cannot have been insincere in their worship.'

The prior shrugged. 'Truly, no one can know what is in another man's heart.'

Ralph lay his spoon down beside his knife. 'Well, I think it is more than that. The fact that it spreads by touching and close contact seems to mean there is something that jumps from one person to another. Why, I hear that even His Majesty the King stopped touching people who suffer from the king's evil.'

Prior Cuthbert clicked his tongue. 'That is a sadness, for there are so many of the king's subjects afflicted by this condition who will be deprived of being cured by the king's divine touch.'

Father Benedict dabbed his lips after sipping some ale. 'I think that you are right, Sir Ralph, although I am sure that Prior Cuthbert is also correct about people not believing and not worshipping as intensely and sincerely as they ought. Yet as a surgeon who has studied physick, I have no doubt that there is a severe disruption of the vital humors.'

'I know something of the doctrine of humors,' Ralph said.

'There are four of these vital body fluids: black bile, yellow bile, blood and phlegm.'

'That is right,' Father Benedict replied. 'An imbalance of them causes illness. The pestilence seems to cause a great excess of blood and also both black and yellow bile, so that it causes glands in the neck, the armpits and groins to bulge as bubos. The excess blood causes bruising of the skin, it makes blood vessels burst and causes the horrible black mottling all over the face and body. Excess black bile, too, so that the sufferer gets a flux of the bowels and will soil themself. If too much yellow bile then it produces nausea.'

'So, bleeding the patient may be the best treatment?'

'And strong emetics to get rid of the yellow bile and purgatives to get rid of the black bile.'

'And much praying,' said Prior Cuthbert. 'The poor souls afflicted with the pestilence need God's help while they live and his forgiveness once they pass.'

'Ah yes, much praying. Which I imagine your sanctuary seeker was busily doing.'

Prior Cuthbert nodded. 'Indeed he was, for that is the purpose of sanctuary, to seek forgiveness for one's sins. He prayed all the time in the sanctum, which is at the end of the north transept. He would have heard us praying and chanting during our services and he would have enjoyed listening to the readings from the Bible.'

'He did not join you in the quire?'

'No, our sanctum is there for a sanctuary seeker to use to commune with and ask God's forgiveness. He would not come out. A bucket would be given for him to relieve himself and it would be taken from him by one of the brothers. But we prayed for him.'

'What was his name? I understand he was a friar.'

Desolation

'He called himself Friar Bruno. He was a Franciscan.'

'From which monastery or house?'

'I do not know. He said he was an itinerant mendicant friar who had sinned badly, which was why he sought sanctuary.'

'What was this great sin?'

'He would not say. All he kept telling us was that he had to atone and make pilgrimage.'

Father Benedict leaned forward and locked his hands together. 'He was a man in great distress. He was full of fear and shook a lot. I think he felt safe in the sanctum.'

'What was he afraid of?'

'That his sin, whatever it was, could lead to his damnation in Hell.'

Prior Cuthbert and the other canons on the high table all made the sign of the cross.

'In the archbishop's letter of instruction to me he said that he needed to make a pilgrimage to atone. Pilgrimage to where?'

'That I do not know,' replied the prior. 'It is not our way to probe. But as he wanted to make abjuration I sent for the coroner, Sir Broderick de Whitby. He came with his two assistants and took the abjuration then left to make arrangements for him to leave the realm.'

'So it is possible that he was going to make pilgrimage abroad?'

Prior Cuthbert raised his hands and shrugged. 'That I do not know.'

'Did Sir Broderick tell you anything about his abjuration of the realm?'

The prior shook his head. 'It would not have been correct for him to divulge it, as it would not be correct for me to ask.'

'Had Friar Bruno made a confession to anyone here? As I

understand all the canons regular are ordained and could take confession.'

'He did not request it of any of us,' Father Benedict volunteered.

A lay brother approached with a jug of ale to replenish tankards. Ralph declined as did Peter and the canons on the high table. Merek smiled and held his out.

9

MORE DEATHS MYSTERIOUS

Axeton
15 May 1361

He had enjoyed killing ever since he was a child. He remembered the thrill of scooping that frog out of a pond and making it squirm and croak as he severed its legs and watched it bleed to death. As he grew older he trapped mice and experimented with different ways of dispatching them. That helped him understand how creatures died, but as he moved up to cats, he instinctively knew they would be harder to kill. They had to be coaxed so he could gain their trust before he made his move. The first time with a black cat resulted in the animal howling and inflicting some severe scratches when he tried to strangle it. Instead, he was forced to dash out its brains.

That experience taught him two things which he had made it his custom to practise ever since. Especially when he finally killed a person. Firstly, he had to charm them and gain their trust. Secondly, he had to either make them helpless or dispatch them instantly. Of the two ways he preferred to have them at his mercy so that they couldn't make a noise. That way he had the pleasure of seeing them squirm, he could feel their fear and terror and he could be creative in how he would kill them.

He had blessed the day he had met the Magister who had instructed him on such an effective way of murdering his victims, and with the village of Axeton he had been given virtually free range. All he had to do was to make each death look like the pestilence had claimed another, and his two searchers did the disposing, along with George the mute. He did whatever the women told him to do and they kept him happy by taking turns in pleasuring him. It helped that he never saw the bodies close up as they wrapped them up and did the lifting of the bodies into the coffins, so he had no idea that they had been murdered and made to look so pestilently dead in such a skilful manner.

And all had been made easy, just as the Magister said he would. The coffin maker had been instructed to keep turning out coffins as fast as he could, and the gravedigger was told to make sure that he had one grave newly dug each day, and that if they started getting more than one death at a time he was to start digging a pit.

Elizabeth Dell, the widow of one of the village pinders, had quickly fallen under his spell as he knew she would. The increasing numbers of deaths in the village and in the hamlet of Underhill had made folk fearful and gullible. Single women were amenable to seduction. He wondered whether it was fear of death that made them desire physical contact, because he was finding it easier to bed them. Elizabeth was in her forties and had lost two children before they were five years old, one from the last plague and one after a cut on her hand festered and she had a fever and died. Her husband had been trampled to death by a bull he had tried to urge somewhere it had no wish to go.

As usual he wooed her in secret, creeping to her house when darkness fell and she was ready for him. She had been wanton in bed and allowed him to take her several ways, so that he had her biting her hand to stifle the shrieks of pleasure that threatened to erupt and which could alert neighbours that she was not alone.

She was atop him and riding him furiously when she reached her peak, the moment he had been waiting for. As he thrust one final time with his own release, he shoved his bodkin up into the back of her skull, into her brain.

Her eyes rolled upwards as she convulsed, her mouth open and saliva pouring down her chin.

'Thank you, Mistress Elizabeth,' he said as he shoved her off him, smiling as he watched her final movements and listened to her death rattle which was music to his ears.

He dressed and prepared her body, cutting the skin about her neck to insert the cheese balls to simulate the bubos of the pestilence. Then he created the bruising around her face.

Megan had chosen her this time and would first thing in the morning paint a red cross on the door and pretend to visit her a few times in the day. The morning after she would discover that Elizabeth was dead and together with Sally they would fill another coffin.

He smiled as he thought how he was going to arrange his next victim, which would be Sally's choice, which was only fair. It amused him that the two women were so full of hate for so many people in the village that they had no qualms about sentencing them to death.

Henry Stone the charcoal burner would be unconscious by the time he let himself into his hovel. The poison that the

Magister had given him to use on the men worked quickly and it worked well mixed in the food and ale he gave as a gift or as part of a barter, whichever was appropriate.

Henry was not conscious when he entered the humble home. That was a pity, he thought, because there was less pleasure in watching his death throes when he introduced him to his faithful bodkin, which he had cleaned of blood and brain matter on Elizabeth Dell's thighs. He much preferred to see the sudden shock in their eyes at the moment he stabbed and macerated their brain.

He snuffed out the tallow candle and then waited and listened at the door before letting himself out into the night.

That was enough work for that evening. Henry Stone would be long dead when Sally called by his hovel in the morning. She would paint his door and then tell the reeve and everyone she had seen that there was another person dying of the pestilence.

The Magister would be pleased with him and another reward would be his.

* * *

Osbert Flood tossed and turned in bed next to Marion. He barely managed to sleep for an hour or so every night, and even then the nightmares tormented him and on several occasions he had awoken suddenly, crying out in alarm and finding himself sitting up bathed in perspiration.

Marion had tried to comfort him, even though she was hardly sleeping either, but on asking him what he dreamed of he could only shake his head and tell her he didn't know, and that it was all because they had lost their beloved son.

Although he wanted to tell her that Dickon lived yet he

dared not. His mind kept conjuring up the moments in the coffin that first time he had been taken.

The Magister – the horrible fiend who had told him that he must tell no one, not even Marion – on this he had been precise. If he tried to alert anyone to get help, then he would carry out his threats of severing fingers. And if he was truly angered, Dickon would be immediately slain.

He felt that his heart could have stopped at that moment. Listening in horror to the orders he was given, he felt nausea overcome him. Yet he had responded by knocking on the coffin lid, agreeing to carry out all that the voice told him he must do.

Then Dickon had been allowed to speak. Just a few words.

'Father – please – help me!'

Then he was silenced and the Magister spoke again.

'The pestilence is coming to the villages and hamlets of Sir Hugo de Braithwaite's manor. Obey my orders and you and your wife and son will be spared. You will be taken back this evening and released, but you will not look at the men who take you. They will also put the body of your ostler in the stables and you will alert the reeve to get the women to collect his body. He has the pestilence, as you will see, but it will not harm you. The men will give you a flask of blessed water. Take a sip every morning and give one to your wife. It will protect you both.'

He had been taken by them twice more, each time forced to get inside the coffin and each time tortured to hear his son. Sounding so frightened and desperate, while the Magister gave him fresh orders.

How his world had fallen apart and now he was besieged by one problem after another. Villagers were dying one or two at a time, and looked most dreadful, all blue and purple with horrible yellow bubos that bled and exuded pus.

Sir Hugo seemed to be losing his wits and Lady Honoria

seemed content to let Osbert carry on overseeing the manor court and handling the affairs of the manor as he saw fit. And the Magister had given him orders about things he should buy from the manor funds and where they should be delivered. Gideon Moor the reeve and all the villagers looked to him for instructions, and he felt bad that he was often irritable with them.

And then there was Father Simon, whom the Magister instructed him to appoint as the new parson. He did not trust the fellow for he had seen the way that he looked at some of the women of the village in an almost lecherous manner. Nor did he like his preaching about the end of the world.

Yet it seemed that it was almost upon them.

10

KING EDWARD THE THIRD OF THAT NAME

Conisbrough Castle, Strafforth wapentake, West Riding of Yorkshire
16 May 1361

His Majesty, King Edward, loved the smell of the northern counties, although he actually loved no place better than Windsor Castle. He had been born in Windsor, founded the Order of the Round Table, which became the Order of the Garter there in 1348, which was based upon and paid homage to the tales of King Arthur and his Knights of the Round Table, and he held his great tournament there on St George's Day in 1349 at the height of the pestilence. He had no doubt that it was the finest castle in Christendom since Camelot fell, and with the building plan that he had put in place it would equal it in time.

Yet he had to admit that Conisbrough was an impressive, well-fortified castle, with a large motte and double bailey, perched high above the River Don and the Don Valley in the Manor of Conisbrough. It had been owned by the old Saxon King, Harold Godwinson, who took an arrow in the eye at Hastings, when it was known as *Cyningesburh*, meaning the 'king's fortress.' Edward's own father had fleetingly owned it and it had seemed a suitable manor and castle for his fifth son. Indeed, so well did Edward think of it that it would make a good home for Edmund and his wife – when he could eventually get him suitably wed.

This was one of the reasons that Edward had on the spur of the moment temporarily moved his court to Conisbrough to allow his twenty-year-old son a taste of hosting the royal court. He had plans to make him Earl of Cornwall in a year, but more pressing was negotiation for his marriage to Margaret of Flanders, a marriage which would have given Edmund control of the continental counties of Flanders, Rethel, Nevers and Artois.

Having said his prayers in the castle chapel, which reminded him of St George's Chapel in Windsor Castle, which he had designed and built with the Round Table in mind, he had been in relatively good spirits when he made his way to the office halfway up the towering cylindrical keep. He sat behind the large oak desk that was covered in plans for his son's marriage proposal and with documents about the three new appointments that were to be made to the Order of the Garter.

On the other side of the desk on a stool sat Martin Ormerod, his clerk, a stack of documents in front of him and quill poised to take orders from the king.

Edward had originally decreed that the Order of the Garter should consist of himself the sovereign, his son Edward the Prince of Wales and twenty-four knights. In his mind it was important to uphold the chivalric code that was the very essence of the Round Table and which he believed to be a link with the divine. By maintaining the Order of the Garter, his recreation of the Round Table, he would protect England and his people from war, famine and even this damnable plague that seemed to have resurfaced.

Only with the death of a Knight of the Order could another be initiated. Until then the Order was broken and England was at risk. With the Treaty of Bretigny and the later ratification of it at the Treaty of Calais he had obtained peace with Scotland and France, enough so that he had released King David the Second of Scotland and King John the Second of France, both of whom had ransoms to pay.

The three new Knights of the Order that Edward had selected were Edward, Fifth Lord le Dispenser, who had fought at Poitiers; Sir John Sully, who had fought at Crecy; and William, Fourth Lord Latimer, who had distinguished himself in the wars in France.

Edward had started to dictate a letter when there was a tap on the door. Edward called to enter and a moment later Sir Basil Gatsby, his chief secretary, entered with a satchel of letters.

Sir Basil strode the length of the office and bowed.

'I beg pardon, Your Majesty, but I bring urgent messages from His Grace John Thoresby, the Archbishop of York. I regret that the messenger is delayed by two days as he was mistakenly sent to Kenilworth Castle.'

Edward sat back and tugged his long beard. 'His Grace is not ill?'

'No, Your Majesty,' Sir Basil replied, taking the messages from the satchel and handing them to the king. 'Sir Broderick de Whitby, your coroner in the north, has been murdered along with his bodyguard.'

'Where?' Edward asked as he opened the first message.

'In the Langbarugh wapentake of the North Riding of Yorkshire, Your Majesty. You will see this in the first of the two messages from the archbishop. In the second he writes that the body was taken to Gyseburg Priory near Whitby. The archbishop sent two messengers one after the first and they both arrived this morning. But I think you must read the whole letter from the archbishop, for he had received news from the Bishop of Durham about the Black Rood of Scotland, which has been stolen. He expressed fears that it could have been the work of Scottish or French spies who would use it as a rallying symbol to raise armies against you. The Black Rood was a national treasure of Scotland.'

King Edward looked up sharply, then he grunted as he smoothed the letter out and read it. His jaw muscles tightened as he absorbed the information written in John Thoresby's own steady hand. He read the greater detail that the archbishop had conveyed in his letter.

'This is devilry, Sir Basil. Sir Broderick was a fine man, and it is a heinous act that he was shot by outlaws in one of my English forests.'

He dropped the letter on the desk and tapped it with an elegant forefinger. Although he was angry inside, yet he controlled any show of temper. He had learned early in his life to control his anger, as he did when he was still in his teenage years and had to watch as his mother, Queen Isabella, and her lover, Sir Roger Mortimer, the Earl of March, ruled England even though he was the ordained king. He had concealed the fury he felt and, putting a plan into action with a small group of loyal friends, he had captured Mortimer in Nottingham Castle and reclaimed his throne.

'I see that the archbishop sent a message to Sir Ralph de Mandeville asking him to investigate both the murder of Sir Broderick and see if there was any connection with the theft of the Black Rood. What news of that?'

'None as yet, Your Majesty. I await any message.'

'Who would dare to steal a precious religious object like the Black Rood?' Edward asked, hardly expecting an answer as he was thinking out loud. 'A piece of the True Cross, it is sacred. Like the Cross of Neith that was also part of the True Cross, that is held in St George's Chapel in Windsor.'

Like the Black Rood, the Cross of Neith had been a treasured sacred relic that had been kept in Aberconwy in Wales by the Welsh kings until Edward's grandfather Edward the First had subjugated the country. It had since then been kept in London until Edward himself founded the Order of the Garter and St George's Chapel, when he had it placed in the chapel as an important symbol of his Order. In his mind it was a link between the Arthurian tales of the Holy Grail and his own reign as king. A link betwixt him and King Arthur.

'I want a permanent guard placed in the chapel of St George to protect the Cross of Neith,' the king said, his mind dwelling upon the importance of the Holy Cross.

Sir Basil looked hesitantly at the king, not wishing to interrupt his train of thought. He waited a moment, then coughed before speaking.

'There is other news, Your Majesty. You will recall from previous letters that the archbishop is concerned about the preaching of a friar called John Ball.'

'I have read about the archbishop's concerns about him in his letter.'

Sir Basil bowed his head in acknowledgement and went on. 'The archbishop wrote to me also, Your Majesty, to say that these friars are telling all who will listen that change is coming to England. That it has been foretold in prophecies by a powerful alchemist who practises necromancy. He predicted that the plague would return and said that it is a sign, just as were the deaths of all those men in your army in France on

Black Monday, that the end of the world is approaching. Well, there are now other preachers spreading these messages outside York and to towns and villages around the wapentakes, and further to the surrounding counties.'

Edward drummed his fingers impatiently on his desk.

Prophecies! An alchemist who practises necromancy.

How he wished that he had his own Merlin like King Arthur, who could foretell the future. His interest in Arthurian tales was well known, for the scholars traced a direct line of descent from King Arthur through his grandfather Edward the First and his father Edward the Second. In addition he was intrigued and had studied alchemy himself and had in his personal library many of the texts on the subject and on the occult arts.

A few years before he had employed a Spanish alchemist called Friar Raymond Lully, whom he had paid a fortune to work for him, and even built for him a spacious laboratory in the Tower of London, and access to the library of the university at Oxford and even of his own library at Westminster. Friar Raymond had convinced him that he and his assistant, a younger Frenchman called Giles de Toulouse, who had studied under Friar John of Rupescissa, a famous French Franciscan friar and alchemist, claimed he could transmute base metal into gold. Edward had tons of lead and tin given to him so that the gold he would produce would fund a new crusade to reclaim the Holy Land.

But it did not happen. The alchemist and his assistant had been happy when they believed the gold would be used to fund a crusade against the Turks, but when he told them that he had decided to use it to finance wars against the French and the Scots they protested that alchemy should not be used for waging war against the French. Their efforts at transmutation came to nothing and Edward grew impatient and was on the verge of having them both made permanent residents at the Tower of London when they both disappeared. As far as Edward was informed, by disguising themselves as lepers. He was told that they had fled the country. He was told later that several important books and manuscripts written by such past alchemists as Albertus Magnus and Friar Roger Bacon had gone missing from both Oxford and his own library.

Yet Edward's pride was such that he could not allow his court and people to think that he had been misled, so he permitted it to be thought that a hoard of gold had been produced and that the gold noble coins that he had minted a year ago to celebrate the signing of the Treaty of Bretigny was from that hoard of gold transmuted from base metals.

'Who is this alchemist?'

'Neither the archbishop nor myself know, Your Majesty.'

'I want it found out, do you understand me?'

'I absolutely understand, Your Majesty.'

Could it be that this alchemist and necromancer is Raymond Lull or his assistant Giles de Toulouse? Edward thought.

'When you find out, do not arrest him, but see to it that he cannot escape. I want to see this fellow.'

Sir Basil bowed. 'Understood, Your Majesty.'

'And as to these friars, do the people listen to the preaching?' he asked concernedly.

'They seem to, Your Majesty. These friars are selective in who they address. They preach to labourers, serfs, villeins in villages, and to guild apprentices in the towns and cities. They tell them that they are being kept poor and they should demand more rights, more wages from their masters and their lords.'

'The labour laws we passed should halt such dissent and make people think hard about upsetting the natural order.'

Sir Basil nodded. 'It should, but whether they do remains to be seen, Your Majesty.'

Again he waited before going on. 'Yet more news, Your Majesty. About the pestilence.'

Edward leaned forward and, putting his elbows on the desk, covered his face with his hands. 'Speak, Sir Basil. Tell me the worst.'

'It has spread throughout London and reached the Midlands and beyond, Your Majesty. And the Archbishop of York said there are rumours that it is already here in Yorkshire, possibly arriving there from the low countries via the ports on the east coast of the county.'

Edward had recently heard himself when riding in his great park in Windsor that one of his oldest friends and a comrade in arms, Henry Grosmont, the Duke of Lancaster, had died of the plague.

'What of the deaths? Are they as horrible or as numerous as the last time?'

'It seems different, Your Majesty. The pestilence this time seems to affect children more than adults, and more nobles and knightly families than the common people. Some are calling it *the pestilence of boys*, and others as *the mortality of children*. I can attest to this, Your Majesty, as my brother is a physician and in the many cases he has seen and treated, more successfully than he did in the first plague, he is convinced that it causes a completely different upset in the humors. It seems to be striking communities and families that were spared from the last plague.'

Martin Ormerod coughed. 'May I interrupt, Your Majesty?'

Edward looked up and nodded.

'We lost a nephew to it in Coventry. He was only eight years old but seemingly it caused a rot in his lungs and he coughed up blood and phlegm and died. My brother tells me that there were other children who died from it in similar fashion.'

Sir Basil pursed his lips. 'The archbishop said he has heard rumours that the pestilence may have reached some parts of the northern wapentakes.'

'Perhaps Your Majesty should consider moving with Her Majesty Queen Phillipa to Beaulieu Abbey in the New Forest again until the pestilence passes.'

'I will consider it, Sir Basil. But we must address the murder of Sir Broderick and the theft of the Black Rood. As for these friars, how are you being informed about them?'

'I have contacts everywhere, Your Majesty, and I receive messages on a regular basis from bishops in all the cities.'

'Then keep me informed about them,' Edward said. His mind again conjured up images of Merlin and how dearly he would like to have a soothsayer who could foretell the obstacles and pitfalls that would occur in the rest of his reign.

He sighed and went on with that thought in mind. 'I want to know anything they say about prophecies and I want to know anything that is discovered about this alchemist. I will write a letter to His Grace John Thoresby, the Archbishop of York and also to Sir Ralph de Mandeville. You said that there were two messengers from the archbishop, so we will send one with a letter to the archbishop and one to Sir Ralph. I know him well for he advised me on the law when we made the Treaty of Bretigny. That is why he was one of my first choices to be a justice of the peace. I know he lost his wife from the first plague, so I shall mention what you have both told me so that he can be on his guard lest the pestilence reaches Yorkshire.'

'I will see to it, Your Majesty,' said Sir Basil.

'But wait, you say your brother is a physician? With experience of the pestilence?'

'He is, Your Majesty. In fact, he is here in the castle at this time. I asked him to come with us from London as I was concerned that my son might be falling ill.'

'And is he ill?'

'Fortunately not, Your Majesty. My brother gave him physick and he is recovered.'

King Edward nodded. 'Then let us send him with the messenger to Sir Ralph de Mandeville. If the pestilence is in the northern counties then his expertise in physick could be useful.'

He clapped his hands then rubbed them together. 'So, to work. Martin, let us do these two letters first.'

11

FRIAR BRUNO

Priory of St Mary at Gyseburg
16 May 1361

It was a chilly morning and even inside the priory one could see one's breath in little clouds.

After the prime service they broke bread before Prior Cuthbert and Father Benedict led the way out of the priory through the gardens to the chicken coops and the tool sheds.

'Young Brother William, who collects our eggs in the morning, said that he thought there could have been a fox on the prowl in the night,' Prior Cuthbert told them. 'The hens laid fewer eggs than usual.'

'Chickens get upset easily,' said Merek. 'But I can honestly say that the eggs your hens laid sit easily on my stomach.'

'I am surprised you could eat this morning,' quipped Peter. 'You must have drunk a barrel of the good monks' ale last night.'

Merek grinned. 'It was fine ale, too.'

They went round the chicken coops and Father Benedict opened the door of the shed. A coffin lay on the floor.

'There is a strong smell of blood,' said Ralph. 'I imagine that your hens may have been aware of it rather than a fox on the prowl.'

'Unless a fox smelled blood and came sniffing in the hope of a killed feed that it would not have to work for,' Merek suggested.

'Let us look at Friar Bruno,' said Ralph. 'Is the coffin lid nailed down?'

'It is not,' Father Benedict replied. 'We knew that you would want to view the body.'

Ralph nodded and he and Merek bent to lift the lid.

'By God's bones!' Merek cursed as they lifted the lid. Ralph and the two monks stared in horror.

'What is wrong?' asked Peter, who had been standing outside the door. He stepped inside and looked into the coffin at the headless body of Friar Bruno.

He clapped his hands to his mouth and ran out to vomit his meagre breakfast.

Merek apologised for his language as he leaned the coffin lid against the wall. The two monks stared aghast at the corpse.

The friar's body was still dressed in his bloody grey cassock, his hands crossed on his chest. The stump of his neck was ragged as if his head had been hacked off with some sort of sharp blade. The great vessels, windpipe and gullet could be seen with the surrounding muscles of the neck. Congealed blood had extruded from the vessels.

Ralph bent closer to inspect it. 'It looks as if the head was cut off while he lay in the coffin. You can see where the blade has cut into the wood as it struck as it was sawed. And I cannot see a separate cut where he slit his throat, so either this was done below it or he cut through the fatal wound to remove the head.'

Merek tugged his blond beard. 'One thing is for sure. This wasn't the work of a fox.'

'We are as astonished by this as you, Sir Ralph,' said Prior Cuthbert. 'This poor friar's body was placed in the coffin with reverence by us as we would respectfully treat any deceased person.'

'But yet he was left in the shed without a lock or bolt,' said Merek, with a trace of sarcasm.

'We have no locks anywhere in the priory,' replied Father Benedict.

'Not even on the door of the sanctum?' Ralph asked.

'There has never been a need,' Prior Cuthbert said. 'The church itself is the sanctuary and no one would dare to steal from it or commit an act of violence. That would be blasphemous.'

Ralph pointed at the corpse. 'Yet someone has done this dreadful thing.' He pursed his lips in thought. 'How does Brother William collect his eggs?'

The monks looked puzzled. 'In a large basket,' the prior replied.

Ralph looked about the shed, stooping to look at the floor, which was made of wood.

'Are you looking for something, my lord?' Merek asked.

'Dust, of which there is a lot on the floor.'

He walked round the coffin and stopped to bend down again and inspect the floor. 'Ah, here it is. The place where whoever cut off the head put the thing he used to carry it off. I can see the outline where it was placed. And here there is soil.'

'A basket, my lord?' Merek asked.

Ralph got on his hands and knees and inspected the circular mark in the dust. 'No, I thought not. Whoever did this would not want bits of flesh or blood clots dripping through a basket. I see the impression of a wooden bucket. And this soil, I think, is from inside the bucket. He probably put that in to soak up any blood. I imagine he also put the head in upside down.'

He stood up and faced the ashen faces of the two monks. 'We have here the headless body of a man in the blood-stained cassock of a Franciscan friar. Are you absolutely able to identify him as Friar Bruno?'

Prior Cuthbert shook his head. 'Father Benedict saw more of him than I.'

The canon regular chewed his lower lip for a moment then knelt down and examined the hands. He rose and shook his head. 'I fear I cannot say for sure. I think I recognise his hands but I may be wrong.'

Ralph knelt and, raising the hands one at a time, looked at the backs and then at the palms. Then pushing the sleeves up, he inspected the arms.

'There are bruises all over both forearms, a strange thing to see on a friar.'

'They look as if he had been defending himself from blows of some sort,' Merek opined.

'I agree,' said Ralph. 'But the skin has not been broken by these blows, so it was not a sword, most probably a club or stick. Very odd.'

He straightened. 'We are going to have to search the whole priory, the frater range, dorter range, the priory, the infirmary and every building and shed in the whole area. I have three questions I need to find answers to. Who did this? Where is the head now? And why was his dead body decapitated?'

A sheepish Peter poked his head round the door while studiously avoiding looking at the coffin.

'Are we to look for a bucket, Sir Ralph?'

'Yes, either one used to carry a head or one with a head in it.'

Peter clapped a hand over his mouth again and dashed back outside.

* * *

Ralph decided that it would be most efficient for him and his assistants to split up and conduct the searches individually, each accompanied by a canon. Prior Cuthbert asked Father Benedict to go with Ralph, and to arrange for two other canons to accompany Merek and Peter. Ralph said that he wanted to search the church itself, the sanctum and the infirmary, while Merek would take the cellarer's range, kitchen and refectory. Peter would search the dormitories of the canons and the lay brothers in the frater and dorter ranges, and the garderobes and latrines.

Ralph asked the prior to instruct the lay brothers to search the stables, the gardens and the area outside the priory walls for any sign of a bucket.

'What should I tell them?' Prior Cuthbert asked. 'They know that Friar Bruno committed self-murder, but they do not know about the decapitation.'

'Tell them the truth, lest they be shocked if they find a head.'

* * *

'Are we specifically looking for wooden buckets?' Father Benedict asked as he showed Ralph around the church, starting in the nave before they looked in the quire and then climbed the tower to inspect the bells.

'Yes, although I suspect the head will not be found, but the bucket may have been discarded once the person was some distance from the priory. Or it may be this moment tied to the pommel of a saddle and be taken somewhere to dispose of it.'

'But why?'

'Perhaps so that no one seeing the body might recognise him.'

'You mean, in case you or your assistants might recognise him.'

'Possibly, yes.'

They looked in the south transept and then the north before entering the sanctum.

'As you see, there is no lock or bolt on the door,' Father Benedict pointed out.

The sanctum floor had been scrubbed so there was no sign of the blood that had been shed. The room was sparsely furnished with a cot, a stool and a table. There was a cross upon a wall, a narrow window covered with a layer of animal hide, but nothing else.

Ralph looked under the cot and the table and felt the walls, looking for any crevice where any small articles could have been secreted.

'What personal possessions did Friar Bruno have?'

'None other than a collection bowl. He had no money and only some dried cheese and bread. The bowl he gave to one of the brothers as he said he would not use it further.'

'A crucifix?'

'Nothing.'

Ralph harrumphed. 'Well, there is nothing here, so let us go to the infirmary. You had buckets in the cell where you removed the arrows.'

They found the buckets of water that had been there the night before, but they had been emptied and filled with fresher water. Otherwise, there was nothing else amiss.

'Prior Cuthbert planned that we should hold Sir Broderick and Adam's funerals today,' the canon said as they returned to the prior's house. 'Will that be acceptable to you?'

'Indeed, and we shall attend them.'

* * *

Neither Merek nor Peter found any sign of a missing bucket, albeit they found many other buckets and barrels for many other uses around the priory. The whole place was kept scrupulously clean by the lay brothers, who cooked, laundered and scrubbed all the floors and steps regularly.

What Brother William did find in one of the tool sheds as he more or less regarded the chicken coops and sheds as his domain, was a sickle. It was hanging on a rack with a number of other similar ones. The only difference was that although someone had tried to clean it, the blade was still sticky with dark, clotted blood.

Brother Alfred, the ostler, reported that none of the horses were missing.

* * *

'So, either whoever did this is still within the priory or they entered and left,' Ralph said when he and his assistants met again. 'But there is no sign of a bucket that might have been used from our search. Since none of the horses are missing it looks as if they must have had horses hidden nearby.'

'Why do you think the friar's head was cut off, my lord?' Merek asked.

'It can only be to ensure that we did not recognise him. I can think of no other reason. Yet the other question is whether he committed *felo de se* or was he murdered. After all, he had sought sanctuary here. I think it highly likely that he was the so-called chaplain with the Earl of Sussex and the squires who stole the Black Rood from Durham.'

'Do you think the murderer could be one of the canons or lay brothers?' Peter asked.

'I think not. It is almost certainly the men who accompanied him, either the earl or the squires, although I think it unlikely that he was an earl. It was either done to silence him or because he had run away from them, possibly with the Black Rood. But I searched the sanctum thoroughly and there was nowhere it could have been hidden.'

'So what now, my lord?' Merek asked.

'We shall attend the funerals of Sir Broderick and Adam, and then I would like to ensure that this Friar Bruno has a respectful burial outside the grounds. If we ever find his head and determine that he was murdered, rather than committed *felo de se*, then he should be re-interred with his body complete in consecrated ground. For now, we must try to follow the head.'

'But how, Sir Ralph?' Peter queried. 'In what direction should we go?'

'We go back. The Black Rood has been taken from Durham and brought south, so it is clearly not the intention to take it to Scotland by road. If it was meant to go by sea there have been so many places it could have been taken to already, so I think there is good reason it is to Axeton that we need return.'

12

THE QUINTESSENCE

16 May 1361

The Magister was used to the smells of the laboratory. He had worked on his own for several days after Sir Boniface had left with two of *les porchers* upon the great task. The third *porcher* had come to him afterwards with news of the arrival of the justice of the peace and his two assistants, and he asked for further instructions.

Le porcher had told him how one of the minions came to him after the justice and his men had gone off to investigate the murders of the coroner and his man, that he had tried to deal with them before they reached Axeton as he had been instructed by the Magister should an official appear, but he had failed.

'I told him he must never fail to carry out your instructions again, my lord,' *le porcher* had said, illustrating how he had passed on the message by dashing a hand across his own throat and making a hissing noise. 'He understood me.'

The Magister nodded approval. This *porcher* was useful, a man with no scruples or morality, who was content to break all the Ten Commandments. At least, he knew that he had broken nine of them under his urging and instruction; the only one he was unsure of was whether he had honoured his father and mother. He suspected he probably had broken that one, too. The other two *porchers* had found him and realised how his lack of conscience could prove useful to him, and so it had proved.

Le porcher had proven a fast learner and had adopted the method of murder that he had taught him to use by killing half a dozen of Sir Boniface's rabbits taken from the well-stocked coney hill. He had even supplied him with the bodkin to do it. It was a twin to the bodkin he had used to dispatch Friar Raymond Lully when they had flown from the Tower of London. Disguised as lepers, a shrewd move for few would challenge them for fear of catching the disease. Instead, guards and gate-keepers let them pass with their scanty belongings in a wheelbarrow with a squeaking middle wheel, often with a curse and a helping shove in the small of the back or the buttocks with a staff or pikestaff. He had tolerated the indignity as he had a plan of escape that did not include Raymond Lully. Besides, it was highly likely that the king's men would be looking for two men, and the most important thing was to ensure that he kept the books and manuscripts that were secreted about his body under the leper's rags. The old alchemist had already started to slow him down and so he chose his time and place and stabbed his bodkin into Raymond Lully's skull. He had taken the other books that Lully carried from under his rags and then shoved the body into a latrine ditch. He knew it would be unlikely that anyone would care about a leper that had died in such circumstances, so there would be no question of the body being recognised.

And he had put his plan into action, which was now approaching fruition. Sir Boniface was playing his part and soon he would be rewarded, while the Magister would soon fulfil his destiny and reap the reward his careful planning deserved. Gradually everything was falling into place.

* * *

The laboratory occupied a large room in the top floor of one of the four towers of Sir Boniface's castle. It was actually a manor house that his father before him had been granted the licence to crenellate and fortify by permission of King Edward the Third's mother Queen Isabella and her lover Sir Roger Mortimer, the Earl of March, when they ruled England during King Edward the Third's minority. Effectively, it had two additional towers built, was battlemented and given a portcullis and drawbridge over the moat.

Sir Boniface had subtly arranged the financing of the vast amount of apparatus needed under the direction of the Magister, so that his own coffers were barely affected, whereas those of Sir Hugo de Braithwaite's were. It was one of the more mundane transformations that the Magister performed which convinced Sir Boniface of the wonders achievable by alchemy, or by an alchemist of such intelligence as the Magister.

It had all started when Sir Boniface had been convinced by his wife, the Magister's sister, before she had died some years before. This was part of the reason that he had willingly become a part of the Magister's plan, and why in exchange for his patronage and sanctuary the Magister was working his alchemical plan on Sir Boniface's behalf.

The laboratory floor had been reinforced in order to sustain the weight of the two *athanors*, the huge six-feet-tall brick and clay ovens that took up one end of the room. Above them both two great chimneys carried away foul-smelling odours and fumes to be blown away on the wind or to rise up and be soaked up into the clouds. Each *athanor* had a number of compartments used in the various processes of alchemy. Each had to be fired to a different heat and kept at that level steadily over weeks to incubate the variety of hermetic vessels of elixirs used in the various alchemical processes the Magister was engaged in at the time.

A furnace for fusing metals and evaporating liquids burned and had to be stocked with charcoal, its fire boosted by hand and foot-driven bellows. Dry baths and wet baths for the different types of alchemy were arranged on the floor, rank odours emanating from many as the *nigredo*, or the *prima materia* was prepared.

Along one wall of the room were long benches upon which various pieces of alchemical paraphernalia bubbled, boiled, fumed and distilled. The apparatus consisted of a mixture of glass, earthenware and copper, depending upon what process they were needed for.

There were *alembics*, *cucurbits*, *stills*, *matrasses*, *aludels* and *hermetic vases*. Many were used singly, others joined together with their junctions sealed with *lute*, a mixture of dung, egg white and clay. There were also pieces with names given by the Magister, such as *angel tubes*, *spirit holders* and *cup of Babylon*.

On the other side of the room, upon tables and shelves, were the various powders, liquids, minerals, ores and substances used in the Magister's alchemical experiments. There was natron, vitriol, lapis lazuli from the east, and cream of tartar. In clay jars, glass bottles and jugs were plants, preserved dead animals, birds, insects and worms, all of them labelled with the special alchemical symbols that had been used since the beginnings of alchemy back in ancient Egypt. And on tables there were various pestles and mortars, baths and crucibles used to prepare them.

Two slit windows were permanently kept with their shutters opened when the Magister was working, for the intense heat was otherwise unbearable. Indeed, he often had to work scantily clad to be able to continue, bathed in a patina of perspiration. He also told Sir Boniface that at times when he had to be entirely alone, the door was locked and bolted and he worked naked, as a particular alchemical ritual would demand.

A huge desk was covered in books and brightly coloured illustrated manuscripts, and a rack with numerous pigeonholes was filled with all the alchemical texts that he had brought with him, he and Friar Raymond Lully having purloined them from London and Oxford. To steal from the king was a dangerous crime, but in his eyes the crime was that these nuggets of wisdom should be readily available to a true scholar and practitioner like himself and not stored in the library of a king or of scholars who did not practise the art.

Among these alchemical masterpieces were such works as the *Tabula Smaragdina*, otherwise known among alchemists as *The Emerald Tablet*, written by the great Hermes Trismegistus himself. Also, the *Corpus Hermeticum*, the hermetic writings of the ancient Egyptian alchemists translated into Arabic and ultimately into Latin. The *Aurora Consurgens*, the *Splendor Solis*. There were works of the Arab alchemist Jabir, known by his Latin name of Geber, the writings of Avicenna, those of Albertus Magnus and most importantly of all, the *Opus Majus* of Roger Bacon, the Franciscan monk.

The Magister had gone to considerable lengths to explain to

Sir Boniface the various processes involved in alchemy. How the *nigredo* had to be placed in a retort at a specific time, worked out using the Magister's astrolabe, as this had to be done under certain constellations and under the influence of particular zodiacal influence. Then the *albedo* or whitening had to be carried out, also under strict conditions, all aimed to purify and cleanse the *prima materia*, which had been a mixture of earth, dung, urine and other ingredients including blood and body fluids. Finally, *rubedo* or the reddening, when the conjunction of what he called the king and queen, the sun and moon, would result in the creation of the *philosopher's stone*. The substance that would permit the transmutation of base metals into gold, and the production of the elixir of life and immortality.

Sir Boniface's eyes had glazed over at the thought of these, but the Magister had told him firmly that this was no light matter. There were dangers if the processes were not handled correctly, with extreme care, precision and attention to the rituals that needed to be carried out according to the timings that had to be worked out for each process.

The Magister had used the manuscripts and books that he kept open at specific pages to convince Sir Boniface of the truth and wisdom of alchemy. Showing him the illustrations of the alchemical symbols of the *hermaphrodite*, the *ouroborous*, the dragon that swallowed its own tail, the knights with sun and moon heads, he explained how the legends of King Arthur and his Knights of the Round Table were allegories of the processes of alchemy. Of how the search for the Holy Grail was no more than the real quest to find the philosopher's stone.

The *Opus Majus* of Friar Roger Bacon he particularly wanted him to see, and he told him of how many had thought him to be a modern Merlin, for it was said that he had made a brazen head, a metallic head that by using his necromantic skills he made talk and answer questions about the future. Sir Boniface had asked if this was possible, to which he replied that there were certainly great things that a disembodied human head could do.

He could see by Sir Boniface's eyes that he had implanted the seed in his mind.

All this he used to show him that the most fundamental part of it all was to understand the nature of the *quintessence*. He explained that all nature was composed of the four elements of earth, air, fire and water and that one had but to watch nature and you would see how each substance would try to return to its essential elements. Thus the flames of a burning torch would reach for the sun. Water would flow downwards towards rivers, and the rivers would flow towards the sea. Smoke or steam would rise into the air and disappear. And a dead person would rot until it was earth and dust. Yet there was an important fifth element, the quintessence that was divine, part of Heaven that could bind and animate them all and produce life.

This was the purpose of alchemical experiments and processes to produce the philosopher's stone to control the elements, so that one could transmute base metals into gold, and distil the essence of any substance to trap and store the quintessence.

Having taught Sir Boniface about alchemy he had shown him how he could turn base metals into silver, mercury or even gold. By changing the colours of substances, he had produced the powder that Roger Bacon had discovered that could explode and produce flashes of light, which so impressed both his minions. By doing so he convinced Sir Boniface that he could wield the power to give him all that he desired.

He told Sir Boniface that he just required a special ingredient to add to the *prima materia*, as well as to the fire that heated the retort it would be placed in. He needed a fragment of the wooden cross to which Christ had been nailed and whose blood had soaked into it in order to prepare the quintessence so he could complete their plan.

* * *

Sir Boniface arrived back at the castle accompanied by his two men. The Magister saw them approach the castle through his open slit window, and soon after heard their horses cross the drawbridge, their hooves then clattering on the cobbles of the courtyard.

It was not long before he heard Sir Boniface's heavy riding boots upon the stone stairs and his fist upon the door.

'Enter!' he called.

Sir Boniface came in, a beaming smile upon his face.

'You have them?' the Magister demanded.

'I have the reliquary and the Black Rood,' Sir Boniface replied triumphantly. He reached inside his surcoat and reverently took out the small cross-shaped, jewel-studded casket. He handed it to the Magister who eagerly opened it to reveal a small finger-sized fragment of aged wood.

He gasped and his hand shook slightly as he took it out and held it up to the light.

'It is wonderful! Why, I... I can feel its power.'

Sir Boniface nodded vigorously. 'I felt it all the time I carried it. To think that it is the wood upon which the Lord was nailed. I confess that I prayed several times.'

The Magister was distracted and did not comment as he examined the precious relic. 'I cannot tell what wood it is. It must be one that grows in the Holy Land. But it will serve us well.'

Reverently he replaced it in the reliquary and put it in a drawer of his desk.

'And what of the head?' he asked.

'It is coming, but we were delayed. The fool fled at night.'

'Not with the Black Rood?' the Magister demanded anxiously.

Sir Boniface gave a short laugh. 'No, it was safe. He fled with guilt, I think. But my men are experts in these matters and tracked him the next day to the Priory of St Mary at Gyseburg. He had claimed sanctuary. But one entered in secret and silenced him, then he waited until the night and cut off his head. I came back with the Black Rood and my men are dealing with the head, as you said it must be.'

'It will be ready tomorrow?'

'It will.'

'Are you sure no one knows of this?'

'No one but us and my two men – and the tanner.'

'But there is yet this justice of the peace, Sir Ralph de Mandeville and his men that the *porcher* told us about. He told me that one of our minions tried to deal with them after they left Paxton-Somersby and he followed them but failed to kill them. He said the fool had not practised his archery enough, but said it was enough to scare them off. He is sure they will think they were attacked by outlaws.'

Sir Boniface sneered. 'My two men would not have failed, but I think it is as well that he failed. The death of another official could bring the king's army down upon us. But never fear. There may be better ways to dispose of this interfering justice than with arrows in his back.'

'I leave him to you, then.'

Sir Boniface laughed. 'It will be my pleasure to do so.'

The Magister nodded. 'But if this tanner knows, then he must be dealt with.'

'I know. One of my men will collect the head in the morning and the other will go to your pestilence spreader and tell him he has another person to dispatch with his plague. Again, it is better that no arrows are the cause of his end.'

13

RETURN TO AXETON

16 May 1361

Ralph, Peter and Merek had carefully retraced their journey without mishap or attack through the forest of Arncliffe back to Axeton.

Before leaving they had attended the funerals of the coroner and his bodyguard and also the burial of Friar Bruno's decapitated body. It was uncomfortable to see his friend Sir Broderick interred, but it bothered Ralph to see the cleric buried without service in a field. Yet he realised only too well that it was canon law and that the friar was to be excommunicated, so his soul could not enter paradise. It reaffirmed his resolve to find the head of the friar and whoever had desecrated his body.

Finding fresh horse dung and recent tracks of at least two horses travelling ahead of them together suggested to Ralph, who was leading, that they were indeed following whoever had taken Friar Bruno's head. Dismounting, he knelt and felt the dung.

'It is still moist and slightly warm, but I would say it is

several hours old.' His eye was caught by some small clumps of red-caked soil. 'And what have we here?' he said, picking up a small clod of earth and raising it to his nose. He smelled the coppery odour of blood.

'It is old blood, right enough,' he announced to the others. 'I can almost see it, the bucket tied to a saddle and buffeting against the horse's side, causing it to spill some of the soil surrounding the head.'

'Do you think they could be the outlaws who fired at us?' Peter asked him.

Ralph shrugged his shoulders. 'I do not think so. Whoever shot at us was no great archer. If I am right, I think that the two who ride these horses with the head of Friar Bruno are very likely to be the same two who murdered Sir Broderick and Adam Dalton. We need to track them as far as we are able.'

They rode on slowly, every now and then either Ralph or Merek stopping to examine tracks, broken twigs or more dung.

'I thought this might happen,' Ralph said as they reached a brook, one of the many becks that eventually ran into the River Esk. 'The horses have entered here, and the riders have done so to lose their trail. So, they are men of some cunning who have taken some precaution lest they are being followed.'

'Might they be waiting to ambush us?' Peter asked anxiously. 'I have no desire to be shot at again.'

Ralph looked grim. 'We will get back to Axeton then we shall get the woodsmen to show us where Sir Broderick and Adam were ambushed in the forest on the other side of the village.'

'Perhaps we could eat before we do that, my lord?' suggested Merek hopefully.

'That was exactly what I was about to say,' said Ralph. 'A tavern is a good place to pick up local gossip.'

* * *

Axeton seemed quite deserted but the Cherry Tree tavern was busy as usual with men wishing to forget, for a few moments at least, the sense of desolation that had descended upon the village. Ralph, Peter and Merek entered its low-ceilinged smoky interior and the landlord known to all as Old Alan, a misnomer for he was not above forty years of age, found them a table and took Ralph's order of ale for all three and bowls of the inevitable perpetual stew that all hostelries kept bubbling away. Some moments later Old Alan came back with a tray on which were three tankards of ale, three bowls of stew and hunks of bread.

'Know that I am Sir Ralph de Mandeville and these are my assistants, Merek of Ryedale and Peter Longwood, my clerk.'

'I already knew who you were, Sir Ralph. You're the justice of the peace,' he said with a slight smile and a deferential bow. 'You won't find any weak ale here, sir.'

Ralph knew that all landlords were worried about the consequences of serving watered down ale. He wondered if Old Alan had heard about the petty session he had held in Paxton-Somersby when he had fined the local landlord for short selling his ale. If he had it was no bad thing that such news was soon passed from one township to another.

'Have there been any other deaths while we were away?' he asked as Merek and Peter began to eat.

Old Alan's lips formed into a tight line. 'I am afraid there have, Sir Ralph. Two more died overnight. Elizabeth Dell, the widow of one of our village pinders, and Henry Stone, the charcoal burner. God rest them.'

He made the sign of the cross.

'They died suddenly, then?'

'They both seem to have done, Sir Ralph. We all are so afeared, because everyone knows everyone in the village.'

Those around muttered similar words and raised mugs of ale in respect before noisily slurping.

There was moaning to them about the curfews.

'Yet everywhere has curfew,' Ralph pointed out.

'Aye, but the bailiff has made them earlier and earlier,' said Old Alan.

'We'll soon be going to bed an hour after we rise,' a wit nearby called out. 'There won't be time to do any work. No work, no wage and no money.' It was greeted by snorts of laughter.

'Aye, and no money, needs to take a bird or two, ain't that so, Walter?'

There was the sound of someone slapping another's back near their table and a muffled curse.

'This is surely a measure the bailiff has taken to curb the pestilence?' Peter suggested.

'Have the funerals been arranged?' Ralph asked.

'They'll be this very afternoon on account of the bailiff ordered that bodies should be quickly buried to try to stop any more deaths.'

'And who will take the funerals?'

'That Friar Simon. The bailiff asked him to stay on as the village parson, so at least there won't be any delays now. But he certainly has a way with words and he talks and talks. He tells everyone that this pestilence is our fault for disobeying the laws of the Lord.'

There was a sudden snort of laughter from behind Ralph's table and a drunken voice cried out, 'We don't need no more law – nor more lawyers of any kind.'

Merek spun round to face the speaker.

'Have a care, fellow. This is Sir Ralph de Mandeville, the justice of the peace for the northern wapentakes.'

'I don't care who he is – or who you are – there's too many and they all think they're better than us.'

He was a large fellow, but not as large or as fast as Merek, who shot up and, grabbing him by the front of his jerkin, dragged him to his feet. 'Shall I arrest this fellow, Sir Ralph, or should I take him outside and give him a lesson in manners?'

Ralph had noticed the hole and healing scab in the fellow's left ear. 'Neither, Merek. Unhand him and I will go outside with him. He has clearly had overmuch ale.'

Old Alan clicked his tongue. 'He does sup a lot, Sir Ralph, and his tongue tends to get him into trouble.'

He addressed the man still held upright in Merek's fist. 'You go and sober up and learn to keep a respectful tongue in your head, Walter Pinker.'

Merek released the man and Peter stood up. 'Shall we come with you, Sir Ralph?'

Ralph shook his head. 'No, you and Merek stay and finish your food and drink. I shall walk with Walter. Just remember what I said about taverns.'

Both his assistants understood and gratefully sat down to eat while Ralph ushered the drunken man towards the door ahead of him.

* * *

Gideon Moor had seen Sir Ralph, Merek and Peter return to the village and arranged for a boy to take their horses and water them in the village trough. He passed a few words with Ralph and watched them enter the Cherry Tree tavern before going himself to notify Osbert Flood of their return. Like all of the village, he was keen to learn whether the justice of the peace had any news about the murder of the crowner.

'Did they tell you anything, Gideon?' Osbert asked.

'No, sir. I thought it would be unseemly to go into the tavern after them and thought you ought to know first.'

'You did the right thing, Gideon. I expect the bodyguard and the clerk will be staying at my house this night. I will get Marion to arrange things.'

He watched the reeve make his way back to his work in the village bakery. Like many others, the reeve managed to juggle his main work baking bread with his duties as the reeve.

I hope they don't hear something that makes them suspicious, Osbert thought anxiously.

* * *

The drunkard seemed to stir himself out of his drunken state as he walked with Ralph.

'Where... where are we walking to, Sir... Sir...?'

'Sir Ralph de Mandeville. I am the justice of the peace.'

'I am Walter Pinker and I beg pardon, Sir Ralph. I meant no disrespect, it is just that my brother and me had some—'

'You had punishment imposed upon you,' Ralph said as they walked across to the pillory. 'I see blood stains on the wood and a healing hole in your ear. I take it you were nailed here?'

Walter hung his head in shame, a hand going unconsciously to touch his healing ear. 'We were both birched in front of the village and were nailed to the pillory.'

'This was a sentence of the manor court, I take it. What was your crime?'

'We took two pheasants from the forest and were caught and reported to Gideon Moor by the woodsmen, Douglas and Luke.'

'The two who are on guard duty at the forest entrance to Axeton?'

'Aye, Sir Ralph. We used to think them our friends and neighbours. I don't think they would have reported us for just taking pheasants a few weeks ago.'

'Why so?'

'Because the bailiff, Osbert Flood, has turned into an angry pig of a man.'

'Have a care what you say, Master Pinker. Explain yourself.'

'Begging your pardon, Sir Ralph. I mean no harm. It's just that he had the pestilence and his boy died of it not long since, and when he got better he seemed his old even-tempered self. Then almost overnight he turned from being a fair man into an angry devil. Since then everyone has been afeared.'

'Afraid of the pestilence?'

'Aye, but I meant scared of the bailiff. He's a changed man. He used to be friendly, lenient even when he first started taking the manor court in Sir Hugo's absence, but since that day he changed he's ruled the whole manor like he was the old boy – begging your pardon, Sir Ralph – I meant like he was Sir Hugo when he was younger and could be very strict. Neither the woodsmen nor Gideon Moor would dare turn a blind eye in case the bailiff heard about it.' He pointed ahead. 'It's only going to be a matter of time before someone swings on that gallows there.'

* * *

Merek and Peter finished their meals and Merek offered to share Ralph's bowl, but Peter was already full so the long-bowman quickly ate his second helping of stew. And to Old Alan's delight he bought another tankard of ale.

Putting Ralph's message into action, they engaged Old Alan in conversation, knowing that a tavern landlord would probably know as much about every villager's business as anyone. Men talked and divulged secrets when they had supped much ale.

'You serve good ale, Alan,' said Merek affably after taking a large swig and wiping his lips with the back of his hand.

'It's good and strong,' the landlord beamed. 'Your Sir Ralph won't find me serving up watery ale.'

'Ah, you know that falls under his jurisdiction?' Peter asked.

'A man who doesn't know how the laws affect him and his living is a fool. We're wary of doing anything wrong here in Axeton. And the bailiff and reeve have put in place all sorts of measures to limit who comes and goes in the village and about the area of the manor. That's no good for my business, but it's understandable with this pestilence. We've lost so many neighbours already. And Friar Simon has said we'll lose more if we don't mend our ways and spend more time worshipping. He told us about some alchemist that's making prophecies that have all come true so far.'

Other drinkers gathered around their table, keen to foster friendships with folk who worked for the powerful justice of the peace.

'Will your Sir Ralph be holding a session here in Axeton?' someone asked.

'He might be,' Peter replied.

'How will that work when we have the manor courts already?' another queried.

'They are different matters entirely,' Peter said. 'The justice of the peace upholds the law of the land, and represents the king. The manor court represents local matters in your manor and is run by the manor lord.'

'Or by his bailiff,' yet another person piped up. 'You ask poor

Walter Pinker that your Sir Ralph is talking to out there. He had the rough side of the manor court.'

Merek offered to pay for more ale for those that would like another mug. It was an offer greeted with many acceptances and cheers, by a broad smile from Old Alan and a look of reproval from Peter.

'Tell us about this alchemist,' Merek asked as Old Alan came round with a large jug to replenish mugs and tankards.

'It's what Friar Simon told us,' an older drinker said. 'He says he's a wise and powerful person who can foretell what's going to happen.'

'He says he's a necromancer, whatever that may mean,' said another ancient sitting beside him.

'It means he can talk to the spirits of the dead,' said Old Alan, making the sign of the cross, as did many of his customers.

'And where does this alchemist live?' Peter ventured to ask.

'You'd better ask Friar Simon,' said Alan. 'I don't want to know that, I'd as soon talk to them that's still alive and I don't want to talk to them that's just passed away neither. He'll be taking their funerals soon enough.'

'What about the crowner and his man?' the oldster asked. 'Did you find out anything about who killed them?'

This opened up a deluge of questions about Sir Broderick's death.

'What I want to know though,' went on the other old drinker, 'is what happened to the coroner's clerk. He was with them, but he wasn't shot and killed.'

'Maybe he was with the outlaws and led them into an ambush?'

'He could have joined their band after the killing?'

'He could be dead?'

'Maybe that necromancer or alchemist could ask him now?' a voice called out in an attempt at wit.

Only one or two laughed; the rest did not think it a suitable subject for jest.

Merek and Peter were politely non-committal to all questions. They knew that it was a question that was very much in Sir Ralph's mind.

14

BURY THE DEAD

Axeton

16 May 1361

The church bell rang, informing the villagers that the coffins containing the bodies of Elizabeth Dell and Henry Stone had been placed in readiness in the cemetery beside the graves that George the mute gravedigger had dug.

Friar Simon stood by the door of the Church of St Agnes.

'Come all, and we shall hold the service inside the church before we commit the bodies of the two victims of the pestilence to the ground.'

Ralph, Merek and Peter entered the churchyard and were immediately greeted by Osbert Flood.

'I had heard that you had returned, Sir Ralph, and have already taken the liberty of informing Sir Hugo and Lady Honoria. May I take it that you will stay with them at the manor house, and Masters Merek and Peter at my humble home?'

'That is kind indeed and we would like to accept your hospitality.'

Osbert bowed his head. 'I have made it known to Friar Simon that you will use the front pew. If you will permit me, I will introduce you to him.'

Friar Simon seemed a humourless young man who had probably never smiled in his life, Peter thought, as the bailiff introduced them all, as villagers flocked past them into the small church.

'You honour us, Sir Ralph,' Friar Simon said. 'You may know that I am merely here as a temporary measure as St Agnes's is without its priest after a most unfortunate accident a year ago. I happened to be preaching in the surrounding villages when the pestilence cast its shadow upon Axeton and started taking villagers.'

'You are doing the village a great service by conducting funerals and blessings for the dead,' said Ralph.

'The Lord calls and we friars must answer the call and serve as best we can. Especially when this pestilence has been foretold.'

'I would like to ask you some questions after the burials.'

'I will be at your service, Sir Ralph,' he replied, his lips curving slightly in the semblance of a smile.

The actual funeral service did not take long. Indeed, it was considerably shorter than the sermon that the friar gave from the pulpit. He delivered his message about the need for worship and penitence for past sins in a voice that quivered as if anger coursed through his body. He told the congregation that he could see their rightful fear and could smell the sins that they had committed.

'If we had but listened to the word of God and obeyed him by abandoning the seven deadly sins then we would not have had these wars, the pestilence and the famine that will come following all this death. Let us go now and bury your beloved, sinful neighbours.'

* * *

Friar Simon led the way out of the church and round the building to the cemetery.

'Mistress Dell is being buried next to her husband and Master Stone beside his mother who passed away two years hence,' Osbert said as they walked to the graveside of Elizabeth Dell where Sally Bringbucket, Megan Prole and George the gravedigger were already standing on the far side of the crude coffin.

The congregation gathered around and Friar Simon this time was quite brief in his words of committal.

'You may lower the coffin,' he said, looking at the two women searchers.

The coffin had been placed over loops of ropes at the head and foot end. The two women prepared to lift them, but Ralph stayed them with raised hands.

'Not yet. Before they are interred, in the absence of the coroner, Sir Broderick de Whitby, I, Sir Ralph de Mandeville, the justice of the peace, would like to know whether these two people were visited by or treated by a physician, apothecary or surgeon?'

Friar Simon stared at him then shrugged. 'That I would not know the answer to, Sir Ralph.'

'They were not,' Osbert replied. 'That is correct, is it not Gideon?'

The reeve, standing a few feet away, nodded. 'That is right. The two only fell ill yesterday and there had not been time for the apothecary to come.'

'Had he been sent for?'

The bailiff and the reeve looked at each other for answer. 'I don't think there had been time, Sir Ralph,' Osbert said.

He looked at the two women searchers. 'What say you, mistresses?'

Megan Prole looked both aggrieved and nervous. 'We would have asked the reeve this morning had they not both been found to have died.'

'In that case, I would like to see both bodies. Please remove the lid of this coffin.'

'It is nailed down,' said Sally Bringbucket. 'I have no hammer.'

'Then I shall open it with my sword,' said Ralph.

He unsheathed his weapon and stepped toward the coffin.

'My lord, is this wise?' Merek said, stepping in front of him to bar his way.

There was a lot of muttering from the congregation gathered around, almost all of whom shuffled backwards away from the coffin.

'I agree, Sir Ralph,' said Peter. 'The miasma may escape and engulf you if you are too close.'

Ralph pulled up his neckcloth from under his surcoat and drew it up and over his mouth and nose. 'It is necessary for I must see, and I shall be wary.'

As he did so he could feel his mouth go dry and a lump formed in his throat. He was sure that he could feel beads of sweat roll down his forehead, for he was truly very uneasy about what he was about to do.

Friar Simon also started to step backwards. 'Your bravery may be foolhardy, Sir Ralph,' he said as he covered his mouth and nose with his hands.

As Ralph approached, the two women searchers and the

gravedigger also moved away from the coffin. Ralph slid his sword under the lid and pushed it through, then levered the lid upwards. It creaked as the nails were pulled from the wood and finally the whole lid slid off and fell on the far side to reveal the body of Elizabeth Dell. She was wrapped in a shroud but Ralph slipped the point of his sword under the part covering her face and moved it aside to uncover her visage.

There was a collective gasp of horror as her bloated face was revealed. Her eyes were open to show the bloodshot whites. Her whole face was mottled purple and her cheeks were grossly swollen. Ralph moved more of the shroud to expose the great swellings on either side of her throat. Her lips were cracked and coloured purple and bruises covered her neck and face.

'I see the bubos on her neck,' Ralph said, adding a hand to his neckcloth to protect his nose and mouth, and also to ensure that he did not vomit. His mind brought images of his father and of his beloved wife Isabella, both of whom had perished with the first plague. Their faces had looked the same and the bubos that protruded from her neck and elsewhere on her body still haunted his dreams at night. He tried not to think about them in daylight, but seeing Elizabeth Dell's body made him feel light-headed.

'She has them under her arms and down near her privates,' Megan Prole volunteered.

'I have seen enough,' said Ralph, his voice husky from lack of saliva. Using his sword to again cover her face and neck with the shroud he signed to the two women searchers. 'You can place the lid on and lower her coffin.'

Sally and Megan did as he bid them and then using the ropes the two robust women lowered the coffin into the grave.

All over the congregation there were sighs of relief.

'In nomine Patris, et Filii, et Spiritus Sancti, Amen,' said Friar Simon as he tossed some soil onto the coffin lid.

Then, clapping his hands together, he pointed to the other coffin. 'And now, let us bury your fellow villager Henry Stone.'

* * *

After Friar Simon said the committal, Ralph once again said that he needed to view the body and once again he used his sword to prise the lid free and then to unwind the shroud from the body's face and neck.

The appearance was much the same, with the large, swollen bubos, the bruising of face and neck, and the purple broken lips. Old, congealed blood was visible on the chin and neck.

Some people started weeping at the sight of this second body, some from genuine grief, others from the fear of the pestilence and seeing people who had died from it in their coffins. People that just a couple of days before had been seen going about their business and trying as best anyone could to avoid the pestilence.

Yet again there was relief when the coffin was interred, and George started shovelling earth into the grave of Elizabeth Dell.

As the villagers started to file out of the cemetery Ralph, Merek and Peter stood watching George working on the first of the two new graves. Looking about, he counted the many new mounds at various other places, some with stones or wooden crosses and all with flowers.

Friar Simon joined them.

'You said that you wanted to talk with me, Sir Ralph?'

'Yes, I wondered where you became a friar?'

'In York, although I have been on the road all year, working and preaching around the northern wapentakes.'

'Preaching such things as you spoke of in your sermon in the church? I was surprised to hear such talk at a funeral. I have always thought a sermon at such a time focused on the lives of the deceased, of how much their lives mattered, no matter how poor.'

'We do not live in normal times, Sir Ralph. The people need to be brought back to God, to understand his wrath and the only way they can avoid it, by abstaining from sin and worshipping the Lord.'

Ralph saw the passion in Friar Simon's eyes and recognised the look of a devout man. He thought that he was the type of preacher that probably flagellated himself with a whip, like the flagellants during the last plague.

'My assistants supped in the Cherry Tree tavern and heard that you also preached about prophecies.'

'The Bible tells of all the prophets, Sir Ralph. They are very real things. Look at the wars with Scotland and France, the killing, the famines and now the pestilence.'

'Are these your own prophecies?'

Friar Simon looked startled by the question. 'Indeed not, Sir Ralph. I have not been blessed enough to receive God's words and insights. I am just one of many that are spreading these words around the country.'

'Are they all from York?'

'Some are, some are from other places.'

'And all are talking of these prophecies? My assistants said they heard that you have told the people that there is an alchemist who by necromancy has made such prophecies.'

'Many people practise alchemy, Sir Ralph. Many are clerics, priests and friars, but it takes a rich man to finance such studies and experimentation.'

'But not many people practise necromancy. Raising the

spirits of the dead is a dangerous undertaking that could cost a necromancer his life and, more importantly, his soul.'

'Like all things that are dangerous, it is less of a danger when that person knows the risks, knows what precautions to take and how to protect himself. Why, the blessed and honoured Friar Roger Bacon less than a hundred years ago practised both the art of alchemy and that of necromancy.'

Ralph stared at him. 'And do you know the name of this new alchemist who makes such bold prophecies?'

'I do not, Sir Ralph. Nor do I know where he lives and works, whether in this wapentake, this riding or even if he is in this country or without. I have merely been told of him.'

'Told by whom?'

'By another friar, but I never learned his name. As I said, there are many of us who move from village to village.'

'Of what order did he belong?'

'He was a grey friar, like myself.'

'A Franciscan then?'

Friar Simon nodded.

'How exactly does this alchemist actually make these prophecies?'

'By necromancy, I was told. But I do not know the method, Sir Ralph.'

'But he claims that he speaks to the dead?'

'So it seems, and yet I was also told that he is at work on an elixir, a healing potion that might cure anything. And that is one of the prophecies. That is the grain of hope amid this desolation.'

'But how does he speak with the dead? Can he hear their voices even though they have no body, no voice box or tongue to make speech?'

'I was told that he may be working on something like that

used by Friar Roger Bacon. Something that can make even more accurate prophecies and that would convince the Church and show them the error of their ways.'

'The Friar, Roger Bacon, made a brazen head, did he not?'

Friar Simon nodded. 'He had a metallic talking head that foretold the future. The friar said it was something like this.'

* * *

Osbert had waited outside the cemetery for Ralph to come out after talking with Friar Simon. He had been glad to leave the cemetery and as he stood at the entrance several of the villagers had patted him on the shoulder.

'I understand why you don't want to stay in that cemetery longer than you have to, Master Osbert,' said Esme Brook, the wife of one of the manor labourers. 'What with you losing your boy and him not buried here but in that priory.'

He thanked her with a nod and averted his eyes. He stepped backwards to lean against the cemetery wall.

'That was horrible to see poor Elizabeth and Henry all black and blue and swollen. It made me feel sick,' Old Alan said as he too passed by. 'I hope that justice of the peace hasn't set the pestilence on us from opening up their coffins!'

The truth was that Osbert felt guilt resurface, knowing that his son lived but was a prisoner of some horrible unknown person and yet villagers were dying suddenly of the pestilence and being buried here in St Agnes's cemetery.

If indeed it was the pestilence, he thought.

So many dying like that, almost quicker than they seemed to have done with the first plague. All of them single folk, widows, widowers or just those that didn't seem to fit in. None of them strong, fit people, but that would be expected, he imagined.

Except the bastard that held his son Dickon made him realise that he wasn't the only one that was under his control, forced to do his bidding.

The things he'd been told to do he had done these past weeks. He'd gone to see the other folk in the bastard's malignant thrall and told them what he had been instructed to say. The messages he gave them made his stomach recoil and he felt bad to give them such orders, but he had to impress every one of them that their task would be a matter of life or death to someone close to them. And each one reacted in the same way, with terror in their eyes, for they each told him they had been taken to meet the man who called himself the Magister. Like him, none had actually seen the Magister, having been beaten, tied up and taken somewhere in a coffin.

Who is he? What is he up to? Are our villagers really dying from the pestilence or are they being murdered? If so, who by? Why?

He shook himself out of his reverie as he saw the justice of the peace and his assistants come out of the cemetery with Friar Simon.

'It is yet another sad day here in Axeton, Sir Ralph,' he said. 'Sir Hugo and Lady Honoria expressed their sorrow over these deaths. Lady Honoria said she will be sending flowers for the graves from her garden.'

'Dead flowers for the dead,' said Friar Simon with a sarcastic edge. 'I do not know your Sir Hugo or Lady Honoria, but attending the church to worship would be a better tribute than flowers.' He bowed to them as they all stood shocked. 'I must go and pray at the altar.'

15

THE TANNERY

16 May 1361

The two men followed the river along and past the Old Stone Bridge over the Esk. For some distance they had been aware of the smell of the tannery even though they were approaching it from downwind. Both were well-armed with bows, swords and daggers and were looking forward to a meal, for they had ridden all the way from Gyseburg without eating, stopping only to water their horses.

'I like the smell of leather, but I hate the stench of a tannery,' said the older of the two riders. He was a man in his mid-thirties, broad of shoulder and with the well-developed forearms of an archer. His face was weather-beaten, and he had an old scar on his left cheek from an arrow that would have bored into his face and killed him outright had its path been but two inches to the side. As it was he had ever since regarded himself as being blessed with good luck and when in need of it when wagering or playing hazard, he would touch the scar several times, depending on what roll of the dice he needed to win.

'Then 'tis a pity you don't wash more often, Quince. Riding with you is like spending time with a tanner who's been scraping flesh and fat from cattle hides all day.'

'You dog, Barrat, I have saved your hide often enough,' Quince replied. He was similar sized but some five years younger and would have been considered not uncomely apart from a nose that had been broken more than once and which deviated markedly to one side. As a result his air passage on one side was permanently blocked and he spoke with a distinctive nasal voice as if he had a permanent cold.

They had talked little on their journey and this was the nearest they came to humour or yet to companionship, even though they had been comrades in arms for many years.

'I will like it when we have discharged the first part of our quest for the Magister,' said Barrat, pointing to the bucket that hung from the pommel of Quince's saddle. 'That head stinks.'

* * *

Jack the Tanner's son Wilfred, who happened to be his only apprentice, was outside the tannery washing several cowhides in the special wooden cage on the bank of the Esk. The boy was nine years old and had a brush in his hand and was washing the blood, dirt and manure from the hide before dragging them one by one into the tannery.

His father had told him to keep his eyes peeled for two men who would be coming with a special delivery. Wilfred was not quick witted and was surprised to see two men riding horses rather than coming in a wagon as most did, laden with sheepskins or many hides from the butchers in the various villages along the riverside.

'Good morrow, masters,' he called out as they walked their horses towards him. 'Art thee the two masters my father expects?'

Quince looked at Barrat and then snorted, before answering in his nasal twang. 'I reckon we are, lad. Is your master within?'

'Aye, master. Shall I fetch him?'

'No, boy! Stand with our horses, we won't be here long,' said Barrat.

They dismounted nimbly and Quince unhitched the wooden bucket from his saddle.

'You haven't got many hides in that bucket, master. What is it, a dog or cat skin for a lady?'

'Wilfred!' a harsh voice called from inside the tannery. 'Who you talking to?'

A moment later Jack the Tanner came out, a large two-handled curved blade in one hand. Then, spotting the bucket Quince carried and realising that these were the two men he had been told to expect, he hurried towards them.

'Come inside, masters,' he said, anxiously signalling them towards the tannery's open door. Then to his son, 'Wilfred, you give every one of those hides another washing, you hear?'

His son's ever-present smile disappeared. 'Yes, Father.' And he set to scrubbing hard.

Jack cast an uneasy eye at the bucket for he had a good idea what was inside it and did not wish his son to have anything to do with it. He had been told that they had a special delivery that he was to prepare. 'Come, gentles.'

They followed him inside and he pulled the door closed after them. They espied a large tree trunk that had been stripped of bark and smoothed. It was buttressed so that it lay at an angle and upon it was a cowhide that was being stripped of the flesh and fat under it. Before them were a series of progressively deeper wood-lined pits, each containing pungent liquids involved in the tanning process. There was a strong smell of excrement and urine, of different animals, and of lime.

Immediately both men started to cough and their eyes began to water. Both cursed.

'I beg pardon for the smell, I am used to it, but—'

'But we never will be,' snorted Quince, holding the bucket handle out to the tanner. 'Here! You know what this is, I take it?'

'The man who told me said I was not to ask questions but do as I was told,' Jack replied.

'And you know what must be done?' demanded Barrat.

'I am to prepare it, but not tan it. It would take some months to do so.'

'You have a day only!' said Quince in his nasal voice. 'We shall return for it then. You know what will happen if it is not done?'

Jack gulped but had some difficulty swallowing. He nodded his head.

Putting the bucket on the floor, he gingerly reached inside, brushed the earth away and lifted out the severed head of Friar Bruno.

'One day,' repeated Quince, screwing his eyes against the stinging fumes from the tanning pits. 'Or when we come again it could go ill for you and your boy out there. Understand?'

Jack could barely speak; his mouth had dried up so suddenly. He gulped and nodded his head rapidly. 'I understand, sir.'

The two men left and Jack immediately replaced the head in the bucket, scooping earth over the severed neck. He felt his heart pounding in his chest and had no doubt that such men were capable of murder. It was clear to him that they knew something about this poor devil's death, whoever or whatever he was, and they had no qualms about carrying his severed head about in a bucket. He had no doubt that one of them had severed the head, but did not dare wonder whether it was cut off before or after he died.

16

BENEFICENCE

16 May 1361

Ralph dined with Sir Hugo and Lady Honoria in the large hall of the manor house that evening. One wall was bedecked with shields, crossed swords and pikestaffs, and another with Flemish tapestries. Sir Hugo sat at one end of the long oak table and Lady Honoria at the other. Ralph sat halfway between them and tried to keep up a polite conversation with them both, as servants bustled about with crockery, food and wine. It was difficult, because Sir Hugo seemed remote and unable to focus on topics, reaffirming Ralph's previous impression that the lord of the manor was not well in himself and his brain was affected by his increasing age. His tremor and facial twitches seemed even more pronounced.

'You must excuse my husband if he does not answer all things directly, Sir Ralph,' Lady Honoria whispered. 'I think he is going slightly deaf and he will not countenance using a hearing horn.'

Ralph had noted how often Lady Honoria answered questions on her husband's behalf and adroitly kept turning the conversation. Nonetheless, there were things that he needed to know and using his own lawyer's skills kept asking questions of her, as well as making light remarks to Sir Hugo that did not call for much concentration.

'I attended two funerals at St Agnes's Church this afternoon,' he told the lady of the manor.

'I understand that you did. Our very able bailiff, Osbert Flood, keeps us informed of all that happens in the village and in the other villages of the manor.'

'Did you know the villagers who died?'

Lady Honoria smiled. 'We know all the people in our manor. I send flowers to the families of those who have died. I cut them myself from my garden here.'

'That is a kindness, Lady Honoria.'

She smiled demurely at the compliment. 'Such beneficence is an obligation upon us that I willingly take on. Sir Hugo and I know how hard life can be for our people and we try to do whatever we can for them. I have bread and cheese delivered to everyone in the village once a week. It is some little help, I believe.'

'A beneficence, as you say,' Ralph replied, smiling at her again. 'I met Friar Simon, who has been serving as the village parson.'

'I – that is, Sir Hugo and I instructed Osbert to appoint him, as our own priest died a year ago.'

'A fall, I heard,' Ralph said. 'He broke his neck.'

'An unfortunate accident,' said Lady Honoria.

Sir Hugo had been swirling his wine in his goblet and looked up. 'A good man, Osbert, our bailiff.' Then he returned his attention to his goblet.

'Have you met Friar Simon?'

'No, we rely on Osbert's opinion and he suggested that it would be a good idea to appoint him, so my husband and I agreed and left the matter to him.'

'Has he told you of the things that he preaches about?'

'I do not recall,' she replied blandly. 'I imagine it is about the teachings of the Bible.'

She seems only vaguely interested, which is strange when villagers have died from the pestilence.

'He tells the villagers that it is their fault that the pestilence has returned, because they have not worshipped enough.'

She shrugged. 'It may be so and it will be good for the people to worship more. Sir Hugo and I try to attend the church when we can. It is not something that we do now that the pestilence has returned. I do so miss my rides out of the village.'

Does she imagine that the pestilence will not trouble them in their manor house? Or is it simply that she is preoccupied with her husband's health?

'Do you ride with Sir Hugo?'

'No, I ride with Osbert. He has a lovely dapple-grey mare and he will accompany me to ensure my safety. I like to visit parts of the manor, but I have not been this last week because of the pestilence deaths.'

She took a deep breath. 'We pray here in the manor house that it will not last long or cause any more deaths. Until then I shall not ride out.'

'I am sure that is wise.' He took a sip of wine, then asked, 'There does not seem to be an apothecary in Axeton, Lady Honoria?'

'Humphrey de Duncombe attends us when needed. It is not far and he always comes when sent for.'

'I do not think he has seen all the cases of the pestilence. He certainly did not see the two people whose funerals I attended today. I was told that he would have been sent for this morning had they not died in the night.'

'I am sure that he would, Sir Ralph,' she said, dabbing her lips with a napkin.

'Then I must call for him tomorrow.'

'Why? You are not ill, I hope, Sir Ralph?'

'Not at the moment, if God spares me,' he replied. 'I would like to have his opinion on matters about physick.'

I wonder whether Humphrey the apothecary has, in fact, been making himself scarce rather than having to face patients ill with pestilence.

Sir Hugo leaned forward in his chair and rapped his goblet on the table. 'More wine!' he called out. A serving man instantly appeared with a jug and replenished his goblet then walked round the table to fill Lady Honoria's and Ralph's.

Once they were all filled Sir Hugo raised his and drained it. 'Good fellow, Osbert Flood. Did I tell you that, Sir...?' He hesitated, looking confused.

'It is Sir Ralph,' Lady Honoria volunteered. 'The justice of the peace.'

'Indeed! A good fellow, too.' He rapped his goblet again and the servant reappeared with the jug.

'Does your bailiff hold the manor court well?' Ralph asked Lady Honoria. 'I mean, does he report back to you on the cases he has heard?'

'On some of them, Sir Ralph.'

'Only on some?'

'On those he thinks we need to know about. On the ones he has collected fines.'

'And what about the ones that he has imposed sentences upon? Corporal punishments, I mean?'

She looked vaguely horrified. 'Oh, he would not bother us

with that. He knows that I have a delicate sensitivity as a lady. If you wanted to know about such cases you would have to look at the manor court rolls.'

'And do you know where they are kept, Lady Honoria?'

She hummed then shook her head. 'You will have to ask Osbert himself.'

'I shall do so, tomorrow, Lady Honoria.'

Indeed, I have tasks for both Merek and Peter on the morrow.

* * *

In the house of Osbert Flood at that same time, Merek and Peter were playing Nine Men's Morris on a board with the bailiff. They had supped an excellent meal of mutton stew with cabbage and leeks followed by cherry pottage all washed down with ale.

Marion had excused herself immediately after they had finished and their serving girl started to clear the table. The three men had then started playing the board game, two players at a time choosing to play the best of three games per pair, the winner playing the third person. Peter beat Merek easily, then beat Osbert two games to one, before playing Merek again. The longbowman had little expectation of outwitting the quick-witted clerk, but realised that Peter deliberately allowed him to win so that he could pose questions while Merek played with the bailiff.

'Did you play this with your son, Master Osbert?' Peter asked.

'I did, and my Dickon was a fast learner. I spent much time with him and tried to teach him all that I know.'

Tears started to form in his eyes and he wiped them away

with the heels of his hands. 'Your pardon, sirs. It is still painful to talk about him.'

'How old was he?' Peter asked.

'He was eight years, but he was like a cloth and could soak up knowledge so fast. He could tally and write.'

Merek made a move, placing a counter down, but Osbert quickly made a line of three and removed another of Merek's stones from the board. 'Had he started to learn how to shoot a bow?' he asked.

Osbert gave a rueful smile. 'Not yet.' He then hung his head. 'I meant no, I had not yet started to teach him. To tell you the truth, I am not much of an archer myself.'

'Did you see him when he was ill?' Peter asked.

Osbert shook his head. 'It is like a stab in my heart to admit it, but I was too ill myself. I did not know anything. What day it was or even if I was alive or not.'

He seemed to lose concentration for the game and made a careless move which Merek took advantage of.

'Where were you? Was this in your house?'

'No, I had taken him on my rounds of the villages in the manor and we both fell ill and were taken to the Abbey of St Leonard. It is on the very southern edge of the manor estate some two leagues distant from here.'

'And the monks treated you both there?'

'They did, although as I said I did not know what they did until I awoke from some fever and ague. They had bled me from my arms and legs.' He moved a stone and then pulled up both sleeves and showed the recently healed scars inside both elbows. 'And I have the same scars above both ankles.'

He showed them to us before, Peter thought. *Did he not realise that?*

Osbert's mouth trembled and he let out a sudden sob. 'They

showed me... I saw his body after he died. He had the most beautiful blond hair, but his face was black and his lips were purple, and he had those horrible bubos and his belly was—'

Peter put a comforting hand on his shoulder. 'I am sorry to trouble you with questions, but where is this abbey?'

The bailiff composed himself. 'You came from Paxton-Somersby, did you not?'

'We did.'

'Then you passed it on your way here. You would have seen it not far from the road.'

'Ah, I remember it,' said Merek. He made a mill and removed Osbert's stone to win his first game.

'Where is your son Dickon buried?' Peter asked.

'In the abbey cemetery. I was so ill, but I was there at his funeral and Father Alban, he was the hospitaller, he took the service over the grave.'

'You say he was the hospitaller?' Peter asked.

Osbert nodded. 'I went back to see his grave about a week later, when I was recovered enough. But in that time Father Alban and Brother John who assisted him in their hospital had both since died from the pestilence. They had lost two or three others before them and their Abbot was ill, too. I do not know if he still lives.'

There was the sound of the church bell ringing.

'That is the curfew,' Osbert said.

'But is it not early yet?' Merek asked.

'Sir Hugo decided that with the pestilence it is right that everyone should be within early and take to their beds early. I had it moved forward two hours.'

17

DISCOVERIES

17 May 1361

Next morning Merek and Peter came to meet Ralph outside the manor house. They walked into the near-deserted village. As they approached the village square, Ralph told them of his supper with Sir Hugo and Lady Honoria. 'I think age is addling Sir Hugo's brain. I have seen it often, and it is clear that he is not able to manage the manor. Lady Honoria tries hard to make allowances and cover for him and they put the affairs of the manor in the hands of Osbert Flood. Yet regarding the manor court, he does not tell her the outcome of all the cases. Especially not those where he has imposed a corporal sentence.'

'Would you like me to inspect the manor court rolls, Sir Ralph?' Peter asked.

Ralph shook his head. 'No, I shall inspect them myself. I would like you to inspect the manor ledgers to see exactly what the bailiff records about the manor affairs.'

Peter nodded. 'Do you suspect him of not being honest, Sir Ralph?'

'I am not sure, but the written records and accounts should give me an idea.'

'Have you a task for me, my lord?' Merek asked.

'Indeed I have. I want you to ride to Duncombe and bring back Humphrey, the apothecary.'

'You are not ill, are you, my lord?'

'No, tell him I merely want his professional opinion about matters of physick. Now let us go about our tasks, they will each take some time, so report back to me in the manor court hall where the court rolls are held at noon. But first, what did you two learn last night? Did anything strike you?'

'Osbert is a broken man emotionally, as we already knew, Sir Ralph,' said Peter. 'He told us again of his return to see his son's grave at the abbey, and seeing the graves of the monks who had caught the plague from looking after them both. It was as if he had forgotten that he had told us.'

Merek nodded agreement. 'It is a most unhappy household, my lord. His wife, Marion, is sick with melancholy and he is still grieving and he does not know how to comfort her.'

'It cannot be easy to lose your son,' said Peter.

'It is hard to lose anyone close to you,' Ralph said understandingly.

As I know only too well. Every night I have to force the image from my mind of my beloved Isabella lying on her deathbed, her face purple and her throat swollen with bubos.

His hand went almost unconsciously to his chest to press and feel the locket that made him feel close to her and which always melted away the image of the bubos and the purple mottling to replace them with her beautiful, smiling visage.

* * *

Merek retrieved his horse from the bailiff's stable where Ned, a young lad of about eleven years, clearly had not been an ostler for long. While Merek saddled his horse himself, not wishing to be delayed and to ensure that it was done correctly, he asked him how long he had been working with horses. The lad told him that it had been only a little over a week, since Old Thomas, the bailiff's former ostler, had been found dead in the hay loft from the pestilence.

'My first task after the women took his body away was to fork out all the straw from the loft and burn it.'

'Did you see his body, Ned?'

'No, sir, but I heard about it. He was almost black he was, his head was covered in lumps and those horrible bubos on his neck had burst and blood and pus had poured out of them. But I've seen all those bodies being taken away. It scares me that my mother and all my sisters might catch it.'

'How many sisters do you have, Ned?'

'Nine, sir. Mary, our oldest, is seventeen and Rose, the youngest, is still a babe. Our father went off with our pig just after she was born and he never came home again. We don't know what happened to him.'

Merek refrained from making any comment. It was a common enough tale, a father unable to look after his own just taking off to start life somewhere else, leaving his wife and family to cope as best they could. In his opinion it took a pretty rotten sort to abandon them, but one never knew. Maybe he'd fallen ill, or been murdered along the way and his pig taken from him. It was a dangerous world even without the pestilence.

'You look after them, Ned,' Merek said as he led his horse out of the stable and put a foot in his stirrup.

'I have to, sir. I'm the man of the family.'

***

Ralph and Peter had gone to the bailiff's house where Ralph told him that he needed to inspect the manor court rolls and Peter had to look over the manor ledgers and tally books.

'You'll find everything is in complete order, Sir Ralph. I look after the manor ledgers and enter everything, and show them to Sir Hugo and Lady Honoria every week. And the court rolls are also recorded by me. Gideon Moor the reeve can read and write well enough, but not enough for such important matters. I've taught my Dickon—'

He sighed, his expression one of sudden pain. 'I mean I did teach my son...' A sob racked his body, but he shook himself and stood straight. 'Your pardon, Sir Ralph. As I was saying, Gideon can help me in many matters, he does some visits, oversees the pinder, the hayward and distributes Lady Honoria's beneficence, but I could not rely on him to help with official manor documents and ledgers, so all that you read is put there by my hand.' He sighed as if weary. 'Let me show Master Peter to the counting house and I will get the manor ledgers, then I will walk with you to the manor court hall. I have the court rolls in a chest that only I have the keys for. I keep them in my pouch here.' He patted it at his side and there was a metallic clinking of the keys.

'There sound to be more than two keys,' Ralph said.

'I have many doors and chests to look after for Sir Hugo and Lady Honoria, Sir Ralph.'

And have you many secrets, I wonder?

***

Ralph made himself comfortable behind the desk in the small office behind the main hall of the manor court. The chest containing the court rolls was open and had pigeonholes containing the vellum rolls. The bailiff had opened the chest and left the key with Ralph, as the justice of the peace had made it clear that he preferred to be left to study the rolls on his own.

'If you require clarification on any case, Sir Ralph, I can give you it when I return,' Osbert had said before leaving. 'I am going to seek out Gideon to see if there have been further deaths overnight.'

Ralph found that the pigeonholes were labelled and that each roll consisted of two years, every session being neatly dated and recorded in the bailiff's precise handwriting. Unlike the court rolls of the assizes and justice of the peace petty sessions which were all written in Latin, Osbert Flood, who signed each session, had written in English.

'So, Sir Hugo stopped taking the manor court sessions three years ago,' he mused to himself. 'But the handwriting has been the same for ten years. The bailiff was the clerk to the lord of the manor, but is now effectively the judge at each session.'

Ralph decided to start looking at the sessions under Sir Hugo. It did not take much reading to see that the lord of the manor had been firm, but also mostly fair. Yet there were many cases where corporal punishment was handed out, and two instances where capital punishment had been the sentence.

'Harsh, but it was his right under the law.'

As the last few years went by, the judgments became less clear-cut and more erratic, as if Sir Hugo's mind had not been as sharp as it had been in the past.

Then there was quite a change as the sessions were held by Osbert Flood on behalf of Sir Hugo de Braithwaite. At first there was hesitation and lengthier considerations, as if he was intent upon being scrupulously fair. The judgments tended to be fair and lenient. And there were no further corporal punishments given out.

Until recently there was a gap, clearly when he was ill with the pestilence. Then, in the last few sessions, considerations were curt. He did not make lengthy recordings, but made brief and concise entries. Fines were larger and corporal punishment was not uncommon, and sarcasm almost dripped from the vellum roll.

Reading on, he came to the last manor court session two weeks ago and the case of the brothers, Walter and Timothy Pinker.

Now, Walter Pinker, let us see if Osbert Flood's record of the trial is different from our own.

He read the bailiff's account that the two brothers had been charged with poaching pheasants from the forest. They had been caught by two woodsmen, named Luke and Douglas.

These are the two who halted us when we came to Axeton, and they reported then to Gideon Moor the reeve.

He saw the remark in Osbert's own hand.

> *I sentence them to spend a day and night in the manor pillory and each to receive twenty strokes of the birch. But an example has to be made. Each shall in addition have an ear nailed to the pillory.*

Ralph sat back and stroked his chin.

What Walter Pinker told me was true. It seems that you have become harsher in the way the court is run, Osbert, but is it all down to the loss of your son? Something does not sit easily with me, for my impression is that you are a man who is suffering, yet you seem gentle and this harshness seems out of character.

* * *

Peter sat in the counting house poring over the ledgers and tally books. It was the sort of activity and study that he was ideally suited to. He liked figures and he enjoyed reading and writing, be it in English, French or Latin. He had a facility with arithmetic and relished the task of seeing how a large manor estate was run.

It was clear that Osbert Flood had a good head for business and kept excellent records. There was a ledger listing all the properties within the manor, village by village and hamlet by hamlet. Then there were separate ledgers for the various activities of the manor, each one having entries for the different villages and hamlets within the manor. Income from rents from fines to the manor court, interest on loans were all recorded, as was expenditure on supplies, crops, wages and loans.

'This is curious, though,' he said, finding several entries for purchases of large amounts of lead, copper and tin. Also purchases of quantities of sulphur and charcoal, several times.

Going back, he found many recurring references for *H de D*.

'Is that Humphrey of Duncombe, that Merek is on his way to fetch?' he mused. 'Are these for medicines for Sir Hugo or Lady Honoria, or perhaps for himself or his wife Marion?'

* * *

Merek rode towards Duncombe and was not surprised to be challenged by some villagers.

'No merchants or travellers are permitted to enter,' one surly fellow said. 'Know you not that the pestilence is here within the manor estate of Sir Hugo de Braithwaite?'

'By whose order are you stopping folk?' Merek demanded, looking down at the three men from horseback.

'On the authority of his bailiff, Osbert Flood.'

'Then stand aside, fellow, I am Merek of Ryedale, assistant to Sir Ralph de Mandeville, justice of the peace. I am sent to bring back Humphrey, the apothecary.'

'Then you should have brought a coffin, Master Merek. He died of the pestilence overnight.'

18

THE FOREST

17 May 1361

After finishing his study of the manor court rolls, Ralph felt in need of air and time to think. He replaced the rolls in their pigeonholes and locked the chest with the key Osbert had left with him.

Osbert was actually waiting for him outside the hall.

'I thought that I should not disturb you while you read through the rolls, Sir Ralph,' he said, patting his pouch again to clink the keys inside. 'But I also thought you might wish to get rid of the key to the rolls chest.'

Ralph smiled and handed it over. 'That must be a heavy pouch.'

'And a hefty responsibility for the things these keys unlock.'

And you are keen to have both keys in your possession once more.

Ralph nodded. 'I am going to ride out to where the bodies of Sir Broderick and his bodyguard were discovered.'

'I will show you, Sir Ralph. Gideon Moor, the reeve, was

called when the woodsmen found them and brought them back to the village. He called for me to decide what should be done.'

'I understood that, but why did you send them on to the Priory of St Mary at Gyseburg?'

Osbert looked perplexed. 'Why... why I... thought it would upset Lady Honoria to know that murdered bodies were within distance of the manor house. And it was there that Sir Broderick had just visited. So I... I thought that if someone came to investigate the murder that there might be a reason to do with his visit to the priory. After all, it was there he had gone to take that abjuration.'

Ralph looked searchingly at him.

A curious thing to do. Was he simply devolving responsibility to the Priory? The murder of an important official should have been treated as a matter of urgency. It would have been a simpler matter to retain the bodies here and send a messenger to the Sheriff of York.

'Had you sought Lady Honoria's instruction?' he asked.

'No, Sir Ralph. I... I made the decision myself. Sir Hugo and Lady Honoria leave me to make many arrangements and make decisions. I informed her afterwards and she seemed relieved.'

'Why did you not ask Sir Hugo himself, the lord of the manor?'

Osbert looked pained before he answered. 'Sir Hugo makes few decisions these days, Sir Ralph. Perhaps you noticed when you dined with him and Lady Honoria. His condition seems to be getting worse and it troubles her, so I try to ease her burden as much as I can.'

Ralph nodded. 'You didn't think it was outlaws who murdered them?'

'That is exactly what I thought, Sir Ralph.'

'What do you think happened to Sir Broderick's clerk?'

Osbert shrugged. 'Luke and Douglas, the woodsmen, said

they think he fell into the beck and could have been swept away into the Esk. Shall we get our horses, and I will show you the spot.'

He now seems eager to show me himself. Is it so he can see if I find anything?

Ralph touched his hand to his chest to feel the locket through his surcoat. His fingertips tingled and he felt Isabella's presence. His mind conjured an image of her nodding her head. It made his mind up to go alone.

'Actually, I know you have much to attend to, so I would like to view it myself.'

'Would you like Gideon Moor to show you?'

Is this him being helpful or would the reeve report back to him any findings I make?

Ralph shook his head. 'No. I understand that the two woodsmen who found the bodies brought them back to Axeton in their wagon. Since they are the most familiar with the spot, I want them to accompany me. I will get my horse and if you would have the reeve send for them to meet me.'

'I think that they will still be guarding the road into the village again, Sir Ralph, but I will check with Gideon.'

'Then if they are, I shall ride to them.'

* * *

The two woodsmen were indeed awaiting him when he rode through the village to the place he saw them when they first arrived in Axeton. Both were robust individuals, their muscles hardened from years of axework and sawing timber in the forest.

Ralph explained that he wanted to be shown the exact spot they found the bodies.

'Were they actually found upon the forest road that leads between Axeton and Gyseburg?'

'No, Sir Ralph,' Luke replied. 'They may have been lying there a-whiles. It was on one of the smaller tracks inside the forest.'

'Then show me.'

The two woodsmen started walking and Ralph rode slowly behind them. To his surprise it was some distance inside the forest that they came to the track, that looked as if it had originally been a deer run.

'It was here, Sir Ralph,' Luke said, pointing to a track that emerged from between two thickets of bushes. 'Sir Broderick was lying face down with arrows in his back and his man was a bit ahead of him, lying on his back with arrows in his chest.'

'How many arrows?'

Douglas answered. 'There were three in Sir Broderick's back and two in the chest of Adam Dalton.'

'Did you pull the arrows out?'

'No, Sir Ralph. We brought our wagon and lifted them as they lay there and took them back to the village.'

'Who took the arrows out, then?'

Both men shrugged. 'I think it was probably the coffin maker when they were put in their coffins.'

'And who took the coffins to Gyseburg?'

'That would have been old George the mute,' Douglas replied. 'We offered, but Gideon Moor told us that our job was to guard the village. He said that Osbert Flood wrote a letter for the prior, on account of George not being able to talk and tell them about it all.'

Ralph pictured the wounds he had examined on the bodies. The description that the two woodsmen gave him accorded with the mental image he had formed when he saw them in the priory cell. Looking back at the bend in the trail and the way it came round the thickets of bushes told him that it was an ideal place to ambush travellers.

Ralph dismounted and tethered the reins of his horse, before walking back towards the thickets. The ground round about had a lot of hoofmarks and was churned up as if horses had suddenly taken to flight.

Presumably the killers had tethered their horses some way about, but far enough so that they would not alert Sir Broderick's party. Yet they must have taken their horses after the murders. First I must see where they attacked from.

Sure enough, he was soon able to find a beaten-down area in each thicket, where the branches had been hacked enough to enable an archer in each to have clear shots at the track.

Searching on his hands and knees, he found what he expected to find: three holes on each flattened patch, each about the width of a finger and the depth of his forefinger.

He pictured each killer making his place ready, and pulling out three arrows from a quiver and stabbing them into the ground in readiness. The killers had been lying in wait for their quarry, their arrows at their side to pluck out of the earth and shoot without having to pull them out of a quiver. The trio passing between the thickets would not have seen their ambushers and their backs would have presented easy targets. They had been given little chance to defend themselves.

So, this accounts for Sir Broderick and Adam Dalton, Ralph thought. Three arrows were used on the coroner and two on his bodyguard. But what of Robert Hyde, the clerk? Did the last of the three arrows despatch him to his death?

* * *

Merek demanded to be taken to see the apothecary's body – from a safe distance. He knew that Sir Ralph would want a full account and description.

One of the men, who told Merek he was called Wilkin, the chief tithing man of the village, led the way into Duncombe. It was a village that was very similar to most of the villages within the manor estates, albeit smaller than Axeton. Stray pigs from one of the households and the ubiquitous hens ran about the main street.

'How many deaths from the pestilence have you had here in Duncombe?' Merek asked from atop his horse.

'This is only the second death this month, and the other was nothing to do with the pestilence. The first was a young boy that had a cut leg that festered. Master Humphrey had been treating him. But that was weeks ago. We've heard about pestilence in Axeton, but so far we've been spared. This is our first and 'tis a pity it is the apothecary himself.'

'And yet you've got guards on the village.'

'Ordered to by Osbert the bailiff of Sir Hugo de Braithwaite's manor. He sent word that we were to do it as soon as the first death from pestilence occurred in Axeton. Humphrey the apothecary had been called and he saw the body. It was upon his counsel, so it seems they was right to do so.'

'How do you know the apothecary died from the pestilence, then?'

'We've all seen it from last time when we lost about half the village.'

'Had the apothecary been ill long?'

'I don't know, master. He must have fallen ill himself because there was red paint on his door this morning. Reckon maybe he wanted to warn the villagers. He had a pot of paint inside his house all ready. I think he must have been waiting for some of us here in Duncombe to catch it afore him.'

'Was he married?'

'No, master, he lived alone in his apothecary's shop. That's where he was found in his bed this morning when he didn't answer the door. His body is still there, waiting for people to come.'

'What people?'

'The people in Axeton that come for the dead. We sent a boy to tell the bailiff or the reeve.'

'I didn't pass any boy on the road.'

'You wouldn't have. He'd been told not to meet anyone but to hide until they passed. In case they had the pestilence or in case he had it and gave it to them.'

Merek nodded and followed the fellow along the near-deserted village.

'Where is everyone?'

'Scared, master. They'll all be indoors not willing to come out until the apothecary's body is taken away.' He pointed to a simple house with a large pestle and mortar on a shelf above the door. A red cross had been daubed on wood.

Merek dismounted and gave the reins to the man. Then pulling his neckcloth up over his mouth and nose, he approached the house. Drawing his sword, he used it to lift the latch and then shoved the door open. He entered and, looking around, saw a counter balanced on two barrels and behind it shelves laden with pots and jars. He was immediately assailed by the smell of spices and herbs and something else. A coppery and foul odour that grew stronger as he went through the apothecary's shop into the living space.

There, lying on a cot, was the body of the apothecary. His

bloodshot eyes stared up at the open rafters of the roof, his face horribly bruised and blue, his neck swollen with large yellow bubos that had burst and exuded blood from around their edges.

Merek had no wish to get too close to the body, but he knew that Sir Ralph would want to know about the scene, so he looked about the room so he could describe it to the justice of the peace. He noted the jug of water beside the cot and a bowl of some sort of potion next to it with a spoon inside.

There was no need to do more than make the sign of the cross and exit. The apothecary, Humphrey of Duncombe, had succumbed to the pestilence.

* * *

'Show me where you found this blood trail,' Ralph ordered the woodsmen.

'We didn't find it until afterwards, when we came back with the wagon after taking the bodies to the village.'

'How did you find it?'

'We knew there should have been three travelling in the party together, so we went looking.'

These are good, sensible fellows.

'We found tracks of a pony and some way through the woods it looked like someone had fallen off. That was where we found the blood.'

On foot they showed Ralph, and indeed there were still brown marks of old blood on leaves and branches.

Ralph pictured the wounded clerk, falling of his horse and staggering along, losing blood.

He had a head start on the killers as he would have been afoot until they either went for their horses or caught Sir Broderick's and Adam's and came on those.

'See, Sir Ralph,' said Douglas, 'there are lots of hoofmarks along the bank. We reckoned his killers followed him all this way.'

Ralph nodded. That was what it looked like.

But why would outlaws go to such trouble to catch one of three men that they had attacked? Did they do so before or after stripping Sir Broderick and Adam of weapons and valuables?

'Here, Sir Ralph,' Luke said at last. 'This looks like the place he entered the beck. Here is blood on the grass on the bank. But I do not see hoofmarks, so it looks as if he had been on foot for some time, mayhap he had fallen from his horse and staggered along.'

Douglas pointed to a tree trunk that was floating down the river.

Luke nodded. 'The river is fast-flowing, Sir Ralph. He may have managed to float downstream on a log like that; we cut a lot of trees and branches and some get washed down when we have storms, so ones like that are common enough.'

'Or he may have been able to swim,' said Douglas. 'Anyways, we followed all the way until we got to the Esk, but didn't find anything.'

'And once in the Esk, he could have been washed right out to the sea,' said Ralph.

What are the chances that a clerk could swim? Again, was it mere robbery that they wanted to disguise, or were they wanting to ensure he had nothing of value on him?

* * *

Peter had many questions in his mind and had borrowed a piece of vellum from a pile on Osbert's desk to make notes, when he turned at the sound of a footstep on the stone floor behind him.

'Have you seen all that you need to see, Master Peter?' the bailiff asked.

'I have, thank you,' he replied with a smile, placing the unused vellum on the pile.

'Would you care for a mug of ale to refresh you?'

'No, I thank you, but I had better go to meet Sir Ralph.'

'Then you may have a wait, Master Peter. He rode off to see where the coroner's body was found.'

Peter nodded. 'Then I will go and wait outside the manor court hall.'

I have some thinking to do, and I shall get my thoughts in order, because I know that Sir Ralph may well have several questions to ask me.

19

THE RIVER

Bishopthorpe Palace, York
17 May 1361

Sir Marmaduke Constable of Flamborough, the Sheriff of York and John de Langton the Mayor of York were both shown into the archbishop's hall together. They had travelled separately from the city after having received the message from the archbishop to attend him in his palace as a matter of urgency for he had received a letter from His Majesty, King Edward.

'Well, Your Grace, what news from the king?' asked Sir Marmaduke as he glanced warily at the cleric's two mastiffs that lay before the mullioned bay window that looked out over the River Ouse. They were powerful hunting animals that the archbishop used to hunt both boar and deer and which were capable of bringing down such prey.

John of Thoresby, the Archbishop of York, resplendent in his purple cassock with a silver cross hanging from his neck, was writing at his desk in the alcove at the end of the hall. He gestured for the two dignitaries to sit on the oak chairs opposite him as he placed his quill in the inkpot in front of him and sprinkled ground cuttlefish bone powder over the letter he had been writing. He tapped and blew it before placing it to his left on the desk.

'His Majesty has moved his court to Conisbrough Castle and he wants to know what progress has been made in finding out who stole the Black Rood and what steps have been made in its recovery.'

John de Langton the mayor was a tall, thin man with a bushy red moustache that he allowed to dangle over his mouth. He waved a hand. 'You said that you wanted us to quash any rumours that may arise about it in York. There have not been any that have come to my ears.'

Sir Marmaduke the sheriff was a sour faced man of sixty years, florid of appearance and much given to speaking his mind. 'I have had guards go to every port in Yorkshire looking for anyone that could possibly be a friar in disguise wanting to sail abroad. I have had no results at all.'

The archbishop leaned forward in his chair and clasped his hands on the desk. 'Nor have I had any substantial news. I have had a further letter from the Bishop of Durham, however. He and Sir John de Coupland the Constable of Roxburgh Castle and the Sheriff of Roxburghshire and Deputy Warden of the East March have a network of guards on all the main roads into the borderlands and he is convinced there is no way that spies could make their way through to Scotland. Bishop John is concerned, however, about itinerant friars preaching about the Church having been guilty of stealing money from the poor, and colluding with the nobility to suppress the labourers and apprentices.'

The mayor nodded. 'Your Friar, John Ball and his ilk, it seems. I have consulted with the guild masters in York and to a man they tell me that they have had to take steps to quash such talk among apprentices. Some have even been dismissed.'

Sir Marmaduke nodded. 'I have heard the same things from Flamborough, Scarborough and the ports, wherever I have sent guards. But they also tell me that these friars are telling people about the end that is coming, and nonsense about some sort of prophecies.'

The archbishop nodded. 'It is as we talked about before. About an alchemist who practises necromancy. I mentioned all this in my letter to the king and he replies that he is most interested in this and orders that he be kept informed. Indeed, he says that two alchemists were employed by him and both disappeared, perhaps disguising themselves as lepers to escape capture, just as he was on the verge of imprisoning them in the tower. He says that precious books and manuscripts written by past alchemists such as Albertus Magnus and Friar Roger Bacon had gone missing from both Oxford and his own library. He believes that they stole them. Their names are Friar Raymond Lully, a Spaniard, and Giles de Toulouse, his French assistant. The Frenchman had studied under Friar John of Rupescissa, a famous Franciscan friar and alchemist who they say could transmute base metals into gold.'

'Surely that is impossible?' Sir Marmaduke asked.

The archbishop shrugged. 'Nothing is impossible if the Lord wishes it. These alchemists trace their history back to ancient days. Arabic scholars are said to have written extensively on the subject and were in advance of ours. After the Crusades, many of their works were translated by scholars in Spanish universities in Toledo, Barcelona and Pamplona.'

'And is the Frenchman also a friar?' the mayor asked.

'His Majesty does not say, but I have looked into this Franciscan Friar John of Rupescissa, and find that he is also a

Spaniard from Catalonia. He was imprisoned because of his prophecies and had written several books decrying the Church and declaring that an apocalypse was coming.'

'A dangerous fellow, it seems, spreading such things,' said the mayor.

'As all these friars are now doing,' agreed Sir Marmaduke.

'His Majesty is concerned that this alchemist could be one of the two who stole from him,' said the archbishop.

'Do you think we should start rounding these friars up?' Sir Marmaduke asked. 'Arrest this John Ball?'

'Not at this time,' the archbishop replied. 'I am certainly reluctant to invoking such action under canon law, as it could have dire consequences if there is a real following, especially as we do not know whether the theft of the Black Rood could be in any way related. And we must not allow news of its theft to become common knowledge for it could undermine faith in both the state and the Church at this very precarious time.'

'Then what do you suggest?' the mayor asked.

The archbishop tapped his fingers together. 'I think we must be creative and do it in secret. Arresting John Ball would be too public. It would be likely to cause a backlash against us at this very delicate time. No, I think we should discreetly remove two of these acolyte friars and interrogate them to find out what they know of this apocalyptic preaching, prophesising, and in particular what they know of this alchemist.'

'You mean one from York?' the mayor asked. He tugged one end of his bushy red moustache. 'Yes, I can see to that.'

'And I can find one in one of the villages outside the city,' Sir Marmaduke said. 'Are you going to take one, too, Your Grace?'

'No, the Church must not be seen to be involved, and you must take care that none know of this or it could affect your own standings.'

'How persuasive do you think we must be?' John de Langton asked.

The archbishop showed his empty palms. 'As much as is needed, although I am told that the threat of violence is often a more powerful persuasion than actual injury. You can use the additional threat of sending them to a consistory court and emphasise that excommunication would be the most likely punishment. For a friar that would be more frightening than being tortured.'

The mayor and the sheriff looked at each other and nodded.

'It might be most effective if we bring two of them together, so that they see each other, and are told that a number of them have been taken and will be interrogated separately,' suggested Sir Marmaduke.

'Yes, I can see that could help,' agreed the mayor. 'It could be staged so that they hear screams as if some are undergoing torture. But they won't be. Yet it must be done somewhere that they do not know about. And they could be told that they are being interrogated because their actions could be treasonable. Threaten them with excommunication and ultimately to be hanged, drawn and quartered.'

'Yet it would not be in public so they could not be considered martyrs.'

The archbishop blew air through his lips. 'I see that you both may have a talent for such clandestine persuasion. Yet it should be done away from York.'

'I know of a place that will suffice perfectly,' said Sir Marmaduke.

'Tell me no more, I pray you,' said the archbishop.

There was agreement then silence for a few moments. Then John de Langton broke the silence. 'What then of the murder of Sir Broderick de Whitby?'

Sir Marmaduke shook his head. 'No news yet. I have yet to hear from Sir Ralph de Mandeville. I imagine he will send word with Merek of Ryedale when he has completed his investigations. He is a good man so I think it will not be long.'

The archbishop sighed. 'Let us hope that he either finds a link or finds that there is none between the sanctuary seeker and the Black Rood. But either way, we need to know if Sir Broderick was murdered by common outlaws or by spies working for Scotland or France.'

He rose from his chair and went round his desk to a side table to pour wine into three goblets on a tray.

'Any further news of the pestilence?' the mayor asked as the archbishop returned a few moments later with the tray. He took a goblet. 'I have had no sign of it as yet in York.'

'Nor I from areas around the coast,' said Sir Marmaduke.

'Then let us hope that Yorkshire has been spared,' said the archbishop, making the sign of the cross.

* * *

Peter Longwood was about to take his leave of Osbert and go back to the manor court hall as Ralph had told them to do, when there was an urgent knocking upon the counting house door. Osbert called out to enter.

The door opened and Gideon Moor the reeve came in, shepherding a red-faced, breathless boy of about twelve or thirteen years ahead of him.

'This is Elric, sent from Wilkin the chief tithing man from Duncombe,' said the reeve. 'He has brought bad news that you should hear.'

'Speak, lad,' said Osbert.

'The 'pothecary is dead, master. From the pestilence.'

Osbert gritted his teeth and thumped one fist into the palm of the other hand. 'Gah! I feared this could happen. Master Humphrey the apothecary must have caught it here and now he's taken it to Duncombe.' He slapped his head with the flat of his hand. 'Oh, Sir Hugo and Lady Honoria will be desolate by this news.'

He breathed heavily a few times to control his emotions, then turned to Elric. 'Where is Master Humphrey's body now, lad?'

'In his shop, master. He lives there and was found this morning. Wilkin said he must have fallen ill and painted a cross on his house himself.'

Peter stared at the boy for a moment. 'A Christian thing for him to do. Mayhap he was treating himself. Did you meet Merek of Ryedale, a big man on horse, as you came here?' he asked.

The lad nodded. 'I saw him as I was running, but Wilkin told me I was to hide if I saw anyone upon the road. Not to get too close to anyone in case of the pestilence.'

Peter nodded. 'It was good advice.' He turned to Osbert. 'But it means that Merek may be there in Duncombe now.'

'Or he may be on his way back,' replied the reeve. 'There will not be anything that he can do.'

'What of the body? Is there any other apothecary, surgeon or physician living nearby who can confirm the death?' Peter asked.

'There is no one within twenty leagues,' Osbert replied. 'And of course, there is no coroner to report the death to. I will send George the gravedigger with the two seeker women, to fetch another coffin and take it to prepare the body for burial. I know for a fact that Humphrey had no family of his own. If there is no cleric there then perhaps I should get Friar Simon to go with them?'

'I think you should await the return of Merek to hear what he saw and thought. Then we should wait upon Sir Ralph de Mandeville's instructions first. After all, he wanted the apothecary's opinion on something and he may yet want to view the body himself.'

Osbert nodded then turned and addressed Gideon. 'You best see that Elric here has food and water before he goes back to his village. He can tell Wilkin the chief tithing man to leave the body where it is until Sir Ralph de Mandeville decides what is to be done. But we will be sending the searcher women and George to do whatever is needed once Sir Ralph has been told of this.'

When the reeve and the boy departed, Peter smiled ruefully at the bailiff. 'I think I will accept your offer of a mug of ale after all.'

* * *

Merek arrived back in Axeton feeling both hungry and thirsty. He found the manor court hall was still locked so he went to the bailiff's house and through the counting house window he enviously saw Peter talking with Osbert and sipping a mug of ale.

Dismounting in front of the stable, he had a friendly word with Ned, the young ostler, before going across the cobbled yard and rapping on the counting house door. Osbert had seen him and opened the door instantly.

Merek responded enthusiastically to the offer of a mug of ale.

'I am afraid that Humphrey the apothecary is dead,' he said.

'We already know,' replied Peter. 'The chief tithing man sent a boy to tell us.'

'Ah, he said he had and that he had told him to make himself scarce if he saw anyone coming along the road. Good advice, since it looks as if the apothecary caught the pestilence from someone here in Axeton.' Merek took two hefty swallows of ale, almost emptying his mug.

'Did you leave any instructions about the body?' Peter asked.

'No, I thought it best to leave it and just close the front door until I found out what Sir Ralph wishes to do.'

'That is exactly what Master Peter thought,' said Osbert. 'So we have instructed the boy to return and tell Wilkin the chief tithing man to do nothing more until Sir Ralph has been consulted. I just hope it will not be too long.'

Merek drained his mug. 'It is past noon; should we go to the court hall to meet him?'

Peter shook his head. 'He saw Master Osbert and said he was going to view the place where Sir Broderick's and Adam Dalton's bodies were found.'

'Should we ride there and meet him?' Merek asked with a slightly troubled expression on his face.

'He is with Luke and Douglas the woodsmen, so he will be safe, if that concerns you,' Osbert said.

He pointed to the large jug of ale. 'Masters, please help yourself to more ale. I must go and inform Sir Hugo and Lady Honoria of this most bad news.'

Merek winked at Peter. 'We thank you for your hospitality, Master Osbert. Another mug of your good ale will go down well.'

'And then we must go and wait for Sir Ralph's return by the manor court hall,' said Peter.

* * *

Ralph had continued his search in the forest with the woodsmen, following the beck until it reached the Esk, and then went along its bank to see if there were any signs of a horse or a man mounting the bank.

It didn't look like he was on horseback when he entered the beck, so I fear he may have been washed out to sea after all.

'How far did you go down the river?' he asked Luke and Douglas.

'To the far side of the Old Stone Bridge, Sir Ralph. It is two miles from Axeton.'

'Is there another settlement on the river beyond that?'

'Not for ten leagues. The only thing after the bridge and the next village is the tannery about a mile further.'

'Did you go that far?'

'No, my lord,' said Luke. 'We didn't think there was any point.'

'It is a long way from Axeton and Duncombe.'

'It is, Sir Ralph,' Douglas replied. 'It's far enough downriver for the stink of tanning not to be too troublesome for the villages. Folk come from all over the manor and the wapentake with their skins and hides to be tanned into leather.'

'And it's at a natural place in the river with a weir that makes it ideal for a tannery, Sir Ralph. Jack the Tanner's family have worked there for three generations, I reckon.'

Ralph frowned thoughtfully. 'Well, I shall search further on my own. You two can return to your watching and guarding.'

He rode on, scrutinising the banks on both sides of the river for any sign of blood or evidence of someone hauling themselves from the water. The further he went the less likely he thought that would be.

A wounded man, maybe not even conscious, pulling himself out of this river? It is unlikely.

Yet he felt that he had to make sure one way or the other.

Ralph smelled it before he saw the tannery in the distance. As he approached it he saw a young boy washing hides in one of the half-submerged frames in the water. He had momentary concern for the youngster working so close to the fast-flowing river and wondered whether the lad could swim if he ever fell in.

The boy had been watching him ride towards the tannery and he stood up and greeted Ralph with a broad grin.

'Good day, master,' he called. 'Art thou looking for some leather? My name's Wilfred. I'm Jack the Tanner's son.'

Ralph returned the smile, thinking how lucky the tanner was to have a son. And then he felt the old pangs of sorrow at having lost his Isabella and any prospect of fatherhood.

Unconsciously his hand went to touch his locket through his surcoat and he almost felt Isabella's hand upon his. It gave him comfort.

'I am Sir Ralph de Mandeville, the justice of the peace,' he replied. 'Is your father within?'

Wilfred's jaw had dropped as Ralph introduced himself, albeit he had no concept of what a justice of the peace was or what it meant. He just seemed to be in awe that a gentleman had come to the tannery.

'Who are you talking to, Wilfred?' came a voice, followed by the wooden door being thrown open and Jack the Tanner emerged, his brawny arms bare from the shoulder and his whole torso covered in a leather apron stained with old blood and all manner of tanning fluids.

'A gentleman, Father,' Wilfred said, turning at the sound of the tanner. 'I asked if he wants leather.'

Jack came forward and tousled his son's hair. 'That's a good lad. But you should come and fetch me first, like I told you, instead of waiting to talk to strangers. Especially these days.'

Then looking up at Ralph he touched his forelock. 'Begging your pardon, sir. I'm teaching my son to be careful these days when there's talk about pestilence. I'm Jack the Tanner. What can I do for you?'

'Good day, Master Jack, I am Sir Ralph de Mandeville, the justice of the peace for the northern wapentakes of the North Riding. I have come for information. I am investigating the deaths of two men, perhaps you have heard about them?'

Jack grimaced. 'I did hear something when Sally from Axeton came with more urine and dung. T'was the crowner and his man, she told me. But worse, she told me there is pestilence in Axeton and she's one of them searchers. Important she is now, so she told me.'

'Working here, do you keep an eye on the river?'

'I have to, and anything I miss, my boy Wilfred sees and tells me.'

'Have you seen anyone in the river? A man, alive or dead?'

The tanner looked shocked. 'A body, Sir Ralph? You mean a dead body floating past my tannery?' He shook his head emphatically. 'No, sir. There's been no body passed this tannery.'

At least that answers my question. If Robert Hyde entered the water, alive or dead, he would have passed here. If alive, he'd have called for help, and if dead, he'd have been spotted by the boy.

Then he mentally cursed himself for not thinking of the obvious.

'Do you and your son live alone here in the tannery?'

'Lord love you, no sir. The tannery is my living, but not my life. We live in a house my grandfather built up in the woods, so we don't have to breathe the smells.'

'So a body could have floated downriver at night and you wouldn't have seen it when you were at home?'

'No, sir, I only meant if it had floated past when we were here, we'd have seen it.'

So he could still have floated past, out towards the sea.

'I thank you, Master Jack. You have been helpful,' Ralph said, turning his horse and waving a thanks to the father and son.

But I am no nearer an answer. Mayhap I must assume he drowned and was washed away.

The father and son watched Ralph ride away, Jack with his arm about his son's shoulders. Wilfred looked up at his father.

'But Father, shouldn't we have…?'

'Hush, lad. You know what your mother said. We were to say nothing. Nothing at all if anyone came asking.'

Life had never proved so difficult for Jack. He was expecting the two men to come back any time soon and he was glad the justice had not tarried, otherwise he feared there could be another dead official. Or worse still, his son and he could be hurt or killed.

Thinking was not his strongest point. It was a good thing he had Polly, his wife, back at home. She was a wise woman just as her mother and her grandmother had been before her. He'd always depended on her to tell him the best thing to do. He just wasn't so sure that she had been so wise lately.

They had their own worries and he had this big problem of his own that he dared not burden her with.

20

MEETINGS

Axeton

17 May 1361

Sir Hugo was sleeping in his favourite chair when Osbert told Lady Honoria of the death of Humphrey the apothecary.

She had been looking out of the great mullioned window, not looking at the bailiff as he addressed her. She suddenly clapped both hands to her face to cover her eyes as she gasped and then let out a sob.

'Our poor Humphrey! What shall we do without his ministrations? My husband has been treated by him these last two years.'

'I can make enquiries, my lady,' Osbert said, conscious of his station so not reaching out to touch her hand, as he would have wished to do. As he tried to do to Marion, his wife, so often these last days only to be rebuffed each time.

When she took her hands away from her face he saw how shocked she was, the colour having rapidly drained from her cheeks.

Desolation

'Should we awake Sir Hugo and tell him, my lady?'

She stared at him suddenly. 'No!' she snapped. 'What good would that do? No, you must say nothing. He will not understand.'

'But I am sure that I can find another—' he began.

'No, you cannot. He has not been well since Father Dominic, our chaplain, left our service. He lost interest in everything, for he was no longer able to continue his studies without him.'

Osbert was well aware of the change in his master since that time. His condition started soon afterwards and his reasoning began to deteriorate.

Lady Honoria's face suddenly hardened. 'I must go riding again. This very evening. The usual way, Osbert.'

'But the pestilence, my lady!' the bailiff exclaimed in protest.

'This evening, Osbert.'

'But the curfew?'

'The curfew is not for me. You will wait until the bell is rung then wait an hour and then accompany me as usual and wait until I return. None shall see us leave Axeton. I will but be an hour or two.'

'I will have the horses readied, my lady.'

'But do so secretly and tell no one. No one at all. Especially not the assistants of the justice of the peace.'

'I would never tell anyone, not even my wife, my lady.' He bowed and took his leave. Lady Honoria had frequently made use of him like this to go riding, albeit he never knew exactly where she went, for he had to accompany her only so far and then wait. There was usually a rider who came to meet her, but whom he never saw clearly for she dismissed him as they approached. He knew in himself it was not the person she wanted to meet, merely someone to accompany her on the second part of her journey.

He had a good idea whom she was actually meeting, but it was not his place to pry or to spy. He knew his place.

Secrets! They dominated his life these days. His son Dickon lived, but only as long as he did as he was told, after each time he had been forced to make that horrible journey inside the coffin, but to where he did not yet know. Each time he had been caught unaware and had a sack thrown over his head and was bound hand and foot before being manhandled into the coffin. He had no idea where he was taken on the wagon but it was always the same. He was told not to talk, but to answer by hitting his head on the coffin lid. He heard his son's plaintiff cries and the same threats were delivered by that same voice as he was given fresh instructions.

He was determined that he would obey everything to keep Dickon alive. Even if it meant that his actions would in some way contribute to the end of the world, that Friar Simon said was coming. Yet thinking that caused the guilt to gnaw away at him and he wondered if he would be brought to the Magister again. If so, would he have the courage to force the coffin open and spring at the monster and stab him? His mind conjured an image of a blade slicing through Dickon's throat, spraying his blood everywhere, and one of the henchmen stabbing him before he could reach the Magister. But at least he would die with his son.

* * *

The killer had enjoyed dispatching the apothecary, the pompous oaf. He always strutted about the place, pontificating and letting everyone know how learned he was, how he could cure all manner of ills with his elixirs and potions. Yet he was just as afraid of the pestilence as everyone else.

As he thought, Humphrey had been amenable to flattery. Especially when wine was given to him. It loosened his tongue and he let his guard down and made him susceptible to seduction. It was obvious to him that he liked men. Especially good, lusty fellows like himself. And that suited him too, because he had found that he enjoyed physical contact, the cuddling, before he shoved the bodkin up into his skull and whipped it round and round inside the stiff jelly of his brain.

It's just like making butter, he had thought with a smirk, as he held Humphrey's convulsing body with one arm while he twirled the bodkin. How clever was the master to teach him such a pleasurable way to kill.

His death may not have been necessary, but it couldn't be chanced to let him live. Not when the justice of the peace wanted him to examine the victims. He had to be killed, of that he was sure. He had confidence in his decision, but he would yet have to inform the Magister.

The beauty was that after he had finished his work and prepared his body, leaving the right touches so that people would think he had been treating himself and had sacrificed himself by painting the cross on his door, no one would be any the wiser.

The pestilence had taken another life. It almost made him laugh out loud, for he was the pestilence! He was the silent bringer of death. He could make his victims look like plague death.

* * *

Jack the Tanner had done all that he could to prepare the head exactly as he had been instructed. It had been necessary to keep Wilfred out of the way while he was working on it, so he had given him the task of going into the woods to collect animal spoors and as much pigeon droppings as he could. He knew it was a thankless task that would take him hours, for he had given him a large bucket to fill. Not only did he not want the lad to see the evil work he was engaged in, but he also did not want him to be around when the two bastards came to collect the head.

He cursed the day that he was first approached and had his wits addled through fear. It had been bad enough during the first time the pestilence ravaged the land. Everyone was afeared back then, but finding himself in thrall to the Magister had opened up whole new meanings about fear. Although the Magister told him that he had been singled out for salvation, because that was what he promised for him and his family, yet something inside him screamed out that it was all against the wishes of God. And Jack, like everyone, else was a God-fearing man. When he had been told that he was to expect men to come with a severed head and what he had to do with it he began to suspect that it was not salvation that he was headed towards, but damnation in Hell.

His wife, Polly, knew nothing of any of this, and that was the best for her.

No, that was how he intended to keep it for he had to keep her and Wilfred safe. Best they know nothing about the Magister and this damned head he had been told to treat. It was bad enough that they had this other secret that Polly had sworn him to keep until she said it was time to do something. A good woman, Polly. So kind and caring.

So, he had done exactly as they wanted and had done as good a job on it as he could. It was impossible to tan flesh in anything less than many weeks, but what he had done was clean it, so that the skin looked as if it still had life in it. There was to be no tar to preserve this head.

It was revolting work to do, and Jack had to break off several times and vomit.

He had flushed water through the mouth so that it poured out of the gullet tube, then he had turned it upside down and poured more into the blood vessels on each side of the neck and through the windpipe to get rid of all the old blood clots, or those that could come out or which he could drag out with one of his fine hooks. Holding it then in a tank of brine he had worked the flesh, washed the hair before taking the head out, drying it and massaging resin and oils into the tonsured scalp and the face. At least it would hold the stench of decay for a few days.

The eyes and lips posed a problem for him.

The eyes because the brine had dried them out and whitened the pupils so they looked like dead fish eyes. These he managed to make lifelike by gently smearing chicken fat over them and teasing the eyelids down so they were half closed, yet the pupils could be seen. The lips were as white as the underbelly of a dead frog, all blood drained from them. To these he applied blackberry juice mixed with fat so they probably looked slightly fuller and redder than they had in life.

Using a tiny amount of this berry and fat mixture, he applied some to each cheek and rubbed it round and round to produce a slight flush in the skin.

Finally, he combed the hair and set it atop a barrel to inspect the grotesque head a final time. The stubble on the chin and upper lip made it look most lifelike, as if the man, whom by the tonsure Jack now knew had been a monk or friar of some sort, was sitting inside the barrel with his head popping out of the top. Almost as if he was waiting for someone to shave him.

Finished, he shuddered again as he knew the time was approaching for the return of the men to collect the head.

He put the bucket atop it to hide it from further sight, then made the sign of the cross. Partly for the dead head that was separated from its body somewhere, and partly for him and the macabre and horrible act that he had been forced to carry out. He silently prayed that his part in this devilry would soon be over and his family would be safe.

* * *

Ralph returned to Axeton and rode to meet Merek and Peter, who were sitting waiting to meet him outside the manor court hall.

'Have you brought Humphrey the apothecary or is he following on his own?' Ralph asked.

'I am afraid to say that he is dead, my lord. From the pestilence. I saw his body myself in his cot behind his shop.'

Ralph looked surprised. 'Had he been ill long?'

'No, my lord. Apparently he was ill in the night and had painted a cross on his own door. I looked at his body and it was just as the others. He had bubos on his neck, he was puffed up, his face was bruised and blue. I noticed he had been taking some potion of his own making as there was a bowl by his cot.'

'What has been done with his body?'

'Nothing as yet, my lord,' Merek replied. 'I told Wilkin the chief tithing man to merely close his shop until I had asked you what should be done. When I arrived back here, Peter had already known about his death.'

'A boy had been sent by Wilkin and he was told to hide if he saw anyone on the road from Axeton,' Peter continued. 'His name is Elric and he seemed a boy with wits. Osbert the bailiff was with me at the time and wanted to send the searcher women and the gravedigger, and also Friar Simon, but like Merek I thought we should await your decision.'

'Had Wilkin made any arrangements about the village? Putting guard on the roads?'

'Master Osbert had already sent word to do that after the pestilence claimed its first life in Axeton. Wilkin told me that Humphrey the apothecary had counselled Osbert to do so.'

Ralph nodded. 'Then I shall go to Duncombe and see the body. Until another coroner is appointed in poor Sir Broderick's place it is only right that I should take over his role and record deaths.'

He looked at his two assistants. 'You were right not to have allowed anything to be done with the apothecary's body until I view it, but we must yet take precautions about the disease spreading, so it must be buried soon. Where is Osbert now?'

'He went to inform Sir Hugo and Lady Honoria about the apothecary's death,' Peter replied. 'He said they would both be upset, since he had treated Sir Hugo for so long.'

Ralph nodded and turned to the longbowman. 'Merek, go and tell Osbert he may instruct Gideon Moor to dispatch the searcher women and the gravedigger to Duncombe along with a coffin, but for them to wait until I have looked at the body first.'

'And Friar Simon, should they arrange for him to go too?' Peter asked.

'Yes, and I shall have some words with the friar while I am there.' His stomach gurgled and he patted his abdomen, realising he had barely eaten that day. 'So let us eat and drink quickly, then we shall all three ride to Duncombe.'

Merek winked enthusiastically at Peter.

* * *

At a table in the corner of the tavern while they ate perpetual stew and drank Old Alan's ale, Ralph asked Peter what, if anything, he had discovered in the counting house.

'Osbert is very neat and tidy in all his penmanship. He is certainly a most diligent bookkeeper, Sir Ralph. He has recorded everything and his accumulations tally exactly.'

'So he seems to be an honest man? There is no evidence of him stealing from Sir Hugo and Lady Honoria?'

'No, Sir Ralph. He keeps separate ledgers for the various activities of the manor. I looked in every one and found that he has separate entries for the different villages and hamlets within the manor. He records fines from the manor court, loans given and interest accrued, wages paid, harvests, rents, sales of animals and all the expenses of the manor. But I was surprised at some of the things that have been purchased, presumably on behalf of Sir Hugo.'

'Such as?'

'Well, there were a lot of purchases of large amounts of lead, copper and tin. Also large amounts of sulphur and charcoal, several times. Many minerals and things that I had not heard of. Strange equipment.'

'Curious indeed,' mused Ralph. 'It sounds like alchemical supplies.'

'I wondered that myself,' said Peter. 'I also found a number of references of payments to *H de D*. I wondered if that could mean Humphrey de Duncombe?'

'That is likely, as I imagine Sir Hugo was in need of treatment from the apothecary. Yet it is odd that the apothecary is now dead.'

He looked at Merek. 'Drink up. It is time we went to see the late apothecary, Humphrey de Duncombe.'

21

THE APOTHECARY

Duncombe
17 May 1361

The road into Duncombe was guarded by villagers as before, but Wilkin the chief tithing man was among them and recognised Merek as the trio rode up.

'Master Wilkin, this is Sir Ralph de Mandeville, the justice of the peace,' Merek said.

Wilkin and the two other villagers greeted Ralph deferentially.

'I've done as you told me, Master Merek, and kept folk away from the apothecary's house.' He looked up at Ralph. 'The searcher women and the gravedigger, George, I think his name is, are at the church already. They came on a wagon and I thought it would be all right for George to start digging the grave.'

'A good idea, Master Wilkin,' Ralph returned. 'Is Friar Simon with them?'

'He came on his donkey and arrived just a few minutes ago,

Sir Ralph. He's gone to the church, too. Shall I take you to the apothecary's house?'

'Lead on.'

A few minutes later they dismounted and approached the apothecary's shop and home. Ralph pulled up his neckcloth and signalled to the others to do likewise. Then he stood a moment and collected himself before opening the door.

There was the spices and herb smell that one would expect in an apothecary's shop, but as Merek had noticed on his first visit there was a coppery smell of blood and a vague odour of excrement. Also, an overriding smell of paint.

Ralph took a few moments to look around the shop, noting how neatly everything was arranged. The counter was made from a large plank atop two barrels. Upon it was a large *macer*, a handwritten book of all the known herbal remedies. Ralph himself had a copy from his own days at university when he had studied medicine along with philosophy and law. Behind the counter was a worktable with pestles and mortars, a cutting and chopping board, bottles of liquid and above it shelves with all manner of boxes, bottles, jugs and caskets. Some were labelled with Latin names, others with English common names.

He recognised the names of various medicines, for like all men who had studied at university he had taken classes in physick sufficient to know the names of remedies if not enough to practise the art. Here were labelled medicine jars of theriac, resin of draco tree, commonly known as dragon's blood, mandrake roots, unicorn horn, although usually consisting of cow or goats' horns, cormorant blood, linseed, myrrh and many others.

Hanging from nails in the wall were strings of onions, garlic and bunches of drying plants.

Looking over his shoulder, he told Merek and Peter to stay

in the shop with the door open while he went through into the apothecary's living space.

'Also, one of you go and fetch the searcher women and the wagon for the coffin so they can take it once I have finished.'

It was not a particularly large area, but there was room for the cot, a table and a chair to eat from, a cupboard with his drinking vessels and his food, a fireplace with a chimney and with a stewing pot hanging over a cold fire.

The body was unpleasant to see, for the skin of his face was mottled and bruised, and he had swollen bubos that had burst and exuded congealed blood around them. His cheeks were swollen as was his tongue, which protruded between his blue lips.

Ralph knew that it was not safe to go too close to a body that had died from the pestilence, so he kept his distance and tried to hold his breath while he was in the room.

He saw the pitcher of water and the bowl with a spoon in it and the potion that Merek mentioned that he had seen.

Reaching out at arm's length, he lifted the bowl and brought it closer to smell. He lowered his neckcloth and sniffed. Immediately he flinched and moved his head away.

It is not theriac, which was what my Isabella's physician forced into her. The wonder cure-all that never seemed to help any.

He sniffed it again.

It's urine mixed with paint, I think. A strange concoction to make and take. Yet I know that some physicians advise drinking their own urine. But paint? What virtue is there in paint as physick?

He took yet another sniff.

And vinegar.

He stared at the piteous sight of the apothecary, with his bloodshot unseeing eyes fixed upwards at the rafters.

'Twas not a remedy that did you much good, Master Humphrey, which I fear is no surprise.

* * *

They watched from the door as Megan and Sally, the two searching women with neckcloths over the lower part of their faces, laid out a winding sheet upon the floor of the apothecary's living space. Then they lifted his body, clothes and all, and laid him upon it.

'Gideon Moor told us the apothecary himself said to always leave them clad,' Sally said, looking at Ralph as they prepared to do the wrapping in the shroud.

Ralph nodded approval. 'It is good sense to do that, so that whatever valuables he has on him if any can be buried with him, and it is less dangerous for you both.'

Megan made a noise that could have been a laugh. 'If it's our time to meet our maker, then we are both happy to have done our work, Sir Ralph. Besides, Master Osbert said the manor will pay us well for our service.'

They were both strong women and their forearm muscles bulged as they went about their work as they wrapped him in the winding sheet. One at the head and the other at his knees, they rolled him over until he was upon his back and completely covered.

Merek felt somewhat guilty about letting the women do such a manual task and was about to offer to help carry the body, but Ralph, sensing his intention, put a hand on his arm and shook his head.

'We'll carry him out to the coffin on the wagon if that's to your liking, Sir Ralph,' said Megan.

'Indeed, pray proceed. We will stand back to give you room.'

The whole village had come out to see the apothecary's body being removed from his shop and home and were standing some distance back.

'Peter, we will make further record of this later,' said Ralph as they removed themselves further back and watched the two women manoeuvre the body first onto the wagon, which George the mute gravedigger had drawn up, then climbing up and lifting it into the coffin.

Wilkin the chief tithing man approached. 'What about his shop, Sir Ralph? Shall we just lock it up, or should it be burned down?'

Sally jumped down heavily from the wagon. 'Master Osbert and Gideon Moor have paid us to fumigate the places we took bodies from in Axeton. We use torches of burning gorse. 'Twas also what the apothecary there, Lord bless him, advised to be done when he was still alive.'

'We can do that if it's your will, Sir Ralph?' Megan offered.

Wilkin raised a hand. 'If you don't mind, Sir Ralph. Humphrey was our apothecary. We'd like to do that ourselves. In fact, I'd like to do it.'

'A good and decent gesture,' Ralph replied. 'Please do so after the good apothecary has had his funeral.'

* * *

Friar Simon had made use of his time while the body was being examined by looking inside St Bede's church to see where he could preach before he took the funeral. It met with his approval, albeit it was a smaller church than that of Axeton. He liked nothing better than a good pulpit where he could look down upon a congregation, however large or small it was.

The villagers crowded into the church, all nodding or

passing a word with the friar whom they all seemed to know quite well. Ralph recalled that it was from Duncombe that he had come and been asked to stay as the Axeton parson by Osbert Flood.

Ralph, Peter and Merek sat on the front pew as they had done in Axeton. Friar Simon said some prayers and then mounted the pulpit and delivered another sermon telling the villagers that it was because they had forsaken the Lord that the pestilence had returned. It was essentially the same message he had given in Axeton in that he talked about the wrath of God and the need to worship and atone for sins.

After the service, in which Friar Simon had actually said kind words about the good work that Humphrey the apothecary had done in his life, the congregation gathered in the small cemetery, where George the gravedigger had worked fast to dig a grave several feet deep.

There were tears and weeping as the coffin was lowered by the two searching women before the friar conducted the interment.

'A good life, Sir Ralph,' Peter whispered to the justice of the peace as they stood listening to Friar Simon intone on.

'But all over so suddenly,' Merek on the other side of Ralph whispered back. 'Healing the sick one day and the next he is dead and being buried. All so neat and tidy. Perhaps that is the way to go.'

Ralph was only half listening to the friar or to his assistants. But then the word 'neat' seemed to strike a note with him.

Neat! Peter said Osbert was so neat in all his penmanship. And Merek thinks this death and burial are so neat. And did I not describe Humphrey de Duncombe's shop as being so neat?

Friar Simon droned on.

Was the apothecary so neat that as he was dying he painted a cross, then made a potion, tidied up after he made it then lay down to die?

He placed a hand over the hidden locket of St Sophia and closed his eyes for a few moments. And in his mind he saw Isabella smiling at him and nodding her head. He mentally thanked her and opened his eyes, resolved in what he must do.

'*In nomine Patris, et Filii, et Spiritus Sancti, Amen,*' said Friar Simon, and threw soil into the grave where it rattled on the coffin lid.

Ralph made a sign of the cross and turned and walked quickly on the path leading from the cemetery.

Peter and Merek were surprised at his rapid exit and after looking at each other hurried after him.

'My lord, where are we going?' Merek asked.

'Back to the apothecary's shop. Something is not right, but I am not yet sure of what.'

* * *

Wilfred had surprised his father by actually managing to fill his bucket with droppings, and as a reward he was sent home to his mother. In fact, Jack was worried about him and wanted him as far from the tannery as possible. He thought it for the best, especially as the lad seemed to be sniffing and sneezing a lot and he wondered if he was coming down with a cold. His Polly would know what to give him if that were the case.

The grizzly head had shaken him considerably. He had been sick several times as he worked on it, but mostly he had been able to think of it merely as a piece of work that had to be done, and kept a secret from his wife and his boy. Yet now, he could barely look at the bucket under which the head sat. When he had lifted it one last time, it frightened him to see the eyes that he had made look so lifelike staring at him. He had dropped the bucket back over it and rushed outside to vomit again.

He was still on his knees when, looking up, he saw a rider.

Only one, he thought with a slight feeling of relief. The sooner the head was taken away, the better.

It was the younger of the two men, the one with the broken nose and the nasal voice. He didn't know either of their names for they had never mentioned them.

Quince smiled affably as he halted and swung himself out of the saddle to tether his horse. He untied a sack containing something from the pommel and took it with him.

'A fine day, Master Tanner. I take it you have it ready?'

'It is inside, master. If you will follow me, I'll be glad to see the back of it.'

'Just as long as you have made a good job of it, I'll take it and be on my way.'

Inside the tannery with all its foul smells, Quince covered his face and coughed. 'Where is your boy today?'

Jack felt himself tense. 'He is at home. He is unwell.'

'Unwell? You must make certain it is not the pestilence, Master Tanner.'

'T'is but a cold, I think. Like the one I have had these past days. But I didn't want him seeing this thing, just like I was told.' He crossed to the barrel with the bucket atop it. 'Are you ready, master?'

Quince laughed. 'Why? Is it going to leap at me and bite?'

Jack forced a smile that he did not feel and lifted the bucket to reveal the head. Despite himself he shuddered.

'You have done a good job, Master Tanner. My master will be pleased with it.'

'Whatever he needs it for you must tell him it will start to stink in about a week. I have prepared it as well as I can, because I only had the one day. I've used resin and oils that will stop it rotting for a while, but if your master wants it properly preserving I'd need—'

'You won't need to know anything about it, Master Tanner,' Quince said abruptly. He placed his sack on the ground and, opening it, reached inside and drew out a large wooden box. Nonchalantly he picked up the head and placed it in the box, which was half full of moss. Reaching into the sack, he took out two handfuls more and dropped it about the head, delicately padding it about the face.

'That's to stop it getting knocked about when I ride back,' he explained as he tapped his bent nose that was still covered by his neckcloth. 'It wouldn't do to break his nose like mine, would it?' He stared at Jack for a few moments. It was clear to the tanner that he expected a response of some sort. Jack didn't know what to say, whether to mention Quince's twisted nose or to say something flattering. He said nothing, but made a snorting noise that he hoped would pass as a laugh.

Quince nodded and placed the box inside the sack and tied its neck. Then he carefully hung it over his shoulder.

'Well, I shall bid you good day, Master Tanner,' he said as he strode out and tied the sack to his pommel before mounting his horse again.

As Jack watched him ride away he felt as if his bowels would squirt, so fearful had he felt. But at least that hellish head was out of his tannery. And he had not been hurt.

* * *

Wilkin had run after Ralph and his assistants, solicitous to any needs they might have. Ralph thanked him and told him to open the apothecary's shop.

'Is there something amiss, my lord?' Merek asked.

'I am unsure,' Ralph replied, raising his neckcloth as he went round the counter and looked at the bottles and jugs. 'Ah yes, vinegar is the first bottle.'

He retraced his steps and noted the paint pot with a brush sticking out. Then he went through to the living space and saw a stack of bowls and a few spoons and a knife on the rough table.

All just a bit too neat, he mused. *And yet it should not be so if he was dying.*

* * *

The Magister had not expected to see his servant killer so soon when he was shown into his laboratory.

'I thought I should report, Magister. I disposed of the apothecary Humphrey de Duncombe last night.'

The Magister stared at him, his eyes blazing. Then he lashed out and slapped him across the face.

'You damnable fool! You might have ruined everything.'

22

A TRYST AFTER CURFEW

17 May 1361

Osbert obeyed Lady Honoria's instructions and waited until after the curfew before going to the stables, where he saddled his dapple grey and Lady Honoria's pony. He walked the horses to the manor house and waited until she came out. Without speaking a word, she permitted him to help her to mount the pony and then they set out into the night.

His life had become full of secrets and he was now used to obeying order without question. He had no doubt that it was a romantic tryst Lady Honoria was going on, for on all the previous occasions he had accompanied her he fancied he saw her smiling contentedly when she returned to the place he had been bidden to stay.

How he wished he could tell Sir Hugo that he was being cuckolded, because the old knight had been good to him and his family, as indeed had Lady Honoria herself, but there was no way he could. He very much thought that Sir Hugo's state of mind had deteriorated too much already to be able to take it in.

And because of that he saw some reason why Lady Honoria was prepared to break the seventh commandment.

Thou shalt not commit adultery!

She was still a relatively young and attractive woman, clearly with physical needs. Osbert understood that, for he missed sleeping with his Marion. But everything had changed since the time they both thought that Dickon had been taken from them. Now, Marion still thought that the Lord had taken him, but he knew that it was the fiend who had him brought to him in a coffin and who made him do things that he never would have imagined himself doing. But at least Dickon was still alive, even though his life hung by a thread.

As he waited for Lady Honoria all he could do was think and sink deeper and deeper into the quagmire of guilt that he now lived in.

* * *

Lady Honoria was met by Quince at the usual place, which was far enough away over a hill to be out of sight of Osbert. In silence he escorted her to the castle. There, in a sumptuous chamber she was able to throw herself into the arms of her lover, Sir Boniface.

They wasted little time and were soon vigorously making love. He was skilled and he made her feel wanton. Her husband had been a kind man, and in the days when they still did sleep together his love-making had been a duty that he performed with less than relish. She thought that in his way he possibly did love her, but he was not attracted to her. She had to ride him hard to make him do his duty. And in a sense he had. She had conceived several times but miscarried with them all except with her only son. Who was taken from her by the plague.

From then on she had barely bothered to share his bed and her own desire fell asleep, until she met Sir Boniface and gradually as their trysts grew more and more passionate he informed her of his great ambitions. He told her of the plan and of how he was about to achieve his dreams with the help of an alchemist.

It was actually Sir Boniface who had helped her to understand why Sir Hugo found love-making so arduous. It all made sense and took away any guilt she had about betraying him for he had been betraying her for some years.

'My God, how much longer will we have to meet in secret like this?' she asked some moments later as they lay spent and naked together.

'As long as your husband lives, my love.'

'His mind is going. It is hard to watch and listen to him. And he trembles and shakes and drools. It... it sickens me.'

'Yet it is necessary that it be done slowly. I think it will soon be the time for him to leave you.'

'I hope so, I have waited so long. He seems so old now.'

He stroked her hair. 'Does he still talk of his chaplain?'

'He does. It is one of the few things we talk about that I can see fills him with enthusiasm, and he usually ends up weeping like a child.'

'And what about his alchemy laboratory?'

'It gathers dust and the kilns and crucibles are long since cold. He never goes there, I think because it all reminds him of his dear chaplain Father Dominic, whom he had the laboratory built for. He spent a fortune on that damned man.'

He leaned over and kissed her passionately. She moved her thigh and felt his arousal. With a sigh of regret she pushed him back gently. 'I cannot again. I must return to the manor. Sir Ralph de Mandeville is staying at the manor house and his two assistants are with Osbert, our bailiff. I had supper with him before I came here. He asked us about the manor accounts. Well of course Sir Hugo could not answer so I did on his behalf, as usual. Sir Ralph said that his clerk Peter told him that there were large payments for metals and sulphur and charcoal and he wondered why, so I told him about my husband's interest in alchemy and that he had a laboratory that he no longer used.'

'Did he now?' he mused, touching his lips.

'He asked why he stopped using it, so I told him it was because our chaplain, who had been more or less teaching him, for he had experience in the art, had suddenly left our service many months ago.'

'Did that satisfy his curiosity?'

'Yes, it seemed to.'

'But why was he looking at the manor accounts?'

'He said it was to do with his investigations. He himself had studied the manor court rolls.'

'Interesting. He seems to be a curious fellow. Too curious, perhaps.'

'But what can I do? He is a justice of the peace and I dare not give him any cause to be suspicious about my husband.' She clasped his hand and shook it. 'None of them must know that I have been out after the curfew. Especially when it is so dangerous with the pestilence returned and all the deaths that have occurred in Axeton.'

He pursed his lips and squeezed her hand before rolling onto his back. 'Talking of the chaplain upset you, didn't it? You don't like thinking of your husband and his lover.'

She sat up. 'It did upset me. It disgusts me. I hated that man and would like to see him dead. When you told me that they were lovers I thought of having someone kill him, only I did not know where he went after I sent him away. Nor do I know anyone who would perform such a task.'

'I know where he went, Honoria. He became a monk at St Leonard's Abbey.'

'How do you know?' she demanded.

'The abbot is a vassal and friend of mine. I am the patron of the abbey. He found out all about Father Dominic and your husband.'

* * *

What Sir Boniface did not tell her was that Abbot Joseph, vassal and friend, had installed his brother-in-law, Giles de Toulouse, as the chamberlain and hospitaller as a favour to him. It was a perfect hiding place for him after he had escaped from the king's men and he had killed Friar Raymond Lully. It was not long before the monks at St Leonard's Abbey heard that Joseph had been taken ill and had taken to his bed in the abbot's house, and that he was looked after by the chamberlain alone. Nor did he tell her that Giles had told him of the wonders he could perform by making the philosopher's stone and the elixir of life. He would be able to bring Boniface untold of wealth and power, and together they had put in motion a plan that would undermine both Church and king.

It all began with their scheme to bring the pestilence to the abbey and then to Axeton, and gradually spread it where needed to keep the people in terror of the desolation it would cause. And so it was that Abbot Joseph was eliminated and his dead body left in his house until the chamberlain eliminated two others and made their bodies look as if they had been plague victims. Since no one would dare get too close to a body it was a simple matter to have them quickly coffined and buried.

The abbot's body was buried too, in one coffin big enough to hold two corpses.

Now, as the plans proceeded, the tricksters and mountebanks were already stirring up the rumours of the impending apocalypse that had begun with itinerant friars of the Franciscan order. A man of power such as he could lead men, as he had done before, and even inspire them to advance him to lead an uprising, a rebellion. He could see himself supplanting the Prince of Wales, whom he hated with a passion, and even King Edward himself, to usurp the throne and wear the crown of England.

Among his many ambitions, Sir Boniface had one in particular, which happened to be making Lady Honoria Braithwaite his wife, along with taking Sir Hugo's manor and estates. All it called for was to kill a few people who did not matter so that the village of Axeton would be full of fear and would keep to themselves amid the desolation that would result as case after case of pestilence occurred and those they knew were suddenly dead.

And that included Sir Hugo de Braithwaite and anyone who dared to stand in his way.

* * *

'Why did you not tell me this?' she demanded.

'Because I know how much it has all distressed you.'

'Do you think I am weak?'

'Not at all, I know you are a strong woman. After all, you have been strong enough to slowly drug your husband these last months. Now it seems that the time is right. He is weak and it will not take much more to finish him.'

She stared at him with wide eyes. 'Do you mean give him a larger dose of the drugs? To... to kill him?' She bit her lower lip.

'I... I am scared to do it. Besides, I am not sure I have enough and now that Humphrey de Duncombe has died...'

'I have more that I shall give you, my love.'

She looked momentarily panicked. 'But I just told you that Sir Ralph de Mandeville stays with us.'

He chuckled. 'I know, but you need not worry about him, I promise you, Honoria.'

She looked suspiciously at him. 'Why? Are you planning something? He is a justice of the peace, which means that he is the law itself. If anything should happen to Hugo he might suspect. He may suspect already. You know the punishment for a wife who poisons her husband. I would be burned at the stake. Our bailiff, Osbert Flood, knows that I ride out on these trysts. He would be able to give evidence against me if Hugo dies suddenly.'

He put a comforting arm about her shoulder. 'Do not worry about Osbert Flood or Sir Ralph de Mandeville. Give him the dose as usual for I have something for you that I guarantee will lay Sir Hugo in his grave. And no one will suspect that he had been given poison.' He kissed her shoulder. 'And you will approve of how this will be done.'

He leaped from the bed and strode naked to a chest and threw open the lid.

'I have something to show you, Honoria. A gift of sorts that I must give you now.'

He came back to the bed with a large casket. 'It will surprise you, but you will like this. Prepare yourself and make no sound.'

Her eyes opened wide as he opened the lid and she looked inside. She was repulsed, confused, yet fascinated by the contents.

'Now is the time we must act, Honoria. You see that don't you?'

He watched her as she stared and chewed at her fist. Then she suddenly looked at him and nodded.

'Yes... yes, I see.'

'I said it is a gift of sorts, but it is indeed more of a loan, for I have other use for it.'

He explained precisely what he meant and why she had to do exactly what he said.

Then she smiled as he knew she would. And, closing the casket and placing it on the floor, he embraced her. This time her passion was inflamed even more than before and she mounted him and rode him hard. Just as he knew she would.

23

MORE QUESTIONS THAN ANSWERS

18 May 1361

The following morning after breaking his fast with milk and a hunk of bread, before Sir Hugo or Lady Honoria appeared, Ralph went out to walk in the fresh air and think. He walked through the village, listening to the clucking of the hens, the grunting of pigs and the odd barking of a dog. He approached the three men who were up already guarding the entry to the village. They all bowed to him as he walked past them towards the woods. The hedgerows looked splendid, the trees were burgeoning with berries and fruit and birds were in song. It was hard to believe that they were surrounded by so much death.

Why would anyone cut off Friar Bruno's head and take it away? he asked himself. *It can only be to prevent him being recognised. And surely that can only mean that someone wanted to prevent me, as the justice of the peace come to investigate the murder of Sir Broderick, from seeing him. But why would they think I would know this friar? It makes little sense, if any.*

He walked on along the path through the woods, seeing

squirrels running up trees and jumping from branch to branch with utter ease. He envied them their simple life. The pestilence did not seem to affect animals, other than farm ones that depended on people to feed and water them.

What of Friar Simon, who I'm meant to speak with after the apothecary's funeral? He said there were many other friars spreading word about these prophecies of doom and the end of the world. And the source of them all is this mysterious alchemist...

He recalled his earlier conversation with Friar Simon and his suggestion that the alchemist might be trying to build something like Friar Roger Bacon. Ralph himself had heard that Bacon had built a brazen head to practise his alchemy.

He heard a sudden noise above him and looking up saw a squirrel rustle a branch as it leapt to another leafy branch. As it did so it dropped a nut from its mouth that fell, and before he could dodge aside it hit him on the head.

Is that a message from someone? Drawing attention to the head. Is Friar Bruno's head destined for some devilish practice? Is this alchemist somewhere near? Does Friar Simon know more than that?

It all added to his growing sense of unease. There was something wrong about all this, yet he could not place it. He turned and made his way back to the village. As he did he put a hand to his chest, seeking the reassuring feeling he usually had from the locket of St Sophia containing locks of his and Isabella's entwined hair. He stopped and closed his eyes for a moment, trying to picture Isabella and hear any counsel she might give him. But he could neither see her nor feel her presence.

* * *

Merek and Peter had taken breakfast with Osbert, who did not look well. His wife Marion had joined them at the table but barely ate, while Merek, ever hungry, accepted a second helping of porridge and a second piece of bread. Peter, as ever, ate fairly lightly because his choleric stomach was easily satisfied and supping overmuch easily upset it.

'You look tired, Master Osbert. Did you sleep poorly?' Peter asked the bailiff.

He noted the sharp look that Marion gave her husband. It almost looked as if she was angry at him for some reason.

I have seen such looks when a wife knows her husband has been sleeping elsewhere, he thought.

Peter also noticed the shift in the bailiff's eyes toward her as if he had sensed unspoken ire directed at him.

'I rarely sleep well, Master Longwood,' Osbert replied. 'With all that has been happening I have much to be concerned about. As I have said before, Sir Hugo and Lady Honoria look to me to manage so many things... all the deaths in Axeton and now the death of Sir Broderick and his man.'

'And Humphrey the apothecary,' Marion snapped.

'Indeed, it was not a pretty sight,' said Merek. 'The pestilence is a curse.'

This time Marion shot him a glance, but it was of fear. Suddenly she sobbed, rose quickly from the table. She curtsied then left.

'I am sorry if I upset your good wife,' said Merek. 'I did not think about your own loss.'

'We will have to get through it, Master Merek. If it was the Lord's will, we must accept it and just keep trying to help the villagers and all the other villages about the manor.' He sighed. 'I must be off to see Gideon the reeve to see if we have had any more folk who have succumbed to the pestilence and lie ill or dead. And as my good wife did say, Humphrey de Duncombe is dead. I do not know how we shall fare. I will have to journey and see if I can find another apothecary or physician.'

'Did you not tell us the other day that there is not one within twenty leagues?' Peter asked.

The bailiff sighed wearily. 'I did, but we may have to make do with any who have some knowledge of physick.'

'Father Benedict at the Priory of St Mary at Gyseburg is skilled in surgery and physick,' Merek said, as he drained his mug of weak ale. 'He might be willing to aid you.'

'I may have to try to see if he could help,' the bailiff replied. 'I would have sought help from Father Alban the hospitaller at St Leonard's, but he and Brother John who assisted him are both dead.'

His voice broke and he hung his head. 'As is my boy!'

They heard boots on the cobbles of the yard followed moments later by a rap on the door and the entry of Sir Ralph. Peter and Merek both immediately stood up. Their master waved them to sit.

'Would you take food or drink, Sir Ralph?' Osbert asked, having also risen.

Ralph waved a hand. 'I have already broken my fast and have been for a walk into the woods. I did not wish to impose overmuch on Sir Hugo and Lady Honoria.'

'Are they not well?' Osbert blurted out. 'Has Lady Honoria said—?'

He stopped himself abruptly and looked embarrassed. He wondered if somehow the justice of the peace had seen Lady Honoria return, especially carrying that large sack that she had tied to her saddle and expressly told him not to question her about.

'I crave your pardon, Sir Ralph, I sometimes feel I must be ever protective of my lady.'

'A good, loyal sentiment, Master Osbert,' Ralph said. Then to his assistants: 'When you are finished I would like us to ride along the Esk beyond where I visited yesterday.'

'How far was that, Sir Ralph?' the bailiff asked.

'To a tannery. Jack was the tanner's name.'

'Yes, Jack the Tanner, he does work for all the villages and hamlets in the manor. Was there a reason you wanted to go beyond, Sir Ralph?'

'I am still investigating the murder of Sir Broderick. I want to check out both sides of the river to see if there is any sign of Robert Hyde, Sir Broderick's clerk, having climbed out of the river.'

Osbert stared at him in open-eyed surprise. 'Do you think he went into the river, Sir Ralph?'

'I am certain of it, and I think he did so deliberately to escape his murderers.'

'Were they not just wolf's-heads, Sir Ralph?'

'Possibly, yet even now I have more questions than answers.'

'We are at your service, my lord,' said Merek, wiping his lips with his finger.

* * *

They rode out of Axeton and followed the river towards the tannery. Ralph told them to look out for any signs on the bank that might look as if someone had come out of the river.

'I supped with Sir Hugo and Lady Honoria again last night and asked about the purchases of metals and sulphur and charcoal. It turns out that Sir Hugo has an alchemy laboratory and many supplies were purchased for it. She also said that he stopped when their chaplain left some months ago. She said Sir

Hugo lost interest and the laboratory has not been used since then. Indeed, he forbids anyone to enter.'

'Really, Sir Ralph. Then it is strange that some of the entries have been very recent, and several times.'

'Are they really deliveries of these things?' Merek asked. 'Could they not simply be entries in his accounts for large sums of money that he labels as being for the metals and sulphur, but perhaps they do not exist? The money could just go into his purse and since he manages the manor who is going to know?'

Ralph nodded. 'That is exactly what I thought, Merek, which is why I wanted to study the manor court rolls and have Peter look at the accounts.'

They had come to the Old Stone Bridge spanning the river. 'Merek, you go across and go down the other bank and Peter and I shall continue here.'

The longbowman nodded and made his way across the bridge while Ralph and Peter continued along their side.

Eventually, the tannery came into sight and as they approached it they heard the sound of wailing and sobbing.

'Come, Peter, someone is in distress.'

They urged their mounts into a gallop and saw a woman and a boy outside the tannery, both on their knees, crying and hugging each other inconsolably.

Ralph and Peter both dismounted and Peter tethered their mounts while Ralph walked over to them.

'What ails you, mistress? I am Sir Ralph de Mandeville, the justice of the peace.'

'My... my Jack is dead.'

She was racked by further sobbing and Ralph waited until she was able to talk. Ralph recognised the boy, Wilfred, from his visit the day before. While Wilfred's sobbing continued and he buried his face in her bosom, she managed to answer Ralph's gentle questioning.

'Jack didn't come home last night. He often didn't when he was worked hard. He'd sleep in the loft, but he'd usually come back to break his fast first thing, but not today. I was worried in case he'd had an accident and didn't want Wilf to come here on his own, so we came on our old donkey. We found him in the tannery, on the ground. He... he died from the plague, sir. It's so... so terrible that I took Wilf away. I only thought he had a cold yesterday. It took him so quick.'

Ralph nodded and signed for Peter to stay with them while he went inside. He also signalled to Merek to come back over to join them.

Drawing his neckcloth up as usual he entered the building and was almost overcome by the mixture of smells, none of them pleasant.

Lying on the ground beside one of the pits in which hides were soaking lay the tanner. His eyes were open wide staring upwards, the whites horribly bloodshot, his face mottled and bruised like those of the other victims he had seen. And like them the horrible bubos that were covered in blood as if they'd burst.

The sight was so distinctive and like the others that there was no doubt in his mind. The plague had taken yet another victim. This time outside Axeton. He felt a shiver of anxiety. The pestilence was spreading.

He was about to turn and go when his eye fell on the barrel and atop it, upside down, was a bucket. Edging carefully around the body of the tanner, he went to look at it, for it seemed slightly incongruous. It was not just any bucket; he had discerned the painted letters on it. They were upside down as he looked, but there was no mistaking the letters 'St M.'

He lifted the bucket and turned it upright. Inside there were dried mud smears. And it looked as if it had contained earth then been washed out. But there was a smell to it. A smell of meat, such as you would find at a butchery as if flesh or offal had been inside and the washing had not removed the smell of flesh and blood.

He sniffed it and was perplexed to find that there was also an aromatic smell like resin of some sort.

He picked it up by its handle and again edged round the body of Jack the Tanner. In his mind he was sure that at some stage this bucket had contained the head of Friar Bruno. But if so, where was it now? He did not feel that he wanted to conduct a search until the body was removed.

* * *

While Ralph was inside the tannery, Peter had managed to find out that Jack's wife's name was Polly and that they lived about a mile inside the forest, far enough from the smells of the tannery. He also found out that she was considered to be a wise woman and collected herbs and made potions and remedies for any that wanted them, as her mother and grandmother had done before her.

'Mistress Polly,' Ralph said after Peter had given him this information, 'it may be best for you to come back to stay in Axeton for a while. I am sure that the reeve or the bailiff could find accommodation for you and Wilf.'

She looked at him almost in horror. 'No! No, I thank you, sir, but we need to be in our own house. But I... I need to do something about...'

She looked at the tannery.

'Have no fear, we shall arrange for your husband's body to

be taken to Axeton. There must be a funeral and a burial as soon as possible. His body must not be long out of the earth.'

'No, please, Sir Ralph. I... I know that Jack would not want to be buried in that cemetery. He'd want to be buried in the forest near our home, where his parents and grandparents lie.'

'But it is not consecrated ground,' Ralph said.

'Please, Sir Ralph! I beg you.'

He thought for a moment then acquiesced to her plea, for he saw no good reason to refuse her. With that he gave instructions for Peter to ride back to Axeton to get Osbert or Gideon Moor to send the two searching women, Sally and Megan, to come with George the gravedigger to take the body to their house in the forest, and also get Friar Simon to come with them on his donkey. Then he told Merek to accompany Polly and Wilf to the house and then return to the tannery to await the searcher women with the coffin, so that he could lead them to the house.

When they had gone he went back into the tannery and, keeping his distance from the corpse, he started a cursory search for the head. He did not expect to find it.

24

THE LETTER

18 May 1361

The funeral that took place later that day was a strange occasion. Merek had helped George to dig the grave in the small area behind the timber and dried mud house, where four simple stones marked where Jack's parents and grandparents had been similarly interred. Friar Simon had desisted from preaching and simply said prayers and conducted the funerary rites in as simple a fashion as he could. The only people in attendance apart from the friar were Polly the tanner's wife and his son Wilf, Ralph, Merek and Peter, the two searcher women and the gravedigger.

The house had a thatched roof and shutters covered with cured animal hides. It looked as if it had been built and rebuilt several times according to the needs of the family. It was sheltered and in a way looked comfortable and safe.

It was clear to them all that the wife and son wanted to be on their own as soon as possible. Indeed, Ralph was so conscious of this that he made sure that they respected her

Desolation

wishes, so that they could be alone with their grief. Young Wilf had not let go of his mother's waist and had wept the whole time.

Yet it is very odd that she does not want to be with other people overnight. Ralph touched his locket through his clothing and, closing his eyes, felt a prickling sensation on the back of his hand as if Isabella's hand rested momentarily on his. And this time he could picture her and she was nodding her head. He opened his eyes. *Very odd, indeed.*

Once again Merek had helped George to fill in the grave and they left a small mound which they covered with the turf they had cut and laid aside when they dug it.

'Shall I look for a stone for you to mark it, mistress?' Merek asked.

'No, thank you, Master Merek. It is a task that Wilf and I want to do ourselves. It will give us something to think about.'

'And flowers, Mother,' Wilf said softly. 'I want to pick flowers for Father.'

'Of course, Son. We shall do that as soon as these gentle folk have gone.'

'I can call again to bless the stone if it is your will,' Friar Simon offered.

'Thank you, but if we decide we want that we will come into Axeton,' Polly replied quickly.

Ralph had noticed the fact that Wilf was sniffing and recalled that when they first came upon them outside the tannery she had said her husband also had a cold. He considered telling her that she and Wilf should isolate themselves from others, but as they lived here so remote from anyone he decided it would be as well to let them grieve on their own. She and Wilf had gone through enough. Besides, there was no apothecary to call upon them and Peter had found out that she was a wise woman herself so would undoubtedly be giving her son some sort of remedy. He decided to simply call back himself on the morrow.

But I shall not tell her my intention. It would be better that I arrive unannounced and not cause them undue anxiety. That apart I need to know why she is adamant that she does not want to go to Axeton, and why she refuses Friar Simon's offer to bless the stone.

George and the two searching women climbed on the wagon and were the first to leave, followed by Friar Simon on his donkey.

'We will leave you now, Mistress Tanner,' Ralph said as he mounted his horse and joined Merek and Peter.

She forced a smile but he could see the relief on both her and her son's faces that they were going.

* * *

As they made their way back through the wood to the tannery Peter pointed to the bucket that hung from Ralph's pommel. 'Do those letters upon the bucket mean it is from the Priory of St Mary, Sir Ralph?'

'They do, and it smells of blood and flesh and some sort of spices or resin. I have no doubt that it contained Friar Bruno's head. I had a look in the tannery while his body was still there, but I want to have a more thorough check now. While I do that I want you to carry on the search along the two banks of the river for at least another league.'

'Are we looking for a floating head now, as well as signs of someone leaving the river, my lord?'

Ralph shook his head. 'I doubt that you will find either, just as I doubt that I will find the head in the tannery. I shall be here when you return as that will give me time to conduct a thorough search.'

* * *

Rather as Ralph thought, neither Merek nor Peter found anything after following the Esk downstream for two leagues. Nor did his search give any further clues. There were barrels of scraped flesh and lots of old congealed blood from the cleansing of hides, but there was no way of knowing if any of those scrapings could have been human flesh or blood. Certainly, he did not find a human skull.

He did not know how the tanner could endure spending so many hours inside the tannery with all those obnoxious odours, so he took some moments after completing his search to sit outside upon a boulder where the air was fresher.

What would you have made of this, my lovely Isabella?

He went to touch the locket, then felt a prickling on the back of his hand. Instead of touching it through his surcoat he reached inside and drew it out. It seemed strangely warm and he ran a thumb over the image of St Sophia upon its front. He recollected Isabella's reason for venerating the saint and having her image engraved upon both lockets for them.

'St Sophia of Rome is the patron of wisdom, judgement and knowledge, my love. A good saint for you, a lawyer.'

'Tell me of her,' he had urged.

'She was a good Christian woman who had three daughters – Faith, Hope and Charity. The Emperor Hadrian wanted them to convert to the Roman gods, and had the daughters tortured in front of Sophia. But they all held to their faith, as did Sophia, even when the emperor had the daughters beheaded.'

Ralph closed his eyes and pictured Isabella standing in front of him, holding her locket containing their entwined hair. Her face was deeply troubled and he heard her voice repeat over and over, *'Beheaded! Beheaded! Beheaded!'*

Then he felt that prickling sensation again, this time on his cheek. He snapped his eyes open and touched his cheek. It felt as if Isabella's lips had just kissed him.

* * *

Ralph talked with his assistants as they rode back to Axeton.

'I have no doubt that Friar Bruno's head found its way here in this bucket,' he said, tapping it as it hung from his pommel. He did not tell them anything so personal as his connection with Isabella through his locket.

'But why take it to a tannery? It takes weeks to tan a hide to turn it into leather, yet it was here but one or two days, so that cannot have been the purpose. Unless it was merely brought here in the bucket and taken away again in some other container.'

'Do you still think the head was taken to prevent you from recognising it, Sir Ralph?' Peter asked.

'No, I am sure it has been taken for a definite purpose, since it would be easy to merely bury it in the forest. It was taken for some purpose and the more I think about it the more it seems it was for some devilish reason. And I am sure it has some connection with the Black Rood and the murders of Sir Broderick and Adam Dalton.'

'And perhaps also with whoever attacked us, my lord?' Merek suggested.

'Highly likely, I think,' Ralph replied. 'If they intended to kill us then they must have something they consider of high importance that they did not want Sir Broderick to know about and that they did not want his death investigated. That thing must be very important and also fairly imminent, so they must have been trying to make time to do it without interference.'

Peter looked puzzled. 'How so, Sir Ralph?'

'The murder of a coroner and of a justice of the peace. King Edward would send a whole army to find out who would dare kill his officials. It would surely be dangerous to them to antagonise the king, unless that is something they wanted to happen.'

'Or it could be a diversion, my lord.'

'It could be. But all things now come back to these prophecies Friar Simon has been preaching about. And perhaps this alchemist who practises necromancy. Mayhap that is why Friar Bruno's head has been taken.'

Merek signed the cross over his heart. 'It sounds the work of the devil, my lord.'

* * *

Gideon Moor was busy unloading loaves from the oven in his bakery using a long-handled wooden shovel, when Osbert called upon him.

'I have an important task for you, Gideon. I have one of the Archbishop of York's messengers who says he bears an important letter from the king, and an important physician from the king's court at Conisbrough Castle. They have arrived to see Sir Ralph the justice of the peace. I need you to take them to the tannery.'

'Why there, Master Osbert? It must be an unhappy place after the death this morning. Will they be not coming back soon enough? I saw the searching women return with George, followed by the friar, but they have not brought a coffin back for burial. I talked with the Friar Simon and he said they had buried poor Jack the Tanner in the woods behind his house. His wife and son are distraught as there's no wonder.'

'They will be, but it is not for us to question the archbishop's messenger with a message from the king and this physician, Gideon. They want to see him immediately, so you must take them to him. Go, get your horse and meet us at my house.'

The reeve hesitated, pointing to the open door of the oven and the wooden shovel in his hands. 'But I have these loaves to take out and another batch in the second oven. I need to—'

'You need to do as you are ordered,' Osbert snapped. 'Now go and saddle your horse. I am giving them drink as they have come from Paxton-Somersby where they have been delayed because the physician has been treating some cases of the pestilence.'

Gideon looked shocked. 'More outside Axeton? First Jack the Tanner, now some more in Paxton-Somersby. Are the victims any that we know?'

'I don't know yet, they were led here by Henry Faker the butcher, so that they did not get lost. I will find out from him while you take the king's messenger and the physician to meet Sir Ralph.'

'And the loaves, Master Osbert?'

'I will find someone to take them out. If I can find anyone who is not afeared to leave their homes. If I can't, I shall do it myself. Now go!'

* * *

Peter was the first to see the group of riders coming towards them along the trail.

'That's Gideon the reeve leading two men, Sir Ralph. One

looks like a messenger and the other is dressed in scarlet and purple. He looks like a physician.'

'Which is just what we need here, my lord,' said Merek.

'Indeed, it is,' agreed Ralph.

Some distance off the reeve hailed them and waved.

'Here we are, gentles,' said Gideon to the messenger and the physician.

'Are you Sir Ralph de Mandeville?' the messenger asked as they drew to a halt in front of them. 'I am Samuel, one of the Archbishop of York's messengers, and I have a message from His Majesty King Edward.'

He noticed and recognised Merek and gave him a smile, which was reciprocated.

'And I am Doctor Guy Gatsby, a physician and brother to Sir Basil Gatsby, chief secretary to His Majesty. You will see from the king's letter that he sent me in case my services are needed if the pestilence has reached this far.'

He was a man in his late forties, thin and clean shaven, wearing the usual wide-brimmed hat that marked his profession. He tapped his bulging saddlebags. 'I came well-prepared with physick of all kinds and have already had to treat cases of the pestilence in the village of Paxton-Somersby.'

Ralph clicked his tongue then bowed his head to them both. Reaching over in the saddle he took the sealed letter from the messenger. 'Your skills are most welcome, Doctor Gatsby. Sadly, we have had many cases in Axeton and unfortunately the apothecary in the next village of Duncombe died from it yesterday. And so too did another this very morning in a nearby tannery. We are returning after the burial of the local tanner.'

He held the letter up and nodded to the messenger. 'Thank you for this. Please now go with Gideon Moor the reeve and we will meet you at Osbert the bailiff's counting house in due course, lest there is a message I need to send.'

The messenger and the reeve both bowed and then rode off.

'Now excuse me, Doctor Gatsby, but I will read His Majesty's letter.'

He broke the wax seal and read. As he did he hummed and then stroked his chin. 'Most interesting. His Majesty has been informed by Archbishop John of Thoresby of the theft of the Black Rood, which alarms him greatly, for it was an important symbol of England's sovereignty over the Scots, that he personally had arranged should be held in Durham Cathedral. He wants to know about what progress has been made in the murder of the coroner, and also he is concerned about these prophecies that are being made, seemingly about the country.'

'I can attest to that, Sir Ralph,' the physician interjected. 'My brother has accounts from many parts that wandering friars are preaching about prophecies of doom. Also, they agitate about the labour laws and the failure of the Church to protect people against the plague and prevent wars. I have heard it myself from patients both rich and poor.'

'That is useful to know,' said Ralph as he read on. 'His Majesty also says that these friars say that the prophecies come from an alchemist that practises necromancy.'

Peter coughed. 'Excuse me for interrupting, Sir Ralph, but this is exactly as we have heard from Friar Simon.'

'Yet there is more. His Majesty names two alchemists who worked in his service, who he says absconded when he was about to arrest them for failing in their promises and whom he thinks were charlatans. They stole precious manuscripts and books from libraries in Oxford and in the Tower of London, among them works by Friar Roger Bacon.'

'How were they named?' Doctor Gatsby asked.

'One was Friar Raymond Lully and his assistant was Giles de Toulouse. The first was Spanish and the second French. They were said to have escaped disguised as lepers and are thought to have made it abroad to France.'

He turned to look at the physician. 'Do you know much of alchemy, Doctor Gatsby?'

'I do, since alchemy, astrology, philosophy and physick are all interlinked.'

'I thought you would. I studied the law but also have a little knowledge of physick, but not the match of your own. I know less of alchemy and astrology, so there are things I must discuss with you when we get back to Axeton.'

Then to Peter and Merek, 'You two can both ride ahead to the village. I want to talk to Friar Simon. If you find that he is preaching, then arrest him immediately and take him to the village cells, which we saw next to the manor court.'

'Arrest him, Sir Ralph?' Peter asked in surprise.

'That is correct. I want no more preaching about prophecies in the light of this news from His Majesty. And I want to know exactly what he does know about this alchemist.

'By the Justice of the Peace Act I have the power to arrest any who are spreading dissent. I make you both my deputies with that authority.'

* * *

Osbert had a passing acquaintance with Henry Faker, for Paxton-Somersby was one of the villages within the Manor of Axeton owned by Sir Hugo de Braithwaite. He placed orders for meat from butchers in different villages as it had always been Sir Hugo's way to spread his custom equally about the manor.

Accordingly, he had dealings with the Paxton-Somersby butcher once or twice a year.

As they sat drinking ale in his counting house he was surprised to learn that his son had disappeared several weeks before.

'Why was this not brought before the manor court?' he asked Henry.

'Your pardon, Master Osbert, but I did report it to Jethro Turner the reeve and he said he'd have it reported but I never heard no more about it. The whole village knows about it, but what could I do? I started drinking heavy, that's what. And that's how I ended up in front of that justice, Sir Ralph de Mandeville's petty session court last week, on account of I was fighting. I drink then I think then I don't think well enough not to fight, if you get my meaning.'

'And what did Sir Ralph make of it?'

'Well, he let me off when he could have had me flogged or birched, but he didn't.' He looked uncertainly at Osbert. 'I do hear that you are not as lenient as you used to be in the manor court.'

Osbert felt a pang of guilt, knowing full well that to be harsher than usual was one of the instructions he was given on one of the three occasions he had been taken to the Magister. He had not been able to see the two men who caught him unawares each time and forced him into the wooden box. Nor was he able to discern where he was taken, although he did know that it was somewhere over a wooden bridge of some sort into a cobbled courtyard.

'Tell me about your loss, Master Henry,' he urged.

He listened intently, his jaw dropping open in shock to hear that they found his bow and arrows with blood on them in a ditch.

He sat feeling helpless as Henry Faker wept as he told him of the hue and cry, of the searching and the raw emptiness he had felt inside him ever since.

'My lovely Tom was just eight years old and as good-looking a lad as there could be. He took after his mother, and had beautiful blond hair, not like me. But he...'

Osbert listened as if he was in a trance. Eight years old with blond hair, just like his son, Dickon. But Osbert's son was still alive and held captive while Henry the butcher's boy had disappeared.

The image of seeing what he thought was his son's body, bloated and disfigured by the plague, came to mind.

He had wondered about that dead body he had wanted to touch and kiss. Now he knew it was someone else's son. And he could say nothing about it.

25

ILL HUMORS

18 May 1361

Osbert had tried to console Henry Faker and felt an urgent need to be on his own long enough to think what, if anything, he should do. He offered to find somewhere for the butcher to stay overnight. The trouble was that no one was going to be willing to have a stranger stay with them in case they carried the pestilence.

Of course, one of the village cells.

Henry Faker was not averse to the idea, having spent two nights and days locked in the single cell at Paxton-Somersby after his fight and damage to property at the Blue Sow tavern. At least he would not be locked in and he was going to have food brought to him.

Osbert had taken him to the cells by the manor court hall and arranged with Old Alan at the Cherry Tree tavern for him to have stew and a jug of ale brought across, when the door opened and he saw Merek and Peter come in, each holding one of Friar Simon's arms.

'Young Ned, your ostler, told us you had come here,' said Peter. 'This is fortuitous since we must lock Friar Simon in a cell until he can be questioned.'

'I don't understand,' said Osbert.

'Nor do I, Master Osbert,' said the friar. 'I have done nothing wrong.'

'You were preaching more dissent,' said Peter. 'Sir Ralph ordered your arrest.'

Merek and Peter both recognised Henry from the session court at Paxton-Somersby. 'Are you also a prisoner, Master Faker?'

'No, master, merely taking a bed and some food and drink overnight.'

'I will arrange food and drink for you too, Friar Simon,' said Osbert.

'And for me, too,' said Merek. 'If you will give me the keys of the cells I shall stay overnight to keep an eye on the prisoner and keep your guest, Master Faker, company.'

* * *

Ralph and Doctor Gatsby let themselves into the counting house and sat down either side of the bailiff's desk.

'As I told you earlier I was going to consult with Humphrey de Duncombe the apothecary about the nature of the pestilence. The Church view as espoused by the friar that you heard me tell my assistants that I wanted to detain or arrest, is that the pestilence is purely a punishment from God. These prophecies seem to reinforce that belief as these friars are telling people that the only protection is to worship the Lord. What is your view, Doctor?'

The physician smiled. 'I think they may be partially correct, for all things are God's will. Yet I do not believe that everything that happens is already ordained by God. Wars happen, but who wins is surely not God-divined. After all, both sides pray to the Lord, so why is it that the side with the more able commanders tends to win? So, in physick I think that the pestilence is a result of a miasma or bad air. Foulness, putrefying material and decay taint the air, and if breathed in can cause pestilence.'

'So it is important to cover the mouth and nose if near a case of the plague? I do this with all of the cases that I have seen here.'

'Have there been many, Sir Ralph?'

'About a dozen, including the apothecary in Duncombe and the tanner we buried this morning.'

'I saw three cases in Paxton-Somersby but I am hopeful that the bleeding I did and the physick I have given will bring recovery.'

'You have seen people recover? In the first plague those thirteen years ago it seemed it was virtually a sentence of death to get it, just as it seems to have been here in Axeton.'

'Yes, I have seen and treated over twenty cases in the south. And I wear this special headpiece that I have made.' He reached into one of the saddlebags he had taken into the counting house. He pulled out a beekeeper's liripipe hood. 'You see that I have had this basket-woven mask sewn into it to cover my face and it has a smaller basket like a large nose that fits over my own. I can see well enough through the basket gaps and I have packed the nose bulge with a variety of herbs and a sponge with vinegar that filter and sweeten the air. It has protected me so far.'

Ralph thought of the potion that the apothecary had been taking. 'Does vinegar have an effect against the pestilence? In a potion, I mean?'

'A small effect, but it depends what else is given.'

'What about paint and urine?'

Doctor Gatsby shook his head. 'Many physicians and apothecaries advise drinking one's own urine, but I am not so inclined to believe it has any beneficial effect. But paint, certainly not. Why so, Sir Ralph?'

'The apothecary had a potion made from it, but it did not help. He was dead in the morning.'

'Had he bled himself?'

'I do not know. I did not get close enough to look for cuts. But there was no sign of a bleeding cup or of a lancet or fleam.'

'Peculiar, I would say.'

'Exactly what I thought, which is why I wanted to understand better about the imbalance in humors that occur in a case of the pestilence. I talked with a Father Benedict at the Priory of St Mary in Gyseburg. He is the hospitaller there and seemed to have wide knowledge, so I asked him. His view was that the pestilence causes a great excess of blood and also of both black and yellow bile, so that it causes glands in the neck, the armpits and groins to bulge as bubos. Excess blood causes bruising of the skin and makes blood vessels burst and produce the horrible black mottling all over the face and body.'

Doctor Gatsby frowned as he listened.

'He also said that if there is excess of black bile, then the sufferer gets a flux of the bowels and will soil themselves. If too much yellow bile then it makes them sick. He thought that bleeding is the single best treatment, for it gets rid of excess blood, but also strong emetics to get rid of the yellow bile and purgatives to get rid of the black bile. So, in the case of Humphrey de Duncombe, could the paint have been used as an emetic, to make himself sick?'

Doctor Gatsby rubbed his chin and sucked air through his

teeth. 'A person with partial knowledge like an apothecary may think so. Yet all that you describe could fit a case of the pestilence that occurred in the last plague, but not this pestilence.'

Ralph frowned. 'What do you mean, Doctor Gatsby?'

'Well, if we are talking about humoral imbalance, I agree that excess blood is a problem and I would always bleed a patient, but the yellow and black biles are not as evident as excess phlegm. That is the fourth humor. So, excess of it causes all of the lung symptoms as the lungs rot inside. The patients can drown in their own phlegm and cannot breathe so they suffocate. In these cases the excess blood can cause them to cough up blood from the lungs, a bad sign.'

'But you said *this* pestilence?'

'Well, it is very different. It is affecting the young more than the old. And also those of higher birth for some reason. This is why some physicians have termed it *the pestilence of boys*, and others as *the mortality of children*. So far I have not seen cases with the bubos that you mentioned. They get lung and breathing problems instead.'

'All of the cases I have seen had the extensive bruising, the bleeding and the bubos,' Ralph said.

'That is indeed strange, Sir Ralph,' the physician replied.

'Tell me also, are some people less likely to catch the pestilence? Can they be in some way protected? I am thinking of the searchers who identify the ill and clad the dead in winding clothes and lift them into coffins, are they not at great risk?'

'They would certainly be at great risk. They are fortunate to have avoided it.'

'That is what I thought also. One final question. How long before a body that died from the pestilence is safe to be looked at?'

The physician gave a short laugh. 'A question that I do not

think has ever been asked, and therefore I have no knowledge how to answer it. My opinion would be not until the flesh has rotted from the bones after many years.'

'Is this an opinion all physicians would give?'

'I would think so, Sir Ralph.'

'It is as I suspected. The pestilence is a fearful thing.'

There was a knock on the door and Peter entered at Ralph's command. He told them that they had arrested Friar Simon as he had been preaching to drinkers outside the Cherry Tree tavern.

'We saw Osbert the bailiff as he has given Henry Faker, the butcher that we saw at the petty session court at Paxton-Somersby, a cell for the night. We locked the friar in the other cell. Merek thought he should stay the night with them.'

'Have they food and drink?'

'Osbert is arranging that, Sir Ralph.'

'Good, it will do the friar good to have a night under lock and key. I will question him tomorrow.'

He sat drumming his fingers on the desk for a moment, then addressed Peter.

'Since Merek will be sleeping at the cells, tell the archbishop's messenger that he may sleep on Merek's cot this night.'

Then to Doctor Gatsby, 'Now we shall go to the manor house and see Sir Hugo and Lady Honoria, for we shall be staying with them. I would value your opinion on Sir Hugo's state of health.'

* * *

At supper that evening, Ralph and Doctor Gatsby sat opposite each other in the hall with Sir Hugo and Lady Honoria at the ends of the long table. The food was excellent, if the conversation seemed stilted. Ralph took the lead by asking questions of Sir Hugo, most of which were, as before, answered by Lady Honoria. Yet still he kept up his questioning, his purpose to demonstrate to the physician that the lord of the Manor of Axeton had limited memory. His mannerisms, twitches and erratic utterances were obvious, as was his tendency to drool. Twice he spilled his wine and thrice he dropped his spoon.

'I understand that you have an alchemy laboratory, Sir Hugo?' he asked.

The knight's rheumy eyes momentarily brightened. 'Ah yes, I did. It was my great... love.'

'But you no longer use it?'

'No, my chaplain left us. He... he was skilled in alchemy. I learned from him. A most intelligent and educated young man.'

'Where did he go, Sir Hugo?' Doctor Gatsby asked, so it did not seem as if Ralph was interrogating the knight.

Sir Hugo looked at Lady Honoria for assistance.

'We do not know, Sir Ralph,' she replied. 'He said he was called by the Lord to move elsewhere.'

'Could we see this laboratory?' Ralph asked.

'I... I... do not go there now,' Sir Hugo returned. 'It is too painful. I miss my chaplain.'

Ralph noticed the two points of colour that suddenly appeared on Lady Honoria's cheeks.

'Then excuse my question, Sir Hugo,' said Ralph.

He glanced across at Doctor Gatsby, who returned his look with slightly raised eyebrows.

Things are beginning to become clearer in these murky days.

'Certainly there is no need to open it unnecessarily,' he added.

Yet I will have to put my ideas to the test.

Desolation

***

Lady Honoria had been shocked the night before when Sir Boniface had shown her the casket and told her what she needed to do. He had also said that she had to go ahead with the plan despite the fact that Sir Ralph de Mandeville was staying in the manor house, and that it would be even better if he was there when it happened.

The supper had been a torture to her because she had not expected a physician to be staying with them as well. She had been extra careful to answer questions for her husband and not to betray her own nervousness.

In their chamber later that night, hours after the curfew, she had given him more wine containing more of the drug her lover had supplied to an even greater effect than she had seen before. Sir Hugo had become more suffused, his cheeks going very red and he had become drowsy, and even more twitchy than usual.

She had helped him to undress and put on his nightgown.

He could barely stand, so she got him to sit in the chair by the window.

'I have something for you, husband,' she said in her most solicitous manner.

From under the bed she drew out the casket.

'A gift, my dear.'

She placed the casket on the bed and turned it so that the lid was facing him. Then she opened it so that he could see inside.

His eyes widened and he opened his mouth as if to scream, only for her to clap a hand across his mouth. His body shook and trembled and she felt his mouth suddenly drooping on one side.

The last things on earth that Sir Hugo saw were the severed

head of his lover, Father Dominic, staring at him from inside the casket. And his wife with a look of triumph on her face. He fell back in the chair, his eyes no longer seeing, yet fixed on the equally unseeing eyes of his chaplain.

It was a matter of a few moments for her to pull him off the chair and arrange his body on the floor.

She kissed his forehead then closed the casket and put it in the sack she had brought it in back from the castle. Tying a rope round its neck, she went to the window. Opening the shutter and looking out she saw the shadowy figure that she knew from her lover would be there. It was wearing a cowl as it came forward into the moonlight and waved. She could not see the face but she had a good idea who it was.

She lowered the sack, saw him take it and then dropped the rope.

She waited a quarter of the hour then went to the chamber door and started to scream.

* * *

Doors opened all over the manor house and servants came running. Ralph and Doctor Gatsby also came dashing from their chambers to find Lady Honoria in her night attire standing at the open door of her chamber, tears streaming down her face and her hands clamped over her mouth.

'My beloved husband, he is...' She pointed inside the chamber where Sir Hugo lay upon the floor.

Doctor Gatsby rushed to his side and performed some examination and put his ear to the knight's chest and his hand in front of the mouth. He called for a hand mirror, which Ralph spied and gave to him. Placing it over Sir Hugo's face he looked at it after a few moments.

'He does not breathe. His mouth has fallen crooked. I am sorry, but Sir Hugo has died of apoplexy.'

Lady Honoria started to sob and was comforted by two of her maids.

'It was an act of God,' Doctor Gatsby announced.

Ralph looked at the lord of the manor's body over the physician's shoulder. He sniffed, having caught a scent of something familiar. From the bed. It seemed to be coppery and yet resin-like.

It gave him considerable qualms.

* * *

Some hours later the Magister was awakened by a knocking on his chamber door. Sir Boniface opened it and marched in.

'It is done and here I have it again.'

The Magister threw his cover off and jumped off the bed. 'Let me see that it has not been damaged.'

Sir Boniface opened the casket and they looked at the head of Friar Bruno, who had several names: Father Dominic, the chaplain to Sir Hugo; Father Ignatius, the chaplain to the erstwhile Earl of Sussex; and Brother John of St Leonard's Abbey.

'The traitorous dog deserved to die. Only now will he be useful. Come, Sir Boniface, I have prepared the apparatus and the quintessence of the cross upon which the Christ was crucified.'

They went to the laboratory where the strangest accumulation of alchemical equipment had been arranged into a pyramidal structure, with a retort stood over a crucible, alembics above it and tubes and bellows attached.

The Magister removed the head from the casket and placed

it atop the structure, placing it so that the gullet and windpipe fitted over the alembic tubes.

'We shall burn the remains of the wood in the crucible to transform it from wood into fire and then into holy smoke which will fill the head. Then I will anoint the head with the quintessence when the appointed hour arrives tomorrow night. Then we shall make the philosopher's stone and you shall have whatever you want, Sir Boniface.'

26

THE MISSING PIECE

Axeton

19 May 1361

There was not the sense of urgency to dispose of the body of Sir Hugo de Braithwaite, since he had not died from the pestilence but apoplexy. Lady Honoria expressed the wish that her husband should be dressed by her and her maids and left to lie upon the bed that he had shared with her for some twenty-five years.

She, of course, wanted to be left alone to sit with him as was the custom.

The news quickly went around the village and Osbert arranged for Marion to call upon Lady Honoria and sit with her for a few hours. His wife had looked horrified at the prospect but as a good and dutiful wife she had agreed, mainly because Lady Honoria had been so kind to her when Dickon had been taken from her.

Osbert's mind was in a state of turmoil. There were so many things to be done, yet his guilt about the things he knew and yet had to keep secret threatened to overwhelm him. He wondered if he would go mad erelong. It was only the thought that Dickon was still alive, albeit the lad must be terrified out of his wits, that kept him going.

Each day seemed to bring something that dragged him deeper and deeper into the quagmire of desolation. And yet, he knew that he had to think of some way that he could save his boy.

Yet the seed of an idea had started to form, but it would depend upon trust. A difficult word for him for he felt he had betrayed trust, just as he had his trust betrayed, of that he was sure. When it came to it he would have to think fast and act quickly.

* * *

Lady Honoria had expressed surprise when in the morning she was told that Friar Simon was currently in one of the manor cells. Yet she could say little as she knew she had to act out the bereaved wife to the best of her ability to convince everyone. She was anxious because she thought there was one person who may not be deceived by her.

* * *

Ralph and Doctor Gatsby had broken their fast together and discussed the death of Sir Hugo.

'Apoplexy can happen at any moment. It is an act of God,' the physician said.

'What did you make of his health at the table last evening?' Ralph asked.

'He was suffering from softening of the brain as was

apparent from his memory difficulties, his tremors and twitches, and his erratic conversation. I think he was on the verge of an apoplectic attack, which clearly he was.'

'What was the cause of this brain softening?'

'Age, probably.'

'Yet could his alchemy experiments have had anything to do with it? Working with metals and minerals?'

The physician scratched his cheek. 'That is possible, if he had worked with a lot of mercury and quicksilver and lead. All metals used in alchemy experiments.'

'That is what I thought,' said Ralph. 'I must leave you now as I have matters to attend to, but I would ask that if anyone comes with news that someone is ill or has died from the pestilence, that you look at them and treat them if possible?'

'But of course. It would be my duty, and His Majesty informed me that I am to stay until you decide I am not needed.'

'I have a feeling that you will not be troubled,' Ralph said, leaving the physician looking perplexed.

* * *

Peter had gone to the manor court jail after he had partaken of a mug of milk and a hunk of bread with beef dripping upon it. Osbert had told him of the death of Sir Hugo before he had gone to give instructions to Gideon Moor. When Peter transmitted this sad news to all three men in the cells they were shocked.

'I must go to Lady Honoria and say prayers with her,' said Friar Simon.

'No, you will stay here until Sir Ralph says otherwise,' Merek told him, much to the friar's discomfiture.

'But I have done nothing wrong. I have merely preached, as preachers do,' he protested.

'It is the things you preach about that is the problem,' said Peter.

Henry Faker nodded. 'About death and the end of everything. That's all we hear from you friars. We had one of your fellows saying that in Paxton-Somersby, and he said he'd come back with some holy water that we could have if we made a donation. I'd heard it before, then my boy went missing. I don't need to hear prophecies of that kind any more.'

Ralph came into the cells and Henry and his two assistants stood and bowed.

'Are you returning to Paxton-Somersby, Master Faker?' he asked the butcher.

'Soon, Sir Ralph. I thought I should stay to pray for Sir Hugo, if there is going to be a service.'

'There cannot be a service while I am locked up here,' Friar Simon said sullenly.

'I understand from my assistants that you were preaching dissent again,' said Ralph. 'That is something His Majesty the King has forbidden. Now answer me some questions.'

He turned to Henry Faker. 'I would be grateful if you would leave us.'

The butcher nodded. 'Willingly, I've heard enough of his praying, preaching and prattling.'

Ralph waited until the butcher wandered away across the village green towards the village pinder to look at the animals. Then he turned back to the friar. 'Well?'

'I spent all evening answering your man's questions, so ask him,' Friar Simon said almost spitefully.

'Disrespect to a justice will not serve you well. Tell me

where did this other friar you mentioned the other day, tell you the alchemist was based?'

'I do not know.'

Merek cracked his knuckles. 'Would you like me to persuade this friar, my lord?'

Friar Simon looked up sharply, fear in his eyes. 'A castle, that is all I know.'

'Where?'

'Somewhere in this wapentake, but I swear I do not know where.'

'His name?'

Friar Simon shrugged. 'He calls himself the master or the Magister or some like, but I promise you that is all I have heard. I know no more.'

'Is this castle the alchemist's own?'

'I think he has a patron, a noble of some sort.'

Ralph signed to Merek. 'He may go free to call upon Lady Honoria and give what comfort he can, as long as there is no talk of the end of things. She has lost her husband.'

Then to Friar Simon, 'There, that was simple, was it not?'

* * *

Ralph and Peter rode out to Jack the Tanner's home to pay a call upon his wife Polly and his son Wilfred. They tethered their mounts some distance from the tanner's cottage and walked the rest of the way through the woods.

'Why do we not ride right up to the cottage, Sir Ralph?'

'Because it is important that they do not know of our coming. Now, no more talking, we must approach as quietly as possible.'

Reaching the cottage, Ralph knocked loudly with his fist upon the door.

'Mistress Tanner, it is Sir Ralph de Mandeville, the justice of the peace. I need to talk to you.'

He heard whispering inside then the door slowly creaked open. Polly looked round the edge.

'I pray you come another time, Sir Ralph. We are not well.'

'In that case, as I have some knowledge of physick I had better come in,' Ralph replied. He did not hesitate but opened the door forcefully, moving her backwards. He and Peter stepped inside and saw Wilf squatting on the floor beside a cot containing a wide-eyed and clearly frightened young man, whose face was as white as alabaster and covered in perspiration.

'You are Robert Hyde, clerk to Sir Broderick de Whitby, I take it?' Ralph asked, not unkindly.

He turned just as Polly was picking up a rolling pin, and Peter was placing a hand upon it with a shake of his head.

'You will not need that, Mistress Tanner,' said Ralph. 'I have been hoping to find Robert alive and have been looking for him. I surmised that he was here. I promise we mean him no harm.'

* * *

Before he left, Ralph had given instructions to Merek. First he wanted him to find George the gravedigger and the two searcher women.

'Tell them only that I may have need of them later. If the women ask if it is for Sir Hugo you can tell them it is not, for a proper funeral service and a burial with honours will be required for him, probably with a marble tomb in St Agnes's Church, but tell them nothing more.'

Then he had a further thought. 'No, impress upon them they are to talk to no one about this. Then keep out of their sight but watch to see if they do talk to anyone and mark who that is.'

Merek did as he was bid. He found George who, being mute could not speak, but he nodded his understanding.

Then he went to seek out Sally and Megan. The two women both looked anxious when he found them together drinking cider behind one of Megan's styes while her pigs rooted in the earth around them. When he declined to tell them what it was about, they tried flirting with him, which he quickly dissuaded by telling them he was an assistant to the justice of the peace. His expressions of distaste may also have had something to do with it.

'But I repeat, you must say nothing of this,' he warned them. 'This is the direct order of Sir Ralph de Mandeville, the justice of the peace.'

'Is there something we should know about, master?' Sally asked.

'No, just stay in the village so that I can easily find you if Sir Ralph wills it.'

* * *

Ralph went over to the cot and sat on a stool that Wilf had fetched for him. Robert Hyde tried to sit up, but Ralph raised a hand to prevent him. 'I can see that you are unwell, Master Hyde, so do not try to move. I am Sir Ralph de Mandeville, the justice of the peace, and this is Peter, my clerk.'

Peter leaned over Ralph's shoulder. 'I am a lawyer's clerk, like you, Robert,' Peter said affably in an attempt to put the wounded clerk at some ease.

'I know something of what happened to you,' said Ralph, 'but I need to know all that happened.'

He noted the arrow that lay on the floor beside the cot.

'Where on your body were you wounded?'

The clerk looked terrified as well as weak, but he managed to talk. 'In my side, sir. They... they shot Sir Broderick and Adam and I... I tried to get away. I couldn't... couldn't help them.'

'I saw where they ambushed you and where you went into the beck.'

Robert looked amazed, and nodded. 'I thought it was my only chance. I... I heard them coming for me. I did not think I could outrun them on my small pony so I slid off it, taking my writing chest, patted its rump to make it run on and then I staggered along to where I heard running water.'

'And you swam?'

'Barely, Sir Ralph. But I held on to my writing chest with all Sir Broderick's documents. Luckily... it floated and I was able to swim a little as I was carried down until the beck entered the river. Then... then I can't really remember.'

'You must have blacked out and drifted downriver until you reached Master Jack's tannery.'

'He did, sir. I saw him,' said Wilf. 'I called Father and he got out a long hide hook and pulled him in. I helped him haul him out.'

'You are a good lad, Wilfred,' Ralph said. 'You saved Robert's life.' He looked at the arrow and turned to Wilf's mother. 'And I take it you removed the arrow, Mistress Tanner?'

Polly was looking slightly less anxious now. 'I did, Sir Ralph. My Jack and Wilf brought him back here and he told me what Master Robert just told you before he passed out again.'

Peter grinned and tousled the lad's hair, eliciting a nervous smile from the boy, whose tear-stained cheeks made it obvious he was still distraught at losing his father.

'You knew how to remove an arrow without leaving the arrowhead inside?' Ralph asked Polly admiringly.

'Yes sir, Jack showed me on animals that he'd brought in that had been shot. We have all sorts of tannery tools here. It was a simple thing to do when he was unconscious.'

Ralph nodded and urged her to continue, aware as he was that she meant animals that had been poached in the woods, and the meat from which they presumably had lived on. And the hide he had tanned. He ignored the fact that was against the law.

'Where was the arrow?'

She pointed to her left lower loin.

'I hear you are a wise woman, skilled in making potions.'

'I am, sir. I made him willow and all-heal to help him heal and break his fever, and a poultice of porridge and crushed comfrey to draw out the poison.'

Ralph picked up the arrow and examined it. It looked very familiar. He looked round at Peter who took it from him and nodded agreement.

'And your husband brought the writing chest that Robert mentions?'

'I did that, sir,' said Wilf. 'My father carried the master.'

'Jack told him to bring the chest that he was clinging on to because he thought it must contain important things. We opened it and saw all sorts of written things, not that either of us could read or write, but we spread them out and dried them off as if they were hides.'

'And where are they?'

'They are in the chest, all dried. It is under the cot.'

'My master, Sir Broderick... is he...?'

'He is dead, I am sorry to tell. I knew him and am investigating his murder.'

The clerk put his hands to his face and sobbed. 'I am so grateful to Mistress Tanner and her husband,' he said at last. 'They understood that evil men... were trying to kill me. I begged them to let me stay.'

Polly put a comforting hand on the clerk's shoulder. 'My Jack said we must protect him until he was strong enough to travel. My blessed son has not given anything away, not even to you, Sir Ralph. We owe it to my husband, who the Lord allowed to catch the pestilence and took away from us.' She let out a sob and covered her mouth. 'Now he is in Heaven.'

Peter smiled at her. 'And you have done a fine thing and he would be proud of you both.'

'What were your plans, Robert?' Ralph asked the clerk.

'I... I was going to make my way to York to see Archbishop John of Thoresby.'

Ralph nodded. 'So, tell me, Master Hyde. Did Sir Broderick take the abjuration of Friar Bruno?'

'He did, Sir Ralph. It is in my chest.'

27

ENLIGHTENMENT

19 May 1361

Ralph sent Peter back to Axeton with the arrow to give it to Merek to keep with the others that had been removed from the bodies of the coroner and Adam his bodyguard, and instructions to fetch Doctor Gatsby and his medical accoutrements and some other things, while he settled down to read through the abjuration of the realm as recorded by Robert Hyde.

Polly took Wilfred outside to go and collect berries in the wood while Ralph talked with the clerk as he read.

'You write well and neatly, Robert,' he said.

'Thank you, Sir Ralph. Sir Broderick has always – I mean, he was always satisfied with my penmanship.'

Ralph read the abjuration of the realm with growing interest. 'Is this an accurate record of the abjuration?'

'It is, Sir Ralph,' the coroner's clerk replied, his face clearly pained. 'I... I sat in a corner of the sanctum, the sanctuary cell at the priory in Gyseburg and wrote everything down just as it was said. Sir Broderick would ask questions and then Friar Bruno would give his reply.'

'But here he begins by stating that the name of Bruno was one he had assumed.'

'Yes, Sir Ralph. He stated that his real name was Dominic, but that he had also been known as Brother John, when he had served as an assistant hospitaller at St Leonard's Abbey.'

Ralph read on out loud. 'Sir Broderick asked him why he sought sanctuary at Gyseburg Priory and wanted to make an abjuration. He stated that he wanted to atone for abominable sins of sodomy, stealing and simony, and that he wanted to make pilgrimage to the shrine of St Dismas in the Church of the Resurrection in Jerusalem. Sir Broderick asked why this shrine, to which he replied that St Dismas was the repentant thief who was crucified on Golgotha Hill in Jerusalem along with the Lord, Jesus Christ.'

'I... I had never seen anyone so full of guilt and so repentant, Sir Ralph,' Robert said. 'He... he said he felt like a repentant thief.'

Ralph read the rest of the abjuration, which was lengthy as the coroner had permitted the friar to say as much as he wished. It was full of confessions.

'What did you make of his last piece when he said that he *"... must make penance for my sins but pray that the theft from thieves may be better than the transmutation of lead into gold, or wood into smoke. I bear the cross of both sinner and thief. Let any who seek my sin seek the cross that bore our Lord."*'

'I... I did not understand it, Sir Ralph. I am not sure if Sir Broderick did either, but my task as ever was simply to transcribe it as my ears heard it spoken and as Sir Broderick instructed me.'

'No more do I, yet there is still much here that makes sense now,' Ralph said with a frown as he finished reading and carefully replaced the document in the writing chest. 'I will need to keep all this for my investigation and as evidence.'

'Evidence, Sir Ralph? Of... of what?'

His face contorted as the effort of talking and the pain from his wound was clearly taking its toll on him.

'Of the murders of Sir Broderick de Whitby and Adam Dalton, and also that of Dominic, who sought sanctuary as Friar Bruno.'

The coroner's clerk gasped. 'He... he was murdered, too?'

Ralph nodded. 'It appeared that he committed self-murder, or *felo de se*, which is, of course, a sin.'

He did not mention that he had been decapitated after death or that his head had been stolen and brought to the tannery where Robert himself had been rescued.

'You must rest awhile. Mistress Tanner has done well by you, but I have a physician coming who will look at and treat your wound.'

* * *

'You were correct, Sir Ralph, no new cases were reported to me,' said Dr Gatsby later when he arrived at the Tanner's cottage with Peter.

'I hoped there would not be any,' Ralph replied.

'Peter, your clerk, explained to me that you have a patient who was shot with an arrow.'

Ralph explained more about Robert Hyde and the murder of his master Sir Broderick de Whitby the coroner and his bodyguard, 'Jack the Tanner's widow, Polly, removed the arrow and treated him with herbs and a poultice.'

Polly and Wilf arrived back with a large basket of blackberries and Ralph asked that they sit with Robert Hyde while Doctor Gatsby examined him and treated him. He suggested that Polly should assist the physician if needed.

Outside the cottage, Ralph explained to Peter all that was in the abjuration.

'The sanctuary seeker's real name was Dominic, not Friar Bruno, and he had been Sir Hugo de Braithwaite's chaplain and his male lover. He was skilled in alchemy and taught Sir Hugo about the subject, but Lady Honoria discovered that they were lovers and sent him away. From there he went to St Leonard's Abbey and became the assistant to the hospitaller, who called himself Father Alban, but who was a far more experienced alchemist than he. This man was also adept in necromancy. Dominic fell under his spell and teaching about the coming apocalypse, and was convinced by him that he was going to change the Church from within by sending friars all over the county and country to tell of the impending end of things, and spread the message that all the ills were because of the corrupt and ineffectual Church leaders.'

'This was St Leonard's Abbey, where Osbert Flood fell ill and his son Dickon was buried?' Peter asked.

'It was, and Dominic, or Brother John as he was then, helped Father Alban to treat them. But then he told him of a powerful noble who was going to help them and would raise a following that would topple the crown, which was equally corrupt and had brought nothing but war, famine and now pestilence on the country. To do this he was going to build a brazen head as Friar Roger Bacon did half a century before and which he had the esteemed Friar Bacon's instructions to do so.'

'A brazen head, Sir Ralph?'

'A mechanical head that can talk and deliver prophecies when the spirits of the dead are infused within it. In order to perform the rituals to raise the dead and animate the head, they would need to obtain sacred wood instilled with divinity. With part of this wood the alchemist would make the quintessence and part he would use to burn to raise the spirits of the dead with the holy smoke that would pass through it. In other words, they would have to steal the Black Rood of Scotland from the shrine of St Cuthbert in Durham Cathedral. Dominic would accompany this noble who disguised himself as the Earl of Sussex. This they did, along with two of the noble's men purporting to be squires, two tough men who frightened Dominic.

'But overnight, as they returned by a circuitous route to avoid any who would have been sent to find them, Dominic's conscience overcame him. He thinks it was the Black Rood itself that turned his mind and made him realise the terrible things they had done and yet were about to do. So, he took the Black Rood and absconded. When he realised they would come for him he left the reliquary for them to find and sought sanctuary with the intention of leaving England to travel to the Holy Land to make penance at the shrine of St Dismas, the penitent thief in Jerusalem. He was one of two thieves crucified with our Lord on Golgotha Hill.'

Both of them made the sign of the cross, then Peter whistled softly. 'Do you think these two men killed Friar Bruno?'

'Probably one of them did, entering the priory and wandering about in a cassock. It would be a simple thing to do. There are no locks in the abbey so he could have slipped in and slit the friar's throat. Later, he decapitated the body as it lay in the coffin in the tool shed behind the priory chicken coops. The head was brought here and I presume was treated in some way by Jack the Tanner. I now do not believe that Jack the Tanner died from the pestilence.'

'But we saw his body, Sir Ralph?'

'That was when we would not go too close to a body thought to have died from the pestilence. Doctor Gatsby has told me that the pestilence this time is quite different and produces very different symptoms and signs of disease.'

He took the mask Doctor Gatsby had given him as he left the cottage.

'Have you brought the shovels?'

* * *

Ralph had wanted Polly and Wilf to be occupied while he and Peter went to the grave, which was why he had asked them to stay while Doctor Gatsby treated the clerk. First they removed the turf that had been laid across the grave and began to dig. Working together it did not take too long before they struck the wood of the coffin lid.

'I shall do the rest on my own now, Peter. Stand up above and just watch.'

Pulling on the beekeeper's liripipe that Doctor Gatsby had devised as a protection, Ralph breathed through the herbs and vinegar that packed the small basket nose and placed a hand over the locket concealed under his surcoat.

I pray that St Sophia and you, my beloved Isabella, protect me if I am wrong in my surmise.

He uncovered the lid enough to be able to prise it free of the coffin.

There was a rotten, pungent odour that rose from within, which despite the herbs and vinegar in the mask Ralph recognised as part putrefaction of the body and part decaying cheese. Looking at the bloated face and neck, the buboes were covered already in green and blue mould.

'Watch, Peter,' he said, using the edge of the shovel to touch one of the bubos. It moved and was squelchy. With a little more teasing it actually rolled off the neck, where it had rested within a large slit in the skin. As it rolled onto the chest, the two skin flaps started to close like the lips of a grotesque mouth.

Peter gagged as Ralph repeated the process with another large bubo on the other side of the neck, but he managed to stop himself from retching.

'They are balls of cheese pushed into a slit on each side of the neck. They looked like bubos that had bled.'

'The bruising though, Sir Ralph?'

'That is real enough, but it is from having been beaten.' He bent down and sniffed through the hawk-like mask. 'The eyes are bloodshot from having vinegar poured into them.'

He looked up and pulled off the beekeeper's liripipe. 'Jack the Tanner did not die from the pestilence; he was brutally murdered. But yet I need Doctor Gatsby's opinion. So go now and see if the good physician has finished treating Robert Hyde. If he has, I want you to stay with the widow and boy but ask Doctor Gatsby to attend on me here. Yet do not say what we have been doing in front of them.'

* * *

Doctor Gatsby was used to seeing dead bodies and did not flinch as he looked down into the grave at the exposed body of the tanner.

'He was made to look as if he died from the pestilence,' Ralph explained as he straddled the coffin and showed the physician the rotting cheese balls on the shovel. 'See, where the neck had been cut and the balls pushed in. No one, myself included, would dare examine the body too closely. He has been beaten, but that may have been after he was dead. What I need to know is how he actually met his death.'

The physician's curiosity aroused, he replied phlegmatically, 'Then we had best lift his body from the grave so I can look more closely.'

It was not an easy task, but between them they hoisted the stiff body from the grave and lay it on the ground. Doctor Gatsby lifted the clothes to look at the lower body.

'You are quite correct, Sir Ralph. The body was beaten about the head and neck to make it appear that the pestilence had caused bubos and bruises, which would have been consistent with the first plague.'

They rolled the body over to examine front and back. 'There are no stab wounds, so he did not die by a knife.'

'He was a strong man so it would not have been simple to overpower him and strangle him,' said Ralph. 'Could there be any marks or wounds under his hair at the back of his skull? Something that could have been done when he was caught unawares?'

The physician lifted the hair and felt the skin around the nape of the neck and then up to the base of the skull. His eyes widened in surprise.

'There is a hole, a small wound,' he announced. He pointed to his saddlebags he had taken from his horse and from which he had taken physick and treated Robert Hyde. 'If you open the instrument side you will find a long probe, please pass it to me.'

He accepted the instrument that Ralph handed him and inserted it into the hole and encountered no resistance. 'You were absolutely correct, Sir Ralph. Some sort of fine instrument or tool was shoved up into his skull and then it seems it was moved about. It created a conical space in his brain. His death would have been instant and horrible. He would not have been able to resist or defend himself. And it would hardly have bled as the wound was straight into the brain.'

'A most heinous and most effective means of murder,' said Ralph. 'But now we must make the grave as it was and say nothing to Mistress Tanner as yet. But I vow I shall find Jack the Tanner's murderer.'

'But why was he murdered?' Doctor Gatsby asked.

'There has been much devilry done lately,' Ralph replied. He told him of his suspicion that the man known as Friar Bruno had been decapitated and that he was sure that the head had been taken to Jack the Tanner to treat it for some evil purpose.

'And so the tanner was killed to prevent him telling anyone about the head.'

Doctor Gatsby had listened in stunned silence. 'Could the murderer come here for her and her son?' he asked.

'No, I am sure they are safe here. It is not an easy place to find and the killer will have had good reason to take the head to whoever is behind this evil affair.'

Ralph looked at the doctor. 'And what about Robert Hyde, has she treated him well, do you think, Doctor?'

'As good as I, to be honest.'

'Then let us leave them here for now. I have another case I would value your opinion upon.'

* * *

In the cemetery behind St Bede's church in Duncombe, Peter and Ralph again dug down to the coffin of Humphrey the apothecary. And once more Ralph made Peter climb out of the grave and watch from above with Doctor Gatsby. First, he pulled on Doctor Gatsby's modified beekeeper's liripipe just in case he was wrong and the apothecary really had died of the pestilence.

Then he removed the coffin lid to expose the dead body of Humphrey de Duncombe.

Peter watched in horror as Ralph performed the same procedure with the shovel and rolled away two mould-covered balls from the open wounds in the neck.

'They are balls of cheese,' said Ralph, bending slightly to scrutinise them and being no longer worried lest the corpse could have died from the pestilence.

'Remarkable!' exclaimed the physician before he climbed into the grave to help Ralph.

Lifting the body stiff with rigor mortis from the coffin they laid it on the ground and Doctor Gatsby again examined it. As with Jack the Tanner he discovered the wound at the base of the skull.

'The same method of killing, so the same murderer,' said Ralph.

'Did you suspect he had met his death by murder rather than the pestilence?' Doctor Gatsby asked.

'Not at the time, but the potion he had supposedly taken did not make sense. I think the murderer intended us to find a potion to complete the picture that he had tried to treat himself. He had grabbed the nearest things and poured them into a bowl. The paint, the vinegar, and to show his own complete disregard for another person, he urinated in it himself. It shows the arrogance of the murderer, who believed they would not be discovered. I suspected that something was wrong as everything was too neat and tidy in the shop and the room where he died, which it couldn't have been if the man was dying. It was staged by the killer.'

'What now, Sir Ralph?' asked Peter.

'We fill the grave in again and then we go to Axeton. We have a noble, an alchemist and a killer to unmask and find.'

28

PREPARATIONS

19 May 1361

When they returned to Axeton they found Merek was waiting for them outside the Cherry Tree tavern. The door was open and there were several people inside, drinking and trying to forget about the pestilence.

Doctor Gatsby excused himself and returned to the manor house to freshen up and clean off the dirt he had accumulated on his clothes from the graves and the taint he felt he had acquired from handling and examining the dead bodies.

Ralph told his two assistants to walk with him, so that they would not be overheard.

'What did you think of the arrow that Peter brought back?' he asked Merek.

'It is a perfect match with the arrowshafts and arrowheads removed from the coroner and Adam, my Lord.'

'As you would expect,' said Ralph. 'And they are high-quality arrows.'

Ralph told him of all that had transpired that morning and

of how they now knew for certain that Jack the Tanner and Humphrey de Duncombe had been murdered by the same hand in the same manner and then it being staged to look as if the pestilence had killed them.

'Do you believe the other deaths were also murders, my lord?' Merek asked.

'Without a doubt. There have been things that I have been unsettled about. First, these deaths were all people who lived alone, not members of a family. Secondly, their deaths occurred without anyone but the searching women being aware of them being ill.'

'But surely they must have been ill, Sir Ralph?' suggested Peter. 'They would hardly be waiting for death to come.'

'True, which is why I think they were already drugged, incapable of moving.'

'You mean with a drug or poison, perhaps given by the apothecary?'

'Possibly, but not necessarily knowingly by him, if it was by him at all. Yet someone thought he had to die, probably because I was showing too great an interest in seeing the dead bodies and they dared not risk him telling of his involvement by supplying drugs. Yet there has been something else that has bothered me, albeit I had not realised it until I walked in the wood the other morning. It is the animals.'

His two assistants looked puzzled.

'The animals around the village, the pigs, the sheep, cattle and the hens, they are all well. Yet in the first plague they died, because people were not about to look after them. But also because rats gathered and ate diseased bodies. There are no more rats than usual. There is not the actual desolation of the area that occurred those years ago. Yet there is great fear and people are staying indoors when they can and not mixing except in the tavern.'

He stopped and turned to them. 'So, what of the searching women, Sally and Megan? Did they talk to anyone?'

Merek nodded. 'I talked to them as you instructed, my lord, then I told them not to talk. But people talked to them. I saw Sally talk with Osbert and Henry Faker, and Megan talked with Gideon Moor and Friar Simon. But they did not seem to seek them out. It was when the men happened to see them. I know that they are both together now at Megan Prole's piggery.'

Ralph pursed his lips, then said to them both, 'Go now and bring them to the manor court cells. Tell them they are under arrest and I want to question them about the people who have died, but do not be discreet about it. The more people that hear of it the better. And Peter, go and get the cell keys from Osbert the bailiff. Tell him I need to have the two women put in the cells. If he offers to come with you, just say that I only want the keys.'

* * *

The two searching women were locked up in the adjoining cells. They both looked petrified when Ralph came in to talk to them through the bars of the cells. Peter sat with his writing chest on his knees so that he could record the interviews. Merek stood against the wall.

'I know that all of these deaths were not due to the pestilence. They were murdered and their bodies defiled and brutalised to make it look as if they had died from the pestilence. Tell me now by whom? Who have you been working with?'

Neither woman knew how to answer.

'By law if I find you guilty of aiding murders you will be hanged. Tell me all now and you may yet save your lives if not your souls.'

The two women stared at each other and began to cry.

'Was it a lover?'

Their reactions confirmed this to Ralph.

'His name!'

Neither would identify him.

'He... he said he was possessed of a demon, sir,' said Sally, her voice quaking with fear. 'He... he said he had put that demon inside us when he lay with us.'

'And if we... and if we betrayed him the demon would eat us from the inside,' went on Megan. 'I can feel it burning inside me now, master.'

I will get it out of them, but not with torture – unless it is necessary.

'Tell me how he used you,' Ralph demanded.

Slowly they told him in between their weeping and wailing. They told him of how he permitted them to choose a person they wished would die from the pestilence and somehow he would either manage to drug them so that when he called upon them at night he could murder them without any difficulty, or he would seduce them as he had done with them. They recounted how he had gleefully told them how he had killed women and men during the act of making love or immediately after when they were totally unaware.

'He... he enjoyed the fact that their last memory was of him,' said Megan.

'His name?' he demanded.

Both women shook their heads, their expressions of pure terror.

'We dare not say!' muttered Megan as she started to sob.

Ralph glowered at them as they wept. 'Your crimes are heinous so your lives still hang in the balance. But you have given your testimony so that this evil murderer can be caught, so I shall take this into account before making my judgment and recommendation to the King's Bench in York, where you will be tried.'

He turned to his assistants and signed for them to follow him outside.

'One of you keep a watch on them, and the other go and bring one of the men guarding the roads to take over that watch. We do not wish them to attempt to harm themselves or each other. But now I have to pay a visit to see how Lady Honoria is faring. She needs to know from me about Humphrey de Duncombe.'

* * *

Lady Honoria and Marion were sitting on opposite sides of the bed upon which Sir Hugo had been laid out with his hands crossed over his chest. Both women had kerchiefs to wipe away their tears.

Ralph had knocked softly then entered the chamber.

After the usual courtesies Ralph told her that Humphrey de Duncombe, whom all thought had died from the pestilence, had in fact been murdered.

Both women gasped.

'It cannot be true!' Lady Honoria exclaimed. 'Who would harm our beloved apothecary?'

'That I promise to find out, Lady Honoria. I have the two searching women in cells by the manor court hall and they will cooperate with me. There is a murderer in Axeton, who has killed several times. These have not been deaths from the pestilence, but by a human hand.'

Marion sobbed loudly. 'No! You are wrong! My son Dickon died from the pestilence and my husband almost died, too.'

'I am going to investigate this, Mistress. I happen to know that Sir Hugo's chaplain, Friar Dominic was the same person as Brother John, who helped to look after your son and husband.'

The two women stared at each other over the body of Sir Hugo.

'My husband? Hugo did not die of the pestilence.'

'No, that is clear. He died of apoplexy, from a severe shock, I imagine.' He looked apologetic. 'I am sorry to bring such ill news, but I needed you to know before the whole of the village is notified about these deaths. There is a killer at loose that I need to apprehend. I will leave you in your grief and will return in an hour or two to make sure you are safe.'

***

Osbert was alarmed when Merek talked to him but was careful not to show it. He thought of going to talk to his wife Marion, but since he knew she was with Lady Honoria he decided on a different course of action. He sought out Henry Faker who he knew was about to gather his belongings and make the journey home to Paxton-Somersby. He drew him aside out of anyone's earshot.

'Friend Faker, I have been meaning to talk to you about your son. I believe that I know who took him and why.'

The butcher was horrified yet a spark of hope gleamed in his eye. 'You know something?'

'We have not much time, I must ask you to trust me. Are you armed?'

'I have my butcher's knife and my cleaver that I am never without.'

'Then let us saddle up, we must go now, without delay.'

* * *

Ralph strode down the street past the village square and entered the Cherry Tree tavern.

He grabbed a mug from a table and rapped it three times to gain attention. 'Listen, all of you men,' he said in his sternest justice of the peace voice. 'There have been evil intentions in Axeton and I have proof that your fellow villagers did not die from the pestilence, but were each of them murdered.'

The tavern was filled with gasps of astonishment, curses and questions.

'What must we do?' someone called.

'Who is it?'

'Is it one of us?'

'You will do nothing yet. Just be wary of anyone acting suspiciously. I will return soon and when I do there will be a hue and cry, but I will lead it. I will want all of you who have animals to ride to be ready. Can you all shoot a bow?'

'Aye, we practise every week as is the law.'

'Be ready. When the bell of St Agnes is rung get your animals and your bows and arrows and meet me here in the village square.'

* * *

Merek and Peter found Ralph and told him that they had done as he wished. Merek told him that he had spoken to Osbert but could not find Gideon Moor and Peter told him that Friar

Simon had been to see Lady Honoria and that soon after that he left the village riding a horse.

'But young Ned told me that he had seen Osbert ride out with Henry Faker the butcher from Paxton-Somersby,' said Peter.

'None of this is unexpected. We know that the alchemist has based himself in some sort of castle. Peter, I want you to go through the schedule of commissions for all the villages and towns we are due to hold petty sessions in. You also have the information supplied by the Sheriff of York's office on who owns the manors in these northern wapentakes of the riding, do you not?'

'I do, Sir Ralph.'

'Then find out which castles, as well as manor houses which have been licensed to crenellate, there are in this and the neighbouring wapentakes. The owner of a crenellated manor house may well call it a castle. It is to the nearest such place, castle or crenellated manor house, that our killer will certainly be heading.'

He felt a sudden desire to touch his locket to assure him that it was still there – that Isabella was somehow near him. And as he did so he felt that familiar pressure upon the back of his hand as if touched by his beloved wife. Then he had an afterthought.

'Also, bring with you the notes you made on the manor accounts, and the map of the whole manor.'

'Of course, Sir Ralph.'

Ralph himself returned to the manor house and found Doctor Gatsby. He quickly explained what he had told the villagers, that there was no pestilence in the village and that there was a killer on the loose.

'I have told Lady Honoria of the murder of the apothecary,

and I shall now go and tell her of what happens next. If you will come with me, Doctor.'

Once again he tapped on the chamber door and entered. The body of Sir Hugo lay on the bed, but there was no one in the chairs by the bedside.

'Rather as I thought,' Ralph said.

He spied the large chest under the window and threw it open. Inside lay Marion, a cut on the back of her head that was bleeding profusely. Her hands were tied with her kerchief and another was stuffed in her mouth.

Together Ralph and Doctor Gatsby lifted her out. They removed both kerchiefs.

'My lady... she must have struck me when she asked me to fetch her maid,' Marion said, her voice rasping with disbelief.

* * *

Sir Boniface looked up at the head of Friar Bruno atop the alembics and the retort as the Magister prepared various pestles and mortars and arranged a series of pots.

An astrolabe was suspended from a tripod on the Magister's desk, and next to it was the Black Rood.

'I can hardly wait until the appointed hour,' Sir Boniface said.

'You must be prepared as I told you,' the alchemist said. 'You must go now and practise saying the rituals exactly as worded. Have you given the orders as I instructed?'

'I have dismissed everyone from the castle, so there is only yourself and I, and Quince and Barrat.'

He laughed and pointed to the head. 'And Dominic, of course. The fool had no idea that his part in this would be so important, after his death! How it pleases me to use his head, especially after his betrayal.'

Sir Boniface had instructed his men that they were to decapitate the friar, for the Magister needed to see and use his head, which was to be prepared by the tanner first. He had no qualms about them murdering him and taking the head, but had been surprised when he absconded in the night, taking the Black Rood with him. When his men found the reliquary and told him that the friar had made his way to the priory at Gyseburg, he took the Black Rood and returned to the castle to give it to his brother-in-law, Giles de Toulouse. He told them that they would have to do the killing in the priory and bring the head to the tannery as planned.

'And the boy, Dickon. Don't forget him, Sir Boniface,' said the necromancer. 'His blood sacrifice will be necessary, too.'

The knight cringed. 'That is the only thing I am as squeamish as a girl about. Is it really necessary, Giles?'

'The boy has been necessary all along. I have him subdued and ready. We needed him to bind the bailiff to our will so that he prepared all that we needed and made the people fearful of him, and also bound the apothecary to us. His blood will work with the quintessence of the wood of the cross and the smoke it makes as it burns to bring the spirits to make the head talk and give us the philosopher's stone and make the elixir of life for you. So go and prepare yourself, bathe and rest until it is dark when we can perform the great work, for you must be pure in body. Also practise the recitation of the rituals, for you must be perfect in the wording of them. I shall ring a bell when the hour approaches this night. Do not return until that moment.'

* * *

Peter had quickly searched through the documents and met Ralph with the information he wanted in his satchel as he returned from the manor house.

'The nearest manor house that had a licence for crenellation from King Edward's father when he was king belongs to Sir Boniface de Lythe and it is but two leagues away, Sir Ralph. It is to the east beyond Duncombe, just over the border in the Pickering Lythe wapentake. He has extensive holdings as a result of marriage to the Countess Marguerite de Toulouse from whom he received an enormous dowry and was able to buy two other manors. She died and he is a widower of three years.'

'Did you say her name was Marguerite de Toulouse?'

Peter nodded.

'Then this is definitely where we shall find the alchemist. For his name is Giles de Toulouse, presumably her brother. Let us find Merek and get him to ring the bell to begin our hue and cry to pursue the Lady Honoria. And undoubtedly also our murderer.'

'Do you suspect who the killer is, my lord?'

'I know exactly who it is. Lady Honoria herself gave me a clue and now that the murderer has left the village, his guilt is clear.'

29

HUE AND CRY

19 May 1361

Friar Simon had been as scared as everyone else that he might catch the pestilence and die from it. He did not want to go to Hell, which was why he was so emphatic in his preaching that the only salvation was through the Lord. He hoped that if he proclaimed the message loud enough as often as he could, then the Lord would listen and forgive him his sins and permit him entrance to paradise.

Forgive me for my sins, Lord. There have been too many of them. I have not been able to forego the sins of the flesh, even though I have only had carnal knowledge of one wench since I came to Axeton, but I have tried my best to spread the word and I have conducted funerals for these people when there was no other cleric.

Yet even more guilt had been added when he stole the horse and left his donkey in its stead. Quite simply, he had to get away from the village as quickly as possible, for he had been humiliated by the justice of the peace and forced to spend a night in the cell with that butcher and the justice's man, Merek.

And then he had heard that all those people he thought had died from plague had actually been murdered and the services he had conducted in good faith had been wasted. But now they were looking for the killer and who was to say that someone would point the finger at him?

Lady Honoria had worried him as he tried to comfort her as she and Osbert's wife sat with the body of Sir Hugo. He saw something in her eyes, but it was not sorrow. It was fear and it was guilt, an emotion he knew only too well. But yet there was a glint of evil and it terrified him. He could feel its presence and he decided in that moment that he had to flee.

'Friar Simon!'

Startled, he turned in his saddle, afraid that it could be Sir Ralph or Merek, sent to catch him. But it was not. He recognised the rider and stopped to allow him to reach him.

It was to prove a fatal mistake.

* * *

Peter looked puzzled.

'A clue, Sir Ralph? From Lady Honoria?'

'She told me about her beneficence. She has bread and cheese delivered to all the villagers every week.'

'I do not understand, my lord.'

'Osbert Flood told me that he delegates certain responsibilities to the reeve, including distributing the weekly beneficence. I should have realised the significance, but it is clear now. Gideon Moor the reeve is the village baker; he produces the bread and distributes it and cheese to all the village. Clearly he keeps back a supply of cheese which he uses to fashion false bubos to make his murder victims look as if they died from the pestilence. He did this to his fellow villagers and to Humphrey the apothecary.'

* * *

Gideon Moor had ridden for his life.

That dog of a justice knows about my killings! And now those two harlots will have told him who I am. My power over them is no more and I have but one chance to escape.

He had been forced to leave straight away and was conscious that people knew him well and yet he had to somehow disappear.

Seeing the friar riding ahead seemed God-given, if he aligned himself more with Lucifer, or Asmodeus or whatever the Magister called the Antichrist.

'How now, Friar Simon, whither do you go?' he asked as he rode alongside.

'Away from Axeton as fast as I can, Master Gideon. I hear that a killer is on the loose there.'

Gideon looked surprised, then riding close signed for the friar to lean closer. 'A word in your ear, Friar Simon.'

Placing a hand on the back of the friar's head he deftly slid the bodkin up into the skull and held it there as he whipped it back and forth, creating a mushed cavity inside the brain. As the body convulsed he shoved it from the horse onto the ground. The animal startled and reared up and then ran off.

It was but the matter of a few moments to strip the corpse of the friar's gown and don it himself before he dragged the body into the undergrowth. Then he remounted his horse and rode quickly off.

Soon, he approached the castle of Sir Gregory Havelock, he

who now called himself Sir Boniface. He rode towards it and espied Sir Gregory's two men atop the battlements. They recognised him for being fellow *porchers* as the Magister called them; they were used to wearing gowns as was he and waved him in across the drawbridge, being well used to his visits to report to the Magister.

Gideon Moor smiled up at them and waved and hailed them crudely as if he had not a care in the world. Which was the opposite of the truth, for he feared for his life but the less they knew the better.

Inside, he expected that the manor house would be empty for he knew this was the appointed night when the plan was to be carried out. It should have been a simple matter, but this damnable justice had spoiled everything and introduced a sense of urgency. Now it was imperative to talk to the Magister.

He knew the way to the laboratory and could have walked there in total darkness. He let himself in and almost cried out as he saw the Magister talking to the head atop a framework of glassware and the retort above a crucible.

The head did not speak as he knew it would not, but it was a shock to see it thus. The last time he had seen it was when he brought it back to the Magister after Lady Honoria had lowered it to him in the sack. The night that Sir Hugo died of apoplexy.

'Magister, I have news,' he said.

The alchemist spun round. 'You are early. It is not yet dark.'

'I fear that justice of the peace knows everything. One of the searcher women told me he wanted to talk with her, then later he had them arrested and announced that the deaths were murders. I left and came here to warn you and Le Patron.'

The Magister frowned. 'The fool is resting now, probably already dreaming of the philosopher's stone and becoming immortal. We must go now to the yeoman's farm where we can prepare to change and leave. I will get the Black Rood and you can get the boy. We may need him if we are challenged. He is in the cell next door.'

Minutes later, after saddling a horse, the Magister, the reeve and the boy bundled in a blanket laid across the reeve's saddle, crossed the drawbridge and trotted into the now late afternoon's fading light.

Quince and Barrat knew not to question the movements of the Magister. They knew it was late at night when his devilish work would be done and the head would talk and they would become rich men.

* * *

Osbert and Henry Faker saw the two men dressed in gowns like clerics of different orders on horseback riding from the castle as they came from Axeton. Osbert could see Gideon Moor thumping the bundle in front of him with his fist and he fancied he heard a cry.

'There they are, the two devils,' he whispered. 'Did you hear anything?'

'A child's squeal of pain, I thought,' Henry replied.

'I think I know where they are going, but we must follow at a distance and not betray ourselves.'

'That child, who is it?'

'I fear it is my son.'

* * *

After taking care of Marion, Lady Honoria had fetched a maid herself and told her to go in secret and saddle her horse, then bring it to the side of the manor house and toss a pebble up at the window when she was there. She had been a good maid and she regretted having hit her on the head and hoped that she would soon recover, but she had to escape. Sir Ralph de Mandeville had more or less told her that he knew that her husband had died from a shock. She was sure that meant he must know about Dominic's severed head and it would only be a matter of time before he discovered, if he didn't know already, that Gideon Moor the reeve had taken the head away after she had shown it to her husband, causing his apoplexy. And if Gideon was captured, the villain would undoubtedly reveal what she had been doing in drugging her husband and finally in killing him.

An experienced rider, she made her way as fast as she could to the castle where her lover, Sir Gregory Havelock, would know what to do and would protect her, as he had told her that this was the night when he would have power unimaginable.

His two men were upon the battlements and waved as her horse clattered across the drawbridge.

Minutes later she threw open her lover's chamber door and saw him kneeling at the side of the bed they so often made love in.

'Honoria, why are you here? I was not expecting you. I have to prepare for—'

'We are undone, my love,' she said, cutting him off. 'I have had to escape, for Sir Ralph knows all. I struck Marion, the bailiff's wife, and hid her in a chest, but I may also have killed my maid.'

The knight rose quickly.

'Then we shall get the Magister to perform the ritual now and none shall be able to challenge us.'

She saw how his eyes seemed afire with enthusiasm. It

frightened her a little for there was a mad gleam about them. 'The ritual?' she asked in confusion. 'With... with the head. You were serious about this?'

'Yes, with the head. Come! We shall stir the Magister into action to make it speak and produce the elixir and the stone, just as Friar Bacon did those many years ago.'

She followed him along corridors and up another flight of stairs where he threw open the door of the laboratory.

Honoria screamed at seeing the staring head of Dominic, her husband's lover, atop the assembly of strange alchemical apparatus.

Sir Gregory ignored her, seeing instead the large, empty laboratory and the open door into the cell, where he kept the bailiff's boy. It was empty.

Spinning round to the desk he saw that the Black Rood was gone.

'Magister!' he yelled.

There was nothing but silence.

'The bastard has gone. I am deceived by him!' cried the knight. 'I will find him and cut his head off.'

* * *

There were eight villagers of various ages who had assembled in the village square with their horses or ponies upon hearing Merek ring the bell of St Agnes's Church.

'We ride for Sir Boniface de Lythe's manor in the Pickering Lythe wapentake,' Ralph announced, as he addressed them from horseback. 'You are armed with bows, so if you need to use them then take your orders from Merek of Ryedale, my assistant. He is a longbowman of Poitiers and has battle experience.'

Peter and Ralph had studied the route on the map of the manor and riding alongside each other they led the way with Merek following and the village contingent coming after him.

They reached the manor house, which did indeed look like a miniature castle with its battlements and towers and drawbridge over a moat. As they approached they saw two men upon the battlements, each with a longbow.

'The bastards!' cursed Merek, riding alongside Ralph and Peter.

'You know them?' Ralph asked.

'They are the swine who flogged me after Poitiers because I refused to slaughter retreating men. Quince and Barrat are their names.'

'I remember them, too. They were under the orders of Sir Gregory Havelock!' Ralph said with gritted teeth. 'I will wager he is the same person as this Sir Boniface de Lythe. His name was dishonoured so he must have taken this other.'

Suddenly, undoubtedly after some words between themselves, the two bowmen started to fire upon them. A villager was hit through the chest and tumbled backwards against his horse's back. The animal took off and the poor fellow fell off and was dragged by his foot in the stirrup.

More arrows were fired in rapid succession.

'Disperse! Disperse!' Merek ordered. 'Dismount and fire on those two villains. Aim high to clear the battlements.'

The villagers, none of them trained military men, nonetheless gave a good showing of themselves. Their weekly training at the butts showed its worth and they rained arrows over the battlements.

'There is only one of them now,' cried Ralph. 'The other must be heading to raise the drawbridge. Come, Peter!'

The two galloped for the manor house drawbridge.

'Keep shooting, my friends,' yelled Merek, running zigzag fashion on foot. As he did Quince kept showing himself at the battlements long enough to aim and shoot. He saw Ralph and Peter galloping and saw Barrat inside the gateway start to turn the drawbridge wheel. The drawbridge began to rise.

Stopping and selecting a particular arrow from the quiver at his side Merek took careful aim and fired the arrow that had been taken from Robert Hyde's side. It flew true and he grunted with satisfaction as he saw it strike Barrat's arm, causing him to stagger backwards away from the wheel.

'Take that, you vicious dog,' he said, then turned his attention again to the battlements.

'I'm coming for you, Quince!' he cried and, running for his horse, leaped into the saddle and made for the castle. 'Keep raining arrows, friends!' he cried at the villagers.

Ralph and Peter were already charging across the drawbridge into the castle.

Quince, out of arrows, started for the stairs, intending to pick up some of the arrows that had sailed over the parapets. As he charged down he saw his comrade pull an arrow from his upper arm and toss it aside.

Ralph and Peter simultaneously jumped from their mounts and drew their swords.

'You men give yourselves up. I am Sir Ralph de Mandeville, justice of the peace.'

'In that case, defend yourself because I'm going to cut you into pieces,' cried Quince in his thick nasal twang as he tossed his bow aside and drew his sword. He jumped down the last steps and ran at Ralph and made a cut at him. But Ralph was a good swordsman and easily parried the blow, then launched his own attack.

Barrat had drawn his sword in his good arm and made for

Peter, who knew how to wield a sword but had seldom had to do so in a serious fight. He found himself swiftly outmatched and winced as he was struck on the shoulder, making him drop his sword.

He braced himself for the killing blow when an arrow whistled through the air and struck Barrat in the thigh. The wounded man screamed and dropped his own sword to clutch at the thigh and tried to staunch the blood spurting around the arrow that had pierced his leg.

Merek had fired as he entered the courtyard on horseback. He dismounted by raising one leg over his horse's neck and dropped to the ground. 'That's for the flogging. I spared your life so that the hangman can wring your worthless life from your body.'

He advanced as Barrat tried to pull a dagger from his belt, but as he could barely stand Merek had no difficulty in disarming him before he punched him in the face, breaking his nose in the process and sending him flying backwards to land in an undignified heap on the cobbles. 'Now you'll sound like Quince, your fellow mongrel – before we hang you both.'

'Ralph de Mandeville!' a voice bellowed from the doorway of the manor house.

Ralph was busy fighting Quince and did not turn, for he knew the voice belonged to Sir Gregory Havelock even after all the intervening years.

'Let me finish this dog for you, my lord,' said Merek drawing his sword. 'If you would like to deal with your noble and then we can get the alchemist.'

'Merek, we should have flayed you properly,' cried Quince, recognising his one-time fellow longbowman from Poitiers.

Quince backed off a few paces now seeing two swordsmen confronting him. At that Ralph spun round and saw Sir

Gregory, recalling the threat to dash out his brains after their debacle after Poitiers. Behind the lord of the manor Ralph saw Lady Honoria wide-eyed with fear with her hands on his shoulders.

'You murderous harlot! I am arresting you for your crimes,' Ralph called out.

'My love, save me from him!' she cried to her knight.

'I will. Go back to the alchemist's chamber,' said Sir Gregory, and he followed her up the stairs all the while keeping an eye on Ralph and wielding his sword menacingly. 'Come and get me, de Mandeville.'

'Lay down your sword, Havelock. Neither you nor the murderous Lady Honoria have a chance.' He ran after them.

Merek had advanced swiftly and powerfully against Quince, soon forcing him backwards, then with several well-executed lunges and cuts he wounded his adversary twice so that the sword fell from his hand and clattered on the stones. Quince pulled a dagger and threw it at Merek, who merely dodged sidewards. Then, as with Barrat, he stepped in and punched his wounded opponent in the pit of his stomach so that he doubled up, then with the same fist he smashed it into his nose to elicit a satisfying snapping noise and a spray of blood.

'And mayhap that will straighten your nose – for the rest of your short life.'

He turned and looked concernedly at Peter who was clutching his wounded shoulder.

Peter smiled as his comrade came towards him, then he stared past him in alarm. 'Dive to the side!'

Merek did so just in time as Quince, who had managed to pick up his sword, lashed down with it, causing sparks to fly as it struck the stones.

'I'll take you one at a time,' he snarled, raising his sword to hack down on Peter.

But with amazing speed Peter had pulled a string on his billowing sleeve and shot out his good arm. The concealed lead weight in the sleeve struck Quince between the eyes and he fell poleaxed to the ground.

30

THE HEAD

19 May 1361

'I was right, they have gone to Samuel the yeoman's farm that borders the Esk, that the Magister, the swine who controlled me, made me evict – supposedly on Sir Hugo's orders,' Osbert whispered to Henry. 'Then the poor fellow was found to have hanged himself from a tree in the woods, but now I think he was likely killed by that murderous dog who I have known most of my life. But I knew him not at all.'

Osbert and Henry had watched from a distance as the two riders entered the derelict farm and Gideon Moor had manhandled the bundle that he was sure contained Dickon off the back of his horse. The other man had grabbed him and held him while the reeve took the horses into an old barn, returning a few moments later. Then they went inside the farmhouse, shoving and dragging Dickon.

On their way to the castle, Osbert had with great trepidation told Henry his suspicion that the reeve had been the one who had taken Henry's son, and that they had killed the boy and made him look like his own son Dickon so that they could force him to do things. Henry had cried for a while and then choked back further tears as fury took its place.

'I feared that my Tom was already dead,' Henry said, his voice quaking with emotion. 'Now I will avenge him if it is the last thing I do before I meet my maker.'

* * *

Ralph kicked open the door that he had seen Sir Gregory close after him and entered with his sword at the ready. But he stood for a moment staring dumbfounded at the head of Friar Bruno, which seemed to be staring at him from atop the alchemical assemblage of glass and earthenware.

It was the opportunity Sir Gregory had planned. He came from the side and lunged with his sword at Ralph's abdomen.

But Ralph parried almost reflexively and countered quickly, making the knight back into the room. Lady Honoria began picking up jars and hurling them at Ralph, who fended them off with one hand while he fenced with the other.

'What damnable business is this, you witch?' Ralph questioned. 'I know whose head it is and why Friar Bruno, or Dominic, was killed. And I know that you killed your husband by showing him this head, you she-demon.'

'Prepare to die, de Mandeville,' cried Sir Gregory. 'I was going to dash your brains out with a battle axe, but cutting your heart out will do instead.'

'Not when you fence like that,' said Ralph, parrying a blow and then countering to stab the knight in the heart.

'Honoria!' Sir Gregory cried as he crumpled to the floor.

His lover was in the act of throwing another flask labelled oil of vitriol at Ralph, but seeing Sir Gregory sink dying with an expanding pool of blood on his chest, she stayed her hand with the flask above her head.

'Gregory!'

The lid fell off and a liquid cascaded onto her head.

She screamed as her hair started to shrivel and the flesh of her scalp began to burn and smoke as the acid poured down over her face, raising blisters as it scalded her eyeballs and charred her lips.

She staggered back, screaming in agony, and fell against the retort. It toppled over, dislodging the severed friar's head which rolled down just as she dropped to the floor, clawing at her face and screaming in agony. Friar Bruno's head lay on its side, the sightless eyes fixed on her as she writhed in unspeakable pain.

* * *

The villagers rode cautiously into the courtyard and helped Merek to secure Quince and Barrat, and one applied pressure to Peter's wound. There was great anger but also sorrow for their neighbour they had lost.

Meanwhile, Ralph had been careful to avoid the oil of vitriol and did his best to help Lady Honoria by pouring water from a bucket over her burning flesh to try to wash away the residue. She writhed and screamed then mercifully fainted.

* * *

Osbert and Henry crept on foot to the farm and made their way to the old farmhouse. Osbert had felt guilty about evicting the yeoman farmer and confiscating his animals and chickens on behalf of the manor, but now he was grateful that there were no creatures to alert the two men inside.

They could hear them talking. One voice was doing most of the talking, giving orders.

'Tomorrow we shall leave disguised as two lepers and we shall row down the Esk towards Whitby where I know a shipman who will take us to France. No one will challenge us for all fear to touch us, just as much as the pestilence. We could say we make for the leprosy hospital at Spital. Once in France I will be taken to the king and will give him the Black Rood. It is worth a fortune for *La Vieille Alliance*. The kings of Scotland and France will come together and defeat this English monarch for the final time.'

'And I shall be well paid for all my work?'

Osbert recognised the first voice only too well as that which spoke to him when he was in the coffin. The same voice that threatened to slit Dickon's throat. He had called himself the Magister. The second was none other than Gideon the reeve whom he had known all his life, but who he now knew had killed so many of his neighbours.

'What shall we do, Master Osbert?' Henry whispered. 'Should we rush them? One is an older man and between us we can surely overcome them.'

'The younger one has killed many people in my village, I think under the orders of the older one. We must be careful for my boy.'

'Well, I am going in,' Henry said decisively. 'You go to protect your boy, and I'm going to butcher these two swine.'

With his butcher's knife and his cleaver, he crept to the door, listened and then with a single kick threw the door open and dashed inside, yelling loudly.

The Magister and the reeve were sitting on stools drinking ale but both instantly tossed their mugs at the charging butcher and stood. Gideon Moor picked up his stool and threw it at

Henry, but it bounced off his burly chest and he raised the cleaver to chop down at the reeve's head, only for him to throw himself to the side as the cleaver descended to cut merely air and embed itself in the table. Instantly the reeve dodged behind the butcher.

Osbert had entered close behind Henry and spying his terrified son Dickon tied to a chair and gagged, he had launched himself towards the alchemist. Yet older though he was, Giles de Toulouse moved quickly and a dagger appeared in his hand drawn from his sleeve. Before Osbert could reach him he dashed behind Dickon, grabbed his hair forcing his head up, and placed the blade at the boy's throat. The boy's eyes opened wide in terror and he moaned through the gag.

'Drop your weapons or the boy dies,' de Toulouse cried.

Gideon had clutched Henry's hair and was trying to shove his bodkin up into the base of his skull. But the butcher was too strong. He had dislodged his cleaver and spun round, pulling his hair from the reeve's hand. Gideon tried to grab the hand with the butcher's knife and he struggled with it, all the while kicking Henry's legs for all he was worth. Henry dropped his knife, wrenched his hand free and grabbed the reeve's wrist. He forced it down on the table and brought the cleaver down to chop off his hand. Blood fountained across the room and the reeve fell to the floor, squeezing his amputated stump as he stared at his hacked off hand still with his bodkin grasped in it.

Gaping in horror at the blade at his son's throat, Osbert dropped his sword.

'I said drop your weapons! Both of you!' the alchemist snarled.

'And then I shall cut you up like I would butcher a pig's carcass,' replied Henry.

'No, please,' pleaded Osbert, holding up a restraining hand towards the butcher. 'My son!'

'Are you the one who killed my boy, Tom?' Henry demanded, taking slow paces towards the alchemist. He held up the cleaver and blood dripped from it.

'Keep back! I mean it,' the Magister said, albeit with less confidence.

'Did you kill my boy?' Henry demanded again, taking another menacing pace.

The Magister's hand moved with lightning speed, flicking back and then fast forward, throwing the knife he had held at Dickon's throat. It embedded in the butcher's left eye, spurting yellow eye jelly and blood as the blade penetrated through the bony orbit into the brain. Henry's great body shook for a moment before crashing face down on the floor. His legs began kicking up and down as he convulsed.

'Yes! And what matter of it?' cried the Magister. Then to Osbert, 'Now you, move away, or I will...' His hands closed about Dickon's throat. 'It will take but a twist and I will snap his neck as I would wring that of a chicken.'

* * *

When Merek and the wounded Peter came to Ralph's aid and told him of the death of one of the villagers, he gave Merek instructions to have a wagon fetched from the castle's stables to take the villager's body and that of Sir Gregory and the unconscious Lady Honoria, back to Axeton.

'But first, what of Barrat and Quince? Are they dead?'

'No, my lord,' Merek replied. 'I knew you would want them alive to stand trial, and I personally want to see them hang. A quick death would be too good for either of them, so I staunched Barrat's wounds and bound them both. They are still both unconscious.'

Ralph looked concernedly at Peter. 'We must get your shoulder treated.'

'It looks worse than it is, Sir Ralph. I am ready to do your bidding.'

'Then while Merek and I question Barrat and Quince, get your satchel and your notes and map.'

A bucket of water each roused the two henchmen and Ralph questioned them.

'Your master, the Magister, where is he?'

Quince sneered as blood ran freely from his nose. 'Where you will not find him. He left here some time ago.'

'Was he alone?'

Barrat was less contrary, Ralph supposed because he imagined if he cooperated he might escape the rope. 'He left with Gideon Moor and they had the boy.'

'Where did they go?'

'To Hell for all we know!' Quince snarled back.

* * *

Osbert stood stock-still, petrified that the Magister would carry out his threat.

'Master, for pity's sake,' groaned Gideon Moor from the floor, trying desperately to halt the blood escaping from his severed wrist. 'I am bleeding to death. H... help me.'

Giles de Toulouse glanced dispassionately at him lying on the floor, then to Osbert he pointed to the severed hand still clutching the bodkin on the table.

'Push that hand towards me across the table.'

Horrified but swift to obey, with disgust the bailiff shoved the hand across the table towards the Magister.

'Now come and kneel here in front of the table with your hands behind your back. Rest your head on the table.'

The Magister released Dickon's neck and grabbed the bodkin from the severed hand.

'Stay still, bailiff, or I will snap your son's neck.'

Dickon started to struggle as he watched the man who had imprisoned and threatened him approach his father with the sharp bodkin.

The Magister poised with the bodkin a mere inch from the base of Osbert's skull, ready to stab it into his brain as he had taught Gideon Moor to do.

'This is the end of your usefulness, Osbert Flood.'

Suddenly the door was kicked open and Ralph rushed in, taking the scene in at once. He had his dagger in his hand and swiftly whipped it upwards and then hurled it at the Magister. It spun through the air and sliced through the Magister's hand, causing the bodkin to fall onto the floor. As it did so an object fell from the Magister's sleeve and bounced to land beside the bodkin.

Ralph had moved quickly as soon as he had thrown the weapon and unceremoniously smashed a fist into the Magister's face, hurling him back to crash his head against the wall and then slide down in an unconscious heap.

'Sir Ralph, thank the Lord!' Osbert exclaimed, quickly rising. 'You... you saved me and my son, Dickon.'

He rushed to remove the gag from his son and, picking up his discarded sword, used it to slice through his bonds.

'Father! I thought he would—' Dickon began.

He said no more as Osbert crushed him to his chest.

'You have much to explain, Master Osbert,' said Ralph as he

put a foot on the Magister's wrist and yanked his dagger free from his bleeding hand. 'I see that poor Henry Faker is dead, but I must staunch the wound of this murdering dog, the reeve, and of this wicked alchemist. You just look to your son.'

Using a piece of the ropes that had bound Dickon, Ralph tied the reeve's arm tightly to halt more blood loss, then bound his good arm to his chest and with another tied his feet together.

'This friar's robe that you are wearing belongs to Friar Simon,' Ralph said. 'And there is some blood on the cowl, so confess it. You killed him, but where is his body?'

The reeve hung his head. 'In the undergrowth by the trail.'

'You will show us on the way back,' Ralph commanded.

Giles de Toulouse was coming round as Ralph bound his wrists together and also his feet.

When Osbert finally stopped hugging his son and held him at arm's length, scarcely believing that they would see each other thus in life, Dickon's face was ashen white, and he looked in shock from all the horrors he had lived through and witnessed. He looked down and pointed to the bodkin and the object that had fallen from the Magister's sleeve.

'What is it, Father? It looks like a cross. A black and gold cross with pretty jewels on it.'

'Give it to me!' Giles de Toulouse cried. 'It is mine.'

Ralph picked it up and shook his head. 'The Black Rood of Scotland, I believe. But the only thing that you own now, Giles de Toulouse, is your life. And that may not be for much longer.'

31

THE BLACK ROOD

In the failing light, in sombre mood the villagers had accompanied the wagon back to Axeton with a grisly load consisting of the bodies of Sir Gregory Havelock – latterly known as Boniface de Lythe – Henry Faker and the maimed, semi-conscious Lady Honoria, along with Gideon Moor, Giles de Toulouse and the two ruffians Barrat and Quince.

The reeve obeyed Ralph and showed them where he had dragged Friar Simon's body after he had killed him. Angrily, but reverentially, two villagers lifted his body onto the wagon.

Doctor Gatsby was kept busy that night. By the light of torches, he sealed the bleeding vessels of Gideon Moor's amputated stump with red hot cauterising irons and prepared a potion to ease the pain. Thus, the reeve was incarcerated along with Giles de Toulouse in the cells adjacent to those in which Quince and Barrat had been unceremoniously deposited, once the physician had removed the arrow from Barrat's leg. The two searcher women were put in the stocks to make room for them, and left to shiver and cower overnight.

Ralph gave orders that no one was to abuse them by

throwing dung or clods of earth as they had not been tried and sentenced, but were merely there as there was not room enough in the village jail. Not a soul had sympathy for them.

For Lady Honoria the doctor could do nothing to save her sight, for the oil of vitriol had scalded and turned her eyeballs to the colour of marble. Her head and face were badly burned and he made a balm for her which seemed to slightly reduce her agony. She lay simpering in a room in the manor house guarded by two women of the village, since Ralph considered that her own maids might in some way try to assist her, either to escape or to help her take her own life.

All of the prisoners would have to be transported to York to stand trial before the King's Bench, where Ralph had little doubt that sentences of death would most certainly be made, albeit leniency might be given to Sally Bringbucket and Megan Prole. Even that was a slim possibility for they had known that the reeve had murdered all the people and they had colluded in the pretence that they had died from the pestilence.

But before sending them Ralph questioned them all individually on the morrow.

* * *

'I know exactly how you murdered all of these people, Gideon Moor,' he said as he faced him across the table in the manor court hall the next day. The hall was empty apart from them and Merek and Peter.

Peter had his left arm in a sling so was still able to transcribe the interrogation.

The reeve had been tied to a chair, his amputated stump bound to his chest. Ralph lifted the bodkin from the table.

'Osbert Flood told me that this was in your severed hand and you tried to use it on poor Henry Faker.'

'The Magister showed me how to do it and he made me do it all.'

He admitted to all the murders, including those of Humphrey the apothecary, Jack the Tanner and Friar Simon.

'And did he show you how to make your victims' bodies look as if they had died from the pestilence?'

Feeling wretched and breaking down in tears, he confessed everything and told of how he either drugged his victims with the potion the Magister had made for him, and which he had given them either in bread or ale, or he had seduced them.

And he also told them that Jethro Turner the reeve in the village of Paxton-Somersby had been ordered to take care of any official that passed through his village after being notified by a messenger.

'That included myself and Merek and Peter,' said Ralph. 'It is fortunate that he was an incompetent archer.'

He turned to Merek. 'See to it that this Jethro Turner the reeve of Paxton-Somersby is also arrested.'

'It will be a pleasure, my lord.'

Then, returning his attention to the prisoner, he said, 'You killed all those people that you had known most of your miserable life?'

Gideon Moor had shrugged through his tears. 'They were going to die anyway. I just put them out of their misery. The women I made feel happy and they died with a smile on their faces.'

It was clear to Ralph and his assistants that the reeve held no remorse for his victims and only wept for himself and for fear of the end that was likely to befall him after he was tried at York.

***

The man who called himself the Magister admitted that his name was Giles de Toulouse and that for a time he had assisted Friar Raymond Tully while employed as an alchemist by King Edward. He also admitted that he was the brother-in-law of Sir Boniface de Lythe and that after he left the king's employ he made his way to his castle.

'I knew him as Sir Gregory Havelock at Poitiers,' said Ralph. 'How is this?'

'He said he hated everything about that campaign and felt humiliated by Prince Edward – and by you, or so he told me! So, he merely used his second name of Boniface ever after. It was his way of forgetting about Poitiers and his humiliation. He thought that all that disgrace belonged to Sir Gregory, not to Sir Boniface.'

He sneered again. 'He was a vain and avaricious fool. He wanted my secrets to get wealth, power and immortality. The fool also thought he could even be king. And above all he wanted the Lady Honoria. I told him he could get both. All he had to do was install me in the Abbey of St Leonard and also furnish me with a laboratory. And he did. I became Father Alban, the hospitaller and chamberlain of the Abbey of St Leonard, where I was safe from the king's men.'

'And what did you want in exchange?'

'The Black Rood. I could use it to take it to my sovereign, King John, to rebirth *La Vieille Alliance* and drive this accursed English king into captivity. It would be the perfect alchemy. The perfect transmutation and transformation.'

'And why did you have Friar Dominic, also known as Bruno or Brother John, killed?'

'So, you know his various identities?'

'I have talked with Osbert Flood and he told me all. About how you had Henry Faker's son kidnapped and then murdered. He knows it was him because he had blond hair and was the same age as his son Dickon, who you used to make him do everything that you wanted. Of how he was brought to you by Sir Gregory's men in a coffin.'

The alchemist sneered. 'I had it planned to the smallest detail. I had already recruited Gideon Moor and from him knew that the bailiff was due to visit Robert the Hayward, taking with him his son. I had him drug them both and bring them to the abbey where, with poisons and drugs, I kept the bailiff raving. I bled him and made him think that he had the pestilence. But I needed his son to bend him to my will without question.'

'And Henry Faker's son, Thomas?'

'He was of little matter. He looked enough like the bailiff's son so that when he was dead I could transform him into someone that died from the plague.'

'You bastard!' Merek spat, unable to control his disgust.

Ralph looked at him and frowned, causing his assistant to apologise.

'I play chess and I played out my plan as a game,' the alchemist said with another sneer. 'To win, sacrifices have to be made.'

'They were not yours to make,' Ralph replied sternly. 'And I repeat, why did you have Dominic murdered and his head taken to the tannery? I saw it in that laboratory of yours. Was it a devilish plan to make it speak, like Friar Roger Bacon's brazen head?'

The alchemist laughed. 'That is precisely what I told my stupid brother-in-law. It was a way of getting him to steal the Black Rood, because I told him I needed the wood of the Holy Cross to raise the spirits. Brother John was to go with him as the chaplain to the Earl of Sussex and then his men were to kill him and bring back his head. The young fool confessed to me that he had been the lover of Sir Hugo Braithwaite, so it couldn't have worked out better, as Boniface wanted Lady Honoria, so that became part of the plan. I gave her the mercury poisons to gradually soften and addle his brain and being shown the head of his young lover would be enough to finish him off, which it did.'

He smiled contemptuously. 'And I did not want to risk the damned fool one day confessing to some justice of the peace about what he had done and what he had seen me do, so he needed to be silenced forever.'

He laughed again. 'So no, I never had a plan to make a brazen or necromantic head, it was all part of the trick. I even had it arranged that I would perform the ritual and burn the wood of the Black Rood last night, when I actually planned to take the wood and go to Whitby after dark. Boniface would find that I had just disappeared, like smoke.'

'What of all these friars who have been preaching dissent? Like Friar Simon?'

The prisoner laughed again. 'He was not one of mine. This was more misdirection that my fool of a brother-in-law and his men helped me in. They found all the tricksters and mountebanks, men who could draw a crowd. I put the fear of the pestilence into them and told them that I could protect them with an elixir that was no more than water. Greedy fools all of them, they thought they would become rich through the fear I had created. I took advantage of the doomsday preachers to spread more fear.'

'You are a disgusting creature and you shall be taken to York and tried before the King's Bench.'

Giles de Toulouse laughed again. 'I think not. I can speak

Latin as if it was my native tongue. I claim benefit of clergy, and you cannot deprive me of that. I will be tried in a consistory court, as I have been a priory chamberlain and hospitaller.'

Peter and Merek looked at one another and Merek cursed under his breath.

'I told you I play chess,' the prisoner sneered.

'But not well enough. You made a mistake by not knowing about the current pestilence. It is not like the one that killed so many those years before. This one causes a rot of the lungs rather than these bubos.'

'It is of little consequence,' the alchemist said dismissively.

'You will go to York,' Ralph said slowly. 'But an archbishop may decide whether you get benefit of clergy or not. I suspect you will be denied.'

The alchemist sucked air through his lips and looked down at his heavily bandaged hand. 'May I see the wood of the True Cross once more?'

Ralph immediately felt a prickling sensation in his chest and put a hand to it to touch his locket. It felt strange and as he looked past the alchemist he saw Isabella in his mind's eye. She stood and shook her head.

Should I not permit him to see it? he thought as he pursed his lips.

And he still saw her in his mind, but this time she smiled as she shook her head.

I understand.

'Yes, you can see this trinket,' he said to Giles de Toulouse as he reached inside his surcoat and took out the ebony and gold reliquary cross. He opened it and allowed the piece of wood within to drop out onto the table. 'It doesn't look very sacred, does it, Master Giles de Toulouse. Nor very old at all.'

The alchemist stared at it and then at Ralph, his eyes open wide in horror. 'Damn you to Hell, de Mandeville.'

'A place you will soon be seeing,' said Ralph as he picked up the wood fragment and replaced it in the reliquary, closing it with a snap.

* * *

Lady Honoria beseeched forgiveness for her sins as she burned up with a fever before quickly falling into a deep, unrousable sleep. Doctor Gatsby tried to revive her with *sal volatile* smelling salts, and by trying to bleed her from vessels behind her knees to draw the malignant humor down from her head and body, but to no avail.

She died but a day after having effectively killed her husband. The villagers mourned his death, but not hers.

* * *

Ralph wrote letters to King Edward, Sir Marmaduke Constable the Sheriff of York and Archbishop John of Thoresby. In them he explained all about the murder of Sir Broderick and Adam Dalton, the wounding of Robert Hyde and the diabolical plan of the alchemist Giles de Toulouse and Sir Gregory Havelock, otherwise known as Sir Boniface de Lythe, to steal the Black Rood and to create the illusion that the pestilence had taken them all. He told of the murders of the good people of Axeton, and of Jack the Tanner, Humphrey the apothecary and young Thomas Faker, and of the deaths of Henry Faker and also that of Friar Simon. And also of the ploy to spread dissent by the bogus friars that he had employed by coercion and bribery.

Most importantly, he told them all that the Black Rood of

Scotland had been recovered and that he was holding it for safety and would himself return it to Durham Cathedral.

To Sir Marmaduke Constable he specifically requested that he send armed guards and wagons to transport the prisoners back to York and that he was referring them all to the King's Bench.

The archbishop's messenger was fresh so he gave him all three letters instructing him to ride to York to deliver first to the sheriff and the archbishop, and then to ride to Conisbrough Castle with the letter to King Edward.

Yet as Ralph watched the messenger go he had an unsettled feeling. The matter was as yet unfinished.

* * *

The villagers were only too keen to rally round. There was terrific anger at the cruel deceits that had been played upon them in making them believe that the pestilence had arrived, and that their neighbours and friends had been so callously and brutally murdered. Ralph was made aware of the mutterings about exacting justice themselves, but he instructed Osbert to call a meeting in the manor court. There he informed them of what had happened in Axeton and that justice was going to take place, but in York not in the village, as the crimes of all the prisoners were so serious they were beyond his jurisdiction.

Sir Ralph exonerated Osbert Flood, for he had not been involved in any way, other than as someone who had to carry out instructions under the threat of his son being murdered. As his wife Marion was also present, her face telling of the joy of having her son Dickon home alive and well, there was forgiveness and warmth expressed for them as a family.

Ralph then arranged for Robert Hyde to be brought back

from the Tanner's house with Polly and Wilfred so that they could all be looked after. They were all offered room in Osbert's house.

'It will be company for the two lads,' said Osbert.

'Will you return to Whitby when you are recovered, Master Hyde?' Ralph asked as he looked down at the clerk in his bed.

'I think not, Sir Ralph. Not after Sir Broderick was murdered. Perhaps I will see if I can get an appointment in York.' He looked at Polly and smiled. 'Or perhaps in a while.'

'I can look after him a while more, Sir Ralph,' said Polly enthusiastically.

Ralph saw her smile and also that of her son beside her, and wondered if there might be a growing reason for the while becoming longer.

The village settled back into some form of normality as they waited for the arrival of the guards from York to take the prisoners away. It was a relief to Ralph and his assistants when they watched the wagons trundle out of the village surrounded by the guards.

'What of these bogus friars that have been preaching around the wapentake, my lord?' Merek asked. 'Should we round them up and arrest them?'

Ralph shook his head. 'I think once they learn about their master that they will all disappear like rats.'

* * *

The body of Henry Faker was not taken back to Paxton-Somersby, but was taken and buried in the graveyard of the Abbey of St Leonard's beside the grave thought to have been of Dickon, but which they now knew to be Tom Faker's.

And Friar Simon was interred beside the grave of

Humphrey the apothecary in the cemetery behind St Bede's church in Duncombe, where he had preached before being called to Axeton.

'Which leaves us with the head of Friar Dominic,' Ralph said to his two assistants as they and the villagers who had attended the funeral left the abbey. 'We must return it to his body, as I vowed to do.'

And so they made the journey once more to the Priory of St Mary at Gyseburg with the head of the young monk, this time in a chest that the village carpenter made specially. There, Ralph explained to Prior Cuthbert and Father Benedict all that had happened and with the prior's agreement Dominic's coffin was exhumed from the unconsecrated ground, opened and his head repatriated with his body. Then he was buried and given a proper funeral in the priory cemetery.

Prior Cuthbert himself conducted the service. Ralph, Merek and Peter stood by the grave as the prior finally tossed soil into the grave atop the coffin.

'*In nomine Patris, et Filii, et Spiritus Sancti, Amen.*'

Ralph suddenly had that unsettled feeling he had experienced before and reaching into his surcoat, took out the Black Rood reliquary.

'Are we going on to Durham now, Sir Ralph?' Peter asked, his arm still in the sling.

Ralph didn't answer immediately but opened the reliquary and took out the piece of wood.

Prior Cuthbert stared at it in amazement. 'Is... is that a piece of the True Cross? May I hold it?'

Ralph handed it over as the prior held it reverentially in his hand.

'It looks just like an ordinary piece of wood, does it not?' said the cleric. 'Yet what it could tell if only there was a way.'

Ralph nodded. 'I agree. I have been carrying it around and not once have I felt as if I was carrying something special.'

He was suddenly aware once again of the prickling sensation around his locket. He placed a hand on his chest and his mind conjured an image of Isabella. She touched her brow.

Think! I must think. That is what you are saying, is it not, my love. What was it that Friar Dominic said in his abjuration?

He imagined himself back in the tanner's cottage reading out loud with Robert Hyde lying in the bed.

I must make penance for my sins but pray that the theft from thieves may be better than the transmutation of lead into gold, or wood into smoke. I bear the cross of both sinner and thief.

It had seemed like a riddle. But what else had he said?

Let any who seek my sin seek the cross that bore our Lord.

'May I take this back?' he asked, and allowed the prior to drop the piece of wood back into the reliquary box. There was padding inside but he closed it and then shook it.

'It rattles,' he said enigmatically.

Of course, when he said 'seek his sin' he meant it literally. His sin was to steal the wood of the True Cross, not just this reliquary box. His sin was the wood itself.

Turning to his assistants, he said, 'Come, we must revisit the sanctuary cell.'

Somewhat mystified, they followed and soon after Ralph opened the door of the cell. He looked at its bare interior then walked over to the wooden cross nailed to the wall. Reaching up he felt along the horizontal crosspieces and with a cry of exultation took down a small piece of wood that rested there.

The wood looked truly ancient. 'Hold out your hand, Peter.'

With some trepidation and excitement, the clerk did so. Ralph opened the reliquary box and tipped the wood inside out onto Peter's hand. Then he placed the wood he had picked up from the cross and laid it inside. He closed the box and shook it.

'This is the true Black Rood,' he explained. 'Listen, there is no rattle, it fits perfectly as this box was meant to hold it. Friar Bruno as he was then known as a sanctuary seeker had tried to repent and prevent the villains from carrying out their devilish plan.'

Prior Cuthbert and Father Benedict came into the cell looking perplexed. Ralph explained.

'Friar Bruno achieved what he tried to do. He saved the piece of the True Cross, so it would be fitting if the piece he deceived the villains with could be blessed and buried with him. Is that possible, Prior Cuthbert?'

'*Sic vero*,' replied the prior. 'Yes indeed.'

* * *

MORE FROM KEITH MORAY

Another book from Keith Moray, *Sacrilege*, is available to order now here:

https://mybook.to/SacrilegeBackAd

GLOSSARY

Abjuration

This is the solemn repudiation, abandonment, or renunciation of an idea or belief by the taking of an oath. It often meant giving up any rights the individual has. It comes from the Latin *abjurare*, meaning to 'forswear'.

Abjuration of the Realm

This was a specific type of abjuration in medieval English law, whereby someone seeking sanctuary in a church or church ground would swear to leave the realm never to return. Only the sovereign could permit the individual to return. It was often taken by a coroner, who would then arrange for constables to accompany the person to a port to leave the country.

Alchemy

An archaic study that is often seen as a proto-science where great discoveries were made, and which laid the foundations for the legitimate study of chemistry. On the other hand it is often also seen as a pseudo-art or science where fraudsters and charlatans deliberately preyed on the gullibility of rich patrons and pretended to have the ability to transmute base metals into gold, and produce the philosopher's stone that provided the elixir of life and immortality.

The ancient Egyptians and Mesopotamians practised alchemy. As such they developed techniques to extract various elements and prepare metals. The Arabian alchemists believed that combinations of the four elements *(see Doctrine of Humors)* plus sulphur and mercury made up the various metals.

European alchemists like Friar Roger Bacon, Nicholas Flamel, Paracelsus and Johann Gauber experimented with the various elements in the hope of discovering the philosopher's stone, which they hoped would allow them to turn base metals into gold, and to discover the elixir of life.

They discovered the process of distillation and discovered sulphuric, nitric and hydrochloric acids, sodium bicarbonate, as well as the elements bismuth, arsenic, antimony and phosphorus.

King Edward III was interested in Arthurian legends and did associate himself with them, advocating the code of chivalry, and likened himself to King Arthur or one of his knights, hence he had formed the Order of the Round Table, which he later termed the Order of the Garter. He did employ alchemists and had his own alchemy laboratory, and a collection of alchemical texts. He reputedly employed Raymond Lully (albeit the dates of their lives do not correspond), but also one called John de Walden, whom he did have sent to the tower.

(See Bacon, Friar Roger)

Apoplexy

In about 450BC, the ancient Greek physician, Hippocrates, known as the father of medicine, described the condition of stroke. He called it apoplexy, which literally meant 'struck down by violence'. This archaic term was used right up until the twentieth century.

Apocalypse

In medieval society, the concept of the apocalypse was deeply rooted in Christian belief, and was often associated with the imminent end of the world or a cataclysmic event leading to a new age. The Black Death was such a cataclysmic event that stretched across the known world, devastating populations and creating desolation. Coupled with the wars against the Scots and the French and the horrifying hailstorm of Black Monday in 1360 that reputedly killed a thousand Englishmen, it would indeed seem as if the end of all things, the apocalypse, was nigh. With it, preachers prophesied the second coming, the day of judgement and the end of the world.

Such influential preachers as the Franciscan Friar John de Rupescissa (1310–1370), and alchemist and apocalyptic thinker, influenced many across the continent and England. He taught that alchemy could actually be a defence against the apocalypse.

Apostacy

The abandonment of one's belief, a serious sin according to Church law.

Apothecary

The medieval equivalent of a pharmacist and doctor. They were originally members of the grocer's and spicer's Guild. They were trained by apprenticeship and were not as highly trained but could be more technically skilled than physicians who usually had a university education and degree.

Bacon, Friar Roger (1219–1292)

Born in Somerset in 1219, he studied at Oxford and became a Franciscan friar. He was a polymath, philosopher, theologian and alchemist. He was known as Doctor Mirabilis, which means amazing, wondrous doctor, as an accolade to his learning. In later years it was said that he was a sorcerer who practised alchemy and necromancy. The legend is that he did actually manufacture a brazen head, an artificial mechanical head that could prophesy and tell the future. A version of this legend is told in the play *The History of Friar Bacon and Friar Bungay*, written by the English playwright Robert Greene, who famously referred to William Shakespeare as '...*an upstart crow.*'

He also described the formula for gunpowder. While gunpowder was invented in China centuries earlier, Bacon detailed its composition and method of creation in his writings. He also made discoveries in the field of optics and suggested use of spectacles as well as describing the principles of reflection, refraction and spherical aberration.

Ball, Friar John (1331–1381)

Although he is only mentioned in this novel yet he is the model for Friar Simon. He was a real and significant figure in the fourteenth century. He trained as a priest in York and preached in York and Colchester. He preached against the Church and advocated a classless society. He was excommunicated in 1366, but continued to preach. He became one of the leaders in the later Peasant's Revolt of 1381 in England. When the revolt was put down he was hanged at St Albans.

Benefit of Clergy

In the early days of the English legal system clergymen

could claim the right to be tried in a consistory or ecclesiastical court according to canon law. Originally this right was restricted to churchmen, but it was extended to any who could read and write a passage from the Bible. Thus such people as pardoners, summoners and vergers could evade the harsher sentencing of secular courts.

Black Death

The name given in later years to the plague that devastated the world. It began in 1346 and reached England in 1348, burning itself out in the 1350s after spreading to Scotland. It was to recur in 1361. At the time this novel is set in, it was referred to as the pestilence, or the Great Death.

Black Monday, 1360

On Easter Monday, 13 April 1360, before the gates of Chartres, which was under siege by the Black Prince, King Edward III's eldest son, a freak hailstorm killed over 1,000 English soldiers during the period that came to be known as the Hundred Years' War. It was regarded as an inauspicious sign and led to the signing of the Treaty of Bretigny three weeks later.

Black Rood

After the Stone of Scone, the Black Rood of Scotland was the most precious treasure of Scottish royalty. It was an ebony and gold, jewel-studded box in the shape of a cross, that contained a fragment of the Holy Cross upon which Jesus Christ was crucified.

It was taken to Scotland by St Margaret, a Saxon princess of the House of Wessex, who was born in Hungary. When King William conquered England in the year 1066 she fled to Scotland and married King Malcolm Canmore. Ever since then it was known as the Black Rood of Scotland and it was kept at Holyrood Abbey near the city of Edinburgh. Queen Margaret died with it in her arms and it was considered a crown jewel of Scotland.

In 1296 King Edward I conquered Scotland and captured the Black Rood and took it, along with the Stone of Scone, as spoils of war and kept them in Westminster Abbey. Then in 1328 and the Treaty of Edinburgh–Northampton, King Edward III returned the Black Rood when he renounced all claims to sovereignty over Scotland.

In 1346 as part of the Auld Alliance with France, King David II of Scotland invaded England but was defeated at Neville's Cross near Durham. King David was held captive for eleven years, during which the Black Rood was taken to Durham Cathedral and kept in a wainscoted cupboard in the shrine of St Cuthbert.

It apparently disappeared never to be seen again during the Reformation in 1540. There are several theories as to what happened to it after that.

Bodkin

A long needle used in leatherwork, tapestry making and sewing.

Brazen Head

During the medieval era there was much interest in producing mechanical figures, automata and what can only be described as robots. Talking heads were an example of this, and the famed brazen head was supposedly made by Friar Roger Bacon, albeit it is probably more mythic than real.

(See Bacon, Friar Roger)

Caput Lupinum or Caput Great Lupinum

Both terms in medieval law for an outlaw, or wolf's head. *Caput lupinum* was Latin for 'wolf's head', and *caput great lupinum* was Latin for 'may he wear a wolf's head'. It meant that an individual was to be considered a dangerous criminal, whose legal rights had been waived, and who could be killed by anyone without penalty.

Coroner

In medieval times, a coroner was a Crown official whose duty it was to investigate deaths and establish the identity of the person. They had the power to conduct inquests to determine the manner of death of the person. The position was created by King Richard I in 1194. They were commonly referred to as crowners.

Consistory Court

A church or ecclesiastical court. One claiming benefit of clergy could be tried by this court. It had various personnel including judges, registrars and scribes, proctors and apparitors, or summoners. In general they handed out lighter sentences than the criminal courts.

Cordwainer

In medieval times, a cordwainer was a leatherworker, a maker of quivers, jerkins, saddles.

Constables

These were upstanding individuals, often members of respected families, appointed for a year, like churchwardens. They were unpaid, wore no uniforms and could accompany abjurers from the realm to a port to leave the realm.

Courts

There were a variety of courts that dispensed the law in medieval England. It was often confusing with overlapping jurisdiction. The administration of the law was thus often piecemeal. The Justice of the Peace Act of 1361 was an attempt to rationalise one part of the legal system and bring the law to all.

Royal Courts, or the King's Bench, was the highest court which heard the most serious cases. Serjeants-at-law, forerunners of the modern barristers, prosecuted or defended before the High Court Judges. There were King's Benches in London and York.

County assizes were held in each two or three times a year, and were visited by judges from London, to try serious cases referred to them.

Quarter sessions were run by justices of the peace every quarter of the year. They tried cases brought to them before a jury.

Petty sessions were frequently held by justices of the peace, without jury, in smaller towns and villages.

Manor courts were held in the lord of the manor's own court. They ran the lord's lands and dealt with offences by the people living in his manor. They had extensive powers.

In all courts the court rolls were transcribed as a record of the cases. Usually in Latin, but also in legal French and ultimately in English. These often provide us today with an insight into life during those days. Some court rolls in the country have been kept since the eleventh century.

Cotehardie

A tight-fitting garment for both men and women. For women it was a long garment that reached to the ground, with slimming seams from the shoulders to the hips and often with loose sleeves. The man's cotehardie was close-fitting in the waist.

Crenellation, Licence to

A right granted by the sovereign to fortify their building or manor house with towers and battlements.

Curfew

This was a rule that everyone should remain indoors after a certain time when a bell would be rung, at usually 8 or 9 p.m. It comes from the old French *couvre-feu*, meaning 'a covering for fire'. William the Conqueror imposed curfews to reduce fire risks and to maintain public order. In the fourteenth century, the curfew meant that fires had to be banked and the householders should prepare for bed. People out after curfew had to answer to the nightwatch. Respectable people would carry a lantern, to show they were not up to nefarious activity.

Doctrine of Humors

The Ancient Greeks had developed the Doctrine of Humors or the Humoral Theory, which was the dominant medical theory of medieval times. It was believed that there were four fundamental humors or body fluids (from the Latin *umor* or *humor*, meaning 'moisture' or 'fluid') which determined the state of health of an individual. These humors were blood, yellow and black bile, and phlegm. Treatments aimed at removing excess of illness producing humors by bleeding, purgation and the use of emetics.

Felo De Se

The Latin term for suicide, or self-murder. The term suicide did not come into use until 1643 when Sir Thomas Browne used it in his book *Religio Medici*. It was regarded as a sin in medieval times and would be followed by posthumous excommunication. As a result, burial in consecrated ground would not be permitted. Indeed, often a burial would take place at a crossroads, perhaps with a stake being hammered through the heart.

Fleam

A specific sharp instrument used by doctors, apothecaries and surgeons to bleed a patient.

Fletcher

An arrowsmith.

Garderobe

A medieval toilet. In castles these often took the form of seat-covered holes with long drops into cesspits, or shafts dropping into the moat. Buckets for handfuls of moss were used as cleaning agents.

Hazard

The game of hazard is a gambling game played with two dice and two or any number of players. It was played during the days of Geoffrey Chaucer. It is thought to be even older than that and may have been played by bored crusaders during the lengthy siege of an Arabian castle, called *hazarth* or *asart* in 1125. Sir William of Tyre is reputed to have invented it and the name of hazard is a corruption of the castle's name. It was popular in medieval times and became hugely popular in the seventeenth and eighteenth centuries. It evolved into 'craps', one of the most popular casino games in America.

Hue and Cry

In medieval times the law said that upon discovering a felony the individual was obliged to raise the hue and cry. Everyone hearing the call was equally obliged to join in the chase to catch the miscreant.

King's Evil

Otherwise known as scrofula, a tuberculous condition of the lymph glands in the neck and hardening of the skin, which was common in medieval times. It was believed that the royal touch, a laying on of hands by the monarch, termed 'touching for the King's Evil' could produce a cure. It had been a tradition since the times of Edward the Confessor. King Edward the Third is recorded to have touched 500 people a year and given each a penny to cure the King's Evil, albeit he stopped during the times of the plague.

Justice of the Peace

The Justice of the Peace Act, Westminster, 1361.

Who shall be justices of the peace. Their Jurisdiction over Offenders; Rioters; Barrators; They may take Surety for good Behaviour.

First, That in every County of England shall be assigned for the keeping of the Peace, one Lord, and with him three or four of the most worthy in the county, with some learned in the Law, and they shall have Power to restrain the Offenders, Rioters, and all other Barators, and to pursue, arrest, take, and chastise them according their Trespass or Offence; and to cause them to be imprisoned and duly punished according to the Law and Customs of the Realm, and according to that which to them shall seem best to do by their Discretions and good Advisement; ...and to take and arrest all those that they may find by Indictment, or by Suspicion, and to put them in Prison; and to take of all them that be not of good Fame, where they shall be found, sufficient Surety and Mainprise of their good Behaviour towards the King and his People, and the other duly to punish; to the Intent that the People be not by such Rioters or Rebels troubled nor endamaged, nor the Peace blemished, nor Merchants nor other passing by the Highways of the Realm disturbed, nor put in the Peril which may happen of such Offenders.

Lancet
A double-edged blade with a pointed end for making small incisions or drainage punctures.

Latrine
A simple toilet, often a hole in the ground, or a trench with seats which multiple people could use simultaneously. These were common in monasteries, priories and abbeys.

League
A non-specific measure of distance in medieval times. It was anything between two and three miles, or about the distance one could walk in an hour.

Liripipe
A long dangling tail hanging from a hat or hood. A classic head garment of the medieval era.

Macer
A word that came to be accepted for a herbal *Materia Medica*, or medical text book. The Macer Floridus 'De viribus herbarum carmen' was an eleventh-century Latin hexameter poem. Each chapter describes the medicinal uses of a particular herb. It is attributed to Macer Floridus, but rather like the works of Hippocrates it is probably an accumulated work with several

authors. Hand-copied versions would be found in many hospitals and in physicians' and apothecaries' possession.

Memento Mori

This is a Latin term which means 'remember you must die'. The ancient Greek Stoics introduced the term, and it was used to refer to objects that reminded the person to consider their mortality, so that they might invigorate their life and be sure to give it purpose. They were much used in the medieval period after the Black Death.

Mercury Poisoning

Mental deterioration, twitches, drooling tremors and unsteadiness are all symptoms of mercury poisoning.

Perpetual Stew

Food that was kept cooking day after day, more being added every day, so that it became perpetual.

Pilgrimage

A journey, often a spiritual one, to a place of worship or veneration. The pilgrim hopes to pay respects or gain enlightenment or forgiveness by the visit. In medieval times, pilgrimages were common to the tombs of saints, or to religious houses that kept relics of a saint. Geoffrey Chaucer's *The Canterbury Tales*, the great classic of English literature, is a collection of twenty-four tales, each told by a pilgrim on the way from London to Canterbury to worship the tomb of St Thomas Becket at Canterbury Cathedral. Other popular medieval pilgrimages were to Walsingham in Norfolk, St Winifred's Well, Lindisfarne, Glastonbury, St Albans and Pontefract.

Pillory

A wooden framework on a post with holes for the head and hands, in which offenders were locked, so that they could be exposed to public ridicule and humiliation.

Sanctuary

A sacred space protected by ecclesiastical immunity. Effectively a church or holy house and the grounds belonging to it. It is from the Latin *sanctuarium*, meaning holy safe place. It came to mean the safe place around the altar, but there could be a sanctum, a specific safe cell where a sanctuary seeker could remain for forty days beyond the jurisdiction of the sheriff.

Simony

A heinous crime in Church law, stealing relics or reliquaries or defrauding the Church.

Stocks

A wooden framework with holes for the feet and hands. Often seen in villages in England to this day, albeit they are reproductions.

Wapentakes

Medieval Yorkshire was divided into three Ridings, East, North and West. The term 'Riding' comes from the Norse word 'thriding' meaning a third. In addition, the county was further sub-divided into administrative areas called wapentakes. This too was derived from the Norse, as this part of the country was conquered by Danish Vikings and they had a different legal system from the Anglo-Saxons. This was the Danelaw, and the wapentake was their equivalent of the Anglo-Saxon 'Hundred', the administrative units of most other counties in England. The word meant an assembly or meeting place, usually at a crossroads or near a river, where literally one's presence or a vote was taken by a show of weapons.

There were thirteen wapentakes in the North Riding, twelve in the East Riding and fourteen in the West Riding. As York was the capital of Yorkshire and situated at the junction of the three ridings, it and the wapentake of Ainsty had its own neutral area, and was not considered part of any of the three ridings.

Wimple

The classic medieval head garment for women, consisting of a cloth which went over the head and round the neck and chin.

WOLFSHEAD or WOLF'S-HEAD

An archaic term for outlaw. As an outlaw someone was considered outside the law and could be hunted and killed. (*See Caput lupinum*)

ACKNOWLEDGEMENTS

Writing this book has been an adventure in itself. One begins with the germ of an idea, and quite literally the germ for this one began during the COVID-19 pandemic. Before the development of the vaccines there was an overwhelming sense of anxiety everywhere, as the virus claimed lives across the world. Once the vaccines came, as a doctor I spent much time vaccinating. I asked people, as they rolled up their sleeves in readiness to receive the vaccine, how the pandemic was affecting them. So many had lost friends, relatives and neighbours and the feeling that was described to me time after time was that of desolation.

I write a newspaper column and over the years of the pandemic I wrote extensively about the coronavirus, the history of vaccination and of past epidemics. I wrote about the plague epidemics that devastated Europe, and for which there were no adequate treatments, far less any defence against it from medicine. I researched the various plagues quite extensively and visited Eyam, a village in Derbyshire, famously known as the 'plague village' for its courageous act of self-imposed quarantine during the Great Plague of 1665. The experience of the pandemic and my research into the history of the plague just cried out to be the theme of a story.

And so, I have several people to thank for allowing me to write this novel. Firstly, my wonderful agent, Isabel Atherton at Creative Authors, who liaised with Vic Britton, editorial director at Boldwood Books, who commissioned the novel, the first of four featuring Sir Ralph de Mandeville, Justice of the Peace. I am grateful to Vic for her initial advice and suggestions about the story, all of which enhanced the tale. Then to Candida Bradford, my copyeditor, who knocked off many of the rough edges from it to make it a smoother read, and to Gary Jukes, my proofreader, who provided the final tweaks and made many very helpful suggestions to produce the finished work. I must also thank Dan Mogford, the book designer, for the splendidly atmospheric cover, and John Telfer for a wonderful job as the narrator of the audiobook.

I am grateful to Amanda Ridout, the CEO and founder of Boldwood Books, and all of the team for taking my work on their list and getting it out there to the most important person for any writer – you, the reader. I hope you enjoy the first of Sir Ralph's adventures.

Keith Moray.

ABOUT THE AUTHOR

Keith Moray is a Scottish author of historical crime fiction. A retired GP and medical journalist, his medical background finds its way into most of his fiction writing. Having studied at the University of Dundee, and then worked in Wakefield in Yorkshire, Keith now lives in Stratford-upon-Avon with his wife.

Download your exclusive bonus content from Keith Moray here:

Visit Keith's website: www.keithmorayauthor.com

Follow Keith on social media here:

- facebook.com/KeithMorayAuthor
- x.com/KeithMorayTales
- instagram.com/souterkeith
- tiktok.com/@cactus.jack511
- pinterest.com/keithsouter1

ALSO BY KEITH MORAY

Ralph de Mandeville Mysteries

Desolation

Sacrilege

POISON
& pens

POISON & PENS IS THE HOME OF
COZY MYSTERIES SO POUR YOURSELF
A CUP OF TEA & GET SLEUTHING!

DISCOVER PAGE-TURNING NOVELS FROM
YOUR FAVOURITE AUTHORS &
MEET NEW FRIENDS

JOIN OUR
FACEBOOK GROUP

BIT.LYPOISONANDPENSFB

SIGN UP TO OUR
NEWSLETTER

BIT.LY/POISONANDPENSNEWS

Boldwood

Boldwood Books is an award-winning fiction publishing company seeking out the best stories from around the world.

Find out more at www.boldwoodbooks.com

Join our reader community for brilliant books, competitions and offers!

Follow us
@BoldwoodBooks
@TheBoldBookClub

Sign up to our weekly deals newsletter

https://bit.ly/BoldwoodBNewsletter